Not Like Other Boys

K.A. Merikan

Contents

Foreword

Despite being set in a high school, this story is definitely out of the realm of Young Adult fiction, instead, crossing into New Adult, where sexuality and topics of becoming an adult are explored. We hope you enjoy this twisted love story as much as we enjoyed writing it.

Kat & Agnes Merikan

(K.A. Merikan)

Chapter 1

ETHAN

ETHAN DIDN'T WANT TO take part in the primitive mating ritual going on inside the house. With the music loud as thunder, he felt he was much better off outside where he sat on the porch with a token red cup. As a single weasel in a rat house, he felt as out of place as ever. He wondered if he had made the right decision going out tonight. He didn't socialize much so a party seemed like a good opportunity to have some fun with people who were supposedly his friends, but all he could think of were the things he'd rather be doing. Like stuffing a squirrel or something. No, really, stuffing a squirrel for his new taxidermy project had been on his mind quite a lot. In contrast, the party wasn't all that much fun, though he did find himself some entertainment. There was a reason for him to sit on the porch of all places, and it wasn't the need to escape yet another Katy Perry hit single.

From his strategic spot, Ethan was watching Robert Hunter. The glow from the fire gave Rob's skin a healthy tint, which only made

Ethan wonder what the rest of that bulky body looked like beneath all the clothes. He never imagined actually dating Rob. It would have been silly with the guy being straight as a flagpole, and Ethan himself was too young and busy to be tied down to a guy anyway. But watc hing... watching was good.

He sank farther into his hoodie to protect himself from the chilly air and raised the cup to hide his face when one of the jocks pulled on Rob's sweater, exposing the perfect abs in the process. That hard six-pack belonged in an underwear ad, and now that Ethan was looking at it, he could practically see the honey-colored skin breaking out in goose bumps. He squeezed his hands around the cup but that didn't stop him from feeling a phantom touch on his fingertips. It made Ethan shiver, but he never stopped watching Rob get free and flash his friends that trademark grin. If there was anything about Robert Hunter's looks that was *not* perfect, it was one of his fangs, slightly crooked at the edge of his smile. But that tiny imperfection always remained in the background, with the whole package attracting 90 percent of the female student population. Rob was the quarterback of their high school's football team but also a decent student, with a smile so contagious Ethan felt both overwhelmed and happy looking at it. Add to that a gorgeous, athletic body, eyes so bright they seemed almost celadon, and big, veiny hands, and you had the most eligible bachelor at school. The guy was so perfect it bordered on ridiculous.

The crowd around Rob consisted mostly of other football players and their girlfriends, who were only invited here because they were friends with birthday boy's sister, Kelly. She was a slim girl with bright blonde hair and a stud in her nose. She was pretty enough for the popular crowd to accept her despite her somewhat alternative, artsy style. Ethan watched her sneak up on Rob and dip her hands under his shirt, tickling him with a half-drunk chuckle. Rob laughed out loud but playfully slapped her hand away and finished his drink in one go. Rob's face was reddened from the alcohol he'd drunk so far. Ethan pulled his knees even higher up to his chin and watched the group, surprised by the composition of the image in front of him. Rob was in the center, and most of his friends focused on him with just a few guys at the flanks talking to one another. It occurred to Ethan that the setup was a bit like the positioning of characters in Leonardo da Vinci's 'Last Supper'. A diorama of stuffed rodents dressed up in letter sweaters and posed like in the famous *fresco* could sell. He needed to add this new project to his never ending 'to-do' list.

He smiled to himself at the idea and drank some beer from his cup, only to realize Pat (or 'Pat the Rat' as Ethan liked to think of him) was looking his way.

"Hey, Edward! You got a cup of blood there?" Pat laughed at his own unrefined joke. Ethan rolled his eyes. Ah, the perks of being goth in the state of Washington. Worst thing was that he wasn't even all that flamboyant. No fake fangs, no black makeup, none of that wearing a cape to school shit. He did have long black hair, pale skin, and an affection for morbid jewelry, but that was hardly a crime.

"Nope, it's full of come. Wanna try some?" Ethan yelled back.

Pat's broad, unpleasant face reddened, and he scowled, shaking his head. "Save it, fag."

Chris, the biggest guy on the football team, hurried to slap the back of Pat's head. It was starting to become the school meme since he'd become obnoxiously gay-friendly after his sister came out several months ago.

"What did you say?"

Pat scowled at him, but at least his attention was off Ethan. "Oh, come on! He's the one talking about cups of spunk. It's disgusting!" Pat spat to the ground.

Ethan swallowed hard, and when he looked up, Rob's eyes were on him. Fuck. He shouldn't have baited Pat. Now Robert, who probably hadn't acknowledged Ethan's existence before, would forever associate him with 'come-drinking fag'. Great. Just perfect.

Chris was slowly getting up on somewhat wobbly feet, and two of his friends were already tensing up, as if prepared to hold him back. "Fuck that, told you there will be no fag-jokes around me!"

Pat spread his arms like a rabid gorilla. "Dude, your sister's a chick. No one minds two chicks making out!"

Ethan wanted to barf out the little beer he'd had have so far.

Another one of the jocks stood up in front of Chris. "Yeah, come on. Like, I don't care if he's a fag or not. What matters is that he's Edward."

Ethan got up with a sneer, his skull a closed pot of boiling brains. "I'm not. Fucking. Edward!"

"See, he's getting sparkly already!" Pat laughed and took a few steps closer.

Robert rolled his perfect pale eyes. "You'd have to wait till morning to see more of it anyway, so come back here."

Chris, who apparently had no problems with bullying that wasn't related to sexual orientation, laughed so hard he spilled some beer on his shirt. He wiped it up with a string of curse words on his lips.

"Hey, where you going, sparkly boy?" Pat asked when Ethan tried to sneak away from the porch while the jocks kept themselves busy. No such luck.

"Piss off," Ethan snarled, wishing he'd never come to this party in the first place. Keiran, the birthday boy, who considered Ethan part of his social circles despite not talking to him much at school, was probably having fun in the hot tub anyway. Surrounded by all the girls with piercings and crazy-colored hair the town had to offer, and having already forgotten that Ethan was even present. When Ethan got invited, he thought that maybe Keiran was bisexual or something, but that turned out to be a dead end. Story of his life.

"I think he's afraid of something. Werewolves?" Chris laughed like a madman, only to raise his head and let out a low, throaty howl that could make one's skin crawl in the dark. Ethan was not amused, even less so when the other football players joined in, throwing their heads back and howling so loudly, the base rhythm coming from inside the house drowned in their voices. Ethan inched closer to the door, but his blood ran cold when one of the jocks ran up to block his way with his huge form.

He was not about to wait to find out what they were actually capable of when drunk. Maybe he wasn't as fit as they were, but he wasn't all that useless either so he did the first thing that popped into his mind.

He ran.

Ethan rushed to the side of the porch, jumped over the wooden railing, and with his heart pounding as if it really were a pack of wolves pursuing him, he sprinted toward the trees around the house, hoping he could lose the hunters in the dark. He was now the little black weasel hunted by a pack of rats on steroids, and no one would help him. All he could depend on was the hope that his body was quick and nimble enough to escape.

The loud howls, laughs, and yelling told him that it might not have been a good move. Like a pack of hounds, the big bulks of muscle chased after him into the dark forest that smelled of rotting leaves and cold. He ran as fast as he could, dodging trees and closing his eyes at the last moment, just as something scratched the side of his face. All he could see were the familiar shapes made somehow eerie by the moonlight, but it was too late to go back with the wolves having smelled blood.

"Run, Edward, run if you want to keep your pants!" howled Pat wit a loud cackle.

Ethan's blood boiled, and fear pumped adrenaline into his veins. Pat was the kind of guy who would actually do something like stripping someone naked in the snow and leaving them in the forest. The mere idea of Rob seeing him humiliated like that made Ethan run even faster. His muscles ached already, but he wouldn't give up. He would *not* be a victim.

It only occurred to him after a while that he'd left the howling pack far behind him. He'd never outrun Robert Hunter on the football field while the guy was at the top of his game, but it seemed that drunk jocks weren't as much of a threat as he'd thought. He bent in half and put his hands on his thighs, panting for all the air he didn't realize he needed. His heart wouldn't stop drumming in his chest.

The wind was slowly moving the treetops high above him back and forth, filling the air with a loud rustling, but the chill was welcome and worked like a balm on his aching lungs and strained muscles.

And then something hit his back, making the brown leaves on the ground come at Ethan with the speed of light.

"Got you, Ed," groaned a breathless voice just as the big, heavy body of a football player molded itself to his back.

Ethan screamed as he fell but then went completely silent with panic when he realized which footballer he had been caught by. Even the cold ground couldn't help the heat flushing Ethan's face. Rob Hunter was spread out on top of him, and Ethan had no idea what to do about it. As much as he would like to claim otherwise, it wasn't beneath Ethan to fantasize about a configuration like this one. What he'd imagined though, was a cozy bed and kisses, not a shove to the ground.

Rob's body shook with laughter, sending vibrations all over Ethan's back and ass, now pinned under Rob's hips. This was a porn scenario waiting to happen. Only this wasn't porno so Ethan wouldn't get any.

"Rawr, I got you, Edward. What do I get for letting you go?" Rob asked in that warm baritone. His speech was only slightly slurred, but Ethan could easily smell beer on his breath.

Ethan whimpered and started struggling underneath Rob's heavy body. What had he done to deserve this?

"Get off, you jerk." It came out less stern than Ethan would have wished, but it would do. With the way Robert smelled, with his body heat on top and sheer closeness, Ethan needed to get out ASAP, or he would get a boner and become the laughing stock of the whole school.

"Don't be like that. I won." Rob slowly rolled off him with a silly grin Ethan could see in the sparse moonlight. "I'd be eating you now if I were a real wolf," he said matter-of-factly.

Ethan swallowed, struggling to get up with his knees soft as butter. He'd love to kiss that handsome smile, even if Rob was an ass. "Won in what?" he hissed. "Chasing me through the woods with a pack of jocks and threatening me with God knows what? You really are an overachiever."

"Oh, come on. It's all plain good fun. Don't be so stuck-up." Rob rose from the ground, patting his jeans to get off some of the dirt.

Ethan gritted his teeth. He supposed it could be fun if he were six feet tall and had a bunch of equally large friends at his side, instead of being a short and slim loner. "I never asked for this so-called fun!" Without thinking much, Ethan shoved at Rob's chest and bounced off with Rob standing there like a rock.

"Jeez, don't be so whiny," growled Rob and shoved back, sending Ethan off like a catapult.

Ethan barely held his ground, but came right back at the lump of a man with a vicious punch at his chest that made his hand hurt. "Don't you dare call me that!" Ethan was short, but not willowy and hated being underestimated. He'd rather get punched in the face by Rob than have the guy consider him a wimp.

"The fuck?" Rob grabbed his wrists, looming over him like a menace as he forced Ethan back with a single movement. "You're only gonna hurt yourself like this," he said with a snort.

Ethan struggled in the grip as he was forced to take a few steps back. This was exactly why he hated confrontation, hated social interactions, and *hated* people. He groaned, trying to push back, but it was no use. "I'm fine!" He could hardly breathe from the tension. Dead animals never gave him such grief.

"Maybe you should lose your pants as a warning then?" growled Rob.

Ethan's face pulsed with heat, and it had to be adrenaline and fear that helped him free one of his hands and hit Rob's arm again. He was never going to any stupid party ever again. "Fuck off!"

In response, Rob pushed him back so hard Ethan spun in the air on his way to the ground. Breath caught in his throat when he noticed a dark shape right below him, but just as he pushed his arms forward, a sharp pain stabbed through his skull and everything became dark.

Chapter 2

ROB

EVERY DAY, THE SWELLING and bruises faded away just enough to uncover new, unknown bits of Ethan's delicate face. Tiny birthmarks and new contours emerged out of nowhere, surprising Robert at each visit. Never before had he known a face so well, from the fair grown-out roots right over Ethan's forehead, to the full pale lips slightly open now that the tube that had previously helped him breathe had been removed. The regular, soothing beep of the heart monitor was like a balm on Rob's nerves, and in his own bed, he sometimes heard the phantom sound just before his mind shut down for the day. Ethan's parents visited their son every day, and Rob always brought some snacks for them. Whenever he didn't get to see them, he simply left the food on the bedside table, right next to the flower vase that was always filled with a fresh bouquet.

He was shocked at how happy they were to learn that Rob was Ethan's 'friend'. To have Ethan's own parents say that they thought their son didn't have *any* friends was like a punch in the gut. Robert had never wanted any of this to happen, he had just been playing around, teasing the guy. They had all been drunk, having a bit of fun. All and any fun ended the moment Rob saw a branch sticking out of Ethan's eye socket, and it was a sobering experience. He didn't remember much from the frantic run with the unconscious body in his arms. His breath still hitched at the memory of sitting in the backseat with his hand over Ethan's chest, and the other holding the slim wrist to make sure the pulse was still there. Though he wasn't sure what he would have done if it had disappeared. What can you possibly do when someone has a branch buried where an eye was just moments earlier? You don't just pull it out—that's what Rob's mom always told him, worried that her son would eventually do something stupid. This time, she had actually been right.

Rob reached out and squeezed Ethan's hand. It was oddly rough, like that of someone who didn't take much care of their skin, but looking at the pristine face, Robert doubted that was the case. For the first few days, when the doctors weren't sure if Ethan would make it, Rob was afraid to even touch him. It hadn't been about Ethan's parents being there all the time but because he became convinced the hand would be icy cold and stiff. Or that Ethan's heart would suddenly stop. Now he was starting to recognize the patterns of shallow lines on the inner side of Ethan's hand and considered clipping his nails. It seemed appropriate after putting him in this situation.

For the past few days, Ethan had been opening his eye now and then, and had even spoken a few times, but it wasn't all that coherent. For someone who had a branch stuck into his brain though, it was impressive and reassuring. The doctors said Ethan had been incredibly lucky to survive, not to mention recover so well. There was a long way ahead of him, but with Ethan waking up for longer periods of time every day, the prognosis was that he'd be able to leave the hospital in a matter of weeks. Without his second eye.

Robert bit his lip, squeezing the slim hand in his palms. It seemed so small and frail between his own long and thick fingers. He couldn't believe he'd let himself go crazy like that and chased the poor guy down like the wolf he was pretending to be. It had all seemed like good fun, but Ethan was different, frequently picked on at school. Who knew what he was imagining during the chase? Maybe he really was afraid they'd beat him up. Didn't stuff like that happen all over the place? Robert had never thought of himself as a bully, but now he was forced to face the facts.

His chest constricted as he chewed on his lip, playing with Ethan's fingers. He had small scars on his hand, all looking a bit like paper cuts, but Rob had no idea how they got there. He hoped he could ask Ethan soon.

And there it was. That twitch of eyelid that Rob had come to know as a sign of Ethan opening his eye in a matter of moments. The first time it had happened, Rob had been so overwhelmed, his eyes had welled up.

He got up to have a better look at his victim but never let go of his hand. "Ethan?" he whispered, a tingle running down his spine. They'd never been alone when this happened so far. "Hi?"

The single blue eye opened, and unlike some of the times, there was a glint of recognition in there. Ethan stared at him, eye widening, as if he weren't aware that he could speak.

"You're in a hospital. Just a sec, I'll get the nurse, yeah?" Rob whispered. He wanted to speak normally, but his voice was too choked up so he just pressed the button on the wall and gave Ethan a small smile. "They'll call your mom and dad."

Ethan nodded slowly but pulled his hand out of Robert's. He'd lost so much weight in the last two weeks that all Robert wanted was to sit him down and feed him anything he'd want. Rob could start with the Oreos he got from Ethan's mom.

His train of thought was interrupted by a nurse, who walked in with a serious face, but she relaxed when Rob smiled at her.

"He wants to speak," uttered Rob, even though somewhere at the back of his mind was dread that he'd be taken away by police the moment Ethan told everyone what had happened.

Ethan frowned and closed his eye again when the nurse gently touched his forehead, chirping to him with a smile. Ethan took a few deep breaths and pressed his eyelid closed again. Everything seemed to take ages, but Robert would wait. Even though he could now speak, Ethan's lips were sealed, opening only to cough. The nurse hurried to give him some water, and Rob didn't even notice when he backed away to stand against the wall. The small room suddenly seemed eerie, like every piece of equipment was waiting for its chance to get him. It wasn't the case, of course, but he still had the urge to just flee before Ethan's only remaining eye settled on him again. He didn't watch the nurse work, but she left with a promise of informing Ethan's parents he was awake. The sound of the door sliding shut behind her felt like a guillotine smashing into Rob's neck only to turn out blunt. With a sudden tightness in his throat, he watched Ethan, unsure if he should talk or stay quiet and wait for him to tell everyone what actually happened back there in the woods. The mere thought of it made Rob's insides constrict and turn into a bundle of hardened wire.

"Why are you here?" Ethan finally rasped, slowly looking around, to the comforter, to his hands, to the machinery around him.

"I—" Robert's shoulders were like screwed tight to the wall. "It's my fault you're here."

"Are you here to finish the job and blind me or something?" whispered Ethan, gritting his teeth as he eyed Rob. "Where's my mom? My head hurts."

Walking over to the bed seemed like an almost impossible task, but Rob pushed himself and crossed the distance that kept Ethan safe from him. His mind went blank when he saw accusation in the fair eye.

"She... she said she needed to go to the bank, but she's always here," Rob assured him, shifting his weight from one leg to the other and back. His body was numb, with only his chest and throat aching like he had a noose strapped around them. "I'm so sorry. I never wanted for this to happen. I'd never do this intentionally," he uttered, his voice less steady than he'd like it to be.

"I've woken up before, haven't I? And... they know you did this and let you stay here?" Ethan frowned even harder but then hissed and put his hand on his forehead.

Rob's face heated up. "Should I call the doctor? Oh, fuck, what do I do?"

"I don't know. You tell me." Ethan took a deep breath that sounded like he was trying to grasp at particles of air. "I just wanna scowl at you, but I can't because my face feels like shit. And I can't see properly," he added in a broken whisper, his eye suddenly welling up.

Robert swallowed and pulled out a paper handkerchief, which he wet with the water from the plastic cup and put it on Ethan's forehead. He had thought seeing him unconscious was bad, but in pain? He wasn't sure what was worse. "I'm so sorry, it was an accident. I didn't want to hurt you."

Ethan took a deep breath but didn't say no to the handkerchief. "Sure you didn't. You just wanted to pull my pants off. Fuck. You. And now I'm feeling all weird, and probably have scars, and no one's gonna want to see me without my pants. I'm probably gonna get some stupid nickname at school. Like Captain Edward."

Robert's face tingled as blood drained from his face. "No one's gonna do that. I'm personally making sure of that. No one's gonna be bothering you, I swear."

"Why are my parents letting you be here?" Ethan tightened his fingers on the comforter. "Did you tell them you're my boyfriend?" Robert wasn't even sure if it was a joke or not, with Ethan's face lacking much expression.

"N-no, everyone thinks you... fell," uttered Rob in a small voice and hugged himself. "I carried you back and made Tina drive my car to the emergency room." He didn't dare look up, but the judgment was coming.

The long silence told him Ethan was processing this. It wasn't fair. Wasn't a jury supposed to be more than one person? But the moment he thought that, Ethan spoke again.

"You're just feeling guilty. You don't really care. For once, things didn't go your way and now you want me to lie for you?"

"But it was an accident. I really didn't want to hurt you." Robert's jaw tensed so hard that the sides of his face started hurting. "And I do care. You have no idea how sorry I am about what happened." With a loud exhale, he raised his hands to cover his face. "I didn't want this."

"Well, if it was an accident, you shouldn't be guilty, right? There will be no witnesses of you idiots chasing me into the forest. No witnesses of our animosity?"

"Ethan, I fucked up, I know." Robert shook his head, his stomach knotting. "I will do anything to make it up to you."

There it was. That spine-chilling silence again. Robert dared to look at to the slim fingers playing with the comforter. Squeezing it and letting go.

"Anything?"

Robert swallowed hard, hardly able to breathe from the tension. "Yeah. Don't... tell anyone, please. I will do anything you ask."

When Ethan started speaking, each word came out quieter than the one before it. "Would it disgust you if I asked for a blow job?"

Rob's hands fell to his sides. "Say again?"

"You heard me the first time!" Ethan raised his voice but his throat was so dry he started coughing. "And actually, I don't want just one. I want one every week until graduation, and I'll let you off the hook. So there. Take it or leave it. I wouldn't tell anyone, so you wouldn't lose your reputation or anything."

Robert stared at him, his heart hammering in his chest so hard he suspected Ethan could hear it. "Reputation? I don't want to go to jail," he whispered even as his mind started envisioning Ethan lowering his pants. Robert would feel the warm smell of his body and taste a cock for the first time. He would have been over the moon if the proposition came under different circumstances.

Ethan finally looked up at him again, with his eye slightly widened. As strange as it was, the bright blue iris radiated fear. "I mean... about the blow jobs. I wouldn't tell anyone."

"Oh." Robert's head was pulsing like crazy, but he couldn't look away from the bruised face. He would do it. Ethan deserved whatever he asked for, and Robert would lose his virginity in exchange for lack of a criminal record. It wasn't the way he imagined it would happen, with his hypothetical first boyfriend in college, but there was no way around it. Ethan had every right to hate him, and it was time to pay up.

Ethan took a deep breath. "Have my parents been called? I wouldn't want them to walk in on us." His voice trembled slightly, but other than that, he was right to the point. Was this really happening? *Now*?

"Wh—" Rob's face went aflame, and his stomach dropped at a rapid speed. "But... someone could walk in on us here..."

Ethan pouted, his pale face getting some color. "Yeah, I suppose so. But as soon as I get out, yeah? I woke up before, right?" *Didn't he already ask about that?*

Robert took a shaky breath. "Y-yeah. But you were out of it. I... and yeah." He hung his head, too ashamed to look Ethan in the eye.

"How long have I been here for?" Ethan slowly tried to sit up but just fell back to the pillow with a hiss.

"Oh, God, don't move, please." Robert grasped his own hair. "Two weeks. But don't move."

"I just wanna check if I can." Ethan slowly lifted up his feet under the comforter. "It would suck to get a promise of blow jobs from the handsome quarterback only to find out I have spinal cord injury or something. I wouldn't feel it then, would I?"

"Then move your toes." Robert hurried to the footboard and uncovered the pale feet.

The way Ethan wiggled his toes, watching them with a serious face, would be quite amusing if it weren't for the situation.

"Can you get me a mirror? I probably look like shit." Ethan reached up to the gauze over his eye, making Robert's heart stop again.

"Don't touch that!" Rob was next to him within seconds. "Ask the doctor first." But the truth was, he himself was afraid what was underneath. What if Ethan not only lost the eye but was also scarred for life? How would they cope with *that*?

Ethan groaned. "Okay, okay. I'm not made of porcelain, you know. Just get me the mirror anyway."

Robert spread his arms. "I don't wear a pocket mirror... you okay with a photo?" he asked, hesitantly fishing out his cell phone.

"Yeah, go on." Ethan clenched and unclenched his fist.

Robert switched on the camera and swallowed, staring at Ethan, increasingly unsure if that was such a good idea. Ethan looked much better than he did immediately after surgery, but that did not mean he looked well. "Maybe you'd like to wait till daytime?"

Ethan closed his eye, his jaw muscles twitching. "I look so shit that you don't even want me to see it?"

"No, but you're still bruised and stuff." Rob swallowed hard. In the back of his mind, the blow job matter became a bit more prominent, the imagined cockhead poking his brain and begging for attention. He didn't know what to think.

Even with the bruises, Ethan's face was extremely attractive. As if Ethan were a drawing in all the wrong colors, but with the perfect lineart. A shapely, slightly rounded nose, one wide, dark eyebrow over the clear blue eye, and well-defined cheekbones, now slightly too sharp because of the weight loss. "Whatever. Not like seeing it will help anyway."

Rob was spared the awkward conversation when Ethan's parents stormed in, walking right past him. He backed away to the wall and watched the happy family reunion with his stomach sinking. Should he leave now, or wait for a moment longer to say his good-byes? Would Ethan even want him to show his face in the hospital again? A thousand bitter thoughts tumbled through his mind as he watched Ethan's mom cry with joy. He was out of place here, yet he couldn't just slip away without feeling like a coward. And what would Ethan think of him if he disappeared? Would he rat him out right away? And even if Ethan didn't say a thing, would Rob be able to look himself in the eye if he fled?

All of a sudden, Ethan's dad was by Rob and patted him on the back with a wide smile. His ever-tense face suddenly bright and relaxed, and even the graying hair at the temples seemed more youthful. "It's so good that you were here."

Robert's eyes immediately went to meet Ethan's icy gaze. "Y-yeah ..."

Ethan's mother looked back with a wide grin, stroking her son's hand. "Yes! Exactly. Why didn't you tell us about your friend before?" For such a petite woman, she had lots of energy now that she knew her son would be okay. It was strange just how much hope and joy changed their appearance. Ethan's parents looked like... well, like the lawyers they were. Always dressed properly, rather stern, but now it all seemed to disperse. No wonder they lost it when they discovered the tattoo of rats dancing around their son's mid-section.

"It's... I... Well, you know now," Ethan finally choked out, casting a glance to the blanket.

"He's been here every day," added Ethan's dad, patting Robert's back again. His eyes shone with joy. "He even remembers my coffee order."

Robert wished he could crawl under a rock. He didn't even want to imagine what Ethan was now thinking of him, the bully who be-friended his victim's parents to ensure his own safety. That was what this had to look like. He wanted to flee so bad.

"Robert is going to be helping me out with what I've missed at school, he's promised already." Ethan actually had a small smile on his face, and it suddenly occurred to Robert that it was an expression he'd rarely seen on his face.

"Yeah, that's it." Robert bit his lip, out of breath. "Maybe... you'd like some privacy?" he asked, trying not to let hope leak into his tone.

Ethan eyed him with that blue eye, which seemed to stare right into the depths of Robert's dirty soul. "That's a good idea. But come over again. Leave your number."

Robert's temples drummed. "I'll come here after school, okay?"

Ethan nodded, his flat expression hard to read. "Can't wait."

Robert turned to the door and pushed it open, voicing his good-byes on the threshold, shaken. Only then he realized that his T-shirt was drenched with sweat. What was he to do now?

Chapter 3

ETHAN

ETHAN COULDN'T BELIEVE THIS was finally happening. Robert would come over and touch him. It boggled his damaged brain. The two weeks he'd spent in the hospital after waking up properly had seemed to extend into eternity. He had an awful scar where his left eye used to be, but most of the bruising was gone. Headaches came and went, but the most unexpected and disturbing problem was random lapses in memory. Only short-term. Sometimes they encompassed a few seconds, sometimes even a few minutes. It made Ethan nervous that something in his head was rotting from the inside like some mental gangrene that no one could cut out, even though the damage to the brain itself was supposedly minor. The doctors told them it could possibly get better with time, but there were no certainties for him, so he was set on grasping each hour, each day.

When he came back from the hospital, he had to clean up all the rats that rotted in the fridge in the basement, since his parents refused to enter his 'den', as they liked to call Ethan's workshop. Ethan went down there in hope that cleaning would help him ease his nerves before Rob's arrival later that day. The setup was perfect. His parents would be at work till late, so no one would disturb his first ever blow job. Organizing his workspace for future projects unfortunately left him with room for thinking. Some of it was imagining Rob naked and sucking him off with that intense gaze looking up at Ethan. But another part of him worried about the state his body was in. Ethan was still only gaining weight back after the hospital and missing one eye made his coordination shit. He'd actually fallen down the stairs to his workshop just today. It had him worried sick about his craft skills. What if he wasn't as precise anymore?

He scrubbed the metal table in arm length rubber gloves after he was done with the fridge. It wasn't messy, but the vigorous, steady motion, and the smell of chemicals got his heartbeat steadier. The basement under the separate garage building was his kingdom, and he hated the dismissive tone his parents used whenever they talked about it. It was the same tone in which they'd call his passion for taxidermy 'just a hobby'. Outsiders often thought Ethan's parents were incredibly understanding, but they never witnessed any of the crap that was thrown Ethan's way whenever his average grades dropped by even a bit. And as much as Ethan understood his mom and dad's hearts were in the right place, he couldn't stand that they were setting his passion up for failure. It was just so incredibly frustrating to have the one thing he believed could be a career he'd actually enjoy ripped to pieces and diminished during every conversation they'd had about it for the last two years. He couldn't stand the constant fighting and lack of freedom, yet being a teenager kept him in his parents' house, without hope for change anytime soon.

The doorbell had Ethan jerking up his head and looking at the ceiling as uneasiness crawled into his stomach. One look at the clock revealed that he should still have over half an hour left to get ready for Robert. Was this a delivery man, or something of that sort?

He ran up the creaky stairs and pulled the plastic mask below his chin when he left the basement. Since coming back home, every time he had to use the stairs felt like climbing Mount Everest, though walking up wasn't quite as bad as descending. All the things he previously took for granted now proved to be tricky with his depth perception screwed up. The doctors assured him that his brain would get used to it, and he would stop bumping into random things, or trying to grasp items that in reality were far from his reach, but right now he kept getting bruised or embarrassed.

All he could hope for was that Rob would not see him fall over like an idiot. It was his call, and Ethan wouldn't be laughed at. He could still barely wrap his head around what he'd asked of Robert Hunter, but he supposed that someone who had just woken up from a coma was excused from adult responsibility.

Once upstairs, he ran up to the door and looked through the small window on the side wall of the garage, which faced the entrance of the house. It wasn't the delivery man. Just the hottest piece of hunk this town had to offer, all tall and broad-shouldered. Ethan's hair bristled when he saw that handsome profile. Robert had a strong, straight nose and sharp brow line. No wonder so many girls at school wanted him. But it was Ethan who'd get him. (Even if just once every Wednesday at 5:00 p.m.).

He went to the door, took a few deep breaths, and opened it. Rob turned on his heel, freezing with his eyes slightly wide. "Hi."

"Hi, you're... early." Ethan stared at him, but then realized how silly he was being and started a slow pace that would hopefully save him the embarrassment of tripping over something halfway, which at this point in time happened to him even on flat asphalt. This wasn't the entrance he wanted, but after Rob had seen him in the hospital, there was nothing that could possibly seem less dignified. Whatever happened, Ethan was on the way up. What he did not understand was why Robert reported at his door so early. Did he just want to have it over with as soon as possible?

Dressed in black jeans and a green hoodie that complemented his eyes, Robert looked like a model from a catalogue, even with the oddly stiff movements he was now presenting. "May I come in? I didn't know if you had any plans..."

"No, no, I was just cleaning my workspace." Ethan stepped onto the porch, carefully sliding the tip of his leading foot up each of the three stairs to avoid tripping. When he stopped next to Robert, the rush of heat to his face was unavoidable, but he didn't expect his knees to feel so funny when he realized just how tall Rob was, and how big in comparison to him. He rarely had the opportunity to be close enough to Rob for the contrast to be so sharp. He hated how this simple jock turned his usually eloquent self into a mess. It had to be the pheromones, and he could hardly blame *himself* for how amazing Rob smelled. The guy was so tall he had to tip his head when Ethan let him into the house. How could one not be attracted to that?

"Okay. Um... should I leave my shoes here?" Robert turned toward him, his eyes slightly wide.

Ethan had no idea. He never had guests over. Why didn't he think this through? What did normal people do? As a weasel, he imagined this house to be his cage but he never wondered how it would be to invite a rat into his space. His mind drifted off into a vision of a black weasel and a white rat sleeping together in one of those ferret hammocks. It took a moment for him to remember what the question was.

"Yeah, just leave them here, we'll go to my room anyway." Did that sound predatory? Could he even *be* predatory? No, he was the one taming a predator. A predator who after this would never dare bully anyone else.

Robert cleared his throat and lowered himself to one knee to remove his sneakers. They hadn't talked much since Ethan had woken up, even though Robert appeared in the hospital almost every day. Ethan had had high hopes that he'd get the promised blow job before he got out, but with his parents constantly present, the only thing Robert could possibly blow for him was a balloon.

"I got you some handouts," uttered Rob, showing Ethan a generic folder stacked with paper.

Ethan swallowed and took off the plastic mask completely. "Thanks. I'll be back at school next week, I'm gonna need it. And sorry I smell of chemicals, I'll take a shower."

Robert let out a shaky breath and got to his feet. He was towering over Ethan, but there was an awkwardness to his posture that took the intimidation away. "Sure. I can wait."

"You could probably wait forever, right?" Ethan grumbled and led the way up the stairs to his room.

The whole house was in a state of suburban perfection, which made the illusion that their family was normal extremely convincing. Family photos on the walls? Check. Spotless corners? Check. An expensive but tasteful antique vase for decoration? Check.

Robert's footsteps missed the rhythm behind Ethan when they reached the door at the top of the stairs. "Not really."

"Let's just make it civil, okay? It's not like we have to talk for God-knows-how-long." Ethan didn't want to seem needy or desperate even if he was all that and more. Ethan turned around and opened the door to his kingdom.

Robert pushed his hands into his front pockets and shrugged, looking around. His face remained rather blank as he surveyed the attic room, probably looking for somewhere comfortable to sit. Ethan was nervous about what Rob would make of his personal space. He'd never had anyone but his parents here, though with the taxidermy decoration and dark brown walls, even they were never all that keen on coming in. Ethan just hoped Robert wouldn't freak out over the chandelier made out of bird bones and skulls.

Ethan rushed over to the bed and patted the fluffy fur throw over it, feeling as awkward as ever. It was only dawning on him now that in a matter of minutes he'd have Robert Hunter's lips on him.

"I'll be back in a second, okay?" He couldn't stop staring at how big Robert was. He still remembered how it felt to have that body on top of his own, sandwiched between hot muscle and fallen leaves in the darkness, where anything could happen. Only instead of spontaneous sex, he got a branch up his eye back then. Fun times. *Not.*

Robert nodded, combing his fingers through the hair at the top of his head as he lowered himself to the bed. "No stress."

Ethan asked himself if there was anything else he should say, but in the end he just rushed out to the adjoined bathroom and shut the door with his heart beating a lot too fast for his liking. *Fuck.* Robert Hunter was sitting in his bedroom, ready to fall to his knees and give him a blow job, and *now* he was getting stressed? What if he couldn't get it up? No, he would definitely get it up.

Ethan took all his clothes off faster than ever and got under the shower. Sometimes, he thought that his life would be much easier without the oversexed fantasies that took his mind off the things that mattered, but since his hormones weren't cooperating at all, he might as well get it out of his system with no strings attached. The warm water and soap felt like a caress on his skin, but he was in a hurry to claim his injury compensation. By a guy whose face he wanted to kiss all over. Not that it was gonna happen, but a guy could dream. Oh and dream Ethan did. Since the day Robert had accepted his offer, the image of Rob pulling Ethan close and sucking his cock was always somewhere at the back of his mind. Sometimes, Ethan imagined himself standing, sometimes on the bed, with Rob's head between Ethan's thighs, his hot mouth sucking, kissing all the way from the tip to the balls.

He stood in front of the mirror as he toweled himself off and put the eye patch back on. He briefly wondered whether it made sense to put the T-shirt back on, but it didn't seem appropriate. What was he supposed to wear? He'd get naked anyway, right? It wouldn't make sense to cover up his chest if he was gonna show Rob his dick. Or was it? Just the jeans? Just the pajama pants? No, that wouldn't do. He took a deep breath. It was sink or swim.

He would go naked.

Ethan combed his hair, which he'd dyed black again since getting back from the hospital, and gave himself a once-over. Eye or not, he wasn't bad looking. He was still regaining weight after the accident, but then again he'd never been the muscular type. Maybe a bit too pale, but that didn't matter, since he wasn't Rob's target audience anyway.

He walked out with his hair still damp, naked as the day he was born, only to see Rob's pale green eyes widen. Robert had taken off his hoodie and was now wearing just a plain long-sleeve which showcased his assets without putting them on display. It did nothing to hide the sudden movement of Rob's chest when he looked up at Ethan's face. His Adam's apple bobbed when he shifted a bit, as if not sure how to act.

Ethan swallowed, suddenly self-conscious about the decision he'd made, but he wasn't going to back down. He deserved something good in his life, and Rob deserved to be punished for being a stupid ass who nearly killed him. He hugged himself but took a step closer with his goose bumps on fire. "Yeah, so... I thought you're gonna see it anyway."

Rob was pulling on the fingers of his left hand, and the slight creaking sounds were like needles stabbing into the back of Ethan's neck. "So, what do I do?"

Ethan stepped closer, hardly able to breathe at this point. "Just... you know, what you'd like a girl to do to you."

Robert froze, slouched forward with his eyes transfixed on Ethan's crotch, which reacted as predicted. Ethan couldn't remember his cock ever filling so rapidly, and when he was ready to call out Rob on not keeping his word, Robert invited him over with a gesture.

So this was it. Ethan pushed some of his hair forward, to hide the flush that was no doubt all over his face when he stopped just inches away from Rob's face, between his spread feet. "Don't eye it like it's dead chicken or something."

Robert's gaze darted to the window, and he scowled so hard it made Ethan uneasy. "God, don't give me this mental image!" He pulled on his index finger, swallowing as he looked at the cock in front of him again. His face next to a penis was an image made in wet dreams.

Ethan frowned at him. "Oh, I'm sorry, are you feeling a bit intimidated? Well guess what, now you have to suck it up. Pun intended," he groaned, sounding more aggressive than he would have liked. This guy and his friends kept intimidating *him* so he was refusing to feel sorry for him and take back his request. He deserved this.

Rob blinked at the cock, exhaling. Then in one quick lunge forward, he grabbed the base and put the other half in his mouth. It was a warm, moist sleeve that tightened around Ethan's cock and started pulling him in like a vacuum.

Ethan gasped, his body instantly responding. It was a melting sensation in his chest, butterflies in his stomach, and fireworks exploding underneath his eyelids, as cliché as it was. He didn't want to just stand there, so he put his hands on Rob's arms, shuddering at the hardness of the muscle underneath. He tried to be gentle at first so that Robert wouldn't feel forced, but the moment the sucking became more intense, so did the grip of his fingers.

Robert's breath tickled Ethan's pubes when he started bobbing his head over the part of the cock that wouldn't fit in his hand. It sent a powerful surge of heat up Ethan's spine, and it was so good it almost hurt. Robert's handsome face was like cut in stone, the beautiful angles of his cheekbones and brow line sharpening as he sucked on Ethan's cock as if it were his last meal.

Within seconds, Ethan's knees went weak, and when he came, looking at the glorious image that was his own cock erupting in Robert Hunter's mouth, it seemed like the most intense experience of his life. He grasped onto Robert's shirt with a low moan and closed his eye, bending over him. The bliss was so pure that for a moment he didn't even remember who he was.

Robert moved back his head, letting the cock slip out of his mouth and into the cool air, but he stayed in place.

Ethan gasped for air, unwilling to let go and overwhelmed with the sudden urge to return the favor. He could bet Robert's cock was as amazingly hot as Robert himself. "Oh wow," he panted. "That was so great. You want me to do you?" he asked even though he knew he probably sounded overeager. Fuck it, it was his call this time.

Seeing Robert shake his head and reach out for a paper tissue from the box on Ethan's nightstand was like a cold shower. Robert held it against his mouth and spit out all of Ethan's come, never even looking up.

Ethan's heart dropped. Now that it happened, he realized this wasn't how he'd envisioned this encounter. His idea of how it would play out didn't include his own stomach plummeting at the realization that Robert was disgusted by his cock. He wanted not to care and just take his revenge, but it was awful to witness.

Ethan slowly stepped to the side and sat on the bed, too shaky to stand. It felt like a very ambivalent dream. Of course Robert wouldn't want a blow job from a guy. He probably had a whole queue of cheerleaders to serve him.

Unwilling to look at Robert, Ethan let his gaze drift to the desk, and the floor seemed to fall from underneath his feet. He'd prepared a condom for this, in case Robert preferred it, but he'd forgotten to ask, too mesmerized by the situation. He took a deep breath and finally dared to sweep his gaze up the firm thighs and to the handsome, tan face.

Robert's big, strong hands curled around the soiled handkerchief as he took deep, slow breaths, his shoulders tense. He swallowed, opened his mouth only to close it again and repeat. "I gotta go," he said eventually in a voice so dull it made Ethan cringe.

"I'm sorry!" Ethan burst out. "I had a condom, I forgot," he muttered, unable to look up at Rob. He felt as naked emotionally as he was physically. As if he were a skinless carcass, ready to be discarded.

Robert's hand opened and the tissue fell to the floor. He got to his feet and grabbed his hoodie. "See you at school," he murmured, already on his way to the door.

Ethan nodded, too shocked to utter a word. He wasn't satisfied. He'd had a glorious orgasm and now knew how it felt to be blown by a guy, but he knew it wasn't really what he wanted. Then again, what could he expect? That Rob would magically become gay for him? That wasn't gonna happen, and Rob clearly didn't want to stay and chat, which was kind of understandable given the awkwardness of the situation. The thumping on the stairs only quickened, and as soon as Ethan heard the door being slammed shut, he knew he was alone again. Nothing would happen between them until next week. The 'See you at school' had sounded more like a 'fuck you' so Ethan already knew he wouldn't try to approach Rob there.

He wished the encounter could have been more than a moment of pure ecstasy followed by a crash landing in reality. He curled up on the bed, not ready to go back to work yet. Even sewing was harder with just one eye available. Another craptastic fail.

Ethan looked at the tissue on the floor with a deep breath. He'd swallow up all of Rob Hunter's come.

Chapter 4

ROB

ROBERT CHEWED ON HIS pizza. He hadn't had the right mindset yesterday to prepare himself a proper lunch for school so he tried to stuff his stomach with the soggy thing. It was so disgusting and unappetizing he had a hard time getting it down his throat. His eyes kept returning to the lonely figure in black in the far corner of the dining hall.

He didn't feel one bit sorry for Ethan sitting there and chewing on his food with just as much enthusiasm as Rob was. The accident hadn't gained Ethan much sympathy, and no one seemed to approach him, even though it was the first day at school after weeks of absence. A simple black eye patch covering the empty socket made him more unapproachable, even when hidden behind a pair of black-rimmed glasses. He wore a pair of skinny jeans and a fitted long-sleeve top under an oversized black sweater with holes all over. The only brightness on his outfit were bits of silver jewelry on his fingers, and a necklace with the skull of a hummingbird. Wearing it had never won Ethan any favors. Not that Rob cared.

The day before, he'd used up a whole bottle of mineral water to wash the taste of spunk out of his mouth, and then spent over an hour sucking on mints while sitting in his car at the gas station where he got the candy. It wasn't because of the taste of spunk itself, even though it turned out to be less pleasant than in his fantasies. The whole encounter had left him with a bitter aftertaste at the back of his throat, and he didn't seem able to get rid of it completely. It was still there, spoiled the taste of his breakfast in the morning, and even bothered him when he was having freshly squeezed juice, always looming around the joints of his tense jaw. He didn't deserve what had happened. Yes, he had fucked up, he was at fault when it came to the accident, and there was no way he'd ever make it up to Ethan, but it had been a lapse of judgment. Rob didn't want to hurt him, but Ethan himself had no moral objections to force Robert into sex. All of the sympathy he'd felt for the guy had evaporated since.

His mind stopped drifting when he saw two girls stop by Ethan's empty table, and even from where he sat he could hear something about karma. Ethan gave them a blank stare and stood up without a word.

"What a creep. He should be happy any girl wants to actually talk to him." Pat, Rob's teammate and friend by association, laughed, shoving the pizza into his mouth as though it was the best thing he'd had in a month. Already balding, thick in the nape and trunk, Pat was the person whose recently-repaired nose one wouldn't want to see up close in a dark street. And his appalling eating habits were another thing altogether.

Chris, Robert's best friend since childhood, yawned, equally unimpressed. "It's not like he was talking to anyone in the first place. Not even the loser table wants him."

"Aren't those the girls who spilled paint all over Natasha's fur last year because they were convinced it was real?" asked Kelly, slurping her drink next to Rob.

"The freaks. I loved how it turned out it was artificial. The principal went mental," chuckled Chris.

"Do you think that bird head on his neck is fake?" Pat wondered out loud, slouching his large body over his tray as he wiped his lips with a napkin.

Kelly shook her head, pulling on the stud in her nose. "Hello, he does taxidermy. At home. In his basement. The sole idea freaks me out."

Rob stroked his chin, his thoughts drifting to the chandelier of bird bones over the bed in Ethan's room, which by the way looked like something that could well have been located in a haunted mansion. Not to mention the framed posters of still life on the walls. Most of them depicted carnivorous feasts, which were interesting as such, but the context of Ethan's morbid room made the paintings unsettling. He didn't even want to think what that infamous basement had to look like.

"Did he even thank you, Robert?" Kelly looked up at him, her wide blue eyes settling on him with a small smile. "It's amazing that you managed to carry him all the way back to the house. All on your own."

The pizza instantly hardened in Robert's mouth, turning into a piece of chalk that he just couldn't swallow. Back then, he'd spent God-knew how much time trying to decide whether to break the branch that got stuck in Ethan's eye or not. He ended up breaking away all the branchlets before he cuddled the immobile body and ran through the forest, with fear curling in his chest. "Sure."

"It's so stupid." Pat shrugged and pushed away the salad. "Who falls over and impales themselves on a branch? Shit like this only happens to Edward."

"Right?" Chris slurped his slushie and leaned back in the chair. "I knew he sparkled, but not that he was made out of Jell-O and bad luck."

Robert bit his lip and forced himself to swallow. He wouldn't feel sorry for the bastard. Ethan was more of a douchebag than anyone imagined.

"Oh, come on guys, stuff like that happens. People die from the strangest things," muttered Kelly. "That's not cool."

"I just need to go and check if that bird head is real," Pat said and got up without further ado. Chris grinned at him and got to his feet within a split second.

"The guy's just been in a hospital for a month," hissed Kelly. "Leave him be."

"I just wanna ask. Nothing wrong with that." Pat groaned and walked off followed by Chris.

"You wanna come, Rob?" Chris asked, turning on his heel with a grin, which Rob supposed was intended to invite him in to join the 'fun'.

Robert knocked his fists on the tabletop, furious he was being forced to take a stand. "No, and Kelly's right. Leave the freak alone."

Pat shrugged and didn't even turn around, disappearing in the exit, but Chris made a one-eighty and looked back at Rob. "Hey, it's just fun. I wouldn't hurt him or nothing."

"I'm not saying you would, but he just had a piece of wood up his brain. Christ!" Robert made a broad gesture, and his hand knocked down his Coke, which spilled all over the table. "Oh, fuck me!" he grumbled, not even bothering to pick up the empty can. He slumped into the chair and threw a napkin into the wet mess.

Kelly nodded and started clearing up her stuff. "Exactly. It was all the way up there. He barely made it out alive. He'd be dead if it wasn't for Rob."

The praise was cut short by the bell, and the rest of their friends, who were focused on their own conversations anyway, got up.

"Let's just go to class." Chris sighed and brushed his fingers through the thick mane of his hair. "See you later, I've got math now."

"Wait for me," muttered Kelly, who dumped some of the wet napkins onto her tray and gave Rob one more charming smile before getting to her feet. She was pretty, smart, and interested. Too bad Rob was gay.

He dumped the remainder of his pizza slice on the tray and slowly made his way to the trash can. He actually had class with the little bastard now.

But when he got to the door, he froze, because there Ethan was, at the end of the corridor, standing at the bottom of the stairs with his hand on the railing, and looking up as if he were about to climb a steep wall without equipment. Ethan adjusted his shoulder bag, took a step forward, took a step back, gripped the railing only to let go of it. God only knew what he was doing. Robert stopped, watching him when a group of girls ran past him and up the stairs with loud chatter. His stomach twisted when Ethan grabbed the railing, as though it was his lifeline, and leaned into the wall. He didn't know what to do.

Ethan's shiny black hair obscured his face as he started walking up the stairs, as carefully as an old lady. It was pathetic and sad at the same time. With every step, he was dragging his foot up the vertical edge of the step, as if he were afraid to stumble.

"Hey, you all right?" asked Robert, putting his hands in his pockets. As much as he despised Ethan for what had happened the day before, the guy's physical condition was still his fault, and he couldn't let go of the responsibility while still being able to look himself in the face.

His heart froze when Ethan glanced back at him so quickly he looked as though he was about to lose his balance. At the last moment, Ethan grabbed the railing again.

"Yeah," Ethan muttered. "I just... stairs are shit. Like a fucking death trap."

Robert didn't need to listen to this anymore. He stepped forward and offered Ethan his arm. "I'll help you. Go on."

Ethan pulled back, pressing his side into the railing. "I'm sorry, you don't have to," he said but looked up at Rob with utter amazement and took him up on the offer in the blink of an eye. "The doctor said I'll adjust to it in no time."

Robert swallowed. He couldn't believe the helplessness in that face. It was as if Ethan had two different people in him. "Is it, uh, your head? Did this... thing affect your balance?"

"It's the eye. I can't figure out all the distances that well just yet, and on the stairs it's the worst because a wrong inch can make you fall. And because I've had these stinging headaches every now and then, it freaks me out to be somewhere where I can break my neck if I lose my balance. Sorry, am I boring you?" Ethan bit his lip and clenched his fingers over Rob's forearm as though it was the one thing that kept him from sinking into the murky sea of concrete beneath their feet.

Robert shook his head and swallowed, looking at the stairs, just to make sure Ethan wouldn't stumble. He had no idea what to say to this word-onslaught, and it hadn't even ended because Ethan opened his mouth again.

"I really hope it'll get easier because all the craft stuff I was doing before is harder now. But I have some new projects in mind. I'm not going to let this stop me. You know, when Monet started losing his eyesight, he made some fantastic paintings, like, really mind-blowing. He saw the world differently and amazed everyone. It's about trying to find an opportunity in all this," he babbled on as they slowly reached the top of the stairs. At least his voice was pleasant to listen to.

Robert clenched his teeth. He could imagine Ethan viewed the possibility of coercing him into sex as just that. An opportunity. This wasn't how he had imagined his first experiences with another guy, but he would suck it up and be a man about it. It wasn't as if it was something he didn't want to do in the long run. He would have wanted Ethan in normal circumstances. He had this nice, silky hair, beautiful, angular face, and soft skin.

It took Ethan a good couple of seconds too long before he reluctantly pulled back his hand from Robert's arm. "Thanks."

"It's my fault you have this problem in the first place, so it only seems fair," said Rob, looking at the empty corridor. Everyone was already in class, but while he'd wanted to run just minutes ago, now the peaceful atmosphere was drawing him in with promises of time off from all this shit.

Ethan looked at something behind Robert and then back into his eyes. "It would only be fair if you went to prom with me." There was a small smile on Ethan's lips, but at this point in their... *acquaintance*, Rob had no idea what was going on in that punctured brain.

Robert's breath caught in his throat. "Maybe you'd like me to donate my eye for you while I'm at it?"

The smile was gone with a little twitch of Ethan's eyebrow. "It was just a joke. I'd never actually inflict the horror of fake-dating me."

Robert bit his lip. A challenge was on the tip of his tongue, but was it really safe to call Ethan out on the Wednesday arrangement? What if it would piss Ethan off, and he'd report Robert's role in the accident?

Ethan watched him for the longest moment before pursing his lips and walking off toward the classroom, leaving only the fresh scent of shampoo behind him. He had nice legs. It only now hit Robert that Ethan seemed to be gaining back the weight he'd lost in hospital. He stepped toward their classroom but his eyes stopped at the prom poster on the wall. It must have been what sparked Ethan's idea. Robert swallowed, lingering for a few more seconds before following the slim figure. Everyone was expecting him to invite a girl, but the last time he dated one was in his sophomore year, and changing this fact was the last thing he wanted. Being gay sucked sometimes. Though thinking of the next visit at Ethan's home sucked more.

Chapter 5

ROB

ROBERT PARKED HIS CAR in the driveway of Ethan's home. Hidden away from the road and surrounded by trees, it was a well kept detached house with green and burgundy wooden panels covering the outer walls. In a place like this, Rob would expect to see a dog, but it seemed that Ethan's parents settled on keeping three cars instead, each with its own gate to a separate garage built in the same style as the house.

He cleared his throat, watching the skylights that were windows to Ethan's room. The thought that he was here just to get Ethan's rocks off made him beyond uncomfortable, but he had to do what he got to do, so after several minutes of sitting in the car and playing with his cell phone, he rang the bell. Each second seemed to stretch endlessly as he waited for an answer.

At least Ethan wasn't already naked when he appeared this time. All dressed in black as usual, his pale blue eye looked up at Rob, and Rob had no idea what was expected of him anymore.

"Hi," Ethan said with that serious expression on his face. "Come in."

Rob frowned, his stomach plummeting. "What is it?"

"Huh? What do you mean?" Ethan looked around the empty, spacious corridor. The high ceilings in the house gave it a high-class touch.

Rob cleared his throat and walked inside. "Dunno, you're just so… different here." And he already knew why. Here, Ethan was the one holding all the cards.

"I don't get it." Ethan reached out to Robert and slowly grabbed his hand. He did so with caution, as if he expected a slap on the wrist. Next thing Rob knew, he was pulled along into yet another massive room with a table fit for a family of ten.

"You know, you're so quiet at school." Rob looked down at their hands, surprised by the gesture. What was going on? Wasn't it all business this time?

"I'm not the most sociable of people, I agree." Ethan sighed and pulled out a chair for Robert. The situation was pure surrealism, but the food on the table was beyond mundane: some toast with peanut butter and jam on two individual plates.

Robert cleared his throat but slowly lowered himself to the seat. He wasn't sure what interested him more: the fake antiques and real artwork on the walls, or the fact that Ethan seemed to think this was some kind of dinner date at home.

Ethan sat on the opposite side of the table and nudged one plate toward Rob before biting into the sandwich himself. "Go on, have some."

Robert cleared his throat. "Am I too early again?" He reached for the food, wondering if it would be too much to ask for something to drink.

Ethan looked at the large grandfather clock behind him. "No, you're on time. Are you in a rush?"

Robert shrugged. "I just thought I interrupted you when you were eating." He bit into the sandwich and closed his eyes for a moment. The jelly was delicious. Homemade? Maybe. Definitely high quality stuff.

"I made it for you." Ethan went silent for a moment and placed the sandwich back on the plate. His moves were oddly stiff. "I know that what we have is maybe... not optimal, but I don't want you to have a totally horrible time."

"Are you autistic?" Robert leaned back in the chair, but he kept on chewing, in hope that if they ran out of uncomfortable topics of conversation, there was always food talk.

Ethan swallowed and looked at his plate. His eye patch added to the surreal atmosphere. As if he were some archvillain sitting behind the table in his lair, and Rob stumbled upon this place by accident. "Who knows. I do have some brain damage."

Robert hid his face behind his hands and bumped his forehead into the tabletop. No, he would not mention autism was not a result of brain damage. His hands were aching with the need to slap someone. "You really think it's all okay as long as you give me some peanut butter? What the fuck?"

Ethan cleared his throat and leaned back in his chair, with his only remaining eye on the tabletop rather than Robert's face. "N-no... I just... I thought we could talk... Maybe. Not make it so impersonal. I think, maybe I was too eager last time. But I've never done it before, and I sort of panicked."

"Surprise, I haven't sucked cock before either!" Robert uncovered his face and started stroking the edge of the plate, keeping his eyes on its decorative pattern. It was squeaky clean. His life was not.

Ethan took a deep breath, his face gradually pinkening. "But you've been in all sort of sexual situations, I can imagine. Thinking back, maybe I should have worn jeans or something. I'm not sure."

Robert swallowed and pulled on his index finger, just as his throat closed up. If sexual situations meant masturbating to gay porn then he had plenty of experience, but that was about it.

Ethan bit his lip. "You have to talk to me. I'm not best at these things, but I'm sure we can work something out. I just... oh God, I want it so much," he uttered in the end with a deep breath.

Robert shook his head and folded his arms across his chest, his muscles bundling up. This was the most selfish sentence he had ever heard in his life. "What do you want me to say?"

"I don't know. You're this amazing guy. I'd never get a chance to talk to you, and now you're sort of here and... maybe this could be an experiment for you, huh? No one would know. I'm not completely hideous or something." Ethan crossed his arms, mirroring Robert's movement.

Robert's lungs emptied as he stared at Ethan from across the table. That much was true, Ethan wasn't hideous. He was hot. Strange but hot. Like a male, grownup version of Wednesday Addams. But what did this mean for *him*? "Are you saying that I could experiment with you, but you wouldn't tell on me if I chose not to do this?" His throat ached so hard from the tension he had trouble keeping his voice even. It would be so embarrassing if he started talking to Ethan in a falsetto. But the tables turned a moment after, stunning Rob into silence.

Ethan straightened and nodded with so much vigor his hair obscured his face for a moment. "Yes, yes, total secret, no strings attached, all and any bi-curious needs satisfied," he said eagerly, with his eye on Robert. He was advertising himself as if he were a prepaid telephone card. "You don't have to even act like you know me much at school or anything. I'd be your clean secret."

Robert swallowed, pinching his left hand as hard as he could. "That's not what I'm asking. I'm asking if you'd let me off the hook if I said I'm not doing this."

Ethan instantly slumped in his chair with his lips quivering in a way that didn't suggest anything good, but he nodded nevertheless. "Yeah, I suppose so. I'd just... yeah, whatever." He sighed and rubbed his forehead above the missing eye. "I'd just never wanna talk to you again, but I guess that wouldn't be much of a loss for you."

"I thought you were happy to talk to me," pushed Robert. He reached for the sandwich again. Was there a hidden camera somewhere? This conversation was turning more bizarre by the second.

"Not if you totally reject me. I'm not made out of stone, you know," Ethan grumbled with a frown. "I don't expect you to feel responsible for my feelings but respect them. I'd rather not have them, but they exist, and that's that."

"Totally reject you?" asked Rob, leaning forward and biting into the sandwich. He couldn't believe something so weird could be the product of a healthy brain. Then again, Ethan was sort of excused.

"I opened up about how much I like you. If you say you don't want to have anything to do with me, even though I proposed complete discretion and no strings attached, then that's kinda humiliating, don't you think?" Ethan slouched, playing with the tips of his hair, but he was slowly going from deep breaths to hyperventilating. Robert blinked and raised his hands.

"Whoa, calm down here, okay? We're just talking," he uttered, watching the tension around Ethan's remaining eye. The guy was so confused it was painful to watch.

"I thought I could just demand it, but then you helped me at school anyway, and protected me from Pat, and did it all in public so other people took notice as well, and I can't just rationalize it anymore. I can't tell myself you deserve what's coming. Fuck." He started rubbing his eye, all red in the face.

Robert shook his head and took a deep breath, trying to be calm. "Of course I did. It's my fault you got hurt. Do you really think I'm some bully that's out to get people?"

"I don't know. I was so scared back then in the forest. I had no idea what you would do. You were all drunk. Anything could have happened." Ethan stared at the table, unmoving like a statue.

Robert swallowed and got to his feet. Keeping his eyes on Ethan's hunched form, he circled the table to stand next to him. From up close, his hair looked like beautiful threads of silk. "Just tell me if anyone picks on you, yeah?"

Ethan looked up at him, with his lips forming into a dissatisfied pout. "I will," he muttered and quickly slid off the chair in a way that allowed him not to risk brushing against Rob. He took a few steps toward the corridor.

"Where to now? Can I have some water first?" asked Rob, whose eyes trailed down the slim legs. Suddenly, being alone with Ethan didn't feel nearly as intimidating. He was pretty, and lonely, and scared of Rob.

"I-I wanted to show you out. I thought you wanted to leave?" Ethan swallowed, and Rob didn't have to be a mind reader to see there was still a glimmer of hope in that blue eye. Robert cleared his throat, desperately trying not to let any redness leak onto his face, but it was a futile attempt. He couldn't help but think that it was an opportunity for both of them. He had planned not to get involved with anyone until college, but Ethan was a safe option. There was still pent-up anger in him, but at the end of the day, someone as self-conscious and weak as Ethan couldn't possibly threaten him in any way.

"Will you do me too?"

The instantly widening pupil was all the answer he needed. Ethan stepped up to him and grabbed his hand. "I will! I don't have any experience, but I'll give it my best. And if you let me practice now and then, I promise I'll get better at it till graduation." The heat of his fingers betrayed the arousal and need contained in that small body.

"Water?" asked Robert, hardly keeping his smile at bay. This kind of excitement was something he definitely wanted to see in someone he was fucking. Heat spread through his body like wildfire.

"Yeah, sure, sure!" Ethan rushed off to the kitchen, with his bare feet thudding against the wooden floor.

"Just be careful." Robert hurried after him, suddenly hit by the vision of Ethan failing to perceive the depth of something and hurting his other eye. "I'm not dying yet." The moment he reached the kitchen, with the last word still on his lips, glass smashed all over the floor.

"Fuck!" Ethan groaned, but instantly dove to the cupboard under the sink for a dustpan and brush. "Don't worry, I'll get it."

Robert didn't hesitate and pulled him out, pressing him against his chest. "Leave it, yeah? You said you don't see well." He could feel Ethan's heart hammering in his chest, and it was kinda nice, actually. He'd held and kissed girls, but Ethan felt and smelled different altogether. There was more of him somehow, even though he was on the small side, and his scent was richer, sharper.

"It's just grabbing stuff that's been annoying lately," Ethan uttered but didn't move by a fraction of an inch.

Robert sighed, closing his eyes for just a short moment to enjoy the closeness. It was odd, but the moment Ethan had withdrawn his demands, his own anger had dispersed like a drop of ink in a pot of boiling water. " You'll get better at it with time." He spun Ethan around and lifted him to the counter. Pulling glass out of those bare feet was the last thing he wanted.

Ethan blinked at him from behind his black-rimmed glasses, but stayed put. "Wow. I mean... wow. I knew you were strong, but... I'm not all that light."

Robert let out a chuckle and looked at the narrow feet with a smile involuntarily spreading all over his face. "Yes, you are. You lost weight in hospital." He scooted down to retrieve the dustpan and brush, and started quickly gathering the shards.

Ethan's curious eye never left him alone. "I have a big appetite now, I'll get it back."

Robert's gaze swept over the bare toes, but despite the temptation, he didn't touch them, even though they seemed so cold and in need of socks. After disposing of the glass, he got himself some tap water and drank it all in one go, pretending not to notice the attention. But he could feel it, and it tickled his ego all over. He'd be lying if he said he didn't like to be admired. He even liked the way girls spun around him at school. Having a guy so clearly ogle him was new and exciting, since it could actually lead somewhere.

He put the glass into the sink and glanced at the pale face. "Ready."

Ethan's chest rose as he inhaled a big gulp of air, but then he slid down to the floor. "You wanna go to my room?" He stared at Robert as if he were the core of his being, lips slightly parted, the single blue eye hazy.

Robert exhaled and reached out to take Ethan's small hand. "Sure." His skin had a few little cuts and scabs, like he hadn't been careful enough while cutting bread or something. Not all that surprising considering how Ethan had broken the glass just moments ago.

Ethan squeezed Rob's hand and led him out of the kitchen and through the spacious living room, back to the corridor. His moves were rushed, and he almost walked into a standing lamp at one point, but they managed to walk through the house without Ethan hurting himself.

Robert swallowed and glanced at their feet, curious how Ethan would manage with the stairs in his own house. He was ready to help if it were needed, but there was a fair chance this staircase would be familiar enough for Ethan to use it without any trouble.

Ethan himself didn't seem so certain. He looked up the steep way upstairs, tightening his grip on Robert's forearm. He didn't say a thing, but after a few seconds, he started the slow climb, with his other hand resting on the railing. Slow but steady. "My mom wanted me to move downstairs, but I like my room too much," he said, watching his own feet.

"Is it getting easier?" Robert sighed. The covered-up eye was facing him, so he couldn't read Ethan's face as well as he'd like to. Now that they were so close, he could appreciate the soft skin, immaculate and flawless without the aid of any cosmetics. He rather liked that, even on someone who wore freaky bird skull accessories.

The moment Ethan turned to smile at Rob, he stumbled but somehow managed to keep his balance by holding on to him. "It's easier when I know the stairs, and I'm really used to these, so it's not as bad as the ones at school," he explained.

"Yeah, I know what you mean. It's a bit like moving in the dark." Robert was tempted to be a normal guy and just kiss the two soft cushions of Ethan's mouth, but he feared it would be crossing boundaries too sharply. He promised himself to wait till he was in college. Getting attached to someone so close to graduation was a fundamentally stupid idea. Sex would be fine though, didn't other guys hook up all the time? He could do that with someone, who thought he was just bi-curious.

"I won't let it stop me, I'll get used to it. It's more annoying than anything else," Ethan opened the heavy door to his attic room and invited Robert with a gesture. "Do you have a preference? I have condoms, I'm sorry I forgot last time.'

Robert swallowed, feeling his cheeks heat up. He cleared his throat and shook his head.

Ethan walked into that insane room of his, in which he looked oddly at home. Rob couldn't imagine anyone else fitting into this den of crazy. There was a stuffed bat in the corner of the sloped wall and a weasel approaching it upside down. The place could have doubled as a museum of curiosities.

"You sure? 'Cause you seemed... um... not really all that... I mean..." Ethan frowned and bit his lips.

"Because the situation was shit for me." Robert cleared his throat and turned his face away to look at a framed print that depicted various meats laid out on a wooden table next to a pheasant cut in half.

The only answer he got was a little squeak of springs and the sound of a computer starting. He blinked and looked that way, his focus drawn to Ethan's computer wallpaper—a photo of Matt Powers, a famous gay porn star. "You wanna show me something?"

Ethan shrugged. "I just thought it might be nicer for you if I turn on some music," he said from where he sat on the bed, with his back to Robert. The comforter was covered with a black mohair fur bedcover that spread over the large mattress.

"Sure, as long as it won't bust my eardrums." Robert smiled and walked around the bed to sit next to Ethan. Now that they were alone, on the bed, his heart was picking up its pace. He couldn't believe he was doing this. Then again, it was only natural since he was young, horny, and had someone available.

"I'll try not to make it shit this time," Ethan whispered and put on the weirdest music Rob had ever heard. A slow piece with instruments Robert couldn't pinpoint, some sounding harp-like, some like a harmonica, a flute, and a deep-sounding drum. It made Rob think of a group of medieval pagan sorcerers dancing around a bonfire and sacrificing virgin goats.

"It's been nice so far." Rob cleared his throat and moved his fingers down Ethan's arm, feeling the warmth of his soft skin. "What's that band?"

Ethan looked down at Rob's hand. "It's the soundtrack from this new medieval TV show. I googled the band and found they do these musical reconstructions but add their own flavor to it as well." He took a deep breath through his nose, eyeing Robert with growing intensity.

Rob leaned forward and breathed in Ethan's scent. Ginger and orange, maybe some bergamot as well, nice and herby. He followed the aroma and moved his nose over the shell of Ethan's ear. His hair was unbelievably soft, so unlike Robert's cock. "You like stuff like that?"

Ethan looked up at him with his lips parted. "Y-yes. Singing distracts me when I'm working on a project so I like all sorts of instrumental tracks."

Robert doubted talking about music was on Ethan's mind right now, but it was fun to see him try to focus. Robert smiled and moved his hands lower, slipping them underneath the oversized sweater. The moment he touched the fitted top below, his chest and stomach burned up, melting like warm jelly. He was touching a guy. He was touching a guy he was about to fuck, and he still couldn't get his head around it. His cheeks on fire, he pulled up the sweater, eager to see more of Ethan's body. Get a better look at that tattoo on his stomach.

Ethan gave a nervous chuckle and threw the garment to the floor. At school, Ethan never even smiled for more than an obligatory moment, it was odd to see his face light up. "I thought I kinda overdid it last time. You know, with being naked. I didn't know what to do." The top Ethan had been wearing under the sweater was tight, emphasizing the slim but toned body underneath.

"I don't mind naked." Rob cleared his throat and pulled Ethan back against him, burying his face in the sleek hair. With one hand sensing every heartbeat in Ethan's chest, he let the other slide lower, to Ethan's thigh, and squeezed it gently.

He liked this a lot more than being told what to do. Ethan really did seem more nervous than him and was like fresh cookie dough in Rob's hands. It would be impossible to resist when an opportunity like this just fell into his lap. A hot guy to touch with no restraint, no strings, and no consequences.

Ethan swallowed, his chest moving quickly under Rob's hand. "I was never naked with anyone before."

Rob couldn't stop a laugh as he let his hands explore, moving over the warm body next to his, petting, stroking, and squeezing the flesh through the fabric as his own skin burned up. "You would be used to this if you did sports at school."

"I kinda... I'm not all that good at teamwork," Ethan whispered and his pale, long fingers moved to Rob's thigh.

Robert bit his lip to keep himself from saying something stupid. Instead, he cupped Ethan's cock through the jeans and shivered at the sensation of it stiffening in his grip. It was so strange to touch another guy like that, even though that was what he'd always wanted.

Ethan leaned into the touch with a gasp, and tightened his grip on Rob's thigh. His breath hitched, its warmth blooming all over Rob's neck. The room felt like a cocoon of safety now that Robert was free to experiment, nothing like last time. And he would take full advantage of it.

"Would you do me first?" whispered Rob, moving his stubbly cheek against the side of Ethan's neck. Despite the growing arousal, the situation was still very odd, and he did his best not to lose the flow.

"Sure, yeah," Ethan said and slid to his knees in front of Robert quicker than it took an egg to harden on a red hot pan. It was one of the sexiest things Rob had ever seen, and it made him feel like a king, like he'd just scored a touchdown. And Ethan hadn't even sucked him yet. Rob already imagined his cock sliding in between those full, pale lips, the black hair tickling his thighs. Heat exploded all over his body. This was it. He was getting his first blow job ever. He wasn't sure whether he was more nervous or excited. His fingers were on Ethan's lips before he could even think of it, tracing their softness in a slow, sensuous motion.

Ethan opened his mouth without a word and kissed one fingertip before sucking on it in a way that made Rob's dick throb. For a socially awkward kid, he was extremely sexy. Rob parted his thighs wider, and Ethan slid right in between them like water finding a crack in a dam. The mere closeness of his body made the inner side of Rob's legs tingle in anticipation of touch. Lightheaded, he stroked Ethan's hair with his other hand. If he could only rewind this moment and live it over and over.

Rob thought it couldn't get any better, but it did when Ethan looked up at him with a smile wider than ever before and unzipped Rob's fly. Ethan had the most heart-melting set of white teeth Rob had ever seen. And it was *him* provoking that reaction. The mere idea of sucking Rob's dick was so attractive to Ethan that he smiled like never before. It made blood thud in Rob's ears. Like on autopilot, he gently grasped the sides of Ethan's glasses and pulled them off. His breath was coming in shallow, uneven gasps, but he simply couldn't help himself. He wanted to feel Ethan giving him an orgasm so badly.

Some of the black hair fell forward and framed Ethan's flushed face. Ethan took a deep breath and leaned forward to kiss the bulge in Rob's pants. The gesture reminded Rob of all his guy-friends complaining about how hard it was to convince their girlfriends to give head. Rob could hardly believe his luck. His whole world narrowed down to that pale face between his legs, and he opened his thighs wider, coaxing Ethan closer into the trap. Though was it really a trap if the guy wanted it?

Rob pulled back Ethan's hair and slowly moved his fingertips over the scalp, trying not to wheeze. It was like petting a super-cute cat and getting head at the same time.

Ethan pulled down Rob's pants and briefs just enough for his cock to pop out, and the way Ethan's pupil dilated made Robert's chest swell with pride. Waiting wasn't part of the plan, and Ethan kissed the tip of Robert's cock as soon as it was out. The hot fingers were on Rob's stomach before he knew it, and the teasing lap on his cockhead once again made him compare Ethan to a cat.

He stared at the soft mouth moving over the tip of his dick like it was the most precious thing in the world. His eyes couldn't go any wider, but he untangled his hands from Ethan's hair, knowing he was close to yanking him forward, and forcing him into anything was the last thing Rob wanted. Instead, his fingers tangled into the mohair fur on the bed, soft and curly.

Ethan looked up for a fraction of a second before slowly sucking the head into his mouth. It felt gentle and passionate all at once, pleasure simmering instead of boiling. He kept exploring Rob's abs when the heat rose, and Ethan took more of Rob's dick between his lips. It slid over his palate, hugged by the velvety tongue from the underside. Hitting the back of Ethan's mouth was yet another perk sending sparks of excitement all the way to Rob's balls. Heat spread over his body like a flash flood, making him squeeze his hands on the furry bedspread, his back tensing as a warm tingle tickled the base of his spine. It was fucking amazing. He forced his eyes to stay open, but the grunts that left his mouth were all too real. He could do nothing about them with excitement rolling through his whole body

"That's so good."

Ethan looked up with Rob's cock deep in his mouth, and there was a smile in his one eye, its side creasing slightly. Without ever blinking, he moved his head forward but then had to back off when he gagged. That didn't stop him though, and he repeated the motion, his lips spread wide over the base. Each time Ethan took it in until he gagged, Rob's cockhead was squeezing into the tightness of the throat, and it was so good Rob almost felt the upcoming orgasm throb in his gums.

Rob reached out blindly and squeezed the slim arm, gasping for air and already in a world of his own. He was galloping toward the sweet, sweet completion with arms wide open. "I'm... I'm close," he whispered, forcing himself to look into Ethan's eye. His face was now all red, shiny with a thin layer of sweat, and it looked so hot Rob hardly managed to produce any sound.

Ethan only backed off by an inch and sucked on Rob's cock with renewed eagerness. His hands were gone off Rob's stomach, and the metallic clang of a belt opening seamlessly melted into the music. Rob would forever associate whatever this medieval style music was with a mind-blowing orgasm. It was like fireworks exploding behind his eyelids, in his brain, sending a wave of intense, loud noise all over him. Then, there was the heavenly pull in his testes, and the moment his cock twitched against that soft, lovely mouth, his head got so light Rob was close to collapsing on his back. He never came like that. Not ever. He forced his eyes open, looking at the man who had made it all happen.

What he got to see was yet another incredibly hot image, and he almost came a second time. Ethan, still on the floor, was slobbering around Rob's cock, with his hand in his rolled-down pants. From above, Rob had a great view on the pale ass sticking out from beneath the tight top. It was too good, but with the growing sensitivity in his cock, he had to gently push Ethan away.

"Too much," he uttered and looked down at the dark cockhead moving in and out of Ethan's clenched fist. God, it was hot. Was he supposed to tell him to stop? Continue?

Ethan let Rob's cock out of his mouth but stayed between Rob's legs, with his head leaning against the thigh and his lips still so close Rob felt his hot breath on his wet skin. Before Rob could decide what to do, gather his thoughts somehow, Ethan came with a low moan, his buttocks tensing rhythmically as Ethan's body jerked, embracing the orgasm.

Robert leaned down to him and pulled him close, absorbing the last shudders and the delightful heat in his arms. "Good. That was really good," he whispered against Ethan's ear, shocked by the intensity of the moment. He couldn't believe he got Ethan so excited the guy couldn't wait for his turn.

Ethan had his arms around Rob's neck within a split second, and he leaned all his body weight on Robert. "Your dick is so awesome," he uttered, still panting after his orgasm. "I want you to always feel good. Or at least not-shit." Even though Ethan was so much smaller, he had a pleasant tightness to his body, which was compact but with tense muscle under the soft skin.

Robert groaned and pulled him up. With his hands tangling around Ethan's waist, he dragged him on top of himself and dropped to the bed, sprawled on his back. "Say again? I didn't hear that well," he uttered, already smiling. His whole body was in a chaotic tingle, as if there were armies of invisible ants crawling all over him.

Ethan put a hand over his face. "Your dick is awesome," he said with a smile in his voice.

Rob's skin burned with pleasant heat where Ethan's still hot cock was trapped between their bodies. He hugged Ethan closer, doing his best to calm his breathing. He didn't want to seem too affected, even though he was. "But you won't get your blow job now."

"That's fine. You didn't seem to like doing it, which kinda makes sense." Ethan sighed, his heartbeat slowly evening out against Rob's chest. "So I figured I'll just save you the trouble."

Robert wanted to slam himself over the head. What was he supposed to do *now*? "You said 'all bi-curious needs', yeah?"

Ethan's head instantly popped up. "Yes, and all discreet and everything. We can do it with a condom, 'cause you seemed to hate the sperm. Or I could jerk off at the end so you wouldn't have to taste it." He was speaking quickly and rocked against Rob's body, as if he really were a cat rubbing itself against its owner. Rob wished he could stay like this forever, with a hot guy rubbing against him, and then do each other, and then maybe cook something nice to have energy for more fucking. That would be heaven.

"If I need something, I'll tell you. Don't be so tense."

In turn, Ethan tensed up even more, which was all too obvious when he was so close, but he then put his cheek on Rob's collarbone and let out a deep breath, which seemed to relax his muscles. "Okay."

Robert closed his eyes, absentmindedly stroking Ethan's body up and down. Up and down. Next Wednesday couldn't come sooner. The herby smell of Ethan's body got even stronger now, it was like sitting by the oven while having a cake inside. Ethan's weight was comfortable, like a heavy comforter but sweeter, but warmer and much more fragrant. Robert loved it. "What?"

"I stress over trying not to seem like I'm awkward and only end up looking more like it in the process. But you'll tell me when you want me off, yeah?" The soft hair tickled Robert under the chin. "You're not a couple with Kelly now, are you?"

Robert grunted. "No, I'm single." He resisted the temptation to kiss the fluffy hair just below his mouth and closed his arms around Ethan. It could only become more perfect if they could have another go at it later tonight, but that wouldn't happen because he needed to go home at some point. He'd get his share of proper boyfriends in college, he'd made sure his university of choice had a proper LGBT club.

"Okay. I mean, not that it matters, I just wanna know. You want any more sandwiches?" Ethan hugged him closer, and Robert couldn't help but steal a glance at Ethan's ass, bare and sprinkled with goose bumps.

Robert couldn't stop the laugh that shook his chest. "Yeah, that would be nice. And maybe some coffee?" He looked at those buttocks and slowly moved his hand lower, stopping it just above the naked flesh.

"Sure." For a moment, when Ethan rose, Robert thought he was getting a kiss, but all he got was a tickle of Ethan's hair, his mouth getting away all-too-soon. Still, this afternoon had turned out completely different than what Rob had expected. "My parents will be back in an hour. I'm sure they'll be happy to see you as a guest, but they have an annoying tendency not to knock on doors," Ethan said as he pulled on his pants.

Robert scrambled to a sitting position with a goofy smile. "Yeah, all right." The last thing he wanted was to be caught in bed with Ethan.

He put his cock back into his pants and zipped up. It was the sound of triumph, he could almost hear jolly music in the background of his mind. He'd officially lost his virginity. And to a hot guy with a cute butt at that. Was that butt on the table as well? He didn't want to ask just yet.

Ethan pulled his hair up into a bun at the back of his head and put his glasses on with a smile never leaving his lips. "I'll get you that coffee then," he chirped. His whole silhouette looked lean and linear without the oversized sweater. A bit like a ninja, all in black and with an eye patch.

"I'll go with you," offered Robert, stretching on purpose to make Ethan stare at his chest. That hairdo was cute, a bit hipster-ish but really cute.

"Perfect. Going up the stairs with a tray full of hot coffee might be stretching it. I would most probably spill it, burn myself, and then slip on the sandwich," Ethan said. He did stare, just as predicted.

"We can't have that," agreed Rob and offered his arm to him.

Ethan took it eagerly, and the awe Rob saw in his eye when he looked up at him was the best thing a guy could ever get after sex. He'd love to be able to tell his friends how eager his 'girlfriend' was to suck his dick.

Chapter 6

Rob

Robert was surprised that the conversation rolled so smoothly. They ended up staying in the kitchen and chatting over coffee. Ethan's parents were lawyers, who worked together in one of the firms in town, and that meant he usually had a lot of time for himself. Without friends, it sounded a bit lonely, but Robert wouldn't say that out loud.

"What do you do out of school with your friends?" Ethan asked, dangling his bare feet over the floor.

Robert grinned, watching the pale face in front of him. "The usual. We go to the movies, watch TV, sometimes we have parties, and so on. It's nothing... you know, special. Just having fun together."

"What I don't like about parties is that you never know whether you're going to have fun or not." Ethan squinted slightly and had another sip of his black coffee. He seemed too serious for his cute face.

Robert blinked, unsure what to make of it. Wasn't the goal of organizing a party to have fun? How could it not be fun? "What do you mean?"

Ethan cocked his head to the side. "Sometimes you get yourself to go, but no one talks to you, and you just end up wishing you weren't there. But I guess you never have this problem." He poked Robert's thigh with his toe.

Robert drew in a sharp breath as the sensation climbed higher up his leg, but he shook his head. Was *this* why Ethan ended up as the prey to drunk werewolves? He'd been all alone that night.

"My parents push me to go though. They claim it's good 'social hygiene', and they believe in the power of connections. I think my mom's been doing too much yoga." Ethan smirked, looking into his coffee.

"So you don't even like parties when it's just you and some of your friends?"

"Come on, Rob, I don't really have many friends. And my parents are all crazy about the idea that at our age it's 'school time'. So many times I've heard that I shouldn't be thinking of friends or dating now. Which is a bit contradictory to the idea of social hygiene, but whatever."

Robert frowned over his coffee, unsure what to say to that without being insulting. Ethan's parents seemed very nice and concerned for their son's well-being. Maybe they were too concerned though. "I guess you're right. When are you supposed to make friends if not in high school?"

"Through head trauma, of course." Ethan poked Rob with his toe again.

Robert swallowed hard, tightening his fingers around the cup. "I'm so sorry. I'm never gonna drink again."

"Come on, that was a joke. I mean..."

Before Ethan could finish his thought, there was a bang of the door, and two pairs of steps. Ethan's parents' voices resounded in the empty living room.

"Hey, sweetie! Sorry we're late, but we did bring dinner," Ethan's mom said. Rob got a glimpse of ginger as she passed the entrance to the kitchen, but then she immediately came back. "Robert! It's so good to see you."

He raised his hand with a smile. "I thought I'd come by to see how Ethan's adjusting. We don't share many classes."

"Would you like to stay for dinner? We have lots of Chinese." She smiled at him and gestured at Ethan, who instantly slid down from the counter. "Terry! Robert's come round for dinner!" she yelled out into the corridor.

"Ethan's friend?" answered Ethan's dad, still fumbling with something by the door.

Ethan's mom nodded at him and walked into the kitchen with hands full of packaged food. Robert felt his mouth water. As good as the sandwiches were, they were no proper dinner.

"If it's no trouble. We kinda stopped paying attention to time."

Ethan's smile grew, and he started getting out the dishes, which made Rob's blood pump a bit faster. He could already imagine all of them falling to the floor when Ethan miscalculated where the end of the table was.

"Not at all," Ethan's mom said. "I can never give you enough dinners for what you've done."

Robert got to his feet and walked over to Ethan, ready to give him a hand. Every time he heard Ethan's parents expressing their gratitude, he felt like the scum of the earth. He didn't want them to know, yet on the other hand felt they deserved the truth. It was so fucked up. "It wasn't anything special," he muttered.

"Someone else would have yanked out that branch, but you really knew what to do." Ethan's Mother walked up to Robert and gave him a hug, covering him in the sweet aroma of her perfume.

"I wouldn't have been there in the first place if you didn't force me to socialize," muttered Ethan, taking the plates to the living room.

"Ethan, behave," hissed his mother, untangling herself from Rob.

Robert bit his lip and took another sip of coffee. "That's just because my mom's a doctor." He peeked at Ethan, wondering if the guy was okay with him staying, but there was no answer.

"That was so fortunate. It's nice of you to still visit after Ethan's been out of the hospital." Ethan's mother took the cutlery and the bags with food, and walked out into the living room. She was always so proper looking in an elegant suit straight from work, and her bone structure made her instantly recognizable as Ethan's mother.

"We're friends," uttered Rob.

"Ethan could use a friend who is actually alive." Ethan's dad laughed and took off his suit jacket before sitting down at the big table.

"Daaad…" Ethan moaned and rubbed his cheek under the eye patch.

"Is that about your taxidermy thing?" Rob asked, turning his head to Ethan. It was a bit freaky, but it wasn't like Ethan wanted to stuff *him*.

Ethan's mother filled everyone's plates with the efficiency of an army general as they talked. "Have you seen his little den of dread?" She laughed and poked Ethan with her elbow. He didn't seem impressed.

"Yes, it's the taxidermy thing," Ethan said, slouching over his plate. "I didn't think Robert would be all that interested. It's a bit morbid."

"A bit?" His father shook his head.

Robert hardly kept a smile at bay. "A 'den of dread'? That sounds promising."

Ethan's dad shrugged and parted his disposable chopsticks. "It's a harmless hobby."

Ethan's mom nodded. "I even asked Ethan to make a rat ballerina for me, but he refuses. Maybe I'll get one for Christmas."

"I don't do ballerinas." Ethan pinched the top of his nose.

"It can have a black tutu, sweetie."

Ethan just chewed on his food, but Robert would not be discouraged. It sounded weird enough to be interesting.

"A rat ballerina? You dress up stuffed animals?"

Ethan looked up at him over the table, and Rob couldn't work out what his expression meant. "Sometimes. I'm still experimenting. My bird skull necklaces are very popular, but I like dealing with small animals, like rats or squirrels. I also buy vintage taxidermy of bigger animals sometimes and make sculptures out of them. My biggest project this year was making a mouse house inside the neck of an old elk trophy head."

"Isn't that inventive." Ethan's dad stroked his son's head like he were a five-year-old.

Robert raised his brows, biting the inner side of his lips. He was happy his mother didn't treat him like a child in front of his friends. "That... sounds unusual. Is it done?"

"Mostly. There's still finishing touches I need to do." Ethan licked some sauce off his lips and went silent for a moment. "You wanna see it?" he managed to ask before any of his parents sneaked in a word.

Robert did the same. "Sure."

Ethan's dad cleared his throat, but kept a smile on his lips. "I'm not sure if that's such a good idea. Maybe you could show him a picture sometime."

"No, he can see it if he wants." Ethan frowned. "I worked so hard on it."

"Okay, okay, but don't be afraid to say if it makes you uncomfortable, Robert." Ethan's mom added to her son's deep, long sigh.

Robert, whose mouth was at this point packed with chow mein, nodded at her. The food was delicious, crispy, well seasoned, and fresh. He supposed Ethan's parents used a proper restaurant as their supplier. The taxidermy thing was intriguing. He knew Ethan was making jewelry but art? That was new.

The rest of the meal passed on pleasant conversation, with Ethan generally staying quiet but adding his two cents every now and then. He kept looking up at Robert though, which sent imaginary sparks of excitement toward Rob. It was as if they were having an entirely different conversation across the table. One that didn't involve patronizing Ethan, but instead consisted of many innuendos and promises of cocksucking. All silent.

Robert was happy to be released from the table, and even as he helped to stash the dishes on the kitchen counter, his eyes kept returning to Ethan across the room. Would they do it again?

Ethan helped his mom in the kitchen, but he kept dropping things, so in the end she sent him off to show Robert his 'den'.

"I'm not usually this clumsy," Ethan huffed as soon as they left the dining room and walked down the corridor toward the door.

"You know, just be careful for now, yeah? You're still adjusting to it all." Robert cleared his throat, following him out of the house. He was tempted to touch him but it wasn't safe with the parents around. After all, the light coming from inside the living room could be enough for them to spot any suspicious behavior.

"I've read that people with one eye drive cars, but I'm not allowed," he sighed and put on a black hoodie with fur lining.

Robert rubbed his hands together. He didn't know what he'd do without a car. It would feel like losing an arm. "Will you ever be allowed to again?"

"Not in the foreseeable future. You know, the doctors are afraid a headache might hit me when I'm on the road, so... yeah." It sounded more like a general complaint than some attempt at guilt tripping Rob, but it still made him want to apologize.

"You know, if you needed to go somewhere, I could give you a lift."

"You could?" Ethan looked up at him with that glint in his eye. Robert loved being tall enough to see the top of his head, it made him feel all big and hunky. Plus, Ethan's hair was healthy, and for some reason, the pale glint of skin at the parting made him think of that herbal scent he liked so much.

"Sure, as long as you don't ask me to take you across the country for the weekend," chuckled Rob.

"No! No, I'd only ask you when I really need it. Like, really. I wouldn't abuse the privilege," Ethan said in all eagerness and grabbed Rob's sleeve.

Robert couldn't help but look back to make sure they weren't watched before relaxing. "Don't stress about it. I like going places."

They approached one of the three garage doors, and Ethan turned back to smile at him in a way he hadn't at the dinner table. "I might use you then." He frowned. "I mean, in a good way, you know?"

Robert cleared his throat, remembering the repulsion he'd felt a week ago when Ethan made him go down on him. There was still a bit of anger in him about it, but excitement rose under his skin at the suggestion. "I look forward to that."

Ethan took a deep breath and smiled even wider. It was as if Robert turned on a switch in him that no one at school, or even at his home, seemed to be able to. Ethan led him into the garage and put on the light. The car that faced them was an old black Chevy, Ethan's car, but to the left stood a bronze sedan, and a red sports car. Normally, he would be interested in the make and model, but it all dispersed in the background when he noticed something large under a black sheet of plastic in the back behind Ethan's car.

Robert raised an eyebrow at it, resting his hands at his hips. "Is that the moose?"

"An elk." Ethan rushed past the Chevy and to the covered piece of art. "You ready?" he asked, grabbing one end of the sheet with his smile radiating enthusiasm.

The open expression on his sweet face made Rob pay all the more attention to what Ethan was about to unravel. Would it be horrible? The bird necklace Ethan kept wearing to school was creepy but seemed well done, so if that was anything to judge by, this could turn out interesting. He nodded.

Ethan pulled off the sheet with a few swift pulls, uncovering the massive trophy. Dyed completely black, the fur was matte, but the grand antlers shone as if dipped in tar. The fake glass eyes had a foggy quality to them, which gave the whole piece more depth. On the side of its thick neck was a small round wooden door. Like one in a hobbit house.

Robert caught himself staring while stepping forward, fascinated by the sculpture. It was so... different and drew him in like a dish he'd never had the chance to sample before. "That is... impressive," he uttered, scooting down to look into the muzzle. He reached out to brush his fingers over the stiff hairs. "Is that hair coloring, or paint?"

Ethan scooted down next to him and adjusted his glasses. "It's dye, and I covered the antlers with liquid latex, so they have that rubbery, slippery look. Go on, touch them."

Robert exhaled and brushed his fingers over the antler. It had a strange texture, a bit like thick rubber gloves but smoother and finer. "It is nice," he said and moved his hand lower, to the small door. The whole thing smelled of paint, so unlike the dull, stuffy smell he had imagined.

"Wait." Ethan grabbed his wrist. "Are you sure you're ready?" He asked as if it was a door to another dimension.

"Why, will I meet Mr. Tumnus behind that door?"

"Or his mouse cousins." Ethan let go and gave Robert a tiny key.

Robert blinked. Was it actually lockable? That was so creative! A small tingle of excitement spurted in his temples, and he nodded, gently pushing the key into the lock. It was such an eerie feeling. Even with Ethan's serious little face so close and his permission, Rob felt like an intruder to a world he might not understand at all. Ethan's world.

Inside was a land of mice, with a tiny house, with an even tinier balcony. Everything, including a miniature tree and a bench underneath was white. "Pull the little cord on the side," Ethan said with excitement, squeezing close to Robert. The touch of his warm body sent sparks up Rob's arm, and he pushed his fingers inside the neck of the elk, pulling on the thin cord with two digits. The world inside the elk's head lit up with bright white light from a tiny sparkling chandelier hanging from the top. It illuminated the scene, showing more detail. There was a mouse in a white dress looking out from the balcony, while another sat in the milky moss and read a book, a top hat with a white feather on its head.

Robert couldn't stop staring at all the gorgeous detail. It was like finding a whole world where one would least expect it, but it wasn't just about the idea. Ethan's craftsmanship was remarkable. Rob would hardly expect to find something this meticulous and creative in a garage in his home town.

Ethan sighed. "I called it *Of Mice and Elk*. There's lots of stuff I still want to tweak. I'd like to add some stairs in that moss, but cutting wood is a pain now, they all come out uneven. But practice makes perfect, I suppose."

"No, it's fantastic. I had no idea you were doing things this... grand." Robert shook his head and crooked his neck to see more. "Do elks dream about mice?"

Ethan stared at him and blinked a few times before a soft smile stretched his lips. "Maybe after they die?" He lay down on the concrete and also looked inside.

Robert lowered his hand to Ethan's back, just letting it rest there, in the warmth of Ethan's body. "What inspired you to make this?"

"It's a mixture of things, it doesn't have some Freudian meaning or whatever. I just love the visuals of it. The black and the white. The massive and the tiny. The grand and the dainty. I like that you can interact with it a bit, not just watch it. I plan to install a mouse on a swing as well. The viewer will be able to push it."

Robert felt his mouth stretch into a smile. The vision of a stuffed mouse on a swing worked like a large gulp of beer. Was it that strange that he found it somewhat cute? "I'd love to see that."

"I'm gonna be like Scheherazade, adding pieces, so you have to keep coming back here." Ethan poked Rob's bicep with his forehead.

Robert swallowed and pulled Ethan a bit closer. The boy was too sweet for that sentence to sound stalkerish. He just said what came to his mind, not really filtering any of it. For a moment, he wanted to tell Ethan he preferred for him to stay male, but he bit his tongue.

Ethan stared at Robert, and his brows gathered into a slight frown. "Sorry. Was that creepy?"

Robert shook his head.

"Good. You wanna see my workshop?" Ethan picked at a thread coming out of Rob's sleeve.

"Is that the den of dread?" Rob asked with a grin, but switched off the chandelier and locked the door in the elk's neck. He wanted to be a polite guest.

"Please don't call it that." Ethan winced and got up. "My parents do, and it makes it sound like it's something silly. And this is really important for me."

Robert got to his feet. "Sorry, I thought it was just... you know, teasing."

"It is teasing. And I hate it." Ethan was too serious for his own good.

"Oh, come on, why does it bother you so much? You know that what you do is..." He gestured to the elk. "It's amazing."

Ethan scratched his head and opened a door in the back of the garage. "I'm not stupid. Everyone laughs at me at school because of it, and the crazy vegans hate me."

"So? This is great stuff. This is art." Robert couldn't help himself and looked back at the elk. One had to appreciate it as an artwork.

"You like it that much? I haven't shown it to anyone but my parents yet." Ethan turned on the lights only to reveal a narrow corridor leading to the basement. Robert didn't like those steep stairs at all.

"I'll go first, okay?" he asked, putting his hand on Ethan's shoulder to stop him. "And yeah, I like it. It's awesome."

Ethan gave him a crooked smile but let him pass. "See, I'm not completely useless."

"I just don't want you to get hurt on my watch. You'll get distracted and fall. We don't want that," said Robert, descending down a narrow staircase that smelled of concrete and disinfectant. He sure hoped the den wasn't as creepy as Ethan's parents suggested. They made it sound like their son was a serial killer. Of rats.

Ethan put a hand on Rob's shoulder and followed. "You must feel so guilty."

Rob exhaled, focusing on the gray stairs beneath his feet. "You think?"

"'Cause you treat me like porcelain now. Can I get a piggyback ride?"

Robert frowned. Was Ethan making fun of him now? Because it was not funny at all. "Not here."

"Why not?" Ethan followed him down the stairs into the large, well lit basement with too many little details everywhere to take in. A large table was full of art supplies, sketchbooks, jars of pencils and brushes. A freezer and fridge stood next to industrial shelving units and a cupboard with drawers with a few stuffed rats posed on top of it. The smell of chemicals lingered in the air, but that was to be expected.

Robert shrugged, walking over to the rats. This place wasn't nearly as creepy as he had imagined. Actually, Ethan's room was weirder, this space was a proper workshop. "Are you serious or not?"

Ethan shook his head and unraveled his hair from the bun, which left them wavy. "Nah, don't be silly."

"I don't know what to expect of you." Robert crooked his head and gently brushed his finger over the fine fur between the rat's tiny ears. He would have never suspected it was done by someone his own age. Ethan had lots of expertise.

"Well, you wouldn't do it anyway." Ethan walked over to the freezer and opened its door. "I keep some rats and stuff here. They're my favorites."

Robert frowned but didn't comment on the piggybacking. He'd totally do it in the right circumstances, but he wasn't going to tempt Ethan. "Where do you keep the rest then?"

"I only have a few at the moment. But there's this guy who's gonna get me quite a few squirrels soon." Ethan brushed his hand against Rob's in passing, making him turn and stare at Ethan.

"Okay..."

"I have this little online store." Ethan walked up to a wall full of necklaces hanging from nails. "I'm planning a whole new collection with squirrels."

"You *sell* this?" Robert raised his brows, surprised, though it was only to be expected for someone with talent like Ethan's to take advantage of it. "More jewelry?"

"Yeah, I've had people from all over buy them. I thought I could make some hairpieces with the tails... I'm still sketching out ideas. Is this too morbid for you? 'Cause I get it if it is..." Ethan had this attentive stare, like he was always switched to the 'on' setting.

"I will tell you if I think you're overdoing it." Rob smiled and peeked at the labels on bottles and jars in a high but narrow block of shelves. Did Ethan use all of this? No wonder the skin on his hands was so dry.

"Don't open those, some are toxic," Ethan warned him and stayed with his mouth open, as if he wondered whether he should go on or not. "Rob... you're a lot more open-minded than I thought you'd be," he eventually said with a small smile.

Robert snorted. "I just look like a caveman."

"And I look weird, but I'm actually nice, right? So we even out?" Ethan bit his lip and clasped his hands together.

Robert frowned. "You don't look *that* weird." He knew that what Ethan wanted him to say was 'yes, you are very nice', but it wouldn't be the whole truth.

"I'm gonna have to work on it then. Get some eyeliner going and stuff." Ethan walked up to a tiny top hat with a skull on top of it. "I could wear this to school."

Robert sighed. He wasn't in favor of the idea. "I don't know..."

"I'm just messing with you." Ethan poked Rob's chest. "This one's sold already anyway."

Robert leaned back against a table and scanned the space, debating how to express what he wanted to say. Eventually, he settled on, "Will you take a break from it when you go to college?"

"I-I wish I wouldn't have to. I would love to just expand my business." Ethan pointed to the stairs. "You wanna go back?"

Robert shrugged. "To the elk?"

Ethan laughed. "You must really like it. No, back to the house. It's kinda chilly down here, and I didn't turn on the heating."

Robert scratched Ethan's nape, just to feel the soft hair at the base. "I think your parents have had enough of me for one day."

Ethan opened his lips in a way that immediately reminded Robert of how amazing it was to have them wrapped around his cock. He chuckled and flattened his palm over the slim neck. "Will you walk me to the car?"

"Y-yeah, sure, absolutely!" Ethan rushed up the stairs only to trip and climb up the last few on all fours.

Robert didn't know whether to feel sorry for him or laugh. "Why are you running from me?" he asked, following Ethan up the stairs.

"I just didn't want to keep you waiting." Ethan scrambled back to his feet and covered the elk with the plastic.

"Why are you so nervous? Chill out." Robert switched off the light on the staircase and closed the door, watching Ethan, who behaved as if he left a soufflé in the oven back at home.

Ethan swallowed, glancing at Rob over his shoulder as he passed the Chevy. "I just don't know how much I can touch you. I don't want to offend you. Obviously you must have some boundaries that I'm not all that acquainted with yet. I'd want our thing to work as well as it can." It was one of the worst babble-moments Ethan had ever had.

Robert reached him in two steps and pulled him back. It took a slow twist of the slim body to get Ethan standing flat against the wall, facing away from Robert, who melted into him, pressing his shins against Ethan's calves. His hips were against Ethan's lower back. It was enough for heat to start simmering just beneath Rob's skin. With a sigh of relief, he smelled Ethan's hair.

"Not many boundaries then?" Ethan choked out, stiff as the elk head.

Robert smiled against his scalp and moved his face lower, brushing his nose over the temple, ear, jawline, neck... "No."

"I... Oh. That's nice. I'll try to 'chill out'," Ethan whispered as his body lost some of its tension. Even the cold air from outside wouldn't cool Rob down. With the smell of the forest so intense around them, Rob would love to just let nature take its course. Ethan was so *available* it was dangerous. It was good that Robert was too nervous about Ethan's dad popping in at any time because he would try to get into Ethan's pants again otherwise.

Ethan slowly turned in Robert's arms and wrapped his arms around his waistline. "I really enjoyed today," he whispered into Rob's chest. "I think we'll have fun until graduation."

Robert's heart went aflutter but he didn't move, just holding the fluffy head against his chest. "Yes... it's interesting to try out new... things."

Ethan chuckled against Rob and hugged him tighter. "My parents would kill me if they knew what is going on. But after a near-death experience, I don't really care anymore."

"My mom wouldn't be happy either, but she won't know." Robert rubbed his chin over the top of Ethan's head and relaxed to signal Ethan could slip away once he was ready.

When Ethan finally stepped back, he had a wide smile on his face. "It's perfect. A little fantasy world no one needs to know of. Like we're little mice inside of an elk head."

Robert swallowed and patted him on the back before walking out of the garage. His car was right where he left it, but it didn't seem all that tempting. "See you at school, yeah?"

Ethan nodded and followed him like an overeager puppy.

Robert opened the door on the driver's side and slumped inside. "Thanks for the food and the blow job. The best I had."

Ethan put his hands in the pockets of his soft hoodie and smiled with a blush creeping up his neck. "Food or blow job?"

Robert bit his lip. He didn't want to seem ungrateful but Ethan deserved the truth. "Blow job, but I appreciate what you did with the bread."

Ethan glanced at his house before leaning down to Robert. "It's 'cause you have an awesome dick," he whispered and straightened up again.

Robert's eyes went straight to the front of Ethan's fly, and he grasped the door, knowing he had to leave soon if he didn't intend to stay. "I owe you one."

"I can't wait till next Wednesday then."

Robert wasn't sure, since Ethan only had one eye, but he could swear Ethan winked before turning around and going back to the house. It took Rob a full five seconds to force himself to stop staring at Ethan's ass, but eventually he started the engine and fled for home without looking back.

Chapter 7

ETHAN

ETHAN CLOSED HIS LOCKER, unable to think about much else than that awesome cock he had in his mouth the day before. It was exactly like Ethan imagined it would be. Quite large. Thick. Veiny. With a beautiful cockhead, all dark and glistening. Ethan could lick it all day. He put his hand on the closed locker, imagining his tongue sliding into the slit and lapping off the bead of precome. Maybe next time Rob could come on his lips so he could enjoy every drop.

The break bell ringing took him out of the fantasy, but the moment he turned around to go to class, the man of his dreams was right there, at the end of the corridor and coming toward him, surrounded by his friends. Ethan didn't even care all that much that he'd never be a part of that group. He and Rob had a secret that even Rob's best friend Chris would never know of. They were laughing about something as they went through the corridor like a herd of magnificent stallions, big and handsome in their matching sweaters. Ethan melted into the locker, trying to fade into the background, but then he saw a glint of recognition in Robert's eyes, followed by a smile so bright that he stopped breathing. Seemingly uncaring that someone could see them, Robert winked at him. Ethan's eye got half-lidded of its own accord, and he smiled back, his mind drifting off to the vision of licking Rob's cockhead for hours at a time.

Rob's eyes stayed on him for a moment too long, and suddenly he stumbled forward. If it weren't for his quick reflexes, he'd be on the floor.

Ethan bit back a grin. Was that his doing? Was his blow job really that amazing? Ethan would make them even better. If he were to practice on the real thing only once a week, he would still have time to polish his technique. One thing was certain of, he would suck every second out of that experience and enjoy it, no strings attached. He was too busy for proper dating anyway so the thing he had with Robert made everything easier.

He turned around and followed the group of jocks, since they took the same class anyway. Home Economics. Super boring. There was one thing that he enjoyed though. Getting a good view of Rob's ass. The buttocks swayed under the denim just right to tickle Ethan's imagination. Would he get to see them? Maybe he could propose to give Rob a massage next time? Rob did say he had no problems with nudity.

"Just ask her, she likes you," said Robert, patting one of his friends on the shoulder. "Or, you could think of something fancy, but that's up to you."

"Have you asked Kelly yet?" Chris elbowed Rob.

Not the prom again. Ethan wasn't even sure he wanted to go, but his mom was nagging him about just how much he would miss out if he didn't.

"I don't know. She's probably already taken for the prom." Rob stretched with a loud yawn. "We could go together if she doesn't have a date."

"You're such an ass," another one of the guys moaned. "Of course she's waiting for you to ask her."

"We're just friends. I've known her for years, and I'm not gonna blow that by suddenly trying to get into her pants."

Pat groaned. "Come on, man. Why not? There's only a few months left till graduation. Just seal the deal already."

"There is no deal. It would be like dating my sister. I will ask her to go as friends if that'll stop you from nagging me about it."

Ethan watched them as they all entered the class, which already smelled of vegetables. They were supposed to be learning about making some soup today. And Kelly was right there, smiling the moment Rob walked into class. The worst thing was that she wasn't even some stupid cheerleader Ethan could quietly despise. She was a nice arty girl with cute T-shirts and a stud in her nose, yet still had an amazing figure and an ass even cuter than her T-shirts. Fuck.

Robert dumped his bag at his usual station and walked all the way to the back of the class to meet her. Ethan couldn't believe how a guy could be so sexy while trying to be all cool and casual, but Robert was. He leaned his hand on the tabletop and started talking to her. And even though there was no way for Ethan to hear them, the way Kelly's face lit up told him exactly what happened.

Ethan wanted to puke into the pot waiting for him at the desk, but what did he expect? Many girls dreamed of Robert Hunter inviting them to prom, but everyone knew there was no one closer to him than Kelly. Ethan pulled his hair back into a bun, so it wouldn't fall into the food, and rolled up his sleeves. He didn't look up when Rob walked past him to organize his workspace. Ethan wished he could just put on his headphones and stop caring about the stupid lesson. It was nobody's fault that he was crushing on a guy who was mostly straight, but why would it happen to *him* of all people?

Ethan had always thought Rob was hot, no doubt about that, but it was the getting to know him bit (and the sucking his cock bit) that changed the game and slowly morphed out of lust into something he didn't even know how to name. This wasn't what he had planned. He'd planned revenge in the form of getting great blow jobs from a stupid yet irresistible jock. Unfortunately for Ethan, Robert Hunter turned out to be insanely nice. He helped Ethan up the freaking stairs, cleaned up his broken glass, and liked his elk project, and all that after Ethan had forced him into gayness. This was really confusing, and Ethan found it hard to focus on the teacher's instructions. Who cared about some stupid soup, when there were such serious issues to deal with?

The first onion and carrot were the victims of Ethan's rage, though he did have to pay special attention not to cut up his fingers.

The other students were chatting to one another, and their voices blended in with the simmering of water in a dozen kettles, the anachronism of chopping, smells of tomatoes and stock that were becoming ever sharper, the sting of tears in Ethan's eye as the onion started getting the best of him. One thing that stood out was the sharp, regular *staccato* of a knife hitting the cutting board with the precision of a metronome. Ethan's gaze followed the sound until they reached the slightly slouched line of Rob's body. He was motionless, only his right hand making quick, precise movements with the knife.

Ethan was always amazed at Rob's skills in this stuff. They brought Ethan's sandwiches to shame. Even watching Rob wasn't making time go any faster in this stupid class.

But then time did go faster. Next second it was ten minutes later, the water in Ethan's pot was boiling, and he was holding a vegetable he couldn't even name. Panic rose in his throat like bile. *No, no, no, no. Not now.* He looked to the other students, trying to work out what he'd been doing.

"Ethan, are you all right?" asked the teacher, frowning at him from behind her thick-lensed glasses.

He drew in a sharp breath, his vision shaking slightly as he looked around, at all the faces that were now turned toward him as if he were some kind of freak show.

"I'm fine!" he hissed louder than he wanted to and put down the knife, completely confused.

"Ethan, please keep you attitude in check. Just follow the instructions I've given," said the teacher.

What fucking instructions? What was the next step? Sweat beaded on his forehead, his hands trembling, heart thudding like he'd just gotten electrocuted.

There was a loud shuffling from the side, but he didn't care. All he wanted was to remember what happened in the minutes he'd lost. He closed his eye, breathing in and out. In and out. A bang of something hitting the table in front of him jerked his eye open and he found himself face to chest with Robert. There were two sets of utensils on the tabletop in front of him, and Rob bent toward him with a slight frown.

"You all right?"

Ethan's heart instantly started racing. "I-I sort of lost the plot," he whispered, his panic rising along with the excitement about Robert actually talking to him in public.

Robert nodded. "Okay. I'm almost done with mine. Is it okay if I help you?" he asked with that serious, concerned face.

"If you have time, I mean... yes... I don't know what this is anymore." Ethan rubbed his forehead, breathing in deeply, trying to find balance, to find the lost ten minutes. It was like having a rug pulled out from underneath his feet, and Robert was there to catch him.

"Don't worry, it's all good." Robert started swiftly rearranging the items on the worktable to make some space for chopping. "Maybe you want some water?"

How did Robert know Ethan had a problem? Was Robert actually paying attention to him? "No, I think it's all right. Thanks," he uttered and couldn't help but glance back at Kelly, who stared at them with worry in her eyes.

"You okay?" she mouthed, blissfully unaware of what Robert was secretly doing with Ethan. All she saw was that her future boyfriend was caring and helpful. What a dream he was.

Ethan slowly nodded and looked back at Rob, who started explaining to Ethan what needed to be done, but it was hard to focus with the amazing way Rob smelled. Rob's body exuded heat and something so masculine Ethan would gladly kneel for him right here.

Rob himself was chopping Ethan's greens and from this close, it was easy to see how efficient he was at it. Ethan would have chopped his fingers off if he tried to do it at the same speed. Even before the accident.

"How do you like your soup?" asked Rob.

"Huh? Tasty?" Ethan looked at him, still confused by the lost time.

Rob blinked. "But... you know, any spices you like? Do you take it with cream? Pasta?"

"Parsley? Maybe?" Ethan felt like an idiot. "How do you know all this?"

Robert shrugged. "From my mom." He finished the last of the vegetables and slid them into the pot.

"You're so good at it," Ethan whispered with a smile, trying to hide his anxiety.

Robert chuckled, and it seemed that the sound made him radiate more of the delicious scent of his masculine body. "It's nothing. You learn to cook when there's no one to make you dinner, and you want to stay healthy." He walked away to the spice rack and started picking out some pots.

"I can barely boil an egg. The sandwiches were the pinnacle of my skills." Ethan stirred the vegetables in the water so it wouldn't look like he was doing nothing.

Robert ran back to the table and put the spices on the counter. He opened the first one and sprinkled the soup with some dried parsley. "It's a useful skill." He winked.

"I know, I know. I should learn." Ethan licked his lips. "So I can impress my future partner one day." He pouted, unsure of how that came out. Maybe it was too much information for Robert? But all he got was a smile.

"It works wonders."

"Good looking, caring, and cooks? Jackpot, right?" Ethan muttered and stirred the soup like there was no tomorrow.

"Give it a rest, it's on medium heat anyway," said Robert, who was measuring small amounts of each of the spices he took and putting them on a plate.

Ethan instantly stopped, feeling like an idiot. His head still had that weird tingle after the lapse. "Oh. I thought... it would stick to the bottom if it's not stirred?" He looked up into Rob's eyes.

"Only if there's not enough water." Robert added a bit of oil to the pot, put the mixture of spices away, and collected the small jars. "Stir only from time to time."

"Okay." Ethan sucked in his lips with heat building up in his body, and it was not from standing too close to the soup. Everyone had to be watching them, but he was too anxious to look around.

"It would have been even better if we made stock ourselves, but that would take too much time," uttered Rob.

"How can you make stock? Do you dry out broth?" In a parallel universe, Ethan put an arm under Rob's letter jacket and stroked his hot skin.

Robert bit back a laugh. "Come on... no... you cook meat with certain vegetables and herbs and then you filter it."

"Do you have a favorite dish?" Maybe Ethan could try and order it for Rob's next visit.

Robert bit his lip. "I'd have to think about that. I like new stuff, but good beef is always nice."

Ethan bit back a smile. He loved good 'beef' as well.

Ethan sat on the bleachers, enjoying the nice weather. And watching the football practice. The soup Robert had made was so amazing Ethan could hardly comprehend it. It might have been so good because Rob didn't really follow the teacher's instructions and chose his own ingredients. Ethan could have Rob over every day with cooking skills like that.

Technically, Ethan was here to sketch his new rat position ideas, but he was mostly ogling Robert. He didn't even care about the abuse he was getting from Pat every now and then, too happy about drawing a rat in Rob's letter jacket. Maybe he could make one like that and give it to Rob as a graduation present so Rob would have something to remember him by. Not that he would, but maybe he could glance at it every now and then and think of the fun times they'd had.

Ethan enjoyed watching the football players tumble, even with all the armor on their bodies. He wondered how it would feel to be to be tackled by Robert. Into bed. The players were running through large tires, and Ethan almost broke his pen as he stared at Robert's amazing thighs in motion. He couldn't wait to feel them again, one time was enough for him to remember how toned they were. The memory could only be better if Rob would have taken off his shirt and showed off his chest and arms instead of always hiding them in long-sleeved shirts.

Ethan could hardly believe how lucky he was to get a taste of such a first-class hunk. It was totally worth an eye. Maybe not brain damage, but an eye. He looked to the cheerleader team practicing just a few meters to the left. Chris pointed at them, saying something to Robert as they were both finished with the tires, but Ethan couldn't hear what it was. He could guess it was something about their asses, or boobs, or whatever.

"Hi, you," said a pleasant male voice from the side.

Ethan turned his head that way. He thought he was alone, but he must have paid too much attention to Robert because a guy from the cheerleading team managed to sneak up on him. He had a smile so white that in the sun it seemed like one bright line between his lips and a handsome, roundish face. "Ethan, right?"

"Y-yeah. How do you know my name?" He had no idea why this guy would want to talk to him. Wasn't he in the celibacy club, anyway? Hardcore Christians never seemed to like Ethan much.

"Everyone knows you. I'm Derek by the way," said the guy, sitting down next to him and offering his hand. The scent of fresh male sweat got Ethan's senses alert in no time. "Hope you're feeling better."

Ethan shook his hand, still unsure where all this pleasantry was coming from. "Yeah, I'm better. Can they manage without you?" He pointed to the group of cheerleaders. Derek was one of only two guys on the team. His green and yellow uniform fitted his athletic body perfectly, but as yummy as he was, Ethan would rather continue ogling Robert's ass.

Derek nodded. "I can spare two minutes. There's something I want to ask you."

"Oh, okay... yeah?" Ethan watched him intently. With the green eyes and dark hair, Derek looked as if he was made for his uniform.

"Do you already have a date for prom?"

Ethan frowned slightly and had another glance at the gold cross on a little chain over Derek's neck. Was this guy trying to 'save' him? Get him a girlfriend or something? "I'm not even sure if I'm going..." Ethan pulled a few strands of hair behind his ear.

"Wanna go?" Derek leaned closer with a wide smile.

Ethan did another take of Derek, but didn't back away. Was this guy actually gay? Was Ethan being asked out to prom? By a Christian gay boy cheerleader? Maybe this was a parallel universe after all. "Are you asking me out?" he muttered, needing to make sure this wasn't some elaborate joke.

Derek nodded. "Yeah, but just so that you know: no sex. I'm too young for committing to anyone," he said with a bright smile.

Ethan's jaw dropped. This was crazy. Was this a pity thing? "Why me? You've never talked to me before." he gently poked Derek's thigh.

Derek sighed, looking into the sky. "You're not bad looking, and I thought you'd like some cheering up after the accident. When I saw you all alone in the cafeteria the other day, I asked myself: 'What would Jesus do?' Some people are totally cool with eye patches, but if you got fed up with it, I know of a great prosthetics producer in the area."

Ethan swallowed. The skin around the eye, the eyelid, had so much scarring it wasn't even just a question of a glass eye. The whole area looked gross, and he'd need plastic surgery before he'd be brave enough to show himself to anyone without the eye patch. "And who's better to cheer me up than a cheerleader, huh?" Ethan chuckled and let the other comment slide. Why not go with Derek? It could be fun. It wasn't like Rob was ever an option. Rob would come over to Ethan's to get a blow job, but he'd go to prom with Kelly.

"That's what I thought." Derek fumbled with his pocket and produced a card with his photo and social media contacts. "Add me on Facebook, and we can chat about the details."

Ethan's eye widened. Derek actually had a social media business card? Was this a thing now, and he'd missed it altogether? "So what's the boundaries if there's no sex?" Ethan had a weird déjà vu about the question. "I mean, I don't mean anything has to happen. I'm just curious, you know."

Derek pursed his lips. "Err, holding hands, maybe a kiss on the cheek?"

"Sounds good to me." Ethan shrugged and tore out a page with one of the rat drawings. He wrote his phone number on the back and passed it to Derek. "That's actually really nice of you."

Derek grinned and got to his feet, already taking one step down toward the stairs. "It's the Christian thing to do to put a smile on a fellow man's face," he declared and walked away, whistling some merry melody.

Ethan followed him with his gaze, still shocked, but why would he not go with it? They probably wouldn't spend God-knew-how-much time together at the party, but even if he'd be wallflowering, at least he would get to watch other people dance and whatever other prom-y things people did. Though he still couldn't believe a guy invited him to the prom. Ethan just hoped this wasn't some *Carrie* scenario.

When he looked back at the field, the football players were gone. Damn, he'd missed watching Robert some more!

The cheerleaders were already starting to practice again, and he wondered whether he should watch Derek like a good almost-boyfriend would, or call his mom to pick him up. He'd finish the drawing first though. The little rat wore a letter jacket and rolled around with a football. Ethan was almost done with the sketch when he heard loud thumping coming from the stairs. One glance was enough to lighten up his day. Rob was there. Still in those tight and dirty pants, in a too-large long-sleeve, he was walking toward Ethan with a red box in hand.

"What are you doing here?" he asked once they were at comfortable hearing distance.

Ethan grinned at him. "You know, ogling the cheerleaders." His heart melted at how much attention Rob was giving him. Even after Chris had told Rob in class that Ethan wasn't his responsibility, Rob had just shrugged it off and helped Ethan finish that soup.

"Oh, yeah, was Derek bothering you?" asked Rob, taking up Derek's former place. Rob was so much bigger in comparison that it made Ethan want to crawl into his embrace. His body heat rose in direct consequence to Rob's proximity.

"Not really, no. He was actually nice." Ethan slid a few inches closer, wanting to smell him. And no, Robert hasn't showered yet, which made him smell spicier and bolder. Rawr.

"I'm surprised. He's a bit... " Robert shrugged and opened the box, revealing a selection of wonderful sliders in sesame seed buns.

"These look so nice!" Ethan took the opportunity to lean closer for a peek into the box.

"You can have some," said Rob, picking up a small bottle. "Add some sauce if you like. And as for Derek, he's a bit... batshit. Yeah, I think that's the word."

"He invited me to prom. Should I be scared?" Ethan laughed and grabbed one of the buns.

Robert frowned, his face going from sunny to cloudy within a split second. "What?"

"I know. It's a bit weird, 'cause he's never talked to me before. He offered me a contact to someone who does prosthetics. I mean... what's up with that?" Ethan started chewing on his slider.

Rob squeezed some of the brown sauce onto the tiny burger and closed the bun. "I thought he didn't want to get a boyfriend until after college."

"Yeah, he told me it has to be a chaste date. But I didn't even think I'd be going so it's still a step up."

Robert cleared his throat. "So what, are you going to date him now?" He bit into the slider, slicing it in half with those healthy white teeth.

Ethan squinted, watching him for the longest moment, cogs slowly turning in his head. "Would that be a problem?"

Robert shoved the rest of the burger in, effectively shutting himself up for several seconds. He shrugged with a deep, bad frown.

Ethan snorted and had another bite. "Well, good. I don't know. He left me his number and stuff, and said we'll talk through the details. You think he'll want me to wear an eye patch matching his tux?"

"But... you guys have nothing in common. He'd bore you to tears," mumbled Rob, with his mouth still full.

"I don't really know him, so I can't be sure. Maybe if my parents knew he was this good boy, they'd let me date him?"

"Would the good Christian boy be cool with dating a guy who's fucking another guy at the same time?"

Ethan stopped chewing, feeling a flush rush up to his face. He hated how quickly it showed on his pale skin. He looked down to his sketchbook. There had been no time to process any of this yet.

Rob assembled his second slider and raised it to his mouth. "You like the food?"

"It's lovely," Ethan uttered. "Thanks. The beef's really nice." From being friendless to having actual interactions with two different guys was such a big difference he didn't know how to juggle it.

"And the avocado? It's in those thin slices, it just melts in your mouth, doesn't it?" Robert gave Ethan a small smile and bit into the second slider.

"Yeah, I like trying new stuff." Ethan inched away discreetly, trying to put together how he understood the situation.

They sat in silence, with just the sound of chewing as soundtrack.

"I don't know, Rob," Ethan was the first to finally speak. "What we do is kind of like another dimension. No one knows, no one *will* know, so it's as if it's not completely real. Does that make sense? It's like dreaming about having sex with your teacher or something. You can indulge because it's just a dream, and then no one will know. So if, and that's only *if,* I actually date Derek, he won't know anything about it."

Robert exhaled, swallowing the sandwich as he looked at the cheerleaders forming some kind of human pyramid. "If you want to date or fuck someone else, then I want to know about it because it changes stuff. I don't see it like that at all."

Ethan pouted and hugged himself. "How do you see it then?"

Robert sighed. "Well, it would be weird doing this with you if you were with someone else. I think this kind of shit is wrong."

Ethan groaned. Why couldn't he have what he wanted? He didn't want to let go of what he had with Rob, even if it was just this weird *thing*. But he did want to go to prom with Derek, show everyone who mocked him that he could date a cute, popular guy. Even if it involved no sex. "You're dating Kelly."

"I'm not. I'm single, and I'm just going to prom with her." Rob leaned back, watching the cheerleaders perform some uplifting routine.

"And I'm just going to prom with Derek." Ethan huffed and crossed his arms on his chest. "Apparently he's saving himself for gay marriage or some shit, so it doesn't change anything anyway."

"That's all right." Rob presented the box with the remaining slider to Ethan.

Sure it was all right for Robert. Ethan grabbed the slider and put as much as he could bite off into his mouth. When he came up with the idea of getting sex from Robert, he thought it would all be different, that he'd be in control of something he lusted for. Instead, he was becoming a neurotic mess. Making decisions about your love life when waking up from a coma probably wasn't advised.

Robert glanced at him with an unreadable expression, but his eyes settled on the sketchbook and just like that, Ethan's face went aflame. He still had it open on the drawing. "Is that... Robert the Rat or something?" asked Rob.

Ethan cursed in his mind. "I just got inspired," he muttered. "It's random." The last thing Ethan wanted was for Rob to get the idea that he was some obsessed stalker boy.

"It's pretty cute. Did you consider making an online comic with those?" Robert's large finger traced the rat's leg.

Ethan smiled and exhaled loudly. "Not really, no. But maybe I should. Robert the Rat in an illicit love affair with Mr. Weasel or something. Their interspecies love would be doomed."

"Doomed love is overrated. This stuff doesn't happen anymore, you know? Give them a happy ending." Robert grinned and closed his lunchbox.

"And little rat-weasel babies?" Ethan raised his eyebrows. "Sometimes things just can't work."

"Wow, what's that? *Junior: The Sequel*?" snorted Robert.

Ethan elbowed him with a chuckle. "I'm just saying it'd be hard for them."

"Come on, we're in the twenty-first century. Shouldn't gay people be more positive in how they portray relationships? Tragic deaths and loneliness were good in the nineties."

"You make it sound so easy." Ethan shook his head. "Are you my new straight bestie?"

Robert chuckled and hung his head. "I just think that's how it's gonna be."

"If I tell you something, will you promise to keep it a secret and not freak out?" Ethan gently poked Rob's foot under the bench so no one would see it. He wanted to show Rob that he trusted him, show him why it mattered so much that Rob helped him out in class.

Robert snorted. "Shoot."

"I lost a few minutes in class today. That's why I was so out of it. It doesn't happen all that often, but every now and then since the accident. I blank, and then it's a few seconds or even a few minutes later. I don't pass out, but I don't know what was happening either. It freaks me out and I don't like to tell my parents about it every time it happens." He hid his face in his hands, too nervous about Rob's reaction to look at him.

For a moment, there was silence so deep he almost believed Rob fainted... or something, but then came a large, warm hand on his shoulder. "I'm so sorry. I had no idea," whispered Robert in a voice so small, it belonged in the bedroom.

"Only my parents know." Ethan wished he could melt into Rob like he did after he gave Rob head. The guy had no qualms about hugging and lying together for a while, and it had felt so normal. "That's why I can't drive a car. If it happened on the road I'd be screwed, because it's so disorienting."

There was silence again and then, "Do you need a lift?"

Was that all Rob had in him? Ethan sighed. He didn't want to continue the topic if Rob clearly didn't want to talk about it. "It's fine, my mom will pick me up soon."

"Sure, I'll wait with you." Robert cleared his throat. "Does this happen frequently?" he eventually asked, playing with his fingers.

Ethan looked up into his eyes. This was all the hook he needed, not even a worm required for him to bite on it. "I haven't found a pattern. It's been so random. The longer ones I have maybe once a week, and the tiny ones every now and then. It's not that bad if I'm just at the desk or something, but when I'm going somewhere, and then all of a sudden I'm just somewhere else, it's really bad. Maybe I should just treat it as teleportation, huh?" He nudged Rob's shoe again.

"Hope you won't skip the blow job I'll give you next time. That would be a waste."

Ethan gasped and grabbed Rob's arm. "No! Don't say that. That would be the worst. Oh, my God." Even thinking about it got his stomach to twist with anxiety.

Robert cleared his throat, pulling on his index finger in a way that made it crack. "I... uh... you wanna...?"

Ethan leaned closer. "Huh?" *Please Mom, don't call now, stay late at work.*

Robert cleared his throat. "You know, we could... hang out in my car somewhere. I'd just have to take a quick shower."

Ethan licked his lips. "That... oh wow, that sounds good," he whispered, and in this moment he knew he'd never see Derek again if Rob asked him to.

Robert's eyes darkened a bit. "Wait for me here?"

Ethan nodded, unable to choke anything out. He'd wait here forever if there was a blow job from Robert on the horizon.

Rob grinned at him and started running down the stairs, his butt and thighs so perfect Ethan wished he had a spyglass.

Ethan packed the sketchbook into his bag and waited. Even with the horrible memory lapse in class, this was turning out to be an amazing day. He got asked out to prom by a cute (if morally impaired) guy and was about to get head from Robert. And he didn't even have to push for it. Robert was experimenting, and Ethan didn't mind being his lab rat.

The blissful feeling was dispersed by the loud, unpleasant music that he used for his parents' calls.

"No, no, no, no..." he whimpered and picked up the phone. "Hi Mom, what's up?"

"Hi darling, I'm waiting for you in front of the school," she said with a cheer in her voice.

"Mom, it's fine, I was about to call you that Rob will take me home. We wanted to hang out a bit."

There was a brief silence in the headset, and he already knew it wasn't good. "Honey, you do have a lot to catch up on after missing so many weeks of school. You can't play as much as you used to."

"But Mom, I'll make up for it tomorrow, or I'll stay up at night. I already promised Rob." His palms got damp with sweat.

"No, I'm sure he'll understand that you have needs that have to be addressed."

Ethan punched the bench in frustration. He did have needs that had to be addressed, and it wasn't catching up with school. "I'll be there in a moment," he groaned.

"All right," chirped his mom and hung up. This couldn't be happening. And to make matters worse, Robert appeared at the bottom of the bleachers and gestured for Ethan to come down.

Ethan grabbed his bag and pulled it over his shoulder as he made his way down with so much resignation it was pulling his shoulders to the ground. Rob looked so fresh and handsome. So much taller, his hair still a bit wet, a white T-shirt under his letter jacket, and a perfect pair of jeans.

"What's the long face?" asked Rob, pushing his hands into his pockets.

"My mom's making me go home," Ethan moaned, looking up at Rob and standing as close as it was possible while being socially acceptable.

Robert's face froze, but he did kick the ground. "Oh. That's a shame."

Ethan made sure no one would see him from behind Robert and pinched his T-shirt. "You wanna go under the bleachers for a sec?"

Robert drew in a sharp breath and looked around. Even the cheerleaders were off by now so Robert's nod didn't come as that much of a surprise. He bit his lip and gestured for Ethan to go first.

Ethan rushed down the stairs and around the benches until he got to the shade below. He wanted at least a bit of touch before he'd be forced to go home. The crumbling of dirt and gravel under Rob's shoes followed him like a ghost, each sound making his skin burn up.

As soon as Rob was in the shade, Ethan slid his arms under the green and yellow jacket and put his cheek on Rob's chest with a deep exhale. Robert smelled so fresh and clean, killing off the smell of trash, piss, and whatever else was around them. He didn't care as long as they could touch. The moment became perfect when those strong arms slid around him and held him tight. Then, Rob's chin was on top of his head, gently pressing on his scalp.

"I want that blow job so bad," Ethan whimpered into Rob's chest and stroked his back. "My mom's probably gonna call again any second now."

"We should have done that instead of shoving food up our faces." Rob's chest shook with rumbly laughter, and Ethan closed his eye, listening to the strong beating of his heart.

Ethan kissed Rob's pec. "I don't want to finish in five seconds this time."

"We'll work on it," whispered Robert into Ethan's hair, his warm breath doing wonderful things to Ethan's cock already.

"Oh, God, I've got to go or I'll get hard." Ethan gently scraped his teeth over Rob's chest.

"Okay." Slowly, Robert untangled himself from around Ethan and stepped back. He gave a small smile.

Ethan took a deep breath. "You shouldn't be so agreeable," he said and started walking back out. Rob's body heat was still all over him.

"I'm not agreeable."

"Bye, Rob!" Ethan chuckled and shook his head.

Chapter 8

ROB

ROBERT STOPPED HIS CAR in front of Ethan's house and rushed for the door as soon as he was out. Every attempt at getting close to Ethan in the past week had been unsuccessful, mostly because of Ethan's parents picking him up right after school. But this was the day.

Before he even touched the doorbell, Ethan opened the door for him with a wide smile. Rob bit his lip, noticing that Ethan was wearing the studded belt that kept digging into Robert's flesh whenever they stole a minute or two alone, but they could get rid of it soon.

"I thought you'd never come." Ethan pulled Robert in by the long-sleeve under his open jacket. It was as if sunshine itself grabbed him.

Rob grinned, walking in and shutting the door behind himself. He gathered Ethan in his arms with so much greed it surprised him, but he couldn't wait to smell that smooth dark hair. "Sorry, got caught up at practice."

Ethan was the perfect height to have his face buried in Rob's neck. "That's fine, I was doing stuff. I do have a life, you know," Ethan whispered into his neck, his lips brushing the skin in a way that made Rob remember how they felt on his cock.

He cupped the warm head with his hand and hummed, absorbing the warmth Ethan was emitting. "So, what were you doing?" He wanted to know how Ethan managed to open the door so quickly if he couldn't move around well yet.

"I was drawing. I'm slowly getting back to the right level. It's not all that bad, I just need to adjust." Ethan kissed Rob's neck and backed away. He pointed to an armchair by the window, to an open sketchbook in the seat. "I was designing those weasel and rat characters."

"Yeah? Show me." Robert grinned, grasped the warm hand, and brushed his thumb over the inner side of the palm.

Ethan squeezed his hand and pulled him along to the armchair. He picked up the sketchbook and showed him a whole page of weasel drawings. They were just sketches, but very realistic and well drawn, with tiny touches of anthropomorphization. On one of them the weasel sat on a swing and on another pulled on a rat's tail. Ethan must have studied the anatomy of the animals to achieve an effect this good.

Rob smiled and took the sketchbook, looking at all the lines that formed characters so unbelievably cute they belonged in a children's cartoon. "Will you be going to art school?"

Ethan's smile waned. "Nah, I'll probably go into law or something."

Rob stared at him, unsure what to say. "Why?" he eventually uttered. "You've got talent for that."

"It's lame. My parents say that it's a good hobby, but that I should secure a proper job first." Ethan sighed and started playing with the little bird-skull necklace on his chest. "It does make some kind of sense, but I really wish I could do more art instead."

Robert looked at the cute rat staring straight at him from the page. "Won't it be a waste of time to study law when you have talent like that? Seriously, if I had this kind of skill, I wouldn't do anything else."

Ethan rubbed his forehead. "What are *you* planning to do after graduation?"

Rob pursed his lips. "I'll do pre-med."

"See, you're all serious too." Ethan gave him a crooked smile. "If I could grow my business quicker I would just go into it. But it's scary, 'cause my parents say they won't give me a penny if I don't go to college. They're not as nice as they seem to be around you."

Rob frowned at that last comment. "I'm sure they mean well. And my talents aren't as amazing as yours, so that's why."

"Oh yeah? That soup the other day was pure talent." Ethan smiled and poked his stomach.

"Yeah, but I don't want to work in a restaurant or anything like that." Rob smiled.

"They do mean well." Ethan looked down at his sketchbook, returning to the topic of his parents. "And they do support my hobby, but they don't treat it seriously. Maybe they would if I could make more money off it."

"How much are you making now?" Robert slowly made his way toward the kitchen. He was dying for something wet.

"That's the problem. I earned a few hundred when I did a launch of these rat skull necklaces, but then a few months later, I had nothing, so it's very unstable." Ethan followed him and slid a finger into the back pocket of Rob's jeans. It made Rob stiffen a bit, but it wasn't an unpleasant sensation. He chuckled and entered the kitchen, hoping he could get some juice or soda. Instead, a bottle of whiskey appeared on the table, and Robert felt his knees going a bit soft.

Ethan wiggled his eyebrows. "Want some?" He stood close and stroked Rob's back.

Rob stepped back and grabbed the edge of the counter. Drinking in Ethan's presence was the last thing he wanted. "I'll be driving later."

"Oh, yeah, right, sorry, I just kinda thought you'd want some... uh..." Ethan put the whiskey back into a cupboard and rubbed the top of his nose.

"A soft drink should be fine, thanks." Rob smiled and petted the back of Ethan's head, sliding his hand to his nape. It was so warm and fit his palm so well.

Ethan leaned closer, like a kitten, and got Rob some juice from the fridge. Rob imagined giving Ethan some milk in a bowl and watching him lick it all up. He took the juice and drank half of it in one swig.

"Why rats?"

Ethan wrapped his arms around Rob's waist, hugging him like a giant plushie. "Oh, it's an old story. I had three rats when I was a kid." He got to his toes and kissed Rob's collarbone, brushing the soft mane of his hair against the skin. "They got ill, and we had to put them down. I loved them, you know? They were so cute and smart. So I threw this horrible tantrum." Ethan chuckled, stroking Rob's back. "My dad said he'll let me keep them if I wanted to. We went to a taxidermist, and he stuffed them for me. I didn't participate in any of it, of course, that would have probably freaked me out at that age, but it sparked something. They were preserved forever. He posed them so that they look like they were all sleeping together and hugging."

Robert brushed the stray hair away from Ethan's face. "You still have them?"

"Yeah. They're still super cute." Ethan rubbed his forehead against Robert's chin. "Rats are very intelligent."

"So I've heard." Robert chuckled and pressed a kiss to the top of Ethan's head. "Show me?"

"Sure... I just need to sit down for a sec." Ethan took a deep breath and pulled away from Robert.

Robert frowned. "What is it?"

"My head... fuck, not now..." Ethan hissed and started a wobbly walk out of the kitchen while holding the side of his head. With his back hunched, and the whole body crooked to one side, he looked like the picture of pain.

"Ethan?" Robert rushed to his side and hugged him, all worried. His mind was already offering him visions of Ethan bumping into a wall or breaking his nose in the haze he was in.

"It's my head... I get these piercing headaches sometimes. It's like getting stabbed in the brain. Fuck. This can't be happening now," Ethan mumbled, not stopping on his way toward the stairs. "I have pills in my room."

Guilt washed over Robert like a cold shower. He offered his shoulder to Ethan and walked him all the way to the attic. "Where? I'll get them."

Ethan sat on the bed with his hand on the side of his head and his eye closed. "They're on my desk," he muttered, pointing to a pile of books and paper on top of the tabletop.

Robert found a small orange vial and a half-filled glass of water, and returned to the bed, watching tension grow around Ethan's eye.

"I'm sorry..." Ethan whispered and took the pills without even opening his eye.

"What? It's not your fault," uttered Rob, slowly sitting down on the side of the bed and watching Ethan. He was powerless. There was nothing he could do to help Ethan but watch him curl into a ball of pain.

"But I wanted today to be great, and now I'm just wasting your time. Fuck, stupid head. Stop doing this to me," Ethan whimpered, curling his fingers into fists.

Robert shook his head. He kicked off his shoes and slowly lowered himself to the bed. He couldn't stop a silly grin from surfacing when the soft fur bedspread brushed his skin. He still remembered how it felt when he was getting his first blow job. "You're not."

"Will you wait?" Ethan whispered and inched closer to Robert. The tension on his face, the way his breathing sped up weren't good signs.

"For what?" Robert pulled the pillow from underneath the throw and got it under Ethan's head.

"Until I get better." Ethan swallowed and slowly opened his eye, hair all over his face.

Robert hummed and rested his arm over Ethan's stomach. In this position, with his head alongside Ethan's, he could feel his warmth seeping into him like warm cocoa. Ethan was taking deep breaths, but leaned into the hug and entwined his fingers with Robert's. Feeling the little scars on them made Rob realize he'd never gotten round to asking about them, but he assumed they had to be a result of all the crafty stuff Ethan was doing. The studded belt though was right there, like a porcupine, stopping Rob from being as close to Ethan as he would have liked. Freaking chastity belt.

He cleared his throat and gently nuzzled Ethan's temple. "It's fine. I hope you get better, but we could just talk if that's all right with you."

"Yeah, I'll try and focus," Ethan squeezed Rob's hand harder. Ethan's whole body had this nice sturdiness to it. Small, but not bony. Especially his arms had nice definition. He was wearing a tight-fitting grey long-sleeve today, so it really showed. "Can you help me take off the necklace? I don't want to crush it." He pushed some of his hair away from his neck.

Rob nodded and pulled on the chain to find the fastening. It was surprisingly hard to open, but he eventually succeeded and put the necklace away on the nightstand, a bit freaked out by the touch of bone.

"The doctor said it's only going to get better," Ethan uttered, turning to his back with a hand over his face.

"Should I turn off the light?" asked Robert, gently stroking Ethan's chest.

"Yes, please. I should bounce back in half an hour." Ethan's lips trembled slightly.

Robert rolled off the bed and switched off the lamp. In the dark, the room looked like any other... at least before he spotted the shadows of taxidermy. *The Shadows of Taxidermy.* This would be a great movie title. When he lay back down next to Ethan, he got a great view of the sky through the window in the slanted rooftop. No wonder Ethan didn't want to move out downstairs.

"You smell so good," Ethan whispered, and Robert had to smile, pulling him close in the dark.

"You smell of orange and bergamot."

"That's very specific." Ethan leaned in for a hug. "How does it feel to have everyone crush on you?"

Robert frowned and stared into the ceiling, letting his fingers roam through the silky waves of hair. "Okay, I guess."

"Seriously? That's it?" Ethan's grip tensed on Rob's forearm.

Rob groaned. "It's nothing special. I suppose if I wanted to fuck around it would be more useful than it is."

"Why don't you, then? You could." Ethan curled into Rob's body with his eye closed.

Robert sighed, pushing his leg between Ethan's, just for comfort. "No one really caught my attention that way."

Ethan's eye instantly opened. "What's your type then?"

Robert wanted to howl. Those never ending questions. "I don't really have a type. But I like long hair, big eyes and smooth skin." *Like yours.*

"That's why I'm a good substitute?" Ethan pouted, never looking away from Robert in the darkness.

Robert's stomach turned into ice. "Why are you saying that?"

"Because I want to get to know you better." Ethan stroked Rob's chest.

"That just didn't sound right," uttered Robert, gently gathering some of the hair in his hand. "It's not like that. I'm not pretending you're someone else."

A slight smile appeared in the corners of Ethan's lips. "I always thought you were really hot. I just thought you were an ass as well."

Robert groaned, leaning in to lie nose to nose with Ethan. "Why?"

It melted his heart to feel Ethan's hot breath on his skin. "You're friends with Pat, and the other guys can't be any better. You guys mocked me whenever I got into your line of sight. Do you not even remember?"

Robert groaned. He couldn't feel ashamed of that. "It was just teasing. I don't know, like the guys saying I'm a mommy's boy because I always have proper food on me."

Ethan smirked and slowly wrapped his arms around Rob's neck. "It mostly stopped though. I think everyone's afraid that I'm this precious piece of cracked porcelain now."

Robert chuckled and pressed a kiss to Ethan's forearm. "You're Mr. Porcelain now."

Ethan's fingers stroked Rob's nape. "I'm not useless."

"It's not like that. You're just still adjusting after all this, so it's only fair people give you more slack than they used to."

"I like the slack you're giving me." Ethan's smile widened, which had to mean his headache was fading.

Robert reached out and touched his nose with a grin. "Yeah, well, I'm enjoying it as well."

"Rob?" Ethan slowly cupped Rob's cheeks in his palms, watching him intently. "Are you bisexual?"

And just like that, Robert's head spiraled down a hot whirl. "No," he uttered, suddenly breathless.

Ethan swallowed loudly, but didn't look away, tension almost visible in the air between them. "Can I kiss you?" he whispered and leaned closer, his lips already parted.

Robert leaned back right away, inhaling the herbal scent of Ethan's hair. His heart went into a gallop. "No, that's..." He eyed the sweet, warm lips. His stomach melted when he imagined his tongue sliding between them, opening Ethan for the kiss. "That's too much."

Ethan rubbed his forehead, obscuring his eye as well. "Sure, just checking," he sighed and fell back to the fur.

Robert bit his lip and placed his hand over Ethan's stomach. He didn't want to give him the wrong idea. He did want to fool around, but high school wasn't the time for anything more, and with each subsequent step, it would be harder to deny himself. He had to draw a line somewhere. It wouldn't be fair to Ethan to let things progress if Rob wasn't planning to develop this in any way.

"I knew I was gay since, like, forever," Ethan said, looking into the sky. "My first crush was Brandon Lee. You know, from the *Crow* movie?"

Robert sighed. "The one with makeup?"

"Yeah." Ethan laughed and pulled on one of the snaps in Rob's jacket. "He had that whole mysterious aura around him. And he was a safe crush to have. You know, dead."

"Why did you want a safe crush?" Robert grasped a strand of black hair and curled it around his fingers.

"No risk. I'm not really all that good at socializing. Can't you tell?" Ethan raised his eyebrows with a smirk. "Sometimes I wish I could be asexual so I wouldn't have to deal with all this hormonal stuff. But since you can't choose that, I'm happy to get some without actually having to deal with a relationship."

Robert smiled and stopped his hand from gravitating to Ethan's. "Yeah, me too. It's too late for stuff like that anyway."

"And I have so much to do. My parents are pushing for grades, I have my art projects. I only actually chatted to Derek once since he asked me out. We had some coffee together, and all I could think of was that I could be working on my project instead." Ethan laughed and sat up to take off his shirt, revealing all that milky skin and the rat tattoo.

Robert couldn't help but grin. He started drawing circles on the smooth stomach. So Derek was a waste of time? Too bad Ethan always had a moment for *him*. "Busy bees, aren't we?"

Ethan bit back a smile. "Yeah. You're studying for pre-med, doing football practice and stuff. You said you cook at home? Where would you squeeze in a girlfriend, right?" Ethan was generally slim, but his stomach was nicely toned, with some definition. He wasn't that skinny anymore.

Tempted by the smoothness of the skin, Robert quickly leaned in and blew air over Ethan's belly button.

"Lower," Ethan whispered and lay back, spreading out for him.

Robert froze, surprised, but then smiled into Ethan's stomach and kissed it, sliding his hand up Ethan's thigh, gently massaging his flesh through the denim. He couldn't wait to touch his cock.

Ethan parted his legs, giving Rob the mental image of what it would be to see him spread his legs in different circumstances. With the semidarkness in the room, they were enveloped in a cozy cocoon where anything could happen. "Wait a sec." Ethan smiled and rolled to his stomach, to reach out for the laptop on a cupboard by the bed. The fabric of his jeans tightened around his ass, giving Robert a perfect view of those gorgeous buttocks. Would he get to see more of them today?

Ethan fiddled with his computer until he put on some music. Slightly different than last time, but still instrumental and medieval...ish? He turned back with a smile and unbuckled his belt as his chest rose and fell faster. Robert was hypnotized by the motion and reacting to the music as if he were already conditioned to associate it with sex and Ethan's delicious body. He put his hand on Ethan's thigh and pushed his fingers up, cupping his crotch with a low groan. It was just a dream weeks ago, but now that he held a cock in his hand, warm tingles spread throughout his body at rapid speed.

Ethan took a deep breath and lifted his hips to the touch. It felt so much more natural than that first time when Ethan came out at him so full-on, taking the decisions out of Robert's hands. Ethan ran his fingers through his hair, looking down at Rob from beneath the thick black eyelashes.

Rob exhaled, kneading the flesh in his hands. "You're hard."

Ethan gasped, and even in the darkness, the flush on his face was all too visible. "Are you surprised? I get hard just lying next to you."

If that wasn't a Michelin star for Rob's ego, he didn't know what was. He smiled and slowly leaned in, breathing in the aroma of jeans, cologne, and sharp male arousal. It sent a burning flame of excitement straight to his cock.

Ethan pushed up his hips slightly and slid his thumbs under his jeans and underwear, to pull them down. He took big gasps of air when his cock was revealed, all hard and proud. Robert could feel the heat on his face. It was lovely, with a dark head and a good girth. The mere sight of the bulging veins on the underside made Rob's mouth water. With a low sigh, he moved his tongue along the vessel, and the rapid pulsing he sensed corresponded to the one he felt in his own cock.

Ethan raised himself to his elbows and let out a breathless sigh. He spread his thighs wider and his cock moved slightly on its own accord. "Take off your jacket?"

Robert nodded and shook off the garment, remaining in just a thin long-sleeve shirt. He took the side of the cock between his lips and sucked it in. It was all smooth, warm skin, hiding a hardness underneath that made his brain boil.

The little sounds Ethan made only got Rob more horny. He'd never touched a guy the way he did Ethan, and it was all he dreamed it would be and more. Ethan's hot fingers petted Rob's arm, only encouraging him to do whatever he wished to, so he looked up, trying to be as calm as possible, even though it was so hard! He gently squeezed Ethan's balls, marveling at how different they felt from his own, and then licked his cock all the way up from the base to the head.

Ethan's face was a glorious sight, and Rob had a hard time deciding if he should look at it or at the cock. Ethan bit his lip, hair was obscuring his flushed face, and he looked down with that glint in his eye. His stomach was tense and slightly glistening. The rats on his stomach now really did look like they were dancing with each deep breath he took. "Take off your shirt?" he whispered.

Robert drew in a sharp breath and looked at his forearms, hidden beneath the fabric. "Err... my arms aren't all that sexy."

Ethan frowned and stroked the side of Rob's face. "Are you fucking kidding? I bet they're so sexy they can compete with your dick."

"No, they're burnt." Rob bit his lip with, leaning into the caress. Ethan touched him like no one else before, like he wanted to intimately know the texture of Rob's skin.

"Huh?" Ethan ran his fingers through Rob's hair. "Show me and I'll show you what's under my eye patch?" he whispered.

Robert stared at him for the longest moment, his breath getting increasingly shallow. He wasn't all that interested in seeing the results of his stupidity, but it was a fair offer. He sat up and pulled off the shirt. His teammates saw him naked on a regular basis, but he didn't wear short sleeves out of the locker room, much less so in a situation like this.

His forearms were covered by ugly white scars, craters and hills of malformed flesh. He looked up at Ethan, but their eyes didn't meet. Ethan was looking at Rob's arms, already reaching out to touch them. He kneeled on the bed, with his dick sticking out of his pants and stopped his fingertips just millimeters away from the skin. "Can I...?" he asked, stroking Rob's stomach with his other hand.

Robert nodded, moving closer. He was not exactly ashamed of his forearms, but didn't found them aesthetically pleasing. And he wanted to avoid stares and question. "Sure, it doesn't hurt or anything, but it's freaky and hairless. Like the skin of an alien."

Ethan kneeled between Rob's spread thighs and embraced one of his arms before kissing the elbow. "I like freaky." He smiled against Rob's skin and ran his fingertips along the forearm. It tickled a bit, and Robert chuckled, hugging Ethan with his other arm.

"Yeah? You never draw burnt rats."

Ethan melted into the embrace, with his arm wrapped around Rob's waist. He fit perfectly into Rob's form, with his head under Rob's chin. "Maybe I'll start. What happened to you?" He kissed the burnt skin on Rob's arm again, and the touch of Ethan's cockhead against Rob's stomach was bringing his blood to a simmer.

"Shit, that's nice," Robert uttered, pulling Ethan closer and raising his hips so that they could grind against one another. With his shirt off, he could actually feel Ethan's skin all over. It was hot, smooth, and hairless apart from where the curly pubes grew around his cock. Ethan was eager to pick up the hint of motion and responded with a grind against Rob.

"You're avoiding the question." He kissed the burnt skin again, but then it only got better when his hot tongue traced one of the scars.

"Ah... I tried to make fried chicken when I was... ten or eleven." Rob winced at the memory of his skin burning in contact with hot oil. "Didn't work out."

"Poor you. Doesn't make you any less handsome." Ethan gave him a tight hug and brought their skin into contact, rubbing their cocks together. Even though Rob's was still in his pants. Ethan kissed Rob's arm again before backing away slightly to reach for his eye patch.

Robert held his breath as he waited for the big reveal. He could swear even his teeth pulsated with anxiety. Ethan pulled off the eye patch and put it on the bed, but his face remained obscured by the curtain of hair until he finally looked up.

It wasn't pretty. Still reddened, with the lower and upper eyelids scarred badly. It reminded Rob of raw meat, all puffy and tender. "I'm gonna have further cosmetic surgery in the future... probably." Ethan gently stroked Robert's chest.

It didn't help the never ending guilt that bubbled up in Rob's veins every time something reminded him of what he had done. "Will you get a glass eye?"

"Maybe. If it all heals well. Don't you think it's cooler to have an eye patch though? I could make it my unique selling point." Ethan's smile widened, which was kinda absurd but eased some of the tension in Rob's gut.

"You're so... positive about it," uttered Rob, deciding to skip further introductions. He grasped Ethan's cock.

"Oh, oh!" Ethan's eye widened, and he held on to Rob's arms. "I— 'cause..." He took a deep breath. "I can't change what happened."

Robert swallowed and started gently moving his hands over the warm hardness. It was so alive in his grip. "Yeah."

"So good," Ethan muttered and unzipped Rob's fly, still petting his arm with his other hand. Being accepted like that, scars and all, made Rob grin and lean forward to bury his face in Ethan's neck. He bit into the skin with a low groan when Ethan squeezed his dick.

Ethan laughed and gave it a tug, but then pulled Rob down to the fur.

"Not too quick, or I'm gonna come," Ethan moaned at yet another touch, exposing his neck to more kisses and nibbles.

"Yeah," uttered Robert. He spit on his hand and used the saliva to lubricate Ethan's cockhead. His blood was quickly reaching boiling point as he tasted Ethan's bergamot sweat.

"You're so hot. I'm so lucky," Ethan babbled and got some hand cream from the bedside table. The moment his hand was gone, Rob wanted to moan his complaint, but as soon as Ethan's fingers were around his dick again, Rob was sated. He loved to look down at it. Since Ethan's hands were so much smaller than his own, they made Rob's cock look bigger.

He chuckled and stared down at their dicks. Those two beautiful cocks would soon shoot spunk all over him and Ethan. He groaned and pushed Ethan's cock closer to his own. Where was this cream again? "Rub them together..."

Ethan's nose flared, and he nodded like a bobble-head figurine. He pushed his hips closer and grabbed his own cock as well, breathing loudly. When they rubbed together, Rob groaned in appreciation and hugged Ethan closer, feeling up his back, dipping his fingers into its creases on the way down. He made a brief stop above Ethan's ass, but then he chose to go for it and gathered the round buttocks in his palms with a low sigh.

Ethan whimpered. He actually *whimpered* and squeezed their cocks together, working them both with those agile, slippery fingers. The shafts touched, cockheads brushed against each other. It was pure heaven, with Ethan's hair tickling Rob's arm and the soft fur on the bed making Rob feel as if they were the only people in the universe, surrounded by sweet and strange music that took them into another time altogether.

Robert pushed his hands down Ethan's pants, kneading the soft ass like fresh dough. He found it hard to keep his eyes open, so he let them slide shut and kissed the smooth skin of Ethan's neck.

The way Ethan pushed into Rob's hug made him feel so protective, so happy to embrace everything Ethan wanted to give. Not to mention Ethan's raspy moans as he jerked them both off were making Rob so freaking horny he wanted to ravish that sweet-smelling body like a vulture. And there was Ethan's ass. Rob couldn't see it well, but it was surprisingly soft and made Rob's imagination run rampant. He wished he could rub himself off on it and see his come flow right between those sweet cheeks. All of a sudden, it all became too much, and he came, trembling in Ethan's arms.

Ethan muttered something, but Rob couldn't comprehend it, only hearing the rhythmical sound of jerking off. Moments later, Ethan groaned and Rob felt Ethan's come all over his stomach. His buttocks clenched under Rob's touch, and Rob could only imagine what it would be like to have them tense around his dick.

He gathered Ethan close and lapped at his sweaty cheek, his breathing still shaky. "Wow..."

Ethan clung to him, their legs tangled together like a perfect bow. "That was hot," he whispered and wrapped his arms around Rob's waist. The heat between them was yet to cool down, but at least the lust was sated.

"Yeah." Rob smiled into Ethan's skin.

Ethan snorted and nuzzled Rob's cheek. "Your cock is the best pain medicine. I'll call you to come over next time I have a headache."

Robert felt heat spread over his face. "Greedy bastard. You're gonna have them all the time now, aren't you?"

"I can't help it. If there's an itch, you've got to scratch it." Ethan slowly rolled to his back, and Rob bit his lip at how glorious he looked, all sated, half-naked, with his pants pulled down and his cock on show.

Robert rolled to his back as well and used Ethan's arm as a pillow. He was one happy guy. "Sure. That's what you're going to tell yourself."

Ethan leaned over and gave Rob a kiss on the cheek.

It made Rob murmur at the soft touch. He raised his hand and gestured for Ethan to give him his. Their fingers intertwined, and Ethan smiled at him sheepishly as he molded his body to Robert's. Rob could get used to this, even if it was meant to only last till graduation.

Chapter 9

Rob

ROBERT SAT DOWN NEXT to Chris in the middle of the menswear store. They already spent too much time in the prom/wedding dress establishment next door, and enthusiasm was draining out of him with each heartbeat. One glance at Chris confirmed that it was a shared experience. He didn't even know what kind of suit he wanted for the prom and was largely indifferent to the color as long as it looked well on him, so he let Kelly, Ethan, and Derek propose something. He actually wished Ethan would weigh in, but the little bugger was too busy ogling embroidered waistcoats to care.

"This one," Kelly held up a suit jacket with blue lining. "It would go well with my turquoise dress."

Rob didn't comment on the fact that no one would actually see the lining.

Chris gently nudged him. "Why did you ask them to come? Shouldn't Ed be shopping in a goth shop or something?"

Rob groaned and shook his head. "He's here because I like him, and because he has a good eye for colors." He then looked back to Kelly and shook his head. "It's not bad. But isn't it a bit too... dark?"

Kelly raised her eyebrows and glanced over to Ethan who seemed to be comparing two shades of black. "Do you think he has an eye for color just because he's gay?"

"Exactly! That's so prejudiced." Chris snorted and grinned at their reflection in the mirror across the room.

"Nah, but he's an artist. He must have an eye for color, right?" He shrugged and smiled at Kelly. "But I want a normal suit, without one of those weird long jackets."

Kelly put the suit jacket back on the rack and kept browsing. "That's fine. You'll look good in anything."

Ethan rushed back their way with a suit in his hand. Derek followed him empty-handed, since he only came for company. Apparently, he had already ordered some expensive suit online over a month ago.

"Rob, look, I found this tie made out of mole leather the vintage section." Ethan's hair was tied back in a neat ponytail. Combined with the glasses, it made him look like he meant business. "I'm planning to do this textured look, all black but with different fabrics."

Robert stared at what used to be a mole's back or tummy. For some reason, he never had this reaction when looking at cow leather or pig leather, but he supposed it was because they were being killed for burgers and pork stew anyway. It was a nice piece of... skin.

He looked up into Ethan's eye, and something in his stomach made a quick backflip. Was Ethan waiting for his approval? Comments on fabrics he had no idea about? "That's... interesting. Is Derek also doing all black?"

"Glad that you ask," said Derek, touching the top of Ethan's shoulder. Rob frowned. The guy's teeth were the color of print paper, but

Rob did his best to look up to Derek's eyes, which were now wide with excitement. "I chose the school colors. Dark green suit and yellow details. And my mother got me this golden cross pin for the pocket."

Chris nodded with a silly grin. "This makes so much sense. I like the forbidden love affair in the air. You know, Edward, the goth going to prom with the top cheerleader."

Chris barely finished before Ethan growled at him. "Call me 'Edward' once more, and I'll punch your face in."

"Yeah, he looks nothing like an Edward." Robert smiled at Ethan, unimpressed by the idea of a forbidden love affair between him and Derek. They had *nothing* in common anyway. "So, will you have any yellow or green as well?"

Ethan petted the tie in his hands as if it were a living animal. "No. We don't have to look all matchy-matchy."

Kelly pouted at them. "It's different for guys I suppose."

"So you're dead set on that blue gown, yeah?" asked Rob, getting to his feet with a smile. He didn't want to be forced to exchange his suit before the prom.

"It's turquoise. It's all paid for and everything. You wanna try this suit on?" She passed him a set. Ethan was already off to the fitting room with his outfit of choice.

Derek waved at him with a grin. "I'll entertain Chris in the meanwhile."

Robert snorted, noticing the slight shadow of uncertainty on his friend's face but accepted the suit from Kelly and walked straight for the fitting room. He wondered where Ethan was. Maybe they could see one another before presenting themselves to everyone else

Ethan was the only one there, and his feet in black socks were a clear indication of where he was. He actually whistled the song they listened to last time they met up at Ethan's place. Rob knocked on the thin door, remembering how it felt to come by rubbing their cocks together... even though he was a bit sorry he didn't get to suck Ethan's cock again.

"Who is it?" Ethan asked.

"Not Derek," answered Robert with a grin and leaned into the door.

There was a pause, but then the door opened. Ethan was standing in just a pair of socks and black briefs. "Too bad. I was hoping for some hot Christian action."

Robert growled. "Kinky. Can I come in?"

"Sure. Am I getting some hot jock action instead? Exciting." Ethan grinned up at him but reached for a pair of black suit pants.

Rob pursed his lips as he walked into the large cubicle. There was a bench running along one of the edges and several hangers on the walls. "I don't think we have enough time."

"Maybe I'll just call Derek over then." Ethan poked Rob with his foot and put on a fitted black shirt, covering the little dancing rats on his stomach.

"Come on. His teeth are fake." Robert grinned to present his own and pulled off his shirt.

"That's so mean! He could be my future husband, you know." Ethan slapped Rob's arm, but then stopped moving altogether and stared at Rob's chest.

Robert drew in a sharp breath as he looked into the dreamy eye in front of him. It was as if his arousal skyrocketed from zero to 100 percent within a few seconds. "How quick can you come?"

Ethan just stared. "Too quick for my own good?" he choked out.

Robert felt a flash of heat going through his body, and he quickly fell to his knees, reaching out for the fly of Ethan's pants. His ears were pulsing so loudly he missed whatever Ethan would be saying to that. Maybe it was for the best.

Ethan didn't stop him though and leaned against the wall. "But really quick. Fuck. If someone comes over, we're screwed," he whispered, but frantically reached out for his phone when it started ringing. "Or not screwed for that matter," he groaned.

"Come on… we never get to this bit," uttered Robert as he pulled the pants down along with Ethan's underwear. The sharp, somewhat sweet smell filled his nostrils, drawing him in like a puppy on a leash. His eyes were on the beautiful head that was ripe for the taking.

Ethan's eye widened, and he silently pointed to his phone, but didn't actually push Rob away. He only got that pink flush on his pale cheeks. "Hi, yeah, this is Ethan," he said into the phone, as his cock stiffened before Rob's eyes.

Was that a yes? A no? Robert was tired of waiting so he just went for it, sucking the head into his mouth. The smoothness of it was giving him shivers as it lay on his tongue, heavier with every moment. It was nothing like that horrible ordeal over two weeks ago. Like the difference between sipping a cocktail and having moonshine poured down your throat.

Ethan's fingers slid into Rob's hair and gripped it at the top but didn't pull him away.

"Yeah? Oh, wow, that sounds fantastic," he said into the phone in a bit of a raspy voice. "Definitely, e-mail me the details." He spread his thighs wider and Rob could feel the veins throb with heat on his tongue.

He leaned in, snaking one hand around Ethan's thigh and gripped the base of his cock with the other, sucking the dick deep into his mouth. If they weren't in a public place, he'd groan. He wanted to masturbate so bad! Finally, he got to properly suck on that gorgeous dick and be in charge of what he was doing. Ethan's hand was an extra sensation at best, as he didn't try to force his cock deeper into Robert's mouth or direct him. He didn't push him away either so Rob took it as a hint to proceed.

"Sure I can get more. We have loads of squirrels in Washington." Ethan took a silent gulp of air, looking down at Rob just as he started sucking in earnest, licking around the shaft and kissing the head in random order. Even after watching so many porn movies, he had no idea what to do, what Ethan would like most. And even if he did, the knowledge would have all evaporated out of his head the moment he saw Ethan's dick. He chose to let nature take its course and dove in, sucking on the musky flesh and teasing with the tip of his tongue. The fact there was someone talking to Ethan, unaware of what was going on at the other end of the line, made Robert's arousal skyrocket. He never thought of himself as kinky, but there he was, sucking off a guy in a fitting room while said guy was on the phone, with their friends close by.

"Y-yeah... I'll e-mail back," Ethan rasped. "Thanks." He turned off the phone and took a huge gulp of air. "Oh fuck," he whispered, grabbing Rob's head with his other hand as well. "I'm gonna come in, like, five seconds."

Robert made a sound of agreement and bobbed his head forward. His own cock was already achingly hard, but this sensation was new, and he wanted to savor it as much as possible. Ethan had to bite on his hand to stifle the moan when he came, jerking his hips forward. Rob caught him just in time to regain control over the situation. Ethan's seed hit his palate, making Rob squirm with excitement and squeeze his own cock through his jeans. He was so lightheaded he wouldn't even notice if someone walked in on them. The taste wasn't all that pleasant, but he didn't care. It was come he earned with his first proper blow job, and he'd have it. So he swallowed.

Ethan took big gulps of air, trying to be as quiet as possible. His eye was wide and hazy as he looked down at Rob. "I changed my mind," he whispered. "*You* can be my future husband." A smile crawled up his red face.

Rob used the bench to pull himself up, gasping for air. He was puzzled by how oddly satisfied he was, even without having come himself. He'd never felt this way before, so on the edge and so content at the same time. "Good, Derek wouldn't do," he uttered, wondering how much time had passed. But Ethan had already moved on.

"Listen, Rob, we need to get squirrels. A lot of squirrels," he muttered, with his pants still down and he gripped Rob's cock through his pants.

But the moment they heard footsteps outside, he pushed Ethan away, biting back a groan. His heart thumped at the sight of a shadow outside the door.

"Guys, are you alive?"

Rob coughed. "Yeah, Ethan just had some phone call…"

"And this suit, it's really good. I'm gonna take it." Ethan rubbed his face and picked up his pants. "We have to get squirrels," he said as if it was any of Kelly's business.

"Yeah, mine's too small, but I can come over another time," Rob said. It would be easier without anyone trying to help him anyway. Straight to the point.

Ethan leaned over to Rob and silently kissed his chin. It was such a sweet gesture that Rob's hard cock twitched in his pants in anticipation of something it wouldn't get now.

"What squirrels?" Kelly asked.

Rob frowned and gave Ethan the 'what squirrels?' look.

"I'll tell you on the way!" Ethan groaned and started swiftly putting on his clothes. He was out of the sex and back to business.

Robert winced when Chris's pickup truck stumbled over some kind of obstacle. Again. He wondered how Kelly was doing, with her fatless bottom on the naked bed of the pickup truck. She didn't look all that pleased, but unlike Derek, she'd decided to go with them anyway. Ethan was on the front seat, guiding Chris along the roads in the forest. The whole trip was pretty mental.

Apparently, Ethan got a phone call from some boutique in LA, which wanted to buy his 'squirrel jewelry' collection. The one that he had only made a sample of so far. Not only did Ethan agree, but claimed that he could have fifty sets done for them within the next weeks. As soon as they got out of that changing room, Ethan had proper madness in his eye. Robert felt like they suddenly changed into cartoon characters when Ethan shook him, and told him that they had to visit some crazy hunter in the forest to get a whole bunch of squirrels. Ethan took out all his savings from an ATM, and here they were, driving up to nowhere in order to buy dead rodents. His drive was both impressive and scary. Since when did a schoolboy know people who stacked up on dead animals?

"You okay?" asked Rob, trying to send out positive vibes. At least it wasn't raining.

"Yeah, sure. It's just so cold." Kelly sighed and cuddled up in her puffy jacket. "I wasn't really expecting a trip into the woods, but this is too exciting to pass on. Can't believe he talked you guys into it."

Rob shrugged, pondering whether he could stand the cold air without his jacket but eventually pulled it off and handed it to her. It wouldn't have been so bad if it weren't for the car moving. "He can be pretty persuasive."

Kelly shuffled over to his side and put the jacket around her shoulders, cuddling up to him. "Thanks, Rob, that's too sweet." She stared at him, as if expecting something more, but he just smiled and raised his chin higher, so she went on, "So this guy's name is Herbert, and he's a taxidermist? What if he wants to stuff us all and hang us on the wall?"

Robert snorted. "You mean, hang you on the wall? Why would he need teenage guys?"

"Oh, my God! That's so horrible!" Kelly laughed and punched his arm. "Maybe he's gay if he's Ethan's friend. You'll be choking on your own words. He'd feed me to the dogs and hang you up there."

Robert stared at her, surprised she of all people would come to a conclusion such as this. "Ethan *has* straight friends."

"Yeah, one. And by the look of it, he's not making any more." She pointed to the glass between them and the front seats, where Chris and Ethan seemed to be arguing. Ethan with a map in his hand and gesturing wildly with the other; Chris baring his teeth in a way that didn't suggest anything good.

"Come on." Robert rolled his eyes. "This Herbert guy probably doesn't even know Ethan's gay."

Kelly kept her gaze on the inside of the cab. "I suppose he's not gay-looking. I know there's all sorts of gays, but with some, you can really tell. You know what I mean? Ethan's just weird."

"I guess." Rob shrugged, watching the trees pass by. They were on a narrow dirt road, already deep in the woods. He wondered how long it would take them to reach Herbert the Squirrel Man. And if he could get off later too. Ethan's parents had such a tight grip on their son, that he and Ethan barely scraped out some hours together. Now Rob understood why Ethan was so specific about meeting up on Wednesday afternoons. It was the only time when he actually had a few hours alone at home.

All of a sudden, Kelly gripped Rob's T-shirt when they took a sharp turn to the side of the road and parked. Chris rushed out of the car and slammed the door shut.

"I am done with this! He does not listen to me!"

Rob immediately untangled himself from Kelly and looked at him. "What's wrong? Aren't you the one driving?"

Ethan got out from the other side with fire in his eye. "He is! And he's doing a shit job! This is a complicated route, and I've been here so many times. But nooo, Chris knows a shortcut, Chris knows how to get to a remote house he's never heard of before, sure!" Ethan crossed his arms on his chest with a huff.

Robert was sorry he couldn't frown at both of them at once. "Maybe I could take over?" he proposed, turning toward Chris.

"Sure, you deal with that know-it-all," Chris groaned and opened the door for Rob, as if he were a chauffeur, and Rob were a lady.

"Can we just get there already, find out if he's gonna kill us or not, and go home?" Kelly complained, huddled up in two jackets.

"Actually, I do know how to get to this guy's house so I do know all about it!" Ethan hissed. "I'd love to drive myself, but, *oh*, I don't have one eye!"

Robert stumbled on his way to the ground. It was like a stab to the gut. Why would Ethan say this now of all times?

He looked over to the empty space between Ethan and Chris, and put his hands into his pockets. "Are you done?"

Ethan gritted his teeth. "We're running out of time," he said, quieter.

Robert rolled his eyes. "Chris? Will you swap with me?"

"Sure, if you think you can deal with Mr. Bossy, here." Chris pointed to Ethan, who only bristled more.

"It's not me who can't take direction."

Robert turned to Ethan, exhaling, and stared straight into his eye. He couldn't believe the guy was being so ungrateful. It was only Chris's good deed for the day to take him here in the first place.

Ethan took a deep breath and lowered his gaze, but turned around and opened the door like a good boy.

Chris got onto the back and sat next to Kelly. "Good luck," he said with a pout.

With one more look at Kelly's disappointed face, Rob got into the driver's seat and slammed the door shut a bit too hard. "Get in."

Ethan looked up at him and followed the order. "Chris is so rude," he mumbled as he closed his seat belt.

"No. You are." Robert started the car and moved forward, wondering how he could possibly put some sense into that stubborn head.

"You're just taking his side," Ethan looked out the window, his body language as closed as possible. Arms crossed, lips clenched.

"Yeah? Whose car is this? Whose gas is this? Huh?" Rob snapped.

Ethan stayed silent, and when he spoke, his voice was much higher. "I just want those squirrels so much," he uttered, rubbing his eye. "I got nervous."

"That's the same thing you told me when you made me suck your cock for the first time," growled Robert quietly, but his stomach froze at the memory.

Ethan slouched in his seat. "I'm sorry," he whispered.

"I'm sorry too. It's not how I imagined my first time, you know. But that's life. Sometimes, you just have to suck it up," whispered Robert through clenched teeth. By the end of the sentence, his jaw was hurting so bad, he had to open and close it several times to relax the muscles.

Ethan folded his map before speaking. "I'm sorry... You know, it's close now. I can hike from here, and I'll call my mom to pick me up." He unbuckled his seat belt.

Robert stared at the road ahead and pressed the gas pedal. Ethan would not be escaping from here. "No."

"You make it sound so horrible..." Ethan rubbed the side of his head. "It was a first for me too."

Robert forced himself to slowly let out the air gathered in his lungs and focused on the road despite the wave of heat that threatened to scramble his brain and cook his eyes. He didn't know where it all came from, but the memories held on to his neck, choking him with all their power. "I sort of imagined I'd choose who it would be, where, and when, you know?" he uttered. "I lost this and will never get it back."

"And I always imagined I'd have both eyes, no debilitating headaches, and no lost memories!" Ethan burst out all of a sudden. "You shouldn't have done what you did! I'm still in pain, still dealing with the aftermath and praying I won't start losing more memory. You seem to have recovered, and you're all over sucking cock," he whispered the last words.

Robert grasped the steering wheel in an iron grip as the trees and asphalt blurred in front of his eyes. "I didn't do this on purpose, and you know it, you little fuck," he whispered, focusing all his attention on the road.

"Okay, so I'm a greedy bastard! Sue me. For once in my life, I got a shot at being with someone I wanted so I took that chance. So maybe it was a little fucked up, but I didn't know you the way I do now." Ethan knocked his head into the window.

Robert felt a sudden stinging in his eyes and he blinked, breathing hard. "Is that how you see this? Really?"

Ethan sucked in his lips and sat there in silence.

It took Robert at least five minutes to gather the courage to speak. He didn't even want to look at Ethan, much less listen to his selfish excuses. "I'll get you there, but call your mom to pick you up."

"I never wanted to be pushy, I just need those squirrels..." Ethan whispered, barely audibly, never looking back at Rob.

"I don't care about the fucking squirrels. You can fuck Derek for all I care," hissed Robert.

Ethan didn't say another word until they got to Herbert's house. It was a secluded old cottage in the middle of nowhere, and it really did look like something out of a horror movie. The man sitting in front of it had a furry hat and a beard that looked like a living creature, but he greeted Ethan like an old friend. Chris and Kelly didn't even get off the back when Robert told them they weren't waiting for Ethan.

"Thanks for the lift," Ethan uttered, standing next to Herbert with his hands in his hoodie. "And thanks for letting us use your car, Chris."

"It's fine." Chris waved his hand, not as bothered as half an hour ago. Talking to a pretty girl must have tamed his temper, not that he was the type to dwell on conflict anyway.

Robert did his best not to look Ethan's way and crawled onto the back as soon as they had Kelly safely stored in the passenger seat.

But it wasn't the end for Rob. When the wheels of the car started moving, the soft, velvety voice reached his ears.

"I'm so sorry, Rob," Ethan said a bit louder so Rob would hear him over the engine.

Robert drew in a sharp breath and huddled his jacket tighter around his arms. He was freezing all over.

Chapter 10

ROB

"Tonight's gonna be epic!" Chris exclaimed, walking around his tiny room in just his pants. Robert tried not to take in too much air, afraid he'd choke on all the deodorant Chris sprayed himself with. He seemed to have taken the manufacturer's commercial too seriously. Rob was doing his best not to cough.

"So what color of dress is she wearing?" asked Rob half-heartedly. His thoughts kept straying to the last words he heard from Ethan. He said 'sorry'. Was it really what he meant, or was he just playing with Rob again? Sometimes, it was hard to read Ethan's facial expressions. They hadn't spoken for over a week, and Ethan hadn't even approached Rob about coming over on their designated fuck-Wednesday. At school, Ethan avoided him like the plague, even when Rob caught himself looking at him across the hall.

"Red. You know what that means." Chris smirked and wiggled his eyebrows as he put on his shirt over the layer of thick fragrance.

"I do?" he asked, biting his lip. This sudden change of dynamics between him and Ethan was making him feel at a loss, even though they'd never talked to one another before the accident. Only now did Rob realize that they had been spending a lot of time in each other's company since then. He'd been at Ethan's hospital bed every single day, then they'd started fucking, and talking, and hugging whenever they could. He knew Ethan was beginning to like him despite the rough start. And was he himself not overreacting? It wasn't like Ethan *raped* him. As painful as it was, Ethan did withdraw his demands after the first time, so had it really been the right to break up their blooming—whatever it was they had—so suddenly?

"Yeah, like, hello! Red. Girls wear red when they wanna look sexy. It's like a signal that they're ready to go all the way." Chris frowned and shook his head. "Everybody knows that. Oh, but don't think that just because Kelly's doing blue, she's not available. Don't let that fool you." He walked up to a tiny mirror on the wall and started combing his short hair.

"She's a friend," muttered Robert, dragging his hands down his face. He refused to comment on Chris's stupid conclusion. He loved the guy to bits, but Chris wasn't the sharpest crayon in the pack.

"Come on, Rob. She's been a friend for, like, forever. You know she'd date you in a heartbeat."

"I don't want her to date me," grumbled Rob, finding himself obsessing over Derek being Ethan's date. Again. This issue had been on his mind a lot lately. What if they actually end up fucking? Yeah. What then? And Rob was the stupid one to encourage Ethan to do it in the first place. With Ethan not being interested in anything else than just scratching an itch, Robert was expendable anyway.

Chris turned around and gave him that serious look. "Are you dating some married woman or something?"

Robert scowled. "Where did that come from?"

"'Cause you push Kelly away like she's got herpes or something, but you haven't invited anyone else. Are you tapping some cougar and have to keep it quiet? I'd kill you if you are, and you haven't told me." Chris squinted, which made heat rise in Robert's head so rapidly it felt as though it would explode.

Robert exhaled. "I'm gay." There. Out in the open. And even though Rob felt that he had every right to be who he was, his stomach still cramped.

Chris frowned. "Very funny. Who's the girl?"

Robert didn't know whether he should laugh or scream in anguish. "I'm gay," he said, trying to pronounce every syllable perfectly.

"Wait, are you serious?" Chris took a step closer and bowed down to Rob's eye level.

Robert discreetly pulled on his own index finger, and his cheeks tingled. "Do I look like I'm joking?"

"Oh, fuck! You're serious," Chris hissed. "What the fuck? I can't believe you haven't told me! I've been your best friend for fourteen years!" His eyes widened, and he stepped back, spreading his arms wide. "Oh, God. Are you fucking Eddie?"

Robert opened and closed his mouth, feeling uncomfortable with the sudden shower of loud words. "Don't call him that."

"You are!" Chris threw his hands in the air. "I can't believe you would finally do it with someone and not tell me!"

"I'm telling you now. And it's kinda private, yeah?" Robert exhaled, slowly relaxing now than he was certain Chris wouldn't suddenly turn on him. Sure, the guy had a big heart and always tried to defend gay rights, but it was a different matter when a guy who kept seeing you naked after every football practice turned out to be gay.

"Yeah, sure, I'll keep it quiet, but... what? Ethan? Out of all people?" Chris took a deep breath and sat down on his desk. It creaked so badly Rob frowned.

"What is that supposed to mean?"

"Come on, he's like..." Chris made a gesture in the air that said absolutely nothing.

Rob frowned at him. "What?"

"Is this some guilt thing? I mean... he's not like... If *I* were gay, I wouldn't go for him," Chris concluded and folded his arms across his chest.

Was that an insult? Maybe not to Rob but certainly to Ethan. "Well, I did go for him."

"'Did', because he's dating that Derek guy now? Wow, come to think of it, Ethan's doing really well for himself. First, he does the quarterback, and now a cheerleader." Chris stared out the window with a thoughtful expression.

"Shut up," uttered Robert, slouching his shoulders. "Derek's a fucking saint. Nothing'll happen there."

"Huh? Is there something I'm not getting here?"

Robert groaned. "We're kinda... I don't think we are on the same page with Ethan."

Chris jumped off the desk. "What page do you want to be on with him?"

Robert shrugged. "Dunno, he's hot, and I like talking to him."

"And he's dating Derek..." Chris gave Rob a pat on the head.

"He's not. They're just going to prom together, like me and Kelly." Robert stretched to relieve the tension that contorted his back.

"So let me just get this *straight*." Chris laughed nervously. "Are you dating him or not? Are you just fuckbuddies?"

Robert felt heat flooding his face. That last word seemed so impersonal. "I don't know."

"Oh, man, this is not good. You don't even know what you're doing? I mean... what? How am I supposed to give you advice?" Chris shook his head and put on his suit jacket.

Robert mentally rolled his eyes. As much as he loved Chris, the guy wasn't the best person to take advice from. "It's different with guys. Not everything's black and white."

Chris squinted and folded his hands into a triangle. "So let me re-cap this. You're gay. You have a thing for Ethan, but it's not anything official, and you guys just... uh, fool around?"

Robert swallowed. That did help. "Yeah."

"That's cool. I think." Chris pursed his lips. "So since you're not doing Kelly, like, ever, can I ask her out after prom?"

Robert frowned. "Didn't you just say you want to sleep with Sue after prom?"

"Well, it's not like I'm married to her or something. And Kelly's not getting any because of you." Chris raised his eyebrows. "It's only fair I put her out of her misery."

Robert gave him a long, cloudy look. What the fuck was that supposed to mean? "I don't think 'getting some' is all they want, so maybe make a decision, yeah?"

"Oh, come on... Aren't you gonna try and get into Ethan's pants tonight?" Chris winked at him.

Rob exhaled. "He's going with Derek. Besides, I wouldn't be trying to get into someone else's pants if it doesn't work out with him. Those aren't anonymous hookups, it's people we know. Come on, Chris..."

Chris sat down on the bed, next to Rob. "I suppose... Why do you have to be so sensible?" He took a deep breath. "Can I ask Kelly out if I break up with Sue?"

"Only if you don't try to get into Sue's pants tonight." Robert leaned back against the wall, tired of the relationship talk. It didn't look like it was about to end.

"Okay, I'll think about it. So what do you actually *do* with him?" Chris asked with a frown.

Rob drew in a sharp breath, remembering the milky skin, and how that flesh turned pliant against him. He wasn't sure if Chris was just asking out of some kind of weird bro-politeness or whether he was really interested. "All sorts of stuff."

"It's so hard to talk to you sometimes, you know that?" Chris took a deep breath. "Are you eying any other guys?'

Robert snorted. "I have some favorite models, and there is this guy at the café in the mall that I think is hot."

Chris punched his arm. "I can't get over you not telling me. Okay, whatever then, you have my blessing. He's a pain in the ass though, so I hope I never have to drive him anywhere again."

Robert's mouth tingled, and he relaxed with a smile. "He can be a bit overdramatic at times, yeah."

"So I suppose instead of an 'epic' night, this will probably end up being a 'PG' night." Chris sighed at the loss.

"Come on, is that the only reason you wanted to party tonight?" Robert shook his head in disbelief.

"Nah, it's just a strange turn of events. Hey, why'd you leave him at that crazy guy's house in the woods then? Did he piss you off too with that map of his?"

"Something like that." Robert looked at his watch, refusing to let the conversation from the car replay in his mind in all the painful detail.

"Oh, my God! Can I tell him I know?" Chris straightened up all of a sudden with a wide grin.

Robert raised his head and blinked. "No! Jeesus, he can't know I told you."

"Damn, I'd love to mess with him." Chris got up and looked at his watch.

"Don't." Robert sighed. "We need to go anyway." He got to his feet and rushed to the door. Chris rarely made him feel uncomfortable, but this conversation had been horrendous. At least he got rid of the elephant in the room and could now stop worrying whether Chris would turn his back on him if he knew the truth.

Chapter 11

ETHAN

ETHAN'S PERSONAL LIFE WAS shit. Dead squirrels were much better friends than people so he was happy to spend time with them instead of dwelling on his relationship status. Fortunately, Herbert didn't charge him an arm and a leg for those, so Ethan still had some money left to spend on the supplies he needed to actually finish his pieces, but it was running out all too quickly in comparison to what he was earning. He was damn sure his parents wouldn't subsidize this order, and since he didn't get a down payment yet, all he had left was to make do day by day. Good that they didn't know how much his grades fell, or they would make an even bigger fuss about his project than they already did.

Time was running out all too quickly, so even now, on the day of the prom, already dressed to the nines in his sleek black suit with lapels covered with mole leather to match his tie, and a pair of vintage crocodile skin shoes, he was down in his workspace, finishing the engravings on a squirrel skull necklace. He needed to wait for Derek to pick him up so he figured he wouldn't waste time.

Sitting around wasn't something he enjoyed lately anyway. It made him think of the messed up thing he'd had with Rob. It made him feel like the villain of the story, and he didn't like it all that much. In fact, he didn't like it at all. Not to mention how upset he got even thinking about that first time they had. He remembered how disgusted Rob seemed with him, and the way he rushed outside, as if he needed air not to puke all over Ethan. It had been a crappy experience, even if Ethan had come in a matter of seconds.

Robert must have remembered just how repulsive it was because they'd stopped speaking to each other. Without his company, school was once again a pain in the ass, even though Derek did chat to him in the hallway every now and then. They flirted a bit, but it was nothing like the pull Ethan felt for Robert. Maybe Ethan was just a 'bad person at the core of his humanity', like all those vegan girls at school had said. So he figured he wouldn't bother Robert anymore. Rob clearly didn't like being pushed.

He flinched when the door at the top of the stairs opened.

"Honey, what are you still doing here?" asked his mom, her feet already resounding along the concrete stairs. She wouldn't enter the room, but had no problem pestering him from the entrance.

"I'm just finishing a project," he mumbled, gently carving the patterns into the skull with a chisel.

"Really, Ethan, this madness has to end. You should dedicate all your time to school to make up for the missed month, and instead, I keep finding you here."

He groaned in annoyance. Would this topic keep coming back to hit him in the head like a crooked boomerang? He hadn't even told his parents about the order he got, afraid they would freak out that he won't manage or that he shouldn't take it on now, before going to college.

"Mom, I'm doing great at school. And it's not like I'm gonna learn anything in the ten minutes before Derek comes to pick me up."

Mother sighed, rested her slim hands on her hips, and shook her head. "You are obsessed with it. Really, once you're out of home and living on your own, you will realize that you can't let a hobby absorb you like that."

"Oh, God, Mom! Just let me do this now then." He didn't even look up from the skull. He didn't have time for this.

"Is this really where you're going to show yourself to your date? A garage?" grunted Mother.

"No, I'll obviously come up when he comes over. I just need to finish this first."

There was a low sigh, but eventually, her footsteps moved away. "All right but this is the last time. You'll be focusing on your studies starting tomorrow."

Ethan just rolled his eye. He was sick of all this bullshit. And if that wasn't bad enough, Ethan's cell phone buzzed. He had to put away the work and look at the text message. Derek was almost there, so it only made sense for Ethan to put the skull away for now. He could finish it tomorrow. Or when he came from the prom at night.

He turned off the lights, the heating, and made his way upstairs. He didn't really feel all that excited about the party anymore, but at least he would get to wear his new outfit, even if not to impress his estranged crush. The last thing he wanted was for Rob to think he decided not to go because of him. Ethan would go and have fun. Or at least stick around for a few hours, watch the band.

He almost bumped into his mother in the dark garage. "Goodness, what happened?" she asked.

"Nothing... Derek's gonna be here in a few minutes. I don't really know when I'll be back."

"Just don't do anything stupid. You're going to college soon anyway," uttered Mother and hurried outside.

"It's not like I'm gonna get pregnant, you know." Ethan got out into the chilly air outside and straightened up the creases on his suit.

Mother frowned at him and wrapped her arms across her chest. "I don't like your attitude. You should be ashamed to even joke like that."

Ethan sighed and decided to keep his mouth shut. He could already see Derek's car in the far end of the street. Getting drunk tonight didn't seem like such a bad idea.

Derek was very chatty on the way to school. In fact, his mouth never closed, even as they left the car and headed for the door with a never ending stream of students in all their tacky finery.

"I like your shoes," Ethan managed to squeeze in when they got into the building.

"Thanks, they're vintage. I found them in this boutique in Manhattan, and for a moment, I was certain I couldn't afford them, but then..." Derek's babble melted into a buzz when Ethan spotted the familiar tall figure in the corridor. Standing next to Kelly, Rob looked like a giant.

She was too close, Rob was too handsome, so at that very moment, Ethan made the petty decision of grabbing Derek's hand. "They're really cool," he said and kissed Derek on the cheek.

Derek blinked. "What? Her hideous tights?" he whispered, nodding toward a girl with rainbow-striped legs.

"No, your shoes." Ethan refused to look at Rob. If he did, he was worried his throat would constrict too much.

"Ah, yeah." Derek flashed him that blinding grin. It was weird that the guy didn't appeal to Ethan much, even though there was absolutely nothing wrong with his looks, and most people would describe him as very handsome. "They remind me of a pair my late grandfather kept all his life. He had worn them on his wedding day and never even thought of getting rid of them. Such a romantic..."

Ethan wasn't sure what to say to that, so he followed Derek's lead. They walked along the tables full of treats and drinks. Ethan's nape tingled with the powerful gaze he felt clinging to his back. The moment he wanted to say something, ending the flood of words from his date, a whole pack of Derek's cheerleader friends swarmed them with all their taffeta.

"You guys look so sweet!" squealed Jessica, a bubbly blonde in a pink dress. Ethan could smell whiskey on her, which made him reimagine her as a tipsy rat, falling into the arms of some suave rodent.

"We need to post photos of you on Facebook," chirped another girl, overwhelming Ethan with her high voice.

"It's so nice that our school is so inclusive, isn't it?" asked Derek, patting Ethan's arm.

"Yeah, sur—" Ethan didn't get to finish that either.

Pat the Rat, with his swarm of minions, just walked past and threw an empty plastic cup at them. "Inclusive of vampires like our Edward. Too bad you don't sparkle at night, Eddie. That'd be very gay."

One of the cheerleaders muffled a laugh, but Derek... along with his own minions in pastels, just glared at the school gorillas.

"Horrible people," he uttered, sliding his hand to the small of Ethan's back. That actually felt kinda nice. Reminded Ethan of when Rob did it. Only Rob's hand did so much more than just make Ethan feel safe.

"I'm not even goth," Ethan felt the need to add.

All the girls, and Derek, stared at him as if he just confessed to being an alien.

"Of course you are. No need to be ashamed," whispered Derek, pulling him in for a hug.

"Goth is the new gay," confirmed one of the girls.

Ethan frowned but went for the hug anyway. When he had his chin on Derek's shoulder though, his gaze locked with Robert's. Standing over the punchbowl, Rob seemed to have frozen with the cup half-filled, and the ladle in hand. His chest was rapidly rising and falling as he looked into Ethan's face, but soon the charm was gone, and Robert swiftly rushed toward Kelly and his other friends.

Ethan groaned to himself and pulled away from Derek. What was he even doing obsessing about a guy whom he'd only met up with for sex? Maybe it was the guilt that Ethan was so relationship-challenged? Even since that argument they had with Robert in the car, Ethan felt like he'd killed a baby seal with a club or something. He couldn't take back what had happened that first time, and now all he kept thinking of was that Robert was repulsed by him. No wonder he didn't want to kiss.

A hand waving in front of Ethan's face brought him back to reality. "You wanna dance? They're already playing," said Derek, moving his body to the distant rhythm.

"Sure, yeah." Ethan let Derek grab his hand and guide him to the dance floor. At least the music wasn't completely horrible, but Ethan wasn't the best of dancers. Fortunately, one of the cheerleaders had a secret stash of vodka under her petticoat and wasn't stingy about sharing. With his senses slightly clouded, it all became much more bearable, and he enjoyed himself, jumping around and making silly moves along with Derek and some of his friends, who kept reshuffling around them like a carousel of faces. He had no idea how much time has passed, but he was starting to feel sweat beading on his face, and an insatiable thirst.

"I'll be back in a sec?" Ethan muttered and gave Derek another smooch before walking off. He needed a breather. Ethan loosened his tie and made his way down the empty corridors. With the entertainment fast approaching, people were reluctant to leave the temporary ballroom so he sneaked out to the bathroom without any trouble. His head was pulsing with heat and pleasantly light.

He took off his glasses to wash his face and neck. The cold tiles of the bathroom wall were all his forehead needed to relax so he rested it there with a small smile.

The dull sound of an opening door behind him sent a jolt of alarm all the way to his legs, but Derek's smile was all he needed to calm down. So he wouldn't be bullied tonight.

"You okay?" asked Derek, joining him by the wall.

"Oh yeah, I just needed to cool down after all the dancing." Ethan smiled back at him.

Derek never looked away from Ethan, a small smile ghosting across his lips.

"You're a good dancer. Not that I'm surprised with you being a cheerleader and all." Ethan leaned against the wall. He couldn't help but compare Derek's body to Robert's. Rob was so much taller, with wide shoulders, looking and acting older than his age, Derek on the other hand seemed so limber, with the athletic body of a runner.

"Thanks. Not too bad yourself," whispered Derek, slowly turning toward Ethan. He was close enough for Ethan to feel the heat of his body without touching.

"I highly doubt that." Ethan shook his head. "I'm having fun though."

Derek stepped closer, his dark eyes smoldering Ethan's skin. "It might sound strange, but I didn't expect to have so much fun. You're a cool guy."

"Wow. Thanks. Was I a pity date?" Ethan pouted but couldn't help his good mood, which was only fueled by alcohol.

Derek reached out, and moments later, warm hands brushed over the skin at the back of Ethan's scalp. There was a slight pull, and he realized Derek was letting Ethan's hair down.

"No, but I thought all you were was a pretty face."

Ethan wasn't sure where this was going, with Derek playing with his hair and the secluded atmosphere of being alone in the men's toilet. "And I'm not?"

Derek shook his head, sliding his hand over Ethan's nape. He moved until his back hit the wall and pulled Ethan with him. Caught completely off-guard, Ethan practically fell onto Derek's lips. He blinked in shock.

"But I thought you weren't... I mean..."

The soft, minty mouth moved over his in tune with Derek's hands, which pulled Ethan closer. "Your hair is so long and soft. It makes me think of Jesus."

What did one say to something like that? Ethan had no idea. "Is that a good thing in this context?"

Derek bit his lip and looked at the floor, his fingers brushing against Ethan's sides. "I like you. Maybe we could ditch all that and go somewhere? What do you say?" he whispered. There was an odd contrast between the shyness on his face, and the familiar glimmer in his eyes. That look reminded Ethan of the way Robert had stared at him that last time in the changing room.

This wasn't happening. Wasn't it Derek who told Ethan he was saving himself for after college, or for Jesus, or some shit like that? "I'm... flattered, I mean, that technically sounds good. It's just that... I'm after a bad breakup." His voice went quieter. "I don't think I'm ready to jump into anything again."

Derek blinked and leaned forward, brushing his lips across Ethan's cheek. His cologne smelled so tempting, so masculine. "I'm so sorry. But we could just talk, see how it goes?"

Ethan slid his arms around Derek and put his cheek on his shoulder. "Thanks, but I think I'd rather go home soon."

Derek sighed and hugged him back. "Okay. You wanna go dance some more then?"

"Yeah, let's go back and see the last band play." Ethan slipped out of the embrace but pulled Derek along by the hand. He felt numb. Having Derek hit on him like that reminded Ethan just how badly he wanted Robert. This was the last thing he should be focusing on now, with the squirrel project so desperate for all the attention Ethan could give it, but his chest seemed to have changed into lead at the thought of never touching Rob again.

Ethan followed Derek back to the gym where the show on stage was already in full swing. A few guys whom Ethan knew from class were playing a cover of a song Ethan sometimes heard on the radio, and it wasn't all that bad, even with the lead singer killing the high notes. Everyone was jumping around and dancing to the music, and it made him feel like even more of an outsider. Looking at all the smiling faces, all he wanted was to crawl under the table and stay there, unbothered in his cocoon of sadness.

Derek walked off to dance with his friends, sending Ethan one more wink. That was it. Ethan was alone again, and for lack of better things to do, he walked up to the wall and the table with the drinks, even though he knew it wouldn't satisfy the need deep inside his gut. He had to be the first gay teenager on the planet to decline a night of sex with a hot guy. What was wrong with him?

Ethan's eye trailed to the dance floor, and he reimagined the scene before him. The cheerleaders would be little white mice, with taffeta tutus, all gathered around Derek, the little rat in green and yellow. Over in the corner, he could see his nemesis, Pat the Rat, as a big, fat ginger-brownish rat, his paws curled into tiny fists as he eyed the others with a predatory sneer. And then there was him, a lonely black weasel, not really fitting in with the crowd of mice and rats, destined to be alone even if the bright lights reflected by the disco ball under the ceiling encompassed everyone.

He frowned when the air around him began to twinkle, but before he had the chance to react, he was swept by a wave of sparkly dust. It went everywhere: into his eye, into his hair, it scratched the back of his neck where it got underneath Ethan's shirt. And when he opened his eye, there was still glitter sliding off him onto heaps on the floor.

Even though the band hadn't stopped playing, everything seemed muted like in a silent movie. So this was his *Carrie* moment after all. Heads turned toward him, and the smiles on people's faces widened as he just stood there, slowly raising his hands, unsure what to do. It felt like being covered in toxic waste. Ethan looked down at his black outfit, his mole tie, his leather shoes... Every last inch of fabric covered in tiny particles of glitter.

"So you do sparkle at night, Edward," Pat said in a high-pitched voice from a lot too close for Ethan's liking. Of course it would be Pat who'd planned this. Who else?

The laughter around him only got louder, making blood thud in Ethan's ears. He couldn't move, he couldn't breathe, he couldn't bear this. It was as if all the sparkles pinned him to the ground, even though it wasn't glitter glue.

Chapter 12

ROB

Robert's world slowed down. Kelly squeezed his forearm as he stopped dancing, focusing on the lonely figure by the wall across the room. Tall as he was, he was able to look over the crowd and spot the big glittery mess that was Ethan. The stuff was cascading down his head and shoulders, making him look like the lovechild of Elton John and Brandon Lee. The window above him was open and Rob could vaguely see someone backing out from there, so it had to be where the bucket of glitter came from. Deep down though, Rob knew whose plan this was. Pat and his minions were already there, next to Ethan, no doubt making jokes about how sparkly their victim now was.

Ethan was usually the type of guy to talk back to Pat, but now he just stood there like a pile of glittery misery, with his lips parted and arms slightly spread to the sides. He didn't move, he didn't punch anyone. Rob could swear Ethan had stopped breathing altogether.

He looked down into Kelly's eyes and bent so she could hear him. "Need to go," he said and swiftly squeezed through the crowd, snaking his body between his classmates, but his eyes were only focused on Ethan, who stood surrounded by vultures, which were ready to take chunks out of his pride.

The moment their gazes met, it was as if seeing Rob pushed Ethan to action. He turned around, and when he started walking, the crowd made room for him as if he were Moses parting the Red Sea. No one wanted to get glitter all over themselves. It was fun in limited quantities, but Robert didn't even want to start imagining how long it would take to get all that stuff out of Ethan's long hair.

Robert quickly changed his course, following Ethan through the shortest route to the exit. One of the teachers gave Ethan a once-over, but apparently death by glitter was not a serious enough issue to react, which only meant it was Robert's call. When Ethan disappeared from sight, he picked up his pace and ran into the corridor.

"Ethan!" Rob yelled after him to get through all the music that was still playing.

Instead of turning around like any normal person, Ethan ran down the corridor, his footsteps resonating in the hallway. With glitter shaking off him with every step, it was a surreal image, as if Ethan left a trail of sparkle behind him just so Rob could follow.

Robert drew in a sharp breath, his legs feeling warm as he sprinted after Ethan. He almost trampled two girls as he turned into another hallway, but he managed to avoid the collision and sped straight for the main door that was still swinging with the force it had been opened with seconds before. A faint cloud of glitter fluttered in the air like a clue, but Robert tore straight through it and ran outside, into the dark parking lot.

"Go away!" he heard Ethan yell at him from a few feet away. With his slim body hunched into a parody of itself, Ethan was a sorry sight, especially when he turned away and rushed across the empty asphalt. Robert had no idea where to, because Ethan didn't drive anymore.

"No!" Robert ran past him and blocked his way. He was surprised to feel his chest tighten, as he was used to sprints, but it wasn't the only reason why he only uttered one word. Ethan was a mess. Eye patch slightly crooked, hair out of order, and a thousand sparkles all over.

Ethan gave up on running away and stopped, rubbing his eye. "You hate me. No need to feel sorry for me now."

Robert stepped back, staring at the misery personified in the much smaller man in front of him. When did it all go to shit? "I... don't hate you."

"You saved my life, you don't need to feel responsible for me anymore," Ethan uttered and walked around Robert with his eye visibly red, even in the weak lights from the school building.

Robert looked at the slouched shoulders as everything in him twisted and tensed up. "Don't go."

"I'm a joke to everyone," Ethan said without turning around, and Rob could swear he'd heard a sniff.

"Don't say that." He followed Ethan at the same speed, not to intimidate him. "You're not a joke to *me*."

Ethan passed car after car, walking out of the parking lot and into an empty street. "No, I'm a problem for you. You hate what I did to you, and now I can't ever take it back, and you think I'm disgusting, and I thought I wouldn't care, but actually, it's worse than not ever getting to touch you. And don't say you don't hate me because you do, I saw it all over your face when we were going to Herbert's. Fuck. And my injured eye socket hurts when I cry." He stopped, with his shoulders trembling and started rubbing his eye again. "I'm so done with all of this," he uttered, barely audible.

Rob's lungs emptied, his whole body rushing with intense heat that threatened to boil his brain on the spot. He stepped closer and grasped the front of Ethan's shirt. His lips found the soft, salty mouth so naturally like they were meant to be there. His heart sent intense waves of tremors all over his chest, and his lips throbbed with pleasure as if all his senses focused on this one place on his body.

Ethan slowly put his hands on Robert's chest and stood on his toes so it would be easier for them to kiss. His breath tickled Rob's face, every second stretching like bubblegum. Before Rob knew it, he was bending farther down, and Ethan wrapped his arms around his neck, their lips never parting. It was better than any conversation Rob had ever had. When Ethan opened his mouth in invitation, Rob didn't second-guess himself and delved right in, gasping at the sweetness of it. He ultimately forgot where and when he was, caught up in the best kiss of his life. None of the girls he'd kissed made him see bright fireworks, none of them came even close to giving him shivers or fueling a violent urge to go deeper, closer. He pulled Ethan against him with a deep sound that he'd never think could come out of him.

There was no opposition, and Ethan wasn't running away from him anymore, instead, caressing Rob's nape and back as they kissed into eternity. It was better than a touchdown. Better than managing to make his first perfect soufflé. Ethan smelled like heaven, and Rob couldn't care less that he was getting glitter all over himself. Their whole bodies joined in the fun, rubbing against each other in the sparkly embrace.

It was only a horn sound coming from a few streets farther that made Rob pull away. He tried to catch his breath, looking straight into that lovely, one-eyed face. Like a disco-pirate. He stroked some of the glitter over Ethan's cheeks with his thumbs and smiled at him, overcome with joy. "Let's leave."

Ethan nodded, the sparkle of glitter reaching his eye. "I'd like that."

Rob let out a long breath and tugged on Ethan's hand, squeezing it tight, reluctant to stop touching him. He didn't know what to say. He had no idea. He just wanted to be alone with Ethan where no one could interrupt them.

"You don't hate me?" Ethan whispered as if he really needed it spelled out. He squeezed Rob's hand tightly as they walked down the parking lot to Rob's car.

Robert shook his head, choosing to ignore a group of students on the other end of the parking lot. They had no chance to see much from there, and he was beyond caring at this point anyway. He quickly opened his car and invited Ethan in with a gesture, reluctantly letting go of his hand.

Ethan gave him a brief smile and for a moment hooked their little fingers before letting go and getting into the car.

"Just fasten the seat belt," Rob uttered as he started the car, already impatient. He wanted to kiss Ethan again, and the way Ethan smiled back at him only fueled that need.

"Yes, Mom," Ethan said but followed the order.

Robert groaned and moved down the parking lot, eager to leave. His throat relaxed the moment he drove into the street, away from the loud music, and everyone... he only hoped Kelly would have fun without him. It was a good thing he'd muted his cell phone because he supposed he wouldn't have a moment of peace otherwise.

"Sooo..." Ethan bit his lip, playing with his seat belt. "That was nice."

"Yeah." Rob smiled as they drove toward the outskirts of town. "I... ah... are you all right?"

"I'm not sure, to be honest." Ethan frowned slightly and reached out to stroke Rob's arm. "I'm so angry, and so happy all at the same time. They wrecked my suit."

Robert squeezed the steering wheel harder. "Bastards. I'm gonna have a chat with Pat."

"What are you gonna tell him? That he shouldn't mess with your boyfriend?" Ethan snorted, but the smile was gone from his face.

Robert gritted his teeth in anger. "You know what? Maybe I should. The fucker needs a big fuck you from life."

"I mean... I'm just kidding, you don't have to do anything." Ethan slid his hand up Rob's arm and squeezed, as if to calm him down, but it wouldn't do. No one would taunt Ethan on his watch. Not anymore.

"Of course I have to!" Robert shook his head, looking for a convenient place to leave the main road.

"I don't wanna get you in trouble."

Robert frowned and finally made a turn into a dirt road. "What can possibly happen? No one's gonna jail me."

Ethan looked out of the window. "I mean, I don't mind being your sparkly secret. I just wish he would fuck off."

Robert groaned. "You're not sparkly!"

"Even you're sparkly by now. Not to mention your car." Ethan sighed, looking at all the tiny glitter particles.

"Okay, but you won't be tomorrow. Doesn't matter," Robert whispered, leaning forward to see better. He eventually switched on the main beam headlights and finally parked the car behind a bush. It was an immense relief.

"What I'm trying to say is that I know what this is, and I wouldn't expect you to change anything you do because of me. It's fine." Ethand unbuckled the seat belt and looked down to his hands.

Robert bumped his forehead against the steering wheel. He wanted to howl. "No, you don't."

"What do you mean?" Ethan's fingers were at the back of his neck, petting him gently and sending shivers down Rob's spine.

Robert swiftly leaned in, resting his head on Ethan's sparkly shoulder and buried his nose in the warm curve of his neck. His breath was quickening at an alarming pace. Ethan moved closer and stroked his hair with a deep inhale. For once, he settled for silence as well.

"Ethan, this might be weird, but..." Robert bit his lip, angry that words were failing him again.

"Hm?" Ethan shuffled forward, into Rob's lap and wrapped his arms around Robert's neck. It felt a bit awkward in the cramped space, but the closeness was making up for it.

Robert swallowed, looking into the big eye, surrounded by glitter on pale skin, and took the plunge. "I'm gay."

Unlike Chris, Ethan wasn't laughing, his face dead-serious. "What?"

Rob swallowed, unsure whether it was a good or a bad 'what'. "I'm gay, and I like you. A lot."

"Oh. I—" Ethan watched him without blinking, but Rob could feel the heat of his body rising. "Why would you not tell me? I thought I was this horrible person, molesting the straight guy and confusing him all over."

Okay, so it was a good 'what'. Robert breathed in relief. "I kinda... with the way it started I didn't think it would matter."

"Why would it not matter? You lied to me." Ethan frowned and pinched Rob's chest through his shirt. "I thought you were just in it for the blow jobs or something..."

Rob snorted. "We're going to college so I thought that it would be easier this way..." He closed his eyes for a moment and pulled Ethan close. He missed his scent so much, and there it was, the intoxicating bergamot on a bed of lime.

Ethan leaned down and gently kissed Rob's lips. "I wasn't planning this either." Having Ethan sit in his lap was fueling the fire in Rob's body even more. He licked Ethan's lips and pulled his arm around his own neck. Explosives went off in his body again, and he gasped, leaning into Ethan with his whole body.

"Am I your first guy?" Ethan's question was pretty much a kiss at the same time. His hair tickled the sides of Rob's face.

Robert pulled him in, eager to feel the strong heartbeat against his chest. "Uh-huh, I only kissed a few girls before…"

"I know you might not believe this, based on how well you know my incredible social skills, but you're my first too." Ethan smiled at him and slowly ground into Rob's crotch. It felt delicious, and made Robert melt into his seat with a low grunt.

"I know, you told me."

"I talk a lot, don't I?" Ethan laughed nervously, and he never stopped looking into Rob's eyes. "I didn't think you listen to half of it. I've never kissed anyone before either. It was everything I thought it would be."

Robert's heart fluttered. "It is amazing. You're…" He swallowed, unsure what to say. He wanted to say *something* but didn't want to blurt out any cheesy shit. "I really like you."

"Since you're actually gay… Would you have sex with me?" Ethan whispered, his face darkening. "You know, like full-on sex."

For a moment, Robert wasn't sure he heard that right through the furious throbbing in his ears, which suddenly spread to his eyelids and lips as well. He was burning up like a torch, and he'd never swap it for anything else. "L-like now?"

Ethan sucked in his lips and frowned. "Well, maybe not in the car…"

Robert inhaled more of the sweet herby essence of Ethan's and gave him a soft smooch, even though he was getting all fidgety, and his cock was dying to meet that lovely ass first-hand. "Really? You really want to?"

"Would I like to have sex with the hottest guy in school? Um, let me think about it. Yes." Ethan laughed and kissed him again. "I'm a virgin, but I've read about it. I know what to do." As if to emphasize it, he rubbed his ass against Rob again. It was like tiptoeing on a ledge over Manhattan, so Rob forced himself to stop Ethan.

"Yes. Condoms and lube," he uttered, breathless.

"Y-yeah, that will be necessary." Ethan hugged him tighter and kissed his ear. "I'm so hot for you. Did I tell you you have an awesome cock?"

Robert gave him an enthusiastic nod and one more kiss before gently shoving him off. His mind was one big buzz of possibilities, porn scenes, books, stuff he'd read online because he was curious, and lots, and lots, and lots of Ethan's naked body on his bed. Which wasn't even made. Shit. Would he have time to change the sheets?

Ethan closed his seat belt. "You want to rent a hotel room or something?"

Robert grinned at him. He was aroused, happy, but underneath it all, incredibly nervous. What if he'd turn out to be shit in bed? He didn't want Ethan to be disappointed. "We can go to my place. Mom's working all night."

"And won't come back till morning?" Ethan slid his hand to Rob's crotch and squeezed his dick, making Rob's heart freeze and flutter at the same time, like an undead, frosty butterfly.

"Oh, fuck..." Rob let his head fall back. "Don't... yet... I'm so horny already."

Ethan sat back with a smug smile. "Good."

Robert fumbled with the steering wheel. He actually turned it the wrong way when moving the car backward. He was a wreck today, so he needed to stay focused until they got home. "Just don't do it again while I'm driving."

Chapter 13

ETHAN

Ethan watched Robert do the necessary shopping at the gas station and couldn't help but grin. The glitter prank was a horrendous ordeal, but Rob was there to make it all better. In spectacular fashion at that. Ethan would never forget that kiss and couldn't wait for more.

He was getting increasingly anxious about the whole thing. In a good way. Even thinking about Rob's cock, about his hot body, his kisses, his touch made Ethan all tingly. They would have the whole house to themselves, loads of time together. It would be amazing.

His heart leaped when Rob appeared in the door of the store at the gas station, tall, in an immaculate suit, and with an ugly plastic bag in hand. Within seconds, Robert dropped into the driver's seat and exhaled as if he'd done something very tedious.

"Did the guy make stupid comments?" Ethan snorted, eying Rob with a smile. He couldn't believe this was happening. Rob was gay and liked him. Like, *really* liked him. Ethan wasn't all that sure what it would mean in the long run, but he wasn't all that sober, so he guessed he would figure it out later.

Robert buckled his seat belt with a snort and passed Ethan the bag. It seemed pretty packed. "Young guy in a sparkly suit buying tons of sex provisions in the middle of the night. Was bound to happen."

Ethan looked into the bag and laughed at the amount of stuff Rob bought. A whole selection of condoms, lubes, and food. Ethan picked up one of the lubes. "Orange. Good choice."

"I wasn't sure what you'd like." Rob cleared his throat, all red-faced, but this time, he managed to steer the car the right way as he drove off.

Ethan actually liked seeing him so nervous. It made him feel that this night was important to Rob as well. "I like *you*." And he liked that they would be first for each other. Rob wouldn't think of him as a failure if he didn't know what to do.

"Yeah, but it happens that people hate certain smells. Like, a friend of mine feels ill when she smells cucumber." Rob cleared his throat and joined the lazy stream of late-night cars.

"Yeah, I suppose I wouldn't be up for, like, chilli pepper lube or something." Ethan laughed, but it came out more nervous than he'd wish it would. With the provisions in hand, it was becoming too real. Joking about his own ass suddenly wasn't all that funny.

"Yeah." Rob cleared his throat. "Or some freaky condoms, right? With so many, we will succeed at putting one on eventually."

Ethan nodded, realizing it wasn't such a laughing matter. What if they did only buy two or three and broke them? "Y-yeah, exactly. I think I wouldn't want the ones with those nubs on them, you know?"

Rob gave him a fervent nod. "Totally. I only took smooth ones. I wouldn't want one like that either."

Ethan went silent, not sure what to say anymore. He tried to stifle his nerves by rustling in the bag and pretending he was reading the instructions on the lube. Thankfully, Rob lived not far away, and ten minutes later, they pulled into the driveway of a neat suburban house in a street that was filled with its clones.

"Welcome to my crib," uttered Robert with a tight smile.

"Such a nice house." Ethan walked out into the dark night, clutching the bag in his glittery hands.

"Thanks, I repainted some of the rooms this summer." Rob smiled at him and gently pulled Ethan closer as they went for the door.

"I was reading those," Ethan pointed to the bag. "And we have to be careful with some of them. Not to mix them I mean, because one lube is not water based, and some of the condoms are latex, some are latex-free."

"Yeah, I didn't know if you weren't allergic, so I took those as well," said Robert as he fumbled with the lock.

"So caring." Ethan stroked Rob's broad back, already imagining being naked together in bed. He wondered what Rob's room would look like.

The first impression of the house was that it was every bit as polished and pampered as his own, with modern furnishings and a splash of color here and there, but he wasn't as interested in the corridor as he was in Robert's bedroom.

"You want anything… to eat or drink?" uttered Rob, petting Ethan's hair.

"Maybe just some water. I've read sex is better on an empty stomach." He stood on his toes and pulled Rob down for a kiss. Nerves were bundling up in his stomach, and as much as Ethan was excited to get to bed, the fact that he didn't know how anal sex would actually feel like got him anxious all over.

"Sure, I have some upstairs. Whatever you need." Rob pulled him close and cradled his head against his shoulder. Ethan could hear the rapid heartbeat hammering so close to his ear, only reminding him how strong Rob was. He could break him in two if he wanted but instead chose to be gentle, caring.

"I just want to be close to you." Ethan wrapped his arms around Rob's waist, trying to calm down. "Will you give me that piggyback ride?" He smiled into Rob's chest as he smelled the cologne on his shirt.

A small smile curved Robert's mouth. He turned away from Ethan and bent his knees. "Hop on."

Ethan laughed and scrambled onto Rob's back. "Prince Charming." He was trying to find a way to relax, and jokes were great. So was Rob's strong back so close to him. Robert smelled so nice and didn't seem to care that Ethan would rub the glitter all over his suit.

"I live to serve," said Rob, slowly making his way up the stairs with a glass balustrade.

"This will be weird, but it's making me horny." Ethan laughed and hugged Rob closer. Part of the attraction was seeing Rob displaying his strength and Ethan feeling confident that he wouldn't be dropped.

Rob slowed down but kept on walking. They were almost at the top of the stairs when he spoke again, "Should I ask you if you want to be on top, or on the bottom? Cuz... we didn't really talk about it."

Ethan swallowed, and his dick slowly hardened against Rob's back. The idea of having Rob bottom did tickle the flame, but tonight and for his first time, he wanted to have Rob on top, feel how it was to have his dick slide in, to feel it inside. "I kinda thought I'd bottom... You?"

"I felt bad that I assumed you would, but yeah, I'd love to top." Robert sighed and looked back with a small smile. "But I'm gay so I'm gonna try bottoming as well anyway." He moved down the short corridor with white walls and black doors, and kicked one open. It was a large bathroom, with a shower stall, and a fuzzy red rug on the floor.

"With me?" Ethan whispered and bit down on Rob's ear. He didn't think about it all that much, with Rob being so big and confident, but he'd probably want to try it one day as well. He'd take Rob from behind, smelling his hair just like he was doing now.

Across the room, he saw Robert's smile in the mirror. "Yeah, if you want." He let go of Ethan's thighs, signaling it was time to hop off.

"First, I can't wait to see you naked. We never got 'round to that. You've seen me, but you keep being half-dressed." Ethan pulled on Rob's sleeve and looked up into his eyes.

"Yeah? Then unwrap me." Robert raised his brows in challenge and spread his arms to give Ethan free access.

Heat spread all over Ethan's body at the notion of finally being all alone with the guy of his dreams. No interruptions, and all the lube and condoms they could possibly need. He started with the buttons of Rob's suit jacket and took it off him before moving on to the blue tie. Ethan's heart pounded in his chest. Even more so when Rob cupped the side of Ethan's face and brushed his thumb over the cheek.

Ethan stood on his toes and kissed Rob's clean-shaven jaw as he worked his way through the buttons of Rob's shirt. He couldn't wait to reveal every inch of that firm, smooth body. The heat coming from underneath the fabric was already tickling his skin, and as Rob leaned into the kiss, opening his mouth for it, the task of undressing him became much harder. Their gasps resonated through the room, only adding to arousal.

Ethan's moves became more frantic as soon as the shirt was off. Every ridge of Rob's muscle was dying to be kissed, but if Ethan stopped for that, he would have to stall with undressing. He took a glance at the burnt skin on Rob's arms, but it only made him think of how well they fit together, with both of them imperfect in some way.

Breathing hard, he unbuckled Rob's belt, dying to see the cock that had haunted his dreams since he'd first seen it.

"You all right?" whispered Rob, untangling Ethan's tie and taking his time to massage his neck while he was at it.

Ethan looked up at him, slowly sliding his hands under the fabric of Rob's briefs and onto the firmest buttocks he could ever imagine. "I am," he rasped, goose bumps all over his arms. It didn't feel like the impersonal arrangement he'd planned just a few weeks ago. Everything had turned upside down and inside out like a vivisected rat.

Robert gasped, pressing close to Ethan. His hard cock got trapped against Ethan's stomach, throbbing between their bodies like a separate living being.

"You touch me so good," he whispered, lapping at Ethan's cheek.

Ethan's shirt clung to his back where he'd sweated under the suit jacket. Despite his size, he could give Rob so much pleasure his chest swelled with pride. That was probably what made him so horny about giving blow jobs. The moment he looked up into Rob's face to see that lust and excitement, it was as if he were the center of Rob's universe. He didn't waste any more time and gave Rob's pec a kiss before pushing down his pants and briefs.

"I didn't draw you correctly, you know." Ethan took in the sight before him, with his heart pounding like there was no tomorrow. "You're not one of the rats, you're a weasel, just like me."

Rob shook off the underwear and quickly toed off his socks. His hands went straight for Ethan's shirt. Each movement of those warm hands and thick fingers was a caress that only brought closer the moment he'd feel Rob's skin on his. "Is that your term for 'gay'?"

A flush crept up to Ethan's face. The moment the shirt was off, a whole cloud of glitter stuck under it also fell to the tiles. "Not really, no. I think it's... I don't think you fit in with everyone the way you seem to. That there's more to you that the rats don't get. Did I upset you?" He swallowed, all of a sudden nervous that Robert would find him too weird, but Rob only shook his head with a wide grin.

"Yeah, I guess you got that spot-on," he uttered, nuzzling Ethan's ear at the same time as he started unbuckling the belt of his pants. It was almost aggressive, as if Robert couldn't wait to be closer to him.

Ethan grinned, wishing he had two eyes just so he could see Rob with both. "You're a white weasel though. You blend in well." He wrapped his fingers around Rob's cock. He couldn't imagine ever getting bored of it.

"And you are what? A black weasel?" asked Rob as he pushed Ethan's pants and underwear down. He kissed him with fervor and ground his hips into the waiting hand.

"Yeah. Everyone can see I don't fit in," Ethan muttered into the hot lips and gave Rob's cock a tug. It pulsed in his hand in the most glorious way, but Ethan did think of it a bit differently now. He tried to asses the logistics of sex. He was gleeful about getting a mouthful of a big dick, but would he feel the same way about anal sex? What if he hated it?

"You fit in with me," murmured Robert, stumbling toward the shower stall, his body shivering. Ethan felt like the cock was a leash he could use to direct Rob.

"I hope I will." Ethan laughed nervously, but followed into the shower, taking in Rob's glorious shape, his broad shoulders, taut stomach, big dick. Ethan had landed the best guy he could imagine. "I've... you know. I'm not sure how it will feel."

Robert turned back to him with a slight frown. "I wasn't... talking about *that*." He cleared his throat, cheeks immediately going aflame. "Yeah, I'm sure we can work it out."

"I know, I know." Ethan ran his fingers through his hair and shook some glitter out of it. "I fit in with you." He took a deep breath and hugged Rob close just in time before Rob turned on the water. It was a bit on the cool side, but it was heating up like the blood in his veins. Water cascaded down their bodies, sliding over Ethan's ears like soft, caressing fingers as he breathed in Robert's natural scent. His chest was almost hairless, with two meaty pillows, just right for Ethan's head.

"At least you'll have less glitter all over your bed." Ethan loved rubbing himself against Rob's firm muscles. "Have you thought much about it? Sex I mean? That is, I know you have, everyone does, but, you know... with me."

Robert bit his lip and ran his hands all the way down Ethan's back. His hands were so big he had no trouble taking possession of Ethan's ass, squeezing it in a way that made Ethan's cock harden even more. "Yeah..."

Ethan gasped and stood on his toes. "And what did you think?" he whispered, letting his fingertips explore every muscle on Rob's back. He never thought he'd be so shy about it all, especially after he'd assaulted Rob with his nakedness on their first encounter. What would Rob think of him and his body? The way it felt around him, the way it smelled, the way it would fit into those strong arms...

Robert chuckled and reached toward the glass shelf to get some fresh-smelling shampoo. He started rubbing it into Ethan's scalp, but his eyes were so focused on Ethan, it felt like they were the only people in the world. "Wow... that's a hard question. There was so much of it... what do you want to know?"

Ethan smiled at the caress to his scalp. Robert was so caring it melted his heart by the minute. He'd always thought Robert Hunter, the quarterback on the football team, cool and confident, would be more of an aggressive and selfish person. Instead, it was Rob's actions that sometimes brought Ethan to shame for being so greedy.

"How do you want to do it? What position?"

"I think that depends on how you will be comfortable." Rob sighed and kissed Ethan on the forehead. "We can experiment another time."

"I imagined what it would be to have you on top of me." Ethan kissed Rob's nipple with a smile, enjoying how gentle Rob was with the shampooing.

"Yeah? How exactly?" Rob pulled Ethan back under the stream of water and started combing his wet hair with his fingers as Ethan explored Robert's warm skin, the meat on his thighs and stomach.

"You're so hot and heavy. I like that. I imagined your weight on top of me." Breath caught in Ethan's throat from the nerves of saying it out loud. He put his cheek on Rob's chest with a sigh. He hadn't planned to feel so emotional about Robert. Ethan always considered himself a logical kind of person, but it was just so hard now that he actually found another weasel in Rob.

"Like... on your back, or on your chest?" whispered Rob, whose hands started to roam again, spreading liquid soap all over Ethan's back, lower and lower. It made Ethan's breath hitch, yet he couldn't wait for Rob to touch him all over.

"On my stomach." Ethan dared to look up and kissed one of the scars on Rob's arms. "With your dick sliding in back and forth. With your stomach rubbing against my back..."

Robert's body shook in his arms, and Ethan clearly felt the big cock twitch against his stomach. "That's... you're so hot. I can't even..." Rob brought their mouths together, and they kissed right under the stream of water, barely able to breathe.

Ethan closed his eye and gave in to the kiss, exploring Rob's mouth. One of the things he did enjoy about being shorter was that Rob's cock was level with his stomach so Ethan could feel how it throbbed and twitched. Those big, strong arms enveloped him, making Ethan feel completely safe. He didn't worry that Rob would be impatient or do something he wouldn't want. He could bet Rob was the kind of guy to pull out if asked.

Their arousal heightened as they soaped up one another's bodies in the steam, touching even the most intimate places, rubbing and kissing until they both knew things had to progress somewhere more comfortable, or else the deed would be done in the shower stall.

Rob dried Ethan off with a big, fluffy towel, and then led him across the hall. Rob's room was large and airy, with one graphite-colored wall at the back of the headboard of a double bed on a low, squarish frame. Over the bed hung a large print photograph of a woman in a trench coat walking through a sequence of *tori* gates. Rob didn't seem to own much, unless it was all hidden behind a pair of sliding doors that ran along one of the walls. There was a desk with a computer, and a bookshelf, which also housed some obscure figurines.

Ethan looked around with a silly grin, no longer embarrassed that he was butt naked and aroused, with only a towel over his shoulders. "It's so clean." He laughed and walked up to the bed. The rustled bedding was solid black, but made of soft cotton, it felt great on his skin.

Robert cleared his throat. "About that... you want me to change the sheets?"

Ethan picked up a pillow and put it against his face. It was like being gently enveloped by cloves, herbs, with a bit of musk. The scent was warm and soothing, just like Robert's touch. "No, I wanna smell you when we do it."

The answer clearly got a rock off Rob's chest, and he smiled, closing the door. He dimmed the light with a switch and slowly walked over to

Ethan, his god-like body on display for Ethan's hungry eye. He placed the plastic bag on the nightstand, right next to the sleek alarm clock. "Take your pick."

Ethan threw the towel to a chair by the desk and started rummaging through the contents. He finally picked up a tube of lube and a pack of condoms. "Orange and pineapple? Tropical theme?" His eye kept straying to Rob's erect cock. It was so much more beautiful than anything he'd ever seen in a porno.

Rob chuckled and pulled back the comforter, revealing a soft-looking sheet. "Sounds sweet."

"Like me." Ethan looked up at him with a grin and lay down, inviting Rob over with a gesture. It was so natural to slide beneath the cool covers with Robert's hot body to keep him warm. Robert's hand brushed over Ethan's cock even before he settled down completely.

"Yeah."

All warm from the shower, Ethan's body was sensitive to the touch. He arched his hips to Rob, once again diving in for a kiss and running his palms down Rob's chest.

They kissed, and Ethan's world rocked on its wobbly weasel legs as heat spread all over him like liquefied charcoal, all the sensations focusing on the endlessly perfect touch at his dick.

"I'll need to turn over," Ethan whispered into Rob's lips, cupping his face and looking into his eyes. He needed Robert to stop touching his dick, or he risked coming much too fast.

Robert's pupils dilated, but he leaned back, giving Ethan room to move. The deep gasping above was tickling Ethan's pride. With one more kiss, Ethan turned over to his stomach, heat throbbing in his neck at showing his ass to Rob like that. He didn't even notice when he clenched his buttocks.

Rob's hand slid up his spine, making him arch like a cat. He was torn between anxiety and an irresistible pull that had to end up with him under Rob's strong, warm chest. And there Rob was, the cock brushing against Ethan's ass, again awakening that fuzzy feeling across his stomach. Rob reached out for the condom pack.

Ethan looked back at him, trying to look sexy, not like a bundle of nerves. "Maybe I should arch up more?" he uttered and raised his hips, feeling more exposed than he ever did when he was showing Rob his dick.

Rob's eyes were wide as he looked at Ethan from above his cock, which was now covered by a layer of yellow latex. "Yeah, I think that would be comfortable," he uttered. With his pink skin and wet hair, he looked like the picture of 'flustered'.

Ethan wanted to say something, but his breath caught in his chest as he scrambled to his knees and parted his legs. He wanted this with all his heart, but nerves were getting the best of him. On the other hand, being naked and ready for sex with Rob was keeping his excitement at peak levels.

Robert took the bottle of lube with a hollow sound coming out of his chest. "You are simply... wow."

"Just... be gentle. I mean, I know you will, I'm just saying... you know." Ethan took a deep breath and calmed himself down by smelling Rob's pillow. It smelled like his shampoo, and did its job as well as it possibly could, but the mere touch to Ethan's butt was now enough to make him tense up again.

"I know, just tell me if I'm doing bad, cause... you know." Rob's voice was actually trembling a bit.

"Sure." Ethan dared to look over his shoulder, struggling between embarrassment and the visceral need to see Rob's body. "You'll be amazing."

Robert let out a shaky breath and smiled as he squeezed out what seemed like a third of the little bottle into his palm. The room instantly took the smell of artificial orange. "I'll do my best."

Ethan swallowed and now kind of wished he had fingered himself before, just to know what it would feel like. He did want to soothe Rob's fears though. Having them both be anxious messes wasn't going to help anyone. Ethan pushed some of the wet hair out of his face. "I can't wait for you to be even closer to me," he said quietly.

Rob bit his lip, leaning closer, and reached out the lubed hand toward Ethan's ass. It was wet, and some of the lube spilled down Ethan's balls right away, but Rob started slowly massaging his hole in languid, circular moves. "Me too. I'm so horny," he whispered, gently petting Ethan's back with his open palm.

Ethan exhaled loudly, his balls tightening at the touch. He thought he'd get more anxious when the touch moved between his buttocks, but actually, the stab of lust it provoked got him to relax slightly. Before, he kept obsessing about how it would feel to be touched, but now, he wanted to feel the fingers inside. He could already imagine Rob's cock sliding into him, Rob coming in him, in the embrace that was tighter than Ethan's lips were.

"You're smiling," whispered Rob, whose skin now had a golden tint to it. His cock was still rock hard as he swirled his fingers all over the sensitive anus while stroking the rest of Ethan's body with his other hand.

"It feels... nice. The skin is sensitive there. I love your hands on me." Ethan let his smile widen, to reassure Rob he was doing better than fine. "You wanna slide it in?" he dared, taking deep breaths. The way Rob's hand kept sliding to his stomach made Ethan tremble and curl his toes.

Rob nodded and leaned over him while one of his fingers gently pressed against the anus, screwing its way in. Ethan gasped, surprised at how easily it slipped in. It was a strange feeling of fullness and heat going straight to Ethan's cock. The sensation itself though, couldn't be compared to Robert's closeness. Ethan buried his face in the pillow, his shoulders tense with anticipation.

"All right?" asked Rob, slowly moving the finger in and out. It was so slick Ethan barely felt any friction.

"Yeah," he rasped but was getting annoyed that he was stuck with imagining what was right behind him instead of watching it. Robert's freaking washboard abs, and thick cock, firm thighs... "Rob?" he turned his face toward his partner again. "Maybe I could turn after all? I wanna see you."

Rob nodded and gently pulled out his finger to let him move freely, but soon, he was kneeling between Ethan's legs, his hips forcing the thighs apart, with the finger safely back inside. This was much, much better. Ethan thought he would watch all that toned finery, but instead, they were looking into each other's eyes, which made it all so intense that Ethan felt no discomfort at all when Rob started spreading him with two thick fingers.

He bit his lip, and wasn't even all that embarrassed anymore. They were both so excited there wasn't really much space left for shyness. He raised his knees to give Rob easier access to himself, unable to hold back a moan when Rob pushed his fingers farther inside.

Rob rubbed Ethan's chest, and it was as if he was herding blood to this spot as all of a sudden, Ethan felt like his ribcage was going to burn. "Good?" Rob asked, breathless as he scissored his fingers inside of Ethan. It was the strangest feeling to actually sense cool air on his inner walls.

Ethan gasped and ran his fingers up the uneven skin on Rob's arms. "Oh! Y-yeah... it is. It's hot." He looked down Rob's body, all the way to his cock. Even with the yellow condom, it was the most amazing thing Ethan could imagine. He loved seeing it all in the new position, and the steady push and pull in his ass was getting more and more exciting, as if his insides were expanding in need of something bigger.

At first, he was even dubious about two fingers, but with all the excitement building up in the heat between him and Rob, his body turned pliant and ready. Ethan grabbed Rob's arm with a moan when the moves of Rob's fingers sped up into a fucking rhythm. This was it, this was an appetizer for what was coming, and Ethan was looking forward to that main dish.

Rob leaned down and kissed him hard, his back muscles rippling under Ethan's touch. "Just say the word..."

Ethan forgot all about how much he wanted to kiss until it happened. He cupped Rob's face to keep him close and enjoyed the scent of fresh skin mixing with orange lube. Not to mention the fingers, which were continuously fucking him and sending sparks of excitement into Ethan's cock. "I want it," he whispered into Rob's lips with a smile, not bothered anymore if his hair was out of order or if his face was pink. He was tucked into this wonderfully soft, warm bedding, with the hottest man around, who also happened to be a great guy. What was there to wait for?

He gasped when Robert removed the fingers. And then his mouth was on Ethan's again, smoldering his lips like the cock that was now teasing Ethan's ready hole with each stir Rob made.

"Oh, God..." Ethan muttered, shamelessly grinding his hips against Rob's cock. He could feel it throb between his buttocks and it was hotter than he'd ever imagined. The cockhead slid through all the slippery lube, and Ethan couldn't wait for it. He wrapped his arms around Rob's neck and pulled his knees up to make it all easier.

Their eyes met again just as Rob reached down to grasp his cock and pushed. The pressure was a bit more than Ethan expected in all his hazy excitement. He let out a high-pitched sound he couldn't even pinpoint with a name and clawed into Rob's back. Heat stirred in Ethan's body, some in his chest, some in his balls, some all over his face. As much as he tried to relax, his body clenched on the invading cockhead.

Rob froze over him, his warm breath brushing over Ethan's lips. "Sorry..."

"It's... it's fine," Ethan uttered, his body trembling uncontrollably. It wasn't Rob's fault that Ethan wasn't as prepared for it as he thought he was. Not to mention being on the verge of orgasm all the freaking time wasn't helping his assessment of the situation. "Just stay like this for a sec." He took deep breaths, slowly trying to adjust to the pressure as sharp, stabbing pain clenched around the ring of muscle that refused to give in.

Rob shuddered and moved his slick hand to Ethan's cock. The lube created a soft, teasing texture as he gave Ethan's dick a slow pump. Rob bent his head, trailing kisses down Ethan's chest. Then came little, teasing nips that climbed up Ethan's neck, breaking the path once in a while for Robert to brush his cheeks and chin over the sensitive skin. "It feels... so good."

Ethan steadied his breath, melting into the touch. All the blood going right back to his cock eased the tension in his muscles around Rob's dick. "You're the best," he muttered, sliding his fingers along Rob's head and nape where he moved them through the short hair. "I think I'm fine now."

Rob raised his head and supported himself with one hand placed next to Ethan's head as he pushed in deeper. Now that it wasn't hurting as much, Ethan could see the bright eyes above him roll back. Robert's face relaxed, going aglow with a flush of arousal as his cock slid its way inside. Ethan feared the length would be a problem but with the initial muscles relaxed into submission, it didn't seem that his body would resist much more.

"Ethan, you feel so amazing," gasped Rob, opening his eyes halfway.

That was exactly what Ethan wanted to hear. He smiled between one moan and another, but pulled Rob's head down for another kiss. He raised his legs experimentally, and when he was sure nothing hurt, he embraced Rob with all his limbs. His own cock was dripping pre-come between their stomachs, and even though Ethan hadn't come yet, he felt as blissfully happy as ever.

"You can fuck me, don't hold back," Ethan whispered, breathing hard. "You're so hot, Rob. I wanna know how it feels to have you come inside of me." His chest constricted with the smell of lust in the air.

Robert moaned into his mouth and snaked his arms underneath Ethan's back. Sweat was beading on his forehead, and every piece of flesh on him throbbed under Ethan's touch as his cock withdrew slightly, Rob's ass arching and lifting Ethan's feet with it. It felt so good, like a state of complete relaxation descended on Ethan in one rapid wave, only to turn into blissful pleasure when Rob pushed his way back in with a shuddery breath on his lips. "Oh, fuck... gonna be soon..."

"Yeah? Come. You're so fucking handsome," Ethan muttered, hugging Rob close. He watched every inch of Rob's face, the flush, the glistening eyes, his symmetrical features, strong jawline... it all melted into one sensation along with the sweet fullness inside of him. He was getting so much satisfaction just from knowing it was him giving a guy like Robert all this pleasure.

The dick moving with each push and pull of Robert's hips was making Ethan turn into a sighing and whimpering mess. He'd heard it was good, that the prostate gland would feel amazing when brushed over, but the jolts of electricity spreading all over his body were so much better than what he'd anticipated. Robert's body was such a sensuous machine, penetrating him with precision yet so yielding under Ethan's caressing touch.

Rob opened his eyes, looked at Ethan with a tenderness that Ethan couldn't even describe, and breathed, "It's just... I can't..." The last syllable turned into a low grunt, and he suddenly froze, buried deep in Ethan, all his muscles becoming hard as stone.

Ethan trembled against him and reached down for his own cock. He thought Rob was the hottest hunk on the planet, but seeing that hunk come took it to another level. Ethan focused on that face and on how Rob's dick throbbed inside of him. This way, it only took a few strokes on his own lubed up cock to spurt its load between their bodies. He moaned his pleasure, not holding back at all. No one would hear. It was only them, together in a hot bed.

Rob relaxed and watched Ethan come, with a hazy smile playing on his face. "You're so pretty," he whispered, reaching between their bodies to withdraw his spent cock. Ethan was close to whimpering at the loss as his oversensitive body collapsed to the sheets, overwhelmed by all the sensations.

The anxiety from before was gone, and all Ethan wanted now was to snuggle into Rob's arms. He'd never opened up to anyone this way. Not only when it came to sex, but on an emotional level as well. "You made me feel so good," he said so Rob wouldn't wonder about it. He wanted his new *lover* to feel great about himself.

Robert's eyelids fluttered, and he grinned so wide Ethan could see his gums at the sides. "It was so amazing to be inside you. The best thing ever."

Ethan answered with a languid kiss, pulled Rob close and let his legs fall back to the sheets. "I've never felt anything as intense. So much better than any porn."

Robert chuckled against his lips and reached over to drop the filled condom to the trashcan. He didn't even bother to tie it. "No way, I'm better than Matt Powers? I'm honored."

"Hey! Did you actually notice him on my wallpaper?" Ethan laughed and hugged Rob closer, relieved at how natural it felt, how there was not a drop of awkwardness left between them.

Robert nodded and placed a box of tissues next to the pillow. He gave Ethan a lazy kiss and dropped by him like a sack of potatoes. "This is way better than porn," he said with a strange glimmer in his eyes.

Ethan quickly cleaned himself without much care. He'd take a shower later anyway. He pulled the comforter over them and slid his arm over Rob's stomach. "How long can I stay?" He kissed Rob's cheek and was immediately pulled closer to the flaming heat of that fantastic body, inhaling the intense scent of fresh sweat and come.

"As long as you want."

"Can I stay till morning? I want to sleep next to you." Ethan swallowed. Was it too needy? He wasn't sure.

Robert smiled into his mouth, which turned into yet another lazy kiss. "I'd love that. We'll have a hearty breakfast when we finally get up. That sound all right?"

Ethan just nodded and closed his eye, letting himself sink deep into the fragrant warmth of the body next to his.

It sounded perfect.

Robert was perfect.

Chapter 14

ROB

ROBERT WAS IN HIS element. He had two dishes in the oven, the smoothie was done, coffee was almost ready to press, and he was busy chopping zucchini while the oil was warming up in the pan. He'd already prepared the bed table, covered it with yellow tissues, and added a small bouquet of fresh herbs and anise stars, which he attached to small stems cut of celery to form mock-flowers. He was happy with how it turned out.

But would Ethan like it? Rob didn't want him to wake up in an empty bed, and he'd already spent over half an hour downstairs preparing breakfast. No matter what he did, whether it was covering fresh strawberries with powdered sugar or chopping up veg, his thoughts kept straying to last night. It had been the most amazing night of his entire life. He'd been nervous but horny, elated yet it all felt so natural. Ethan had been sweet like the strawberries in the oven. A night such as this deserved a celebratory breakfast, but since he didn't want to leave Ethan alone just to go to the farmer's market, Rob had to make do with what he had at home. He hoped his new boyfriend would like it.

"Mmm, smells lovely," he heard his mother's sleepy voice behind him. He stiffened a bit but turned to smile at her. He had hoped she would stay in bed longer. Was she up so early because she wanted to ask him about prom?

"Hi, mom. How was work?"

Her hair was tied into a messy bun, and she was sporting plaid pajamas that looked far too large for her. "Long night. We actually had one student from your school with a concussion. I hope you were responsible?" She raised her eyebrows, but her eyes were still half-closed and hazy with sleep.

"You can press the coffee and help yourself. I'll have breakfast ready soon," said Rob and shrugged. "I didn't drink, don't worry."

"Is there enough for three?" She gave him an expectant look and walked over to the espresso machine. "I hope you were responsible with more than the drinking."

Robert cleared his throat, but his face immediately flushed with heat. "Um... yeah, I guess."

"Come on, Robert, don't make me tear it out of you. Who's the girl? I wanted to check if you were back in the morning, so I got a flash of her hair, but I left. Obviously." Mom pressed the coffee with a loud yawn.

Robert closed his eyes, took three deep breaths and tossed the chopped zucchini into the pan. The sound of sizzling was like cool yoghurt on his nerves. Great, so she thought he had a girl in. He swallowed and added some chopped almonds to the salad he was preparing. "Mom, I'm gay," he said, raising his eyes at her. This was the third time within the last 24 hours he'd admitted to it... after not saying it ever before. Was that a sign of progress?

She stalled while pouring coffee and squinted at him. "Huh? You found that out after sleeping with a girl? I mean... what? You're not gay."

Robert snorted. "Mom, I am gay. Shouldn't you know? Mothers always know in the movies."

She cocked her head to the side, with that confused look glued to her face as she sipped her coffee. "But... no. No, I never suspected this. So who is upstairs?" She pointed to the ceiling.

Robert raised his eyebrows and mixed the greens in the pan with a wooden spatula. He supposed his mother didn't spend enough time with him to notice the signs. "My boyfriend."

Now that woke her up. She opened her eyes wider. "You have a boyfriend?" she uttered, looking at Robert as if she saw him for the first time in her life.

Rob looked into the oven and quickly wrapped his hand with a towel to pull out the dessert. "Yeah."

Mom cleared her throat, still staring at him and barely blinking. "So... who is this boyfriend? Wait... Didn't that Ethan boy have long black hair? No, Robert, don't tell me it's him."

Robert sighed. He hated intelligent parents. "I made baked strawberries."

"Robert..." There was that warning tone in her voice. "I hope you're not doing this out of guilt? You saved his life, you don't owe him anything."

Well, at least she didn't hate the fact that he was gay, though he had hoped she'd care about it more. Robert shook his head. "Of course not. I just... you know... had a reason to get to know him better," he said in disbelief that he was telling all this to his own mother. How uncomfortable was that?

"He's not like Chris. He's not the kind of guy you usually hang out with. Don't get me wrong, it's kind of sweet, but you know he's got brain damage?" she spoke softer. "I just don't want you to get hurt if his condition worsens."

"Mooom..." Robert gritted his teeth, but the moment he realized Ethan had a branch up his eye still flashed through his memory. "He's fine, he's had those headaches but that's all."

Mother shrugged. After all, she wasn't Ethan's doctor. "If you say so. As long as it doesn't hurt your grades, it's fine by me. But... is this an official thing? Are you going to come out at school and all of that?"

Robert shrugged and turned on the toaster. He already put the sourdough bread slices inside. "Haven't decided yet. Chris knows," he said, not without pride.

"Make sure you think it through." Mom took a deep breath. "If it's going to create conflict, maybe better keep it quiet until you graduate?"

"I'm happy that you support my decisions," said Rob and broke the seal of baked dough with a spoon, shoveling a generous portion of the strawberry pie into a bowl, which he handed to his mother.

She sighed and took the food. "Thanks. I'll go back to sleep, I had a long night. Bring him over some time, yeah? I want to meet him properly."

"Sure thing. Just don't scare him." Rob smiled and decorated the smoothies with fresh basil leafs.

"How could I possibly scare him? Is he a fawn?" She shook her head and put the empty coffee cup into the sink.

"Nope, he's a weasel," said Rob and pulled the cupcake frittatas out of the oven.

"If this is some modern gay sex slang, then I'm not getting it."

Robert grinned, slowly assembling his perfect breakfast. He even put the bread in the toast stand. "No, but he's so slim, and mischievous, and stubborn. You know, like a weasel."

"You're too sweet, Robbie. Have fun. I'll see you in the evening." She laughed and waved at him, exiting with the bowl of steaming strawberries.

"Sleep well," said Rob, and after five minutes, he was slowly walking up the stairs with the foldable bed table in hand. He was so proud of himself. The cupcake frittatas with lean bacon and tomato looked amazing on the small tiered stand, which also housed a few homemade breakfast spreads, both savory and sweet. There were two bowls of strawberry pie, a spinach salad with nuts and warm zucchini, coffee, smoothies, and toast. The light downstairs was so nice he even took some pictures of the food before walking up the stairs. But would Ethan appreciate it? It was high time to find out.

Rob opened the door with his elbow and smiled when he saw Ethan's pale body buried under the black comforter.

There was a slight moan and a yawn, but Ethan turned around and slowly opened his eye under the pile of messed up hair. Only now Robert realized that he'd never seen Ethan's hair like this out of the hospital. The mere memory of the heart monitor beeping made him shiver.

"Hello..." Ethan smiled sweetly and pushed the long black hair back. It took him a second to open his eyes wider. "Oh, wow, what is that?"

Rob exhaled in relief and walked up to Ethan, carefully positioning the table over his lap. "Breakfast. I have more, so just let me know if you want anything." He looked into Ethan's eye and slowly leaned in to kiss his warm lips.

"Robert, this is amazing! Where did you get all this?" Ethan's smile widened, and he looked up at Rob with such awe it would be worth slaving in the kitchen for a lot longer just to get it. Ethan wiggled his fingers over the food, really looking like a little undecided weasel, but finally went for the frittata cupcakes first. Good choice.

Robert walked around the bed and crawled in to join him, also taking a cupcake off the stand. They smelled amazing, fresh but luxurious. Just the way he liked his food. "I made it just now. I wasn't expecting any guests so it's a bit of an improvisation."

"Are you kidding me? This is so good!" Ethan exclaimed with his mouth full. "You are the best host ever. You *made* this? Can I have your babies?"

Robert chuckled, unsure if he was more happy or confused by that last question. "Maybe after college."

Ethan reached out and pinched his cheek. "So responsible. Not like me, already thinking about getting knocked up by the first guy who makes me breakfast in bed." He went back to stuffing his face. It was nice to see him with so much appetite, and Rob was ready to provide all the food Ethan wanted if he was to get so much gratitude in return.

"That's all right, we used condoms." Robert pulled up his pillow and leaned back against it, putting an arm around Ethan's waist. Even after last night, he smelled so incredibly delicious it gave Rob goose bumps.

Ethan smiled at him before moving on to the salad. "I was a bit scared yesterday, to be honest. But you made it all so good. I couldn't have had a better first time," he whispered.

Robert exhaled and leaned in to hug him, resting his head on Ethan's warm shoulder. He kissed the warm, smooth skin, his chest swelling with pride. "Same here. You made it so amazing."

"I bet my mom thinks I spent the night with Derek." Ethan snorted and snuggled up closer, carefully watching the bed table.

Robert bit into the frittata. It tasted just right. "As if. The guy's such a prude."

Ethan shook his head. "He kissed me. He was hitting on me. He said I had hair like Jesus."

Rob was close to spitting out the delicious food. He didn't do it only because it would have been a waste. "He what? Like Jes— *what?*" His head flooded with heat.

"I freaked out. I didn't think he'd do something like that. Doesn't he have a purity ring and all?" Ethan slurped the smoothie with a blissful expression.

Robert swallowed, munching the rest of the savory cupcake. "Do you want me to talk to him?" he asked eventually.

"Why? Do you think I can't take care of my own purity?" Ethan laughed and poked Robert's stomach. "Don't worry. I'd never swap you for him."

"I know, that's not the point." Rob bit his lip and reached for the smoothie while still hugging Ethan.

"What is the point then?"

Rob groaned. "It's so... wrong. Like he's a flytrap or something."

"Oh, come on, he's just horny like everyone else. He doesn't have a Robert." Ethan grinned at him. "No one to make him breakfast."

Rob felt his mouth twitch, and he relaxed, allowing himself a smile. "Maybe."

"So what's up with all of this? This isn't just a guy making himself toast because he has to cook himself." Ethan pointed to the table.

Robert gave a shuddery breath, unsure how to approach the topic. The only people who knew about this were Mom and Chris. He didn't want anyone to think of him as some kind of attention seeker. "Last night was so… good that I thought I would treat you to something nice."

"Can you do a lot of other things? Like the lunches you bring to school look so good. You make them yourself, don't you?" Ethan leaned over for a kiss.

Robert squeezed Ethan's nape gently and smiled into the smooch. Ethan's recognition was a huge weight off his shoulders. "It's a hobby. I love food."

"You are just so perfect it aches." Ethan watched him with a glint in his eye. "I wanna have sex with you all over again."

Robert pulled him closer, his heart skipping a beat. "We can totally do it later," he said, gulping down some of the smoothie. His life was falling into place, and for once he didn't want to pull on the brakes.

"I'm gonna have to go home soon, but I want another meal like this next time I come. Pun unintended."

Robert swallowed, sweat slowly beading on his back. "Can I take a picture of our feet behind the food for my blog? I want to make a post about this breakfast."

"My feet? You have a blog?" Ethan finished the smoothie and went straight for the coffee. He pulled up the covers and gave his feet a critical look.

Robert chuckled and poked Ethan's toes with his broader, larger foot. "Yeah. It's uh, about food that I make, or try." He frowned, wondering if it was a good idea, but then asked, "Would you like to see?"

"Are you kidding? Show me! Why didn't you tell me? Robert Hunter, a foodie?" Ethan laughed, but there was no mocking in his voice, just pure adoration. It made Robert all tingly inside.

"Yeah, I started because my nanny was into food, and we cooked lots of things together for my mom." He walked over to the desk and returned with his laptop. "I got my burns because I tried to cook on my own and spilled a pot of boiling oil all over my hands."

"I like learning new things about you." Ethan reached out to stroke Robert's arms as he switched on the computer and opened the folder his camera automatically sent all pictures to. After the obligatory feet shoot, he opened the main page of his blog and showed it to Ethan. He was proud how the layout looked, with fresh food photographed on wooden boards. He took the pictures himself.

Robert swallowed, his stomach fluttering as if he had a colony of ants developing inside. "And you let me see new things about myself. Before yesterday, I didn't know I was a weasel."

But Ethan's attention was already on the laptop, his eye widening. "This looks so professional. I was expecting something low-key and this... some of these dishes are like out of a catalog." Ethan scrolled down with his jaw hanging low.

Robert bit his lip, his chest swelling with pride. He picked up a piece of toast and added a generous amount of cinnamon butter on top. He deserved it. "I actually earn some money on it as well."

"I can't believe you haven't told me about this." Ethan kept scrolling and checking out Rob's old posts. "Are you gonna develop this further?" Then all of a sudden, he made a rapid turn with his body and leaned closer. "Oh, my God! Would you photograph my elk head?"

Robert grinned, munching on the toast. His hand kept roaming all over his boyfriend's smooth back. *Boyfriend.* Even if just in his mind, it did sound nice. "Sure, I'd just have to take my lamps and arrange a bit of a studio around it."

"There I was, thinking you were a hot football player, an ambitious student heading for pre-med, and now I find out you're also creative and take fantastic photos?" Ethan leaned closer to kiss Rob's lips. "Not to mention you're hot in bed," he whispered with a grin.

Robert's ego was close to bursting. He nuzzled Ethan's cheek, taking the chance to smell him again. "I have more up my sleeve," he promised and scrolled down to the search field. He typed in the name of his most ambitious creation, *The Goddess's Bazaar*, a feast of arabic-inspired foods displayed in the scenery of a restaurant nearby, on plates he'd purchased for the occasion and rented props.

"I really love tasting different things, and if I could pick anything to do, this would be it." He gave Ethan a smile. Only his mother and Chris knew about this obsession of his. "Creating different flavors, reviewing restaurants, and so on."

Ethan stared at the screen and stroked the scars on Rob's arms. "Wow... Robert. Why don't you then? All you told me about your plans was that you're going to college."

Robert blinked, and when he looked at Ethan, it seemed that his vision briefly changed to slo-mo. Was Ethan for real? Did he really think it could work out? "Because... it's an uncertain business. I can't predict if it works out, and if it doesn't, I will regret it all my life."

"Or you would always regret you never tried. Since I got that commission for the squirrels, I started thinking about it. Why wouldn't I try and make it now? All these people who start following their passions at forty make me wonder what they could have done if they started earlier. I know it would be risky, but it's exciting as well." Ethan squeezed Rob's hand, looking into his eyes. "If you make some money off it now, wouldn't now be the time to try and develop it?"

Robert drew in a sharp breath, captured by the depth of Ethan's single eye. He cleared his throat. "I don't know. I don't think I'm *that* good. Everyone can cook."

"I can't. And most people can definitely not cook like *that*." Ethan pointed to the screen. "I still haven't told my parents I'm considering at least taking a year out after high school."

Robert sighed. "A year sounds good. You have an amazing artistic talent, you know. I'm quite jealous." He leaned down and kissed Ethan's arm.

Ethan smiled at him and pulled closer for another kiss, which was cut short by Ethan's cell phone beeping. He let out a moan. "It's my mom. She won't give it a rest. I'm gonna have to go soon."

Robert sighed. "Tell her you're at my place. That you drank a bit too much and crashed with me?" He finished his smoothie and was ready to skip the salad in favor of dessert.

"You sure? No mention of hot gay sex?" Ethan snorted and started tapping a text message on his phone.

Robert chuckled and gathered some strawberry and dough on a spoon, before raising it to Ethan's mouth. "If you must."

"I'd rather them not know. They don't let me date," groaned Ethan, but he opened his mouth wide.

Robert swallowed hard, put the bowl away, and moved his hand across Ethan's tattooed stomach. "My mom knows you're here."

Ethan stopped chewing and finally spoke after he swallowed. "Oh. Is she angry?" He lowered his voice.

Robert shook his head and hugged him tight, his heart speeding up to a furious tempo, as if the emotions only hit him now like a stampeding herd of antelopes. "I just came out to her downstairs. Isn't that amazing?"

"Oh, wow! It is!" Ethan reciprocated the embrace and kissed his ear. "I'm so happy for you. Is she all right with everything?"

Robert snorted and kissed his neck. "I had to tell her because she went into my room and saw your hair. But... yeah, she's fine with me being gay. She even wants to meet you some time, you know?"

Ethan laughed nervously. "Oh, God... But yeah, sure, I'd like to meet her. Your mom doesn't seem as uptight as my parents." He hugged Robert tighter.

"Yeah, she's just... very busy." Robert switched to the picture folder and smiled at the photo of their feet sticking out from underneath the comforter. He was so ridiculously happy.

Chapter 15

ROB

ROBERT SMILED AT THE glitter he tried to clean from the sofa upholstery with a hand wrapped with tape, sticky side out. There was a lot of mess left, but he didn't mind working one bit. The last 24 hours had been bliss. Life-changing. There was still the matter of Kelly, for whom he felt terribly sorry, but he didn't want to approach her unprepared. Before he drove Ethan home, they managed to share a moment in the shower, and now that they had progressed to something more than blow jobs, even those felt different, somehow more… mature.

Rob laughed at himself and went on, bit after bit. He'd posted an entry with just photos and the title 'Breakfast for two' but hadn't dared to read the comments yet. It fact, he hadn't visited the site since. He was torn between being proud and feeling like a tease.

The ringtone he'd set for Ethan brought him back to reality. It was the weird instrumental music that he got his first blow job to. He loved it. Just listening to it brought back so many memories he was getting horny.

He picked the call up immediately. "Hi, have you slept?"

"No! Robert, you won't believe what happened." Ethan's voice was trembling, so hard Rob could barely hear him. "They locked my workshop. I'm grounded for not coming back so long. I'm eighteen, they can't ground me!" A deep sob stopped Ethan from talking further.

Robert froze, looked at his hand, all wrapped up in glittery tape, then a the carpet. He shouldn't have made such an elaborate breakfast, they shouldn't have had sex. Fuck. "I'm so sorry... are you okay?" He dropped onto the sofa.

Another sob crackled through the phone, followed by a long sniff. "No, I'm not okay! I hate them so much! They don't understand shit. I don't want to do things their boring way. I am so angry. I can't do my project. I'm gonna fail the squirrel commission, and they don't care. I miss you so much."

Robert leaned back in the couch and looked around, over the almost pristine room. "Can I help?"

"I just... I want to tell you all this in person, and they wouldn't let you visit, 'cause I told them we're dating and... I know I shouldn't have, but I was so angry. I'm sorry, Robert."

Robert swallowed hard, squeezing and opening the taped hand. His body was stiff, as if all his joints suddenly lacked lubrication. "It's not your fault, baby. They have no right to do that."

"Now other potential customers will think I'm a flake, and I can't deliver. My reputation will be ruined. I think that's what they want. They want me to fail. Robert, I need to see you so bad. Would you come over at night? I could let you in through the window. I just... I need a hug. I need a friend."

Robert got up from the sofa and started pacing around, all tense. So he would be creeping into a house at night to see his lover. Things were getting serious. "Sure, of course. Just tell me if you need anything."

"I just need you. You make me feel so safe." There was another gut-wrenching sob and Robert wanted to be there so bad it hurt. He took a big gulp of air and walked over to the window. His car was there, ready to be driven.

"Maybe I could come over now? I just… don't want to know you're all alone with this."

"I'd want that so bad, but my parents could walk in any time and they could throw you out. I don't know what to do anymore."

Robert pulled off the glove of tape and tossed it to the floor. He didn't even know what to say to make Ethan feel better. He hated being powerless! It was like the moment Ethan had been taken into surgery all over again. Less horrible, but…

Ethan also kept silent for a while, just breathing hard. "Come over around eleven, okay?"

Robert nodded, squeezing the phone against his ear. "How do I get up to your room? Do I need a rope, or something?"

"I have a rope ladder, I'll throw it down to you. You just need to park away from the house."

"Yeah, I figured." Robert sighed, leaning his head against the glass. "I'm so, so sorry, Ethan. You have no idea how much I want to be with you right now."

"Just knowing you're there is so important to me, honey. You can't even know how much. You're the best thing that's ever happened to me."

Robert slowly scooted down, gripping the windowsill hard. That declaration forced all the air out of his lungs. "That's not true. You're ill because of me," he uttered, closing his eyes as a wave of guilt washed over him like a furious storm.

"I would have never found you if it wasn't for that." Ethan's voice was shaky and became more quiet. "You're worth losing an eye for."

Rob sprang to his feet, his head flushing with intense heat. "Don't say that. I'm gonna get you now. Will you go with me?" he whispered, already walking to the door, but he sidetracked to get the plastic bag from the bedside drawer.

"Yeah, I don't care where we go. I just don't want to be here. I feel so trapped."

"I'm gonna walk up to your house. Be there in fifteen minutes, don't worry," whispered Rob as he rushed down the stairs. He wouldn't let Ethan suffer on a day like this.

Robert was slowly creeping between the trees toward Ethan's house. He'd left his car in a small street five minutes away and was already feeling like a bundle of nerves. What if Ethan's parents noticed him? He was keeping to the bushes to avoid the possibility of getting spotted through the window.

He started walking around the house until he saw the windows in the attic. Ethan waved at him and seconds later, opened the window. He rolled out the ladder that went all the way down and Robert's heart stopped when he imagined Ethan slipping and falling to his death. He looked to both sides, relieved that there were no windows on this side of the house but that didn't make watching the climb any easier. He trotted over, hoping if Ethan were to stumble, he would be there to help.

It was hard not to get distracted when Ethan was wearing a pair of gray, tight-fitting skinny jeans, which only reminded Robert of how amazing it felt to have sex with him last night. At least Ethan was being careful on his way down, but the wobbly ladder wasn't making Rob feel any more confident.

He bit his lip and grabbed the lower end of the ladder to stabilize it, but it also provided him with the opportunity to look up at the shapely ass and slim thighs. He'd love to sleep with his head buried between those.

Thanks to the weather being milder than in the past few days, Ethan didn't have to wear a jacket, and he only had a black hoodie. As soon as he was at arm's length, Rob pulled him back into an embrace before Ethan's shoulder bag could hit him on the head. Ethan had gained weight since leaving the hospital, but to Robert, he still seemed so frail sometimes, like he would break if he tripped. The black hair, which had been a mess just hours ago, now was all straight, neat, and smelled of that amazing bergamot shampoo that Rob had come to associate with Ethan. He hugged him tightly, gathering a fistful of the sweet-smelling mane. The kiss that started out of nowhere made him feel like it had been ages since he last tasted Ethan's lips, but they couldn't linger right at the gates of the enemy.

"L-let's go?"

Ethan nodded, but stood on his toes for one more kiss. Glints of glitter still lingered in his hair. "Yeah, I want to get out of here."

Rob exhaled, smiling at Ethan as he squeezed his hand. Without a word, he started running back between the trees, away from the threat of detection and closer to the safety of his car. He wanted to scream with joy.

"I'm so happy you came to get me. I'm sick of that place so much," Ethan moaned as soon as they got to the car. Robert pushed him against the door and molded their bodies together, opening Ethan's sweet mouth with a deep kiss. His body was a warehouse of fireworks, ready to crackle every time he was near Ethan.

Within seconds, Ethan's arms were around his neck, and his lips opened in invitation. He gently petted Rob's nape and rubbed his thigh against Rob's. That alone was enough to start giving Rob a hard-on. He remembered how pliant Ethan's body was, how Ethan encouraged him to come inside its tightness.

"Oh, God, baby," he whispered, squeezing his hands over Ethan's waist. His body was getting worked up, and that couldn't happen here. "We need to go."

Ethan gave Rob's neck one last kiss and suckle before withdrawing. "Take me wherever you want." He looked up at Rob with that single piercing blue eye.

Robert sighed and staggered backward, opening the door for Ethan. "Yeah, let's go. They might find out you're gone," he said, walking around the car.

Ethan quickly got in and threw his bag to the back seat. "Fuck them. I hope they do, and I hope they worry. I had the worst fight with them."

"What happened? Why did you tell them about us after all?" asked Rob, starting the car and driving to the highway as quickly as he could without breaking any traffic regulations.

Ethan buckled his seat belt without prompting and looked up at Rob with a deep breath. "It got out of hand. They locked my work-space, and I went ballistic. So I told them they can't do this, they can't keep me from doing what I want. One word led to another, and I told them we were dating, 'cause I knew it would piss them off. Another thing they have no control over. It made me feel a little bit better to see their outraged faces."

Robert smiled. He knew he shouldn't after Ethan's parents have been so nice to him, but this time, they were wrong. "No, they can't stop me from seeing you."

Ethan reached out to him and stroked his arm. "They can't. It's ridiculous. They treat me like a child. It only opened my eyes about how sick I am of being told what to do and feeling inadequate about my passion."

"So, what do you want to do?" Robert brushed his thumbs over the steering wheel.

"I want to grow my business, learn more about the craft, be a better artist. They tried to guilt-trip me about college, complaining that they offered to pay for it. I don't want them to pay for it because I don't want to go to law school. It's not for me. So I decided." He took a deep breath. "I'm not going to college."

Robert frowned at the road. This conversation was taking a sudden turn for the serious. "Why?"

"It's just a big debt. And for what? There are so many ways to learn if you're doing art. Tutorials on the Internet, shorter courses, meeting crafters. Most of what I know about taxidermy, I learned from Herbert, and he taught me for free. I could move to Seattle and meet people there. If my parents hadn't locked my workspace, I could finish my commission for that store in L.A." Ethan seemed to be speaking calmly, but at the end of the last sentence, he took a deep breath, and when Rob shot a glance at him, he saw tears streaking down the smooth cheek.

He drew in a sharp breath. Maybe this wasn't the best time to get into serious discussions about the future so he settled on trying to calm down his boyfriend. "Okay, I get it. It's terrible, but let them think on it. Maybe you could negotiate."

Ethan got a tissue to rub the tears off his face. "What can I negotiate? They're dead set on unlocking my workspace only after graduation, and I'm not giving you up either."

Robert bit his lip. "You know, maybe they don't understand how serious you are. I'm sure they'll come round."

Ethan sniffed and looked down at his knees, hiding his face behind the curtain of hair. His shoulders trembled with every breath he took.

"Ethan, please don't cry. I can't even do anything when I drive," uttered Rob, doing his best to focus on the traffic. He was a bit overwhelmed by the new responsibility of taking care of a distressed lover.

"I'm sorry... I just feel like such a failure. I won't be able to deliver on my promise to that store, and everyone will know I'm unreliable, and no one will order from me anymore. I'm so embarrassed, and it's all their fault." Ethan didn't look back, but the tissues were hard at work.

Robert gave a shuddery breath. "You could e-mail them, write that you have a family emergency and ask for an extended commission time."

"You think they would have me after I blow a deadline?" Ethan finally looked up at him, with his eye all red.

"Well, it's a small store, not a huge corporation. It's people like you and me. I'm sure anybody can understand that sometimes shit just happens. Why not try?" Rob smiled at Ethan, hoping this could brighten up his mood. Seeing Ethan smile back was like a soothing menthol balm all over his forehead.

"Maybe I could try that. You're right."

Robert went weak with relief. He felt almost guilty that he found the teary smile on Ethan's face beautiful. Hot even. He wanted nothing more than to curl up with him in the backseat.

After about a half-hour drive, they turned into a small road, deep in the woods, and Rob hoped to find a good secluded spot for them. It took another ten minutes, but finally he stopped between the bushes, close to a lake they could see between the trees.

The moment they stopped, Ethan unbuckled his seat belt and went straight for a hug. "Thank you for coming. I needed this so much," he whispered before kissing Rob's cheek.

Rob relaxed into the seat and pulled him closer. They would be safe here. "Have you switched off your phone?"

"I didn't even take it with me." Ethan smiled into Robert's lips before closing in for another kiss. "I don't need to call anyone when I have you here."

Rob's heart exploded with warmth. He gently petted the top of Ethan's head and squeezed his hand. "You want to move to the back?" A promise of arousal overcame his body as soon as those words left his mouth.

Ethan drew in a sharp breath and pulled on Rob's lip with his teeth. "Hell yeah." He slid his hand between Rob's thighs and squeezed his dick through the jeans.

Robert shuddered, spreading his legs without thinking. Heat rushed from his loins, all the way to the toes and head. "Yes, that's..."

"'Good' is the word you're looking for." Ethan gave him one more kiss before pulling back to get out.

"Yeah, sure." Rob scrambled out of the car and quickly dove into the backseat, moving the blue plastic bag to the floor. He hoped they'd need its contents again. He reached out to Ethan with a wide smile. "Come on."

Ethan's smile widened, and it was the best thing Rob could imagine after seeing him cry. Not to mention he really must have enjoyed yesterday. "I'm gonna."

Robert's chest filled with relief. He had been so scared the night before that it would all turn to shit. That he wouldn't be able to keep himself in check, because that was what he had read online, that he'd hurt Ethan, and Ethan wouldn't like to do it anymore. All those things had kept flashing through his mind when he was preparing to make love to Ethan yesterday. But it had been bliss. They were fine. And Ethan, he was so eager for another go.

"How?"

Ethan slid closer to Rob and kneeled next to him. "All the way?" he whispered. "I've got baby wipes and stuff. I just wanna be close to you so bad."

Robert reached out behind him and closed the car, enveloping them in their private love nest, as cheesy as it sounded even in Rob's mind. He gave a frantic nod. "And I've got everything else. We can... you are so amazing," he said out of the blue because the initial thought fled his mind like steam from a pot that was opened too soon.

The touch of Ethan's soft lips was all Rob needed to forget about the whole world. He straddled Rob, and having Ethan's thighs spread wide over his lap made him think of how much he wanted to see them naked. "We can do whatever we want," he whispered.

"I want whatever you want," whispered Rob, kneading his fingers into the slim thighs around him. The heat spreading around his cock was already preparing him for something powerful and sweet.

"I want you in me again." Ethan cupped Robert's cheek as they kissed, his soft hair tickling Rob's neck. "I can actually still sort of feel you today. But not in a bad way. Just... tender."

Suddenly, Rob had a difficulty taking a whole breath, and he nuzzled Ethan's face as a shudder went through them both. The raw need, the acceptance Ethan kept showering him with since yesterday was filing Robert's heart with a warmth that was hard to grasp. "You liked it so much?" He swallowed, brushing his thumbs over Ethan's cheeks. "I'm never gonna do it with you if you don't say something like this," he chuckled.

Ethan slid his hands into Rob's hair, and when Rob pushed his hands under his hoodie, he realized Ethan wasn't wearing anything underneath. "Like what?" Ethan teased him, grinding his body into Rob's.

Robert gasped, moving his hips against him and sank his fingers into the naked flesh. It was so smooth and sweet to the touch. "You know, being enthusiastic, saying stuff like 'I want you to come inside me'... that was amazing," he whispered, never looking away from Ethan's face.

Ethan's smile made his eye almost close. He slid his hands to Rob's neck and they were so hot Rob could melt into them. "I can't help myself when I'm around you. Now that I know you're actually gay? Wow, it's like a whole lifted curtain. I can say things without worrying if they're gonna freak you out."

"That depends," chuckled Rob, moving his hands up Ethan's warm torso, still hidden from his eyes by the hoodie. He cupped his pecs and squeezed them with a low moan. He wanted to see Ethan naked and pliant again. It would surely become his new addiction.

"On what?" Ethan pouted and traced Rob's jaw with his thumbs. "I don't have freaky needs." His growing erection was becoming more and more obvious, and Rob found himself salivating.

He slipped his hands from underneath the fabric and pulled down the zipper, revealing the smooth chest. He leaned forward and buried his face in the fresh scent of skin and bergamot, tracing small kisses over Ethan's breastbone. "What do you need?"

Ethan stroked the back of Rob's head. "I need you to be here for me. To kiss me, suck me, and fuck me. I loved watching you come. It was the hottest thing ever. Made me throb all over. *All* over."

Now it was Robert, who was throbbing all over. With a shuddery breath, he bit into the flesh by his mouth and slid his hands to Ethan's ass. He was the happiest man alive, hands down. He didn't need much else than listening to this coming from a guy he was so fond of. "I want all of that, too."

Ethan's buttocks tensed up under the touch, and it only made Rob want to tease it more. He stirred and rolled his head against Ethan to caress him without pulling his hands away from that lovely ass.

"I like you touching me there." Ethan put his head on Rob's shoulder and kissed his ear.

"Believe me, I like that too," Rob whispered, arching his body at the sweet shivers wandering across his chest and stomach.

"I still can't get over the fact that you actually want me." Ethan tightened his hug. "My pants are getting too tight."

"You can take them off if you want," said Rob, squeezing Ethan's ass tighter. He couldn't believe Ethan was so confident and it was so sexy on him. "It's the same here. Can't believe you like me this much after... everything," he whispered, guilt seeping into his heart.

"Because you turned out to be different than what I've seen you as before. Leaving me at Herbert's was kinda crappy, but I suppose I deserved it." Ethan gave Rob another kiss before rolling over to the side. He pushed off his sneakers and opened his pants, looking all too eager. His cute face was flushed pink, and he was breathing hard. Two strawberry nipples on the milky chest were hard, as if just asking to be sucked on. For now, Rob settled on squeezing one of them. He opened his own jeans at the same time, breathing in the scent of Ethan's hair. He was becoming severely addicted to it.

"Hey!" Ethan laughed, but Rob's gaze headed down when his boyfriend pushed his pants down along with his briefs. His erect dick sprang out like it was eager to play.

"You want me to suck you?" whispered Robert, pulling Ethan close in one swift move, only to bite into the side of his neck. His whole body shuddered when the movement made the hard dick brush against his hand.

Ethan let out a low moan but chuckled. "I can see you want to. Go on, sweetie, have some cock." His fingers slid under Rob's shirt.

Robert blinked, unsure whether he was being made fun of or flirted with. He chose to believe the latter and leaned down toward the gorgeous, veiny dick that was pointing straight to his face, demanding attention. Robert's own cock was begging to be freed so he pulled his pants lower with a sigh of relief. "It looks so good."

"Oh, God, even feeling your breath on it is making me sweat." Ethan slid his fingers into Rob's hair. "In a good way, I mean."

Robert grinned and spat on his hand, which he then slowly moved over the whole length of Ethan's dick. Its musky, mouth-watering scent made Rob shudder even before his lips touched the smooth head. "Sure."

Ethan gasped, stroking Rob's hair. "Natural talent." He closed his eye and leaned back in the seat.

Rob groaned and licked around the head, flicking the tip of his tongue over its edge before diving in and taking the cock in deeper. The hardened flesh was so solid and delicate at the same time. It made him squeeze his thighs in excitement.

"So good," Ethan whispered and bent, curling over Rob. "I can't take much of this though," he laughed nervously, already panting.

Robert moaned, taking the cock as deep as he could, teasing his gag reflex. Despite the discomfort, his limbs went softer each time he bobbed his head, but he couldn't ignore the warning. "Love it," he whispered, looking up at Ethan. There were shivers rushing over the surface of his skin and inside his stomach, tugging on his own cock. He felt honored he was allowed to suckle on that throbbing flesh, to drink Ethan's come, and hold him close.

"I know another thing you'll love." Ethan bit his lips and slowly pushed him away to get the bag off the floor.

"You do?" whispered Rob with a smile. He pushed down his pants to his knees and sat back, slowly stroking his own cock. Each move Ethan was making was like an invitation to take a bite.

Ethan nodded, watching him with hunger crystallizing in his one eye. He got out a condom and carefully rolled it on Robert, giving him a quick kiss in the meanwhile. Things were progressing with the speed of a summer storm, and were just as electrifying.

"You must really want it," uttered Rob, pulling at Ethan to make him straddle his lap.

"I just want to be close to you." Ethan wrapped his arms around Rob's neck and spread his naked thighs over Rob's lap. He looked so hot with his pants off but the hoodie still on. "And I'm horny," he added in a whisper.

"Yeah? And you want me inside?" asked Rob, cupping Ethan's buttocks with a low hum. They were ripe and juicy, and all Rob wanted was to dig in.

"Y-yeah…" Ethan hugged him close and passed him the lube. Robert bit his lip. His breath was hitching and having that hot tightness so close, just slightly above his dick, was like having cookies baking in the oven. You know you have to let them get ready, but you still want to take them out as soon as possible. He chose not to share this analogy with his lover though.

"Tell me, how does it feel?" whispered Rob, dropping the lube to the floor as soon as he'd squirted enough of it on his hand. His fingers delved between Ethan's buttocks, and he was instantly hit by the warmth that was awaiting him deeper, in the hole between the soft folds of skin.

Ethan clung onto him, his breath tickling Rob's ear. "It's stretching, so it's a strain, but then when it's in, and the head brushes over the prostate, it's like 'wow'. And the skin there is so sensitive, every touch is like a tug on my cock."

"Yeah? Is it that good?" Rob was gently rubbing his fingers all around Ethan's anus, slippery with the lube and so warm it seemed to invite him in. His lips found Ethan's, and he traced the sweet mouth with his tongue.

"You make it so good." Every hitching breath that came out of Ethan's mouth was like an invitation for fucking. "Slide them in, I want to feel it again."

Rob pulled him closer by the waist with a low groan and pressed two fingertips against the tight opening. His cock twitched the moment they pressed in. Ethan moaned into the kiss, and his muscles tensed around Rob's fingers. His dick rubbed against Rob's chest, all stiff and demanding. Rob groaned at the damp touch and pressed his fingers in deeper while cradling Ethan to his chest. He slowly turned his fingers inside of him, playing with the smooth, warm flesh.

"That feels right." Ethan slowly rocked against the fingers, kissing Rob's ear. Getting his boyfriend ready was almost as sweet as the sex itself. Watching Ethan's responses, feeling his muscles tense or relax turned Rob on more by the second. He pulled on Ethan's hair, forcing his mouth to meet his in a deep, demanding kiss, just as he pressed his fingers in to the knuckle and moved them to where he remembered Ethan liked being touched inside. His head felt light, as if all the blood in his body gathered in his pulsing dick.

Ethan whimpered and rocked his hips against Rob, but wasn't moving away and kissed him back with even more passion. His hands roamed all over Rob's neck and jaw, petting it, giving Rob all his attention. He was like dough in Rob's hands, all pliant and squeezable.

"Is that it?" whispered Rob against his lips, massaging the nub of flesh inside even as Ethan's sphincter squeezed around the base of his fingers. He couldn't wait to feel it clamp down on his cock.

"Oh fuck! Yes, yes, yes!" Ethan writhed in his embrace, but wasn't trying to get away, instead grinding into Rob with new force. "Fuck, so good," he uttered breathlessly.

Robert groaned and sucked on Ethan's lip while slowly letting his fingers fuck Ethan with more force, quicker. He made long, broad moves with his hand, scissoring the digits and slapping the heel of his hand against the lovely buttocks. He ground his hips up, seeking contact, and moaned into the welcoming lips when his cock brushed against Ethan's balls. He couldn't wait anymore, and Ethan seemed to be reading his mind.

"Yeah, let's do it, I think I'm ready," Ethan said, looking into Rob's eyes. His chest was moving rapidly as he took sharp gulps of air. As soon as Rob pulled out his fingers, Ethan awkwardly turned around in his lap and made Rob feel pure lust when he got a view of that sweet, pale ass. With a low growl, he pushed a finger back in, just to tease Ethan. The warmth inside must have made his brain melt as he didn't have any idea what he was supposed to say.

Ethan wiggled his ass against him and took off his hoodie. He lay back against Rob's chest, stretching out to have his hands behind Rob's head. It wasn't the most comfortable position, but then again, cars weren't exactly meant for this either. Another moan left his lips when Rob teased his anus, but he was ripe and ready for fucking.

"You need to show me how you like it now that you're on top," rasped Robert, slowly pulling out the finger from the slippery, tight hole. He grasped his own cock and positioned the head at Ethan's entrance. A groan escaped his lips at the mind-numbing pleasure that came with the contact.

"Oh, oh... okay..." Ethan uttered, looking back at Rob. He slowly pushed down on the penis, but not strongly enough to have the cockhead pass the sphincter. He rubbed against it in a teasing motion. Robert felt his lips twitch with a smile. What a little devil Ethan was to play with him like this.

He grabbed his cock and patted it against Ethan's hole, shuddering with every touch. He couldn't wait to push in again, to have Ethan ride him for the first time. Ethan took loud, raspy breaths as he lowered himself right onto Rob's dick, accepting it inside with a grunt that only made Rob hotter. With his chin resting on Ethan's fragrant shoulder, Rob had the perfect view on his boyfriend's pale chest and the stiffened nipples. Rob's gaze slid lower, to the tattooed rats dancing on Ethan's belly with every breath he took. The pressure bearing down on Rob's cock was so mind-blowing that he pulled Ethan tight against his chest and clenched his teeth not to come as his dick sank into the sweetest, tightest ass he could imagine. He never even realized initially that his thighs had started trembling.

"Ohh.... it's amazing," he whispered, chaotically petting Ethan's slim body all over. It was burning, as if Rob's cock was the fuel to Ethan's lust. Robert rubbed the angular hip bone with his fingertips, delighting in the sight of Ethan's reddened dick sticking up like it was just asking to be touched.

Ethan slid his arms behind Rob's back, hugging him close this way, as he let his head fall back to Rob's shoulder, plump mouth open, cheeks pink. "I love you," he whispered breathlessly, tensing his ass in the most delicious way.

The words, spoken so softly, were like the smoothest chocolate drizzling all over Rob's heart. He gasped, pushing his hips up, deeper into the pliant body. He hadn't expected to hear this, especially not today, but most of all, he hadn't expected it to feel this good. With a low hum, he pulled Ethan's face back and stifled the sudden pain in his own chest with a deep, gentle kiss.

Ethan was hungry to reciprocate, his hot tongue exploring Rob's mouth as if he wanted to rub his declaration into Rob's gums. They moved together, and it took Rob to a whole new understanding of what sex was, and what he wanted it to be. It definitely wasn't just about something dirty for him, a tight ass and a forgettable experience. With Ethan, it was something they shared, both each other's first, both equally hungry for touch. He wanted to make this as unforgettable of an experience for Ethan as it was for him, even if he couldn't declare anything just yet. It wouldn't be fair to spill out something like that just because of passion. Completely embedded within the warm glove of Ethan's body, he sucked on his lips while gently running his fingers up and down Ethan's chest, thighs, and then his tight balls, his hard cock, which Rob could suck on for minutes at a time.

"You feel so good."

All of a sudden, Ethan's body became stiff and rigid, his ass clenching so hard Rob almost came on the spot. He looked around the car, holding onto Robert with his arms twisted back. "Wait, wait, Rob?" His breath hitched, but it sounded more like hyperventilating than panting.

Robert hugged him tight, suddenly alert. "Did I hurt you?" he whispered, stiff with nerves at the idea that maybe he pushed in too hard, was too enthusiastic and selfish. "Do you want me to stop?" he choked out through clenched teeth, pressing his mouth to Ethan's salty temple.

"I— I don't know, I think I had a lapse," he uttered with a voice so small Robert would do anything to help. "I can't believe this is happening. Just... I... We went here to the back..." Ethan's ass was slowly relaxing, and he stroked Rob's forearms.

Robert's chest clenched so hard he couldn't breathe properly. Was Ethan suddenly finding himself during sex to which he didn't remember he consented? How fucked up was that?

He started raining small, soothing kissed all over Ethan's cheek. "I'm so sorry, baby. Do you want me to pull out? It's not a big deal," he promised, hardly keeping his nerves in check. The last thing he wanted was to have Ethan scared while having sex with him. This was a nightmare, yet he felt guilty for even thinking that because it was surely worse for Ethan.

"Y-yeah, sorry... I'm just... confused..." he moaned, slightly wiggling his ass. The movement wasn't making it easy on Robert. "Just fill me in, please. Oh God, that was a horrible way to put it." He put a hand over his face.

Robert clenched his teeth and pulled out of Ethan, the cool air burning even through the condom. He quickly dropped to his knees on the floor and helped Ethan's stiff form to lie on the seat. He didn't want to be too imposing by crushing him with his own weight now.

But Ethan wasn't pulling away. Instead, he reached out to hug Robert, though his eye had that red tint to it that made Rob panic. "I messed up, I'm so sorry. Was it nice before? I wanna continue, I just... I need to grasp things." He hugged Rob tighter, his body trembling.

Rob moved closer to Ethan's head and gathered it in his arms, sheltering him from all the bad things that could hurt him, at least those he could prevent. He gave him a gentle kiss on the lips and tightened his hands around him. "You didn't, it's not your fault," he whispered into the smooth, soft skin. It was all *his* fault.

Ethan took a deep breath and stroked Rob's back. At least they were safe and alone, with all the time they needed to finish things later. "Coming out of a lapse doesn't feel all that bad with you around," Ethan finally said and kissed Rob's arm. "You wouldn't hurt me. I just wish I could remember everything. If I forgot my first time, it would be the fail of the century."

"That won't happen," rasped Robert, squeezing Ethan's hand. "And even if it would, the next time would have been the first for you, wouldn't it?" He couldn't believe it was him who had irreversibly hurt the one guy he cared so much about. It even hurt him to think about it.

Ethan blinked at him and the one eye he had left welled up, even though his pretty lips curved into a smile, only adding to Rob's confusion. "You're right. I could have another first time with you."

Robert swallowed hard, closing Ethan's fingers in his. His heart was pounding so hard he could barely breathe when he realized that Ethan couldn't remember one more thing—the fact that he had just confessed his feelings to Robert. Just the thought of it sent a piercing pain down Robert's chest. This moment between them happened only seconds ago, and yet for Ethan it was as if it never existed, and it made Robert's eyes sting with the pressure. That wasn't right. This moment couldn't just disappear from memory, he needed Ethan to know what it was all about.

"I love you so much", he whispered, and the moment he said it, it dawned on him that it was exactly what he meant, and in some twisted way, he was the first one to say it. They both got to say it first.

Ethan's smile widened, and he kissed Rob's lips. "I love you too," he said, looking into Rob's eyes, oblivious to having said it once today already. His fingers tightened on Rob's as well. It was as if the car was their cotton candy cocoon where life was only about being together, sticking to each other in the sugary sweetness.

Robert felt a prickling around his eyes. He already knew he wouldn't regret that he confessed to having this bundle of intense emotions that seemed to have spread all over him like a parasite, changing the way he thought and what he did. Would he ever help anyone escape from their parents' home when they were grounded? Of course not, but with Ethan, he seemed to lose some of his reason. As frightening as it was, he rather liked being so passionate about someone.

"I know, you just told me, baby," he added, lowering his voice as it got hoarse.

"I did?" Ethan's smile widened, making him look so cute, so handsome, that Rob couldn't wait to have sex with him again.

Rob nodded and leaned closer, touching his forehead to Ethan's. What he got in return was a kiss so hot it made Rob's somewhat softened cock stiffen to full attention. Ethan ran his fingers over the sides of Rob's side, tickling him. "I'm feeling better now." He rubbed his thigh against Rob's erection.

"You sure?" whispered Rob, closing his eyes. "I just want you to be comfortable."

"That's why I'm sure." Ethan gave him another kiss, his hair tickling Rob's face. "I can trust you." He stroked Rob's skin as they tried to work out a comfortable position in the backseat, with Rob climbing on top of Ethan before he even consciously thought about doing it. It was as if something about Ethan's position gave him a clue.

"What do you want me to do?"

"I think I want to get back to what we were doing earlier." Ethan smiled at him and stroked the back of his head. "But without a bed, I think it'll be better if I turn over."

Robert nodded but didn't let him move yet. He cupped the soft cheek and stroked his fingers over the rosy flesh of Ethan's lip. His chest was a bundle of emotions so powerful he didn't know what to do with them. "I'm so happy we made this arrangement."

Ethan laughed as his hands slid down Rob's back. "Oh, my God! Don't call it that."

Robert chuckled, gently thrusting his cock into Ethan's crotch. "How should I call it? Our first date?"

"My horrible, misguided way to get the guy I wanted?" Ethan licked his lips and moved in a similar way, his fingers dancing over Rob's ass but barely touching it.

Robert smiled at him, breathless. "So when will we have our anniversary?" He started grinding his crotch against Ethan with renewed vigor. He would soon be ready for action again. Sliding his cock over Ethan's stomach felt so amazing he could even get off on it.

"Three months next week." Ethan moved against him, hard as well. A pink blush was blooming on his cheeks, and Robert kissed his way all over it.

"You make me act all crazy, you know that?"

Ethan grinned, breathing heavier again. "Your mom's gonna hate me. I make you break the rules."

"No way, she's gonna love you, I promise." whispered Robert, grinding his now hard cock into Ethan's hip. Just being so close felt so achingly good. And Ethan accepted him in ways no one else did, let Rob inside of his body, baring himself in the most intimate of ways.

Ethan gave him one more kiss and bit his lip. "How about we stay like this, huh? Just rub against each other?"

Robert grinned and raised his hips to pull off the condom. "Baby, you have no idea how much I want to... you know, come on your skin," he uttered, not wanting to sound insensitive.

Ethan swallowed and squeezed Rob's buttocks so gently, as if he was afraid the world would fall apart if he did it harder. His eye was completely focused on Robert, dark and hazy. "We were both virgins, you know... Maybe we could lose the rubbers sometime soon? I mean, I trust you. I'd like it that way. That is if it doesn't... you know, gross you out." He looked at Rob's chin instead of into his eyes, a flush spreading over his cheeks.

Robert frowned, surprised, and his mouth went dry. "I kinda th ought... you'd feel safer with rubbers, you know, because you're bottoming."

Ethan took a deep breath. "I was thinking about it since yesterday. We could do with or without, depending on the situation. Like, in a car, I'd want a condom, for convenience, but maybe if we're at home, in a bed, we can experiment..." His grip on Rob's ass became firmer, and it made Rob's head bob like a puppet's. He did want that, to be closer to Ethan in every way, and for Ethan to accept Robert's come inside seemed like the ultimate sign of acceptance.

"What if I... make love to your thighs, and then suck you off?" he proposed, flooded by heat.

Ethan chuckled and kissed his nose. "That sounds hot. Just please, never again say 'make love to your thighs'. That sounds horrendous." He raised his lips to Rob's ear, soothing his embarrassment. "You can say you wanna *fuck* them," he whispered and rubbed his cock against Rob's stomach.

Robert exhaled and leaned in for a slow, deep kiss, which awakened thousands of nerve endings on his skin, on his torso where their chests touched, his hips and cock, which was so pleasantly tucked between their stomachs, his ass, grabbed hard like bread dough, and his lips, exploding with sensation. "I want to fuck your thighs," he whispered, glad he didn't offend Ethan. He didn't want to be *that* guy.

Ethan licked his lips and turned under Robert, presenting his ass and thighs for the taking. The memory of Ethan riding his cock so eagerly just fifteen minutes ago was still tingling in Rob's balls. Such a tight, hot ass. As if the view itself weren't good enough, Ethan pushed back slightly, rubbing against Rob's cock in a way Rob was sure he would never get enough of. He leaned in, tasting the sweaty skin on the back of Ethan's shoulder and squeezed some more lubricant on his fingers, already grinding against his lover.

"I love it when it gets all hard and throbbing," Ethan whispered, arching his back to the touch. In this position Rob could get his fill of the tangerine and bergamot smell of Ethan's hair. He only wished he had a CD with that weird music Ethan liked so he could put it on.

Slowly, he slipped his hand between those perfect thighs and started spreading the lube all over not to rub his skin too much. "You can keep them together," he whispered, fantasizing about the hot cavity he'd fuck.

"Yeah? So it's tight for you?" Ethan panted against the upholstery and slid his thighs closer. "I'm so turned on right now." Heat evaporated from his body as if he were a portable radiator.

"You like me on top of you? Squeezing in?" whispered Rob, furiously masturbating over the pale thighs. His head was filling with images of how they looked right now, with him on top, spread over Ethan's lovely form. "Squeeze them as tight as you can, baby."

"I do, I like how big and heavy you are," Ethan uttered, and Rob knew those legs tensed the moment he saw Ethan's lovely ass squeeze and get dimples on the sides. This was when he sank in, tearing through the narrow channel with a low grunt. It was so beautiful and strange at the same time, but he slid his forearm under Ethan's cheek and hugged him tight, gently biting into the flesh of his arm.

What he got in return were gentle kisses all over his forearm. Ethan's flesh was so hot and slippery, available for fucking, and the mere thought that Rob would get to come all over that pale skin was like being thrown from the microwave straight into a pan of boiling oil. Overwhelmed, he started thrusting, moving on top of Ethan like a machine, listening to his lover gasping, to the slapping of their skin. It was perfect, and very soon, Rob found himself nearing the peak. Ethan's slim, but firm body was everything he wanted and needed.

"You're so hot," Ethan uttered, moving against him, pushing their bodies together and clamping his tense thighs on Rob's dick, milking him even as Rob grabbed his side, coming with a rush of noise in his head. It was only when he fell on top of Ethan, spent, that he unsqueezed his fingers from his lover's ribs and petted them gently.

"So intense..."

"Oh, wow, I feel it." Ethan reached back to stroke Rob's arm. The smell in the car was intoxicating, and the only thing that would make this better, was having Ethan's stiff cock in his mouth.

Robert moved to his knees and pushed his fingers between the hot, slippery thighs. So good. Anyone who underestimated *frottage* didn't know shit. "I'm thirsty."

"So dirty!" Ethan let out a raspy laugh and parted his thighs for touching, but soon turned around, presenting his arched up cock.

"Why would you say that?" asked Rob with a half smile as he lowered himself to face the beautiful arch of Ethan's cock. No pornstar cock could possibly compete with how flawless, fragrant, and proportionate it was. He gave it a sloppy kiss.

"Just messing with you." Ethan slid his fingers into Rob's hair, his own black mane slightly messy and sticking to his face. He spread his slippery thighs, still wet with come and lube. He looked so appetizing Rob's mouth watered. This was the perfect final course to this excellent menu.

He opened his mouth and sucked in one of Ethan's balls, sliding his tongue over the unshaven skin. The smell of sweat and come elevated the experience to a whole new level.

"Mmm, I like that." Ethan pulled up his legs and put them over Rob's shoulders, it was the sweetest of traps, one Rob had no intention of escaping from.

"Tell me what you want me to do, and I'll be your slave then," chuckled Rob, caressing the tight balls with his tongue. With Ethan, he felt so free, like he didn't have to live up to any expectations. He could just be himself, and Ethan would still want him all the same.

Ethan smiled, sliding lower in the seat. "Suck on my balls. It felt really good." His chest moved up and down, the lean muscles under the skin tensing in a hypnotizing way.

Robert complied and hummed low as he explored Ethan's scrotum, gently nipping the skin, lapping at it, sucking. He was surrounded by the sweetest of smells, and with that gorgeous cock over him, he had no reasons to complain.

"Now lick my dick from the balls, all the way to the tip." Ethan gently massaged Rob's head, and it was all the necessary encouragement. Rob followed the instructions with an openmouthed smile on his face, caressing the thick vein on the underside and finishing the lap with a swirl of his tongue around the tip. He liked how relaxed Ethan was, and how good it felt to receive direct hints like this. He wanted to give him as much pleasure as he could.

"Now suck on the head, I wanna see your cheeks hollow." Ethan's voice became lower, and he looked down into Rob's eyes with his own wide open.

A hot shiver ran down Robert's body, swirling in his stomach, and he did just that, sucking on the spongy head for all he was worth as soon as he stuck the tip of his tongue into the slit at the top. He loved the salty, musky aroma of Ethan's cock.

"Oh wow, flip your tip over there." Ethan bit his lip and pulled Rob closer with his legs, gasping when Rob obeyed his command. His slim body was trembling with a series of shivers as he pushed his hips up into Robert's face.

It was so incredibly satisfying to make Ethan feel so good. Robert groaned over the cock and took more of it in, sucking as hard as he could, and so loud the sounds were giving his own cock a small twitch. Next thing he knew, he had Ethan moaning, gripping his hair and coming into his mouth with a few intense thrusts. One of them went deep enough to make him gag, but he relaxed and drank it all, clutching to Ethan's hips for dear life. With time, he would learn to be a great lover, he was sure of it.

So far, Ethan wasn't complaining. He had a big grin on his face and slowly let go of Rob's hair. "You knew exactly what I needed."

"I need to take care of my baby," Rob said, climbing up Ethan's body to hug him as soon as they were lying side by side on the narrow seat.

This time, Ethan was on top of Rob, kissing his neck and murmuring like a satisfied cat. "You did well. You should get a treat." He paused to look up at Robert. "Oh wait, you already did."

"I love sucking your cock. And balls," confessed Robert, just before planting a sweet, chaste kiss on Ethan's chin. He'd never been so satisfied in his life, and he wouldn't be embarrassed to admit it, especially with Ethan being quite shameless himself.

"Thanks for snatching me away. I really had a hard time today."

Robert sighed and pulled Ethan even closer. "And what now?"

"I don't know. I can't let my parents control me like that." Ethan hugged Rob and kissed his chest. "I really think this is my time to learn and develop, and they completely blocked my plans."

Robert kissed him again, wondering whether they shouldn't put something on. He was starting to freeze. "You know, you're eighteen, you could crash at my place until they calm down." As soon as he said that, his chest went aflame with hope. He hadn't even known before just how much he wanted that. He could cook for Ethan, impress him with his skills, watch Ethan slouch on the couch while he worked on yet another drawing of weasels. And at night, they'd cuddle in Rob's bed and fuck as loud as they wanted because Rob's mom was usually out at night.

"I could? Would your mom allow it?" Ethan's heartbeat sped up so much it was pounding against Rob's chest, and this was when Rob knew he'd made the right choice. He smiled at Ethan.

"She's not home most of the time. I can't imagine why she'd be opposed to the idea."

"I really want that so much. I'm so sick of my parents, all I want is out. There's just the question of my workshop... I'd need your help with that." Ethan looked up at Rob with that big blue eye, and it became clear that he'd do anything Ethan would ask for.

Chapter 16

ROB

ROBERT HAD NEVER STOPPED smiling since he'd driven Ethan back home the day before. He could only imagine how furious Ethan's parents were after finding out their son had fled through the window, but he hoped Ethan would keep his anger in check this time. They'd shared some messages since, and he seemed fine, but Rob still couldn't wait to see his face again. His veins were pulsing with liquid happiness, which warmed him all over and made his heart so light he could fly.

As much as he despised Pat for orchestrating Ethan's glitter shower, if it weren't for that, maybe he and Ethan would still be in the dark about each other's feelings, and he wouldn't have been inside Ethan, held him tight. The blow jobs had been amazing, but going all the way just blew Rob's mind. He had to watch out not to daydream about it too much because the threat of getting a boner at school was ever-present whenever he remembered Ethan's moans, his flushed cheeks, eager moves, and the smell of his hair.

The post-prom blues was in the air as Rob walked down the corridor to the cafeteria. Chris joined him the moment he reached the open doors.

"Man, there's so much gossip around," Chris whispered with his hands in his pockets.

Robert raised his brows and moved to the counters, taking a tray. "Yeah? What did I miss?" he asked, deliberately pretending not to know. He wanted Chris to ask him about what happened.

"You left, like, mid-prom. And Ethan did as well. At one point there was even gossip that he attempted suicide after that glitter thing," Chris spoke quickly, with his eyes wide open.

Robert chuckled and put some milk on the tray, moving along the counter with other students. Ethan was far too driven to try to kill himself because of some shithead. "Nope."

"What happened then?" Chris poked him with an elbow and got three slices of pizza.

Robert bit back a smile and took some salad with croutons and tuna. He couldn't focus whenever he thought about Ethan telling him to come inside of him. "Well, we're a couple now," he said, looking up into Chris's squarish, smiling face.

"I'm guessing I know what that means." Chris snorted. "Your place?"

Robert poked him with an elbow. "Oh, shut up. Tell me about the prom. Did you talk to Kelly after I left?" he asked, fighting the dawning feeling of guilt. He had been too nervous to send her a message. Besides, it would be more gentlemanly to apologize face to face, but now that prospect seemed even worse. He didn't want her to hate him.

Chris smiled even wider than usual. "Yeah, I took care of her, and, you know, not in a sleazy way or anything. I had fun with both her and Sue, and drove them both home. Maybe it was even for the better, you know, because this way it seemed less like a date with Sue. Pat was proud of himself though. That guy needs a shaking. How did Ethan take it, anyway? I know you *cheered him up*, but in general." Chris grinned, and they turned to their table with full trays.

Rob groaned and felt his blood pressure rise. "His suit is ruined so obviously he's not happy. And he has this drive for his hobby, you know. Doesn't deserve to be put down like that," he said.

"Robert!" He heard Kelly's cheery voice from behind, and he froze with his hands tightening on the sides of the tray. There was no way to push this away anymore, and he made himself turn with a slight smile.

"Kelly."

"You didn't answer me on Facebook or anything," she said and gently elbowed him with a glowing smile. "Where have you been hiding all weekend? Cheering up Ethan?"

Chris snorted at the last words, and Rob wanted to slap him for it. He opened his eyes wider, tempted to look at Chris. Did Kelly somehow find out about him and Ethan? The smile on her face, however, seemed genuine, and he relaxed a little. "I'm so sorry that I just left. Forgot my phone from the locker."

"Yeah, I thought you might have needed to leave. It's just too bad you missed the rest of the prom. Is he all right? Is he coping?" She had that concerned look on her face, like when she was telling him about the latest killer whale documentary she'd watched.

The image of Ethan's orgasm face briefly flashed through Robert's mind, and he focused all of his attention on Kelly not to embarrass himself in public. "Yeah, he's doing fine. It's just so awful his prom was ruined so soon after the accident."

"Pat has really outdone himself this time. What a douchebag. Is he afraid of Ethan's taxidermy or something? I mean, it's creepy all right, but that's no reason to pick on a disabled kid. Seriously." Kelly huffed and shook her head.

"It's generally shitty to do that to anyone. He came to have fun like anyone else," muttered Robert and slowly started making his way to the table where all of their friends, including recently un-friended Pat, were already eating their lunch.

"You going into taxidermy now, Rob?" Chris laughed out loud as they sat down.

"What's that about?" Pat joined in with a smile, clearly uninformed about his own undesirability.

"He does pretty cool stuff, actually", Rob told Chris while sitting on the bench across from Pat. He gazed up at him and shrugged. "I was just talking to Chris about your prom stunt," he said, keeping his gaze firmly on Pat's.

The table went a bit more quiet, and all eyes turned their way.

"Oh, yeah? Did you like the sparkles? You didn't say anything." Pat bit into his greasecheese of doom and laughed with his mouth full. Rob stared at him, wondering whether there was any dietary advice Pat followed. The football team was banned from having sodas, but Pat still downed gallons of it out of school. At this rate, the guy was bound to die of a heart attack before his fortieth birthday. But then Pat opened his mouth again, and all of Robert's sympathy for him dissolved in the grease.

"If glitter is 3D, then does Ed actually see it with one eye?"

Rob stared at him lightheaded, and only after a moment he realized how hard he was gripping his fork. It could be used as a murder weapon. "I don't know, why don't you ask him?" he growled, making sure to cover every syllable with just the right amount of frost for Pat to get it.

Pat frowned so some of the cogs in his brain had to be movable. "'Cause I don't wanna get his gay glitter over me," he murmured with less resolve, and Chris stepped in the moment Pat said 'gay'.

"I told you, you shithead, stop it with the offensive comments!"

The conversation continued, but Rob's mind drifted away when he saw the single figure in black carrying a tray full of food.

Ethan wore his hair in a ponytail, wore his thick-rimmed glasses over his eye patch and looked lost with no empty table for him to sit at. There was no sadness on his face though, just this serious frown as he assessed the room.

Robert felt his mouth form a smile. He looked at Pat before raising his hand and gesturing for Ethan to come over. He just wanted to touch him again, even if just with his foot under the table. Instead of a smile he usually got from Ethan, there was uncertainty on his boyfriend's face. Yet Ethan did start to make his way toward them. He'd gone a long way since coming out of a coma: he struggled less with stairs and didn't trip all the time anymore.

Pat kicked Robert in the ankle. "Dude! What are you calling *him* over for?"

Rob raised his eyebrows and moved his ass over the bench, forming a vacant space between himself and Chris. "Get used to him."

Pat's eyes went so wide Rob couldn't help a grin. When Ethan finally came over in all of his lovely self, raven beak necklace included, Rob took his tray so he wouldn't struggle. The silence at the table was worse than the grease on the pizzas.

Despite his resolve not to care, something clenched in Rob's insides and refused to let go, even as he took Ethan's hand to help him maneuver himself into the free space. Even touching that warm, slim hand was making his own skin crawl with joy. He'd never felt like this before, and he refused to hide it. "You guys know Ethan."

Kelly smiled like the angel she was. She deserved a boyfriend far more divine that Robert. "Hi, Ethan."

Ethan's one eye scanned the table, and with his lips in a thin, pale line, he reminded Rob of a one-eyed rabbit about to flee.

Fortunately, Chris was there to help. "Oh, yeah, only the most annoying road captain I've ever had to drive for." He laughed and nudged Ethan's ribs.

"And the king of sparklers," Pat added with a pout.

"Says the pisser of sparkles," snapped Rob, squeezing Ethan's hand as they both settled down comfortably with their hips touching.

"I'm not even goth," Ethan muttered with a frown, and a few people at the table snorted. Ethan never did himself much favors in social situations.

"Yeah, tell that to the goth jewelry on your neck," said Pat and started tapping his fingers on the table in annoyance. He was so easy to read Robert didn't even have to make *assumptions* about his state of mind.

"Are *you* Maori?" asked Rob.

Pat's frown deepened. "What the hell?"

"Don't you have a Maori design tattooed on your calf?" asked Robert in a tone just above mockery. Most of the table would get his point while Pat would not.

"Jesus! It's not the same!" Pat spread his arms, and Rob was happy to see that Ethan's facial expression was getting calmer. With a hint of a smile even. "Why do you protect him so much? He's the same Ed he's always been. You don't owe him anything!"

Robert felt heat explode in his head and grabbed Ethan's hand. "He is the same he's always been, but now he's my boyfriend, and I want him to enjoy his lunch." He stopped, breathless. Coming out number four. And the curtain rose.

Everyone's eyes were on him, including Ethan's, who was staring at Rob with his lips parted. He rarely looked this silly.

"Your what?" Kelly uttered as the only one who managed to find a voice.

Robert swallowed and moved his arm to rest atop Ethan's shoulder. He never remembered it being so stiff. "My boyfriend," he repeated, keeping a straight face despite the panic raging through his muscles.

At least Chris was there to support him. "See? We finally have a token gay couple," he said with a broad grin.

Those words made Rob feel better, but what really had him melt was the way Ethan shyly slipped his arm around Rob's waist with a little smile.

Pat sneered and threw up his arms but wasn't going anywhere. "I can't believe this shit."

"Come to think of it, it's pretty cute," said Sue with her eyebrows up high. She didn't seem to have minded the double date at prom at all.

With his confidence boosted, Rob took a sip of his milk, challenging Pat with his gaze. "I'm not telling you about unicorns. It's all right here for you to see."

Pat shook his head, watching them with obvious distaste. "I don't get it, man. You've changed."

"No, I just started dating." Rob frowned. "Maybe you should take your time thinking about it if you don't get it."

Ethan placed a peck on Rob's jaw, which made all of Rob's insides flutter.

Pat shook his head without another word.

"So... you're gay?" muttered Kelly, nervously playing with her spoon.

Her voice dawned on Robert like a bludgeon, but he managed not to curl his shoulders in shame and looked at her. "Yeah."

Kelly looked away with an annoyed sigh but didn't say a thing. Ethan on the other hand smiled as he munched on his sandwich. In his hair, Rob could still see specks of glitter, which at the moment made him look even lovelier, almost as if there was a halo around that pretty head.

Chris poked Ethan's forearm. "You look as chirpy as a cricket."

"Because it's all going my way," Ethan said, looking up at Rob with his one blue eye.

Robert flushed with heat, unsure how that would be interpreted by his friends, and his eyes strayed to Kelly again. Ethan could be so embarrassingly deadpan sometimes. Who said things like this out loud? "This is my time," he mocked, looking at the tabletop.

"What does that even mean?" growled Pat. "This is so fucking gross."

Ethan looked at Pat, his face suddenly changed, no smile left on it whatsoever. "It means you can take your glitter and shove it up your ass."

Laughter and hissing exploded around the table at the insult.

"I thought it's fags who like to shove stuff up their asses! You can even shove it in your empty eye socket for all I care." Pat made a move like he wanted to get up and slouched over the table toward Ethan.

Robert didn't even notice when he got to his feet, and one look to the side told him that so did Chris. Anger throbbed through his veins and curled his hands into fists. Pat's nose was so out of place on his face, Robert's fingers were all tingly with the need to crook it sideways. "You want to take this outside?"

"No, I'm just going to take myself outside. Fuck this shit." Pat said and got up with a screech of his chair. He shoved Ethan's tray on the way but didn't manage to even spill his drink.

Ethan gave Pat a sneer and the middle finger. All eyes followed Pat across the canteen in a silence so profound no one even dared to chew their food. It was like watching a wounded bull retreat from a fight. Pat even kicked down an innocent chair on his way, as if only to demonstrate that he did indeed *choose* to retreat.

Robert dropped to the seat and stared at the slow swing of the door. He could only hope that would be the end of it.

Ethan casually got back to the sandwich and looked up at Chris. "My day is only getting better. I've got a favor to ask. Would you *please* help us out with your pickup truck in the afternoon?"

Robert tore his gaze away from the faces that demanded he explain himself, and smiled at Chris. "That would be a huge favor."

"I'd owe you," said Ethan.

"Okay, but you don't try to navigate." Chris shook his head with a sigh and bit into his pizza.

"Deal."

And that should have been it. Robert would have loved to just chat about movies or the latest gossip, but unfortunately for him, lunchtime changed into "The Rob Show" with questions flying at him from each side. At least the attitudes were good. Some people excited, some joking around, some curious.

All in all coming out was a great idea. There was no reason to be sorry that he didn't wait till college.

Chapter 17

ROB

ROBERT WAS HAPPY TO slow down now that they were out of the war zone that was Ethan's house. He parked his ass on one of the wooden boxes containing Ethan's work supplies and drank some water from a plastic bottle. Now that he, Ethan, and Chris started unloading the pickup at Robert's house, out of immediate danger, the reality of what they'd done started hitting Rob with more force.

Technically speaking, they'd committed burglary. The garage belonged to Ethan's parents, and with him being locked out of there, they had no right to break in, much less take all the equipment, some of which was expensive, and carry it off. Sure, Robert and Chris were technically just two guys helping their friend move, but Ethan could have problems if his parents wanted to make this hard on him. After witnessing how distressed they had been by Ethan's accident, Robert didn't believe they'd be capable of forcibly reclaiming the contents of the basement just to make their point.

Ethan had already prepared his clothes and the likes neatly packed, but the workshop wasn't nearly ready for them when Ethan opened it with a pair of keys he'd stolen from his mom's purse earlier that day. What followed was two hours of frantic handling of chemicals, and wrapping taxidermy in paper and bubble wrap. Robert and Chris even managed to take the freezer, though they had to remove several dozen dead squirrels, birds, and rats beforehand and carry them upstairs separately. The tiny bodies were completely stiff, and Robert had a vision of their limbs or tails breaking off if they fell to the floor, though the texture of the fur was still there, making Robert feel like he was petting a dead animal. Which was probably because he was.

Ethan moved the corpses with utmost care and put them in boxes. He wanted to help carry stuff, but the thought of Ethan climbing up the stairs too quickly only to fall down and impale himself on something gave Robert such shudders that he made Ethan promise he would let Chris and him finish the job. It was strange how Ethan's accident made death an all too real possibility and made Rob find Ethan so fragile sometimes. Especially that his boyfriend's body bounced back from its frail state and though his frame was small, Ethan was as strong and confident as ever.

Robert groaned and picked up the box he'd been sitting on for the last five minutes and carried it into the open garage, only to walk straight through the door in the back and into the basement where they were establishing a temporary workspace for Ethan. Robert still hadn't figured out what he'd tell his mother, but he doubted she'd notice, as she almost never went all the way downstairs.

Ethan had the most serious expression on his face as he made his way down the stairs, holding on to the railing and with a massive vintage bird cage in his other hand. "I think we're almost done."

Robert gave a nervous laugh. "All weasels back in the freezer?" he asked, and Chris answered him with a low grunt from the farthest corner of the basement. Rob hoped that meant 'yes' because he didn't even want to imagine the smell of so many carcasses thawing.

Ethan put the cage on top of one of the boxes and made his way into the darkness. His quiet presence made Chris yelp and Rob started laughing.

Ethan took a box out of Chris's hands and hugged it to his chest. "These don't go in the freezer! They're stuffed, not frozen. Can't you see the difference?"

Chris scratched his head. "They all look stiff to me to be honest."

"Guys, take it easy." Robert smiled and put the box by the wall, alongside several other containers and bags. The stuff Ethan needed on a daily basis was already stored in Rob's bedroom, which was giving him a permanent silly smile.

"What are you gonna do with this?" asked Chris, picking up the mohair throw that Ethan used to cover his bed with.

Ethan smirked and petted the fur. "I can think of a few things. Rob made me take it."

Robert pressed his mouth shut, moving his gaze between Chris and Ethan as a hot flush spread all over his face. He loved that spread. Just thinking of it took him back to his and Ethan's first time, the proper one. "It's very nice," he said, just to tell Chris something.

"It's *veeery* nice." Ethan snorted and pulled the fur out of Chris's hands. He took a few steps closer and rubbed the mohair over Rob's cheek and neck, causing little sparks of pleasure rush for Rob's groin. "Rob loves how *nice* it is..."

Chris watched them in silence, but with curiosity in his eyes. Robert knew he and Chris were friends, that Chris didn't mind gay people, but that didn't mean he wanted to have any insight into the gay sex life of Robert and Ethan. With a low sigh, he turned to look at his boyfriend. "Yeah, I think we already established that," he said to stop Ethan from making him even more embarrassed.

The silly grin on Ethan's face waned, and he took a step back, hugging the throw. "I'll go check if enything's left in the car."

Robert sighed and brushed his hand over Ethan's shoulder to soften the blow. "Sure. We'll just finish this here and join you."

Ethan put the fur on one of the boxes and rushed to the stairs, making Rob's heart stop for a terrifying moment by tripping over the first step, but the rest of his climb was slow and steady. Sweat still managed to bead on Rob's neck.

Chris sat in an old creaking chair and stretched. "Are you gonna keep him in the basement?"

Robert blinked and groaned, slumping into a chair. "No, he'll be living with me. Upstairs," he said with a slow smile. His arms ached to cuddle Ethan again.

Chris shuffled his feet, looking away from Rob's face. "And your mom is fine with this? I mean... I know he can't get pregnant, but still..."

Robert cleared his throat. Technically, he hadn't asked her about that yet, but was sure she could be convinced. "She wanted to meet him anyway," he said with a small smile and poked Chris's arm. As unreasonable as it all was, he just couldn't bring himself to make detailed plans for each and every possibility. He could just go with the flow for once. It wasn't like the world would end if he made a mistake.

"But... but this is big, Rob. You're gonna live with him? Like some married couple? What if it doesn't work out? You get annoyed with him or something." Chris frowned and looked up at Rob with concern emanating from his face.

The smile died on Robert's face. As much as he wanted to deny it, he knew Chris was right. And the fact that he was actually worried about Rob and Ethan made it even worse. All Robert could do was to suck it up and smile. "I know, it's crazy, but I just can't stand him being so unhappy. Does that make sense?" he asked, looking up at Chris, whose frown deepened.

"Weird, but it actually makes a lot of sense. It's, like, a proper reason. Wanting to bang him every day wouldn't be."

Robert laughed out loud, immediately relaxing. "I fucking love you, man. You just say something, and all trouble goes away," he said with a small smile. He was lucky to have a friend like Chris.

Screams from upstairs had them both on their feet in a split second. One of the voices was definitely Ethan's, but the others were too muffled to recognize. Robert shot a look at Chris, dropped everything, and ran upstairs, ready to intervene. There were rarely any violent incidents in this area, but who knew? What if it was Pat coming over to his house for some crazy vendetta?

Instead, they ran all the way to the driveway, and he completely froze at the sight. Ethan's dad was pulling his son to the car, and Ethan writhed and screamed as if he were being flayed alive. Ethan's mother was no better, her face as red as her hair and voice raised to match Ethan's. Ethan was having a screaming match with his mom.

"I'm not going! I'm eighteen, and you can't make me do shit! I can even quit high school if I want to!" yelled Ethan.

The sight of Ethan being jerked away from him against his will was like rocket fuel to Robert's legs, and he rushed outside without a word. He didn't even need to say anything because the moment Ethan's parents saw him, Ethan managed to break free.

"Robert, you can't be serious about this." Ethan's mom turned to him with a frown and shook her head. "He is completely out of control, his grades have fallen, and he doesn't want to go to college all of a sudden. Who's going to support him if he moves out?"

Ethan ran over to Robert and hugged his waist to an angry groan from his father.

"I'll get a job!" Ethan yelled back while pressing his cheek into the middle of Rob's chest. "I would have gotten paid for my squirrel project if it wasn't for—"

Ethan's Mom stopped him mid-sentence. "Ethan, if I hear the word 'squirrel' one more time, I'm going to stuff you myself!" she screamed. Rob had never seen her so out of control.

He slowly put his arms around Ethan and squeezed him tight. He swallowed hard, straightening his back to be even taller and more imposing, and it was partially to make himself feel better about what he was doing. Being stern toward adults was so much easier when you could look down on both of them. "It's his decision. He can stay as long as he wants, but if he wants to move back, I won't be stopping him," he said.

"Is your mother agreeing to all this?" Ethan's mom asked in a voice that sent chills down Robert's spine. The need to protect Ethan though was too strong for him to deflate even one bit. Ethan was counting on him, cuddled up in the safety of his arms. There was no way Rob would betray that trust.

He gave Ethan's mom a slow nod. "I understand why you're worried, but he is stressed after all that happened. With all due respect, I don't think he's coping with the pressure."

"Christ! All we want for him is to get his grades in order. He is still grounded though for not coming back from prom on time. Whatever it is between you two... we can discuss." She pursed her lips.

Robert stared at her. They had to be desperate to come up with that. What would the arrangement be? A conjugal visit once a week? Before he could speak though, Ethan's dad stepped closer.

"Ethan, you might be eighteen, but you're still a child. You only become an adult when you can provide for yourself," he said, a bit red-faced.

Ethan finally turned his face away from Rob's chest. "I said I'll get a job," he hissed through his teeth.

Ethan's dad groaned. "Where will you get a job, Ethan? Think for once. You haven't even graduated from high school!"

"I'll find a part-time job to support my art freelancing, and I'll be just fine!" Ethan's grip on Rob's sweatshirt tightened.

"What's happening here?" came the all-too-familiar voice from behind, and Robert felt his knees soften like butter in a hot pan.

"Hi, Mom," he shouted back. "Ethan's things are almost unpacked," he added, hardly keeping his voice level.

His mom walked up to them in her pajamas and slippers. "What do you mean?"

He smiled at her, trying to stay as calm as possible, even though his whole body tensed up at the prospect of her denying it all. "We talked about this when you came to the kitchen last night. Ethan's gonna live with me for a while."

Mom gave him a slight frown but slowly nodded and scratched her head. "Yeah, I think you might have said something. I heard shouting though. Is everything all right?"

Ethan's mom came closer. "I am so sorry this is happening. Ethan won't listen. I can't imagine it's fine for him to stay here, right?"

Robert looked over his shoulder and positioned himself so that his mom would see how distressed Ethan was. "He needs a break," he said, looking at her with pleading eyes.

Ethan rubbed his eye and looked up at her as well. It scared Rob that he wasn't entirely sure whether Ethan was actually going to cry or just playing his part.

"I won't be a problem, Mrs. Hunter. And I'm planning to get a part-time job, so I could pay some rent…"

Robert watched his mom's face turn a shade darker, and the frown on her face only deepened when Ethan's dad spoke again.

"I know this is a very inconvenient situation for you. I am so sorry my son put you in this position. We know how much Robert cares for Ethan, but don't you think this is going too far?"

Mom took a deep breath. "Please, let's just calm down and figure this out. We have enough space so Ethan staying here for a while wouldn't be a problem. It's up to him. Ethan?"

Ethan looked to his parents, but stayed cuddled into Rob's body like a little bird looking for shelter during a storm. It made Robert feel lightheaded that it was him Ethan turned to for protection. "I'd like to stay here for a while…"

Ethan's parents stood still, looking at them in silence. Mom must have completely woken up now because she walked up to Rob and touched his arm. "Maybe make Ethan some cocoa, and I'll talk to Mr. and Mrs. Merrick, all right?" she asked, but with the way her eyes seemed a bit narrower than usual, Rob knew she didn't fall for his stupid lies. Not that he really expected her to. She tended to be forgetful and casual about little things, but he had taken it too far.

"Thanks, Mom," he said, swept by a flood of heat in his chest. He hadn't even realized how tense his muscles had become before they relaxed.

Chris cleared his throat somewhere behind Rob. "I… I'll be going, guys. See you at school," he muttered and quickly walked off to his pickup truck, gesturing for Rob to call him.

Ethan looked back at his parents once more, but soon Robert led him back to the house with a heavy heart. He hoped this wasn't all a terrible mistake. What if Chris was right, and they'd fall out after moving in together? He opened the door and let Ethan in first before following. The sound of it closing didn't give him nearly as much relief as he expected.

Ethan on the other hand took a deep breath and rubbed his eye again. "Oh my, God, your mom is gonna hate me," he moaned and pinched the base of his nose. "And now my head is starting to hurt."

Robert's mouth went dry. "Do you want me to help you upstairs? You could lie down while I settle things with Mom."

"No, I'll stay. I don't want her to think I'm weaseling out of talking to her. But I'll need to lie down soon. Thank you for standing up for me." He looked up at Robert and hugged him tight. He seemed so small and delicate nestled in Rob's arms, which were as thick as Ethan's legs.

Robert swallowed and leaned down to nuzzle Ethan's nose, slowly leading him to the living room. There, at least, Ethan could lounge on the sofa until Mom was back. Rob could only hope she wouldn't disinherit him for that stunt.

They sat together on the sofa, with Ethan's head in Robert's lap, which at least gave Robert something to do with his hands as he anxiously awaited his mom's return.

"I hope I find a job soon," Ethan muttered all of a sudden, breaking the heavy silence.

"It'll be fine," said Robert, even though he felt like he was sitting on pins and needles. Slowly, he moved his fingers across the soft skin of Ethan's cheek, swirled them over the ear and brushed away the silky hair. Ethan was so beautiful.

The door slammed so hard the windows shook.

"Robert," his mom called out. "What on earth was all that? Both of you have a lot of explaining to do!"

Robert swallowed and put his hand over Ethan's ear. Loud sounds would be hard for him to stand while having one of those headaches. "We're here, Mom," he muttered.

Ethan put his hand over Robert's and slowly opened his eye. "I'm so sorry Mrs. Hunter. I never meant for this to happen."

Robert's mom pulled an armchair close to the sofa with a vicious screech of wood making a mark on the floor. "Robert, that was so low. How are you going to make it up to me?" She dropped into the seat and crossed her arms on her chest. Her skin was so flushed with anger, Rob half expected vapor coming out of her ears.

He stared at her, his heart beating hard in his chest. "I'm sorry, it was all so sudden..."

She silenced him with a raised hand. "Chris had a pickup truck. That didn't look sudden to me."

Ethan scrambled to sit up, his moves heavy as if he were trapped in molasses. "It's because I have this project I need to finish, and my parents locked my workshop. I need to finish it so bad, there's a store in L.A. waiting for it. I can't do it in my house. I swear I won't be a problem."

"Yeah, I promise you won't even notice there are more people in the house," said Robert, squeezing Ethan's hand gently. "I can bring you breakfast in bed every day for the next month to make it up to you. I'm so sorry, Mom."

Mom groaned and rubbed her face. "Okay. So where will Ethan be staying?" Robert was sure this question was a trap.

He pressed his mouth shut and shrugged. "With me?"

Ethan entwined their fingers, but seemed extremely interested in the carpet.

"Oh, so you're nesting already?" Mom pouted as she looked at them skeptically. "Are you using protection? I doubt the school covers sex education for gay people."

Ethan's grip became so hard it hurt. "We... I..."

Robert looked at her, stunned. "Is this really when we have 'the talk', Mom? With my boyfriend in the room?" he muttered, feeling sweat beading on his back. Was she implying they would both be promiscuous and infect one another with some ugly diseases? Just because they were gay? That was so unlike her.

"Well, you're both going to be staying under my roof. And I'm assuming your boyfriend is involved in the sex, so yes, we need to have 'the talk'."

Ethan groaned. "We know about stuff..."

Mom squinted slightly. "I sure hope you do because the things I see at the hospital are not pretty. Especially men are extremely careless because they think they can do anything just because none of them will ever get pregnant."

"Mom, we're using condoms, and water-based lube, and this is incredibly embarrassing," rasped Rob with his face burning up. Ethan seemed to share his sentiment, as he hid his face in Rob's arm.

Mom rolled her eyes. "Good. So now you know how I felt, put on the spot in front of Ethan's parents. You can go. We'll talk details later. And I won't be forgetting about those breakfasts." She got up from the armchair and walked off to the kitchen.

Robert took in a raspy breath, melting into the couch. "I love you?" he said loudly enough so his mom could hear.

Ethan exhaled and collapsed to the sofa like a puppet without strings.

Chapter 18

ETHAN

ETHAN SAT ON A blanket and watched Robert with a dreamy smile. A week in Rob's house had passed in the blink of an eye, and with graduation less than two months away, he'd never felt as peaceful. They were becoming the 'it-couple' at school, but he couldn't care less, too engaged in his squirrel project and finding new places on Rob's body that he hadn't kissed yet. The idea of topping Rob also kept swirling in his mind, but it just never seemed to be the right moment for it. Oh well, they had time.

In his new workshop in Rob's basement Ethan found the peace to finish his elk project as well. Robert was so supportive it was almost making Ethan feel like a parasite, because he still hadn't found a part-time job. When Ethan showed Rob the finished *Of Mice and Elk*, Rob showered him with so many compliments, it had Ethan's inner weasel doing backflips. Not only did Rob cheer Ethan on, but he also proposed taking proper photos of the finished thing, and it was a godsend. If Ethan were to take photos himself they would be nothing as professional as what Rob could do with the practice he had working on his food blog.

It had been Rob's idea to do the photo shoot in the woods around town, and they came to the place they'd found earlier, where the trees weren't growing too close together, but there were plenty of bushes and little hills for a captivating scenery. Robert kept telling Ethan that he would manipulate the pictures to give them an eerie feel, but that did not mean he wouldn't be careful with the photos themselves. In fact, he brought two lamps, equipped with those weird white umbrellas that, according to Rob, were there to make the light softer. He had considered getting hold of liquid nitrogen to create fog, but he eventually decided against it because it would be too much fuss. It could be photoshopped on, he said, making Ethan even more enamored with him.

And there Ethan was—sitting on a blanket with the post-winter chill barely there and a large picnic basket next to him—watching Rob assume acrobatic positions all over the elk's head.

"Oh yeah, stay like that." Ethan laughed when Rob got into a position in which Ethan could see the top of his ass peeking out above his jeans. The comment got him a low groan, but Robert didn't even turn back, too focused on the task at hand. Ethan had brought along something special he had made for Rob as a thank you for all his help and protection. He could only hope Rob would like it. For now though, he sniggered when Robert rolled to his stomach, with his face dead serious, as if he were hunting that elk, not photographing it.

"You don't know how much I appreciate this. It's gonna look so professional on my new website." Ethan lay down on the blanket, his heart swelling with pride that he had such an amazing boyfriend. Good-looking, kind, talented, a great cook, and an artist as well. He wanted to be sure Rob knew how much Ethan appreciated him, but he wasn't yet sure how to do that exactly. He was working on it though. Maybe some small commitment ceremony or something? It all sounded so cheesy in his mind.

Robert got to his knees and looked back at Ethan with a small smile. He shuffled closer to the head, and Ethan realized he had to be taking photos of the key in the little door in the animal's neck. "I'm enjoying myself. If it can help you get more customers, all the better."

"This is going to be my showpiece, you know, something that will bring potential customers to my site for the 'wow' factor. Then, they will hopefully be excited to see what else I have and buy some of the smaller pieces. But I'll also send out the photos to galleries. They might be actually able to afford it. If I sold it I'd have money to start renting in Seattle."

Robert stalled for a moment, but then gently opened the tiny door and peeked inside. Earlier that day, he had made a miniature photographic lamp, using a small flashlight and white cloth, and he was now positioning it inside the head. "That would be great for your career."

"Have you…" Ethan wasn't sure how to start this conversation, but he had been pondering on it for the last weeks, since he started eating the amazing food Rob prepared, seeing him so passionately updating his website, and interacting with his 'fans' on social media. Ethan had sneakily looked into some of the stats of Rob's blog, *The Secret Foodie*, and discovered that he had over two thousand likes on Facebook. "How are the ads on your site going?"

Robert shrugged. "They're good. I don't need to get another job as long as I keep it up," he said with a small smile, maneuvering the lens to catch the inner side of the elk from a particular angle.

"Maybe you wouldn't even have to go to college." Ethan laughed, but meant every word. His heart rate sped up as he imagined the possibility of a life with Robert, living together in Seattle, both engaging in their passions, having leisurely breakfasts in bed, and always being there for each other.

Robert chuckled. "I don't earn *that* much. And health insurance won't pay itself," he said from where he was lying in the pale grass.

Ethan huffed loudly and rolled over to his back, looking at Rob upside down. Always so practical. "If you put more work into it, maybe it would grow faster," he suggested, but Rob only shook his head and made a few more photos.

"So nice. I would buy that if I owned a gallery."

"You just say that 'cause you love me." Ethan smiled, even though he knew his elk was amazing. He loved teasing Rob.

"Yeah, maybe you're right," said Rob, making Ethan sit up at once and throw a little rock at him, but a little smile never left his face.

"How can you say that!"

"I can't let your head get too big. Your tiny weasel body wouldn't be able to handle it," said Rob, grinning back at him as he slowly withdrew and closed the tiny door.

"I compare my work to others, and I think I really have a shot. Loads of people are loving my stuff online. I sold a pair of earrings just yesterday."

"The ones you made out of tails?" asked Robert, slowly approaching the blanket and switching off the lamps on his way.

"Yes, with the black stone. I worked till two in the morning to finish those. You were asleep when I sneaked in." Ethan's smile widened. Living with Robert was like a never ending sleepover. With sex. God, the sex was amazing. Rob was always so curious about Ethan's body and eager to explore. He definitely wasn't just a dick and ass kind of guy, and being with him, Ethan discovered that his whole body could sometimes feel like a big erogenous zone.

"I felt you coming in." Robert smiled and raised the camera to his face, adjusting the focus with the lens, which was now directed at Ethan.

"I felt you *coming*." Ethan looked straight into the lens and touched his top lip with the tip of his tongue. He noticed Robert swallow just before making a photo.

"Okay, now let's take a picture that I can actually show to my mom," chuckled Rob as he came closer.

"Oh yeah? Was that one going to your spank bank?" Ethan snorted, but kneeled by the basket to look like a good boy.

Robert let out a quiet growl but moved closer, pressing the shutter release over and over, as if trying to find the best angle. "*You* are my spank bank."

Ethan couldn't help breath catching in his throat and blood rushing to his face. "Or am I your *spunk* bank?" he whispered as his gaze strayed to Robert's big hands. Whenever he looked at the veins on Rob's forearms, on how thick those hands were compared to his own, he couldn't help but think about them holding him down, picking him up. Robert's strength turned him on so much.

Robert groaned, hiding his flush behind the camera. "Yeah, that didn't come out right..."

Ethan licked his lips and pushed his hair out of his face. "You have condoms in that basket?" He pulled up the wicker lid.

"No. Let's forget about the spank bank. Smile at me," asked Robert, slowly kneeling down at the edge of the blanket.

"I wouldn't take the quarterback for such a keen photographer." Ethan sat down and gave a wide smile. "I thought you were completely different just a few months ago."

Robert's shoulders slouched, and he put down the camera with a quiet sigh. His brows were low over his eyes as he looked at Ethan. So handsome. Ethan wanted to kiss him. "Don't laugh, but I don't like football all that much."

Those words came as such a surprise that Ethan cocked his head to the side and frowned. "What do you mean? You work so hard to be good at it." Ethan delved his hand into the basket, curious what glorious deliciousness Rob had prepared for the outing.

Robert sat cross-legged opposite him and shrugged. "If I get a scholarship, I won't be in as much debt after college."

Ethan watched him, dumbstruck, with a box of strawberries in his hand. "Huh? You wouldn't do it otherwise?"

Robert sighed and shuffled closer to open the basket. Inside were little packets of cotton, clear jars, and plastic containers with food. Since coming to live with Rob, Ethan had started to eat far too much, and he needed to watch his calorie intake. But it wouldn't be at this meal. "I'm not all that competitive. Don't get me wrong, I like sports, and fitness, and all that, but I'd rather just do running, or play football with friends. For fun, not for the scores."

Ethan cocked his head to the side, unsure what to say, so he decided on a joke. "I wouldn't date you if you weren't a quarterback. School royalty and all that."

Robert smiled at him, and his body relaxed. "So it does have some perks." He reached into the basket and started pulling out all the little portions of food. A 'sample menu', he called it.

"I bet all the closeted gay boys are now hitting on you." Ethan gently punched Rob's arm, which was so freaking firm he wanted to lick it. "You're just not telling me." The truth was that as much as he joked about it, a part of him did wonder if an out-Rob wouldn't get tempted by some other pretty face. One that wouldn't cause him so much trouble. The way Rob stilled for a split second was answer enough.

"Oh." Ethan swallowed, unsure what to say. "They can dream, right?" He laughed nervously, opening one of the boxes to get his hands busy. It contained chestnut-sized white balls, drizzled with a red sauce. They smelled so sweet his mouth went moist the moment the scent hit him.

"Obviously. You're far too much trouble for me to have time for anyone else," chuckled Robert, leaning forward. He caught a strand of Ethan's hair and pushed it behind his ear.

Ethan took a deep breath. Rob always found a way to calm his insecurities. It reminded Ethan that Rob was in fact a weasel like him. That in turn prompted something else altogether. "I've got something for you." He reached for the large travel bag he'd brought his present in.

Robert grinned, leaving the basket for now as he looked down at Ethan's lap, his eyes sparkling with interest.

Ethan unzipped the bag and pulled out the large box wrapped in simple brown paper. "A little thank you for all your help." He said and passed it to Rob.

Robert accepted the gift, glancing at Ethan with those sweet, bright eyes. He was so handsome it hurt. "I like helping you," he said but started gently unwrapping the paper. Each time one layer was off, Ethan felt his heartbeat pick up. Would Rob even enjoy the present?

His anxiety peaked the moment Robert pulled back the lid and froze, his face relaxing into an expression that was hard to read. He pulled out the white weasel Ethan had dressed in a tiny version of Rob's green and yellow letter jacket. There was even a miniature football attached to the weasel's paw. When he was planning this, weeks ago, he wanted it to be something Rob would remember him by when they parted, but now, Ethan hoped they never would.

Robert adjusted on the blanket, gently cradling the piece of taxidermy in his large palm, and stroked the fur on its bare belly. He then touched the ball, the forehead, and his mouth slowly stretched into a smile.

"You like it?" Ethan got closer, eager to hear more about his creation.

Robert slowly looked up, and the sun made his eyes look almost transparent. Only then it seemed that the cogs in his joints oiled up, and he nodded. "It's... really amazing. Wow. I've never got anything like this."

Ethan couldn't help but start laughing. "I can't imagine anyone ever stuffed a weasel for you."

"No, never." Robert's eyes twinkled, and he made a move toward Ethan, but then suddenly seemed to remember about the taxidermy and placed it back in the box with utmost care. As if it were the most precious item he'd ever touched.

"Now you're gonna have something to decorate that empty room of yours." Though since Ethan had moved in, there had been a significant increase in decoration.

"I'm gonna make a display shelf for it," declared Rob, and it didn't sound like a joke at all, especially with the gentle way he moved his fingers over the side of the box.

"Oh, yeah? Maybe you should feed it as well?" Ethan passed Robert a tiny box with sunflower seeds.

"You think he should have lunch with us?" Robert got to his knees and leaned over to press his lips against Ethan's.

Ethan slid his fingers to Rob's nape to hold the kiss for a little longer. "Yes, he likes his food, you know."

Robert's mouth spread into a smile against Ethan's lips, and he pulled back. "Who wouldn't? But those are too big for him," he said, taking a peek into the basket, only to pull out another box and pick up a small knife with his other hand.

Ethan gently put the taxidermy back on the blanket. "You're the best weasel daddy."

A flush bloomed on Robert's cheeks, but he took out a thin tortilla wrap and started meticulously slicing off a few thin pieces of it. "I need to do my job right, now that you delivered."

"Let's give him a little photoshoot." Ethan smiled, watching Robert prepare a tiny meal for the weasel. His heart couldn't be melting any more. It was so cute to see Robert being so responsive to the gift. Within minutes, he created a miniature picnic on the edge of the blanket, with lids of small sauce containers serving as plates, and even a mock-mug made out of cardboard. His weasel version looked amazing in the setup.

"It looks weaselicious. Makes me imagine all the things we can do with stuff like this. We could do a rat tea party or theme foods with my projects..." Ethan came up to Robert on all fours and hugged him from behind. Robert responded with a low hum as he photographed the weasel, leaning back into Ethan's arms.

"Yeah, we could buy some doll pottery."

"We're gonna have fun with this." Ethan nestled his face in the soft fabric of Rob's hoodie and kissed him between the shoulder blades.

Rob leaned back and pointed the camera at their feet again before making a picture. "I think it could be a fun thing to do together."

"I have the best boyfriend in the world," Ethan murmured and nuzzled Rob's back. Now if only he could get Rob on board about the move to Seattle, they would be like two peas in a pod.

Chapter 19

ROB

Two months passed like a summer storm. Robert was surprised how smoothly he and Ethan settled into living together. Mom was popping in and out of the house as usual, and spent some time with them every few days, but for the most part, it was just the two of them. Fortunately, Ethan's parents came around, and even invited them all to dinner, which was an incredibly stiff affair, but it was worth enduring for the sake of mending the canyon of doom between Ethan and his parents.

The photos of taxidermy combined with food were a huge success on Rob's blog, and since then, he and Ethan continued to do more and more elaborate projects together. They fed off each other's energy and bonded over their work in a way that Rob had never even considered possible. Even Chris was starting to get a bit jealous of the time Rob spent with Ethan. They were in love, had amazing sex and intimacy, but through having passions that combined together in such an unusual way, they could never get enough of each other. There was always a new project to discuss, progress to talk about, or an idea that would spur a flood of text messages.

Even school was good. Rob and Pat were carefully neutral to each other, and Ethan wasn't harassed anymore. Some people still disliked him, but that was okay as long as they didn't openly confront him. There was no person in the world who'd be universally loved. Robert was surprised that Derek, Ethan's estranged prom date, actually kept trying to chat Ethan up even after he and Rob came out as a couple. But he wasn't too worried about that since Ethan was clearly not encouraging it.

Robert's grades were good, and he was anticipating the impending graduation. Ethan did find a part-time job at a local Choco Panda, and Rob always served as his chauffeur. It was nice to pick him up and brighten his day with a hug, or a kiss. Not to mention that Rob considered the uniform Ethan hated so much insanely cute. It was a black and white cap with round ears and a fitted black shirt with white sleeves.

Still, Rob was impressed by Ethan's determination. He kept complaining about having no time for himself, yet kept a part-time job in the evening, went to school, and still found time to do his art. Sometimes, Rob was actually worried Ethan didn't sleep enough, but those thoughts were dispersed every time Ethan sacrificed some of his sleeping time in order to have sex. Rob couldn't get enough of this new semi-adult life, and sometimes his thoughts drifted to possibilities of life after college. He knew it was cheesy, but there were people who spent their lives with their first boy- or girlfriends, so why would their relationship be doomed just because they were young? He was positive that whatever happened, they would at least try to make it work.

When Robert parked in front of Choco Panda, he could already see Ethan's lonely figure behind the counter and looking out for him.

He still had five minutes to go, and Rob could bet he was dying to go home. But today, Rob had something to tell Ethan that would cheer up that sad panda.

He closed the car and entered the funky-looking shop, which at this time of night was rather empty. He greeted Ethan with a wave and smiled at him, walking past a group of teenagers munching on donuts. "Can I get some muffins to go?"

Ethan pouted and shook his head at him. "I'm still waiting for Becky to swap with me." He tapped his fingers on the counter.

Robert grinned at him. "So, you're not going to give me any?"

Ethan raised his eyebrows so high they reached above the rims of his glasses. "Oh. That wasn't a joke?" He walked over to a glass display with muffins decorated with sugary ears.

Robert snorted and leaned over the black and white counter. "I just want some cake, sweetie." He looked at the way Ethan bent his body to reach his favorite flavor, caramelized bacon and maple syrup, and smiled to himself, imagining how he could mold his body to Ethan's.

Ethan meticulously packed the two muffins in a cute cardboard box with a manga-style illustration and handed it to Rob. "Here you go, sir. I hope your purchase is pandalicious. Would you like to donate a dollar to our charity and support the conservation of giant pandas in China?" asked Ethan in the most monotone voice imaginable.

Robert ignored the sarcasm and winked at him. "Make it three dollars."

"Three? I am sure it will make some panda really happy." Rob was sure there was a shadow of a smirk on that pale face though. They both knew which panda enjoyed Rob's attentions more than anything. Ethan passed Rob the box with muffins the moment Becky finally stormed in through the back door.

"Sorry I'm late Ethan, my cat pooped in the bathtub," she said as she ran past them and behind the counter, already putting on her cap.

Ethan frowned. "That is the worst excuse I have ever heard."

"Don't worry, I kept him entertained," said Robert, slowly brushing his fingers over the top of Ethan's hand. He couldn't wait to tell him the news. He'd even taken his tablet with him so that they wouldn't have to wait till getting home.

"Oh, I'd love Robert to *entertain* me." Becky laughed and elbowed Ethan with a wide smile.

Ethan put a hand over his face. "See, Rob, this is what I have to deal with."

"Horrible. I bet you just can't wait to get home," said Robert, winking at Becky, who grinned in return and pinned on her badge.

Ethan took off his cap and walked out from behind the counter. "Have fun, Becky. Bye!" He stroked Rob's arm as they walked through the shop.

"Anything interesting happened?" asked Rob like he did every evening. He opened the door for Ethan and followed him outside to his car. He couldn't wait to put his hands on Ethan, smell his warmth, and tell him everything. He was sure Ethan would wrap his slinky weasel body all around him at the news.

"Nah, I was just thinking about all the stuff we can do after school's over. I can't wait."

Robert grinned and got into the car. "About that... there's something I need to show you." He opened the glove compartment and pulled out the tablet.

Ethan smiled and leaned closer from his seat. "What is it?" He already sounded excited.

"Gimme a kiss first." Rob nuzzled his cheek, opening the browser. His heart was pulsing with joy.

Ethan's smile widened, and he leaned over. His lips were all minty, ready for a little mouth-to-mouth action. "I'm always ready for this."

Robert gently sucked on the succulent lips, but eventually withdrew and rested his head on Ethan's shoulder. There it was, the classy layout of the website of one of the most famous fashion magazines in the world, showcasing Robert's new blogpost, the one with taxidermy mice having Victorian high tea. His heart was drumming like crazy every time he read the short commentary. The editor called their work 'unique', 'refreshing', and 'beautifully odd'. And the number of subscribers of *The Secret Foodie* had skyrocketed within hours.

Rob's chest swelled with pride at the way Ethan's eye grew wider. "Oh, my fucking God! Robert! Do you know what this means? Fuck! I need to check my e-mail, see if it got me new orders."

"You're even named. Look." Robert grinned even wider and kissed Ethan's ear, inhaling the sweet scent of the hair. He wanted to celebrate on the furry throw.

"This is amazing. Robert, *this* could be the beginning of something big. Isn't that what we've been waiting for?" Ethan gripped the tablet and pulled it from Rob's hands. "We have to work more now. Maybe contact some other magazines?"

Robert relaxed into the seat and pulled out one of the muffins. Ethan's enthusiasm was endearing, and at the same time, Rob honestly believed his boyfriend could make it as an artist in the future. He had enough talent and drive for a hundred people. "Sure, why not."

"Maybe we could do a project where we take the taxidermy to different restaurants and make mini meals out of their menus, and you could review the restaurants. We could build a business on that, make the ads more expensive." Ethan's eye was glued to the screen.

Robert sighed and rustled the little weasel's hair. Visions of fame and glory sank the moment Rob thought of being a thirty-year-old person with little education and no qualifications. "That sounds interesting, but I don't think I could dedicate enough time to something this big while in college."

Ethan's blue eye turned to him as he gripped Rob's hand. "Rob... I was thinking about this. Isn't this the breakthrough we needed? Doesn't it show you how much people love your website?"

Robert stared at him, the muffin raised halfway to his mouth. Ethan was a dreamer, and while Rob understood that, he also didn't think they could afford being dreamers in this economy. It wouldn't be fair if he tried to convert Ethan to his point of view, but Rob knew he himself needed stability. "What if they stop reading it in a few years? It's not like it means something to a potential employer."

"But it's doing well now. If we don't grab this opportunity, it might not be there in a few years. You can go to college any time. Just think about it. We could be living and working in Seattle, you could expand your website, I am already working on all sorts of projects for sale. I earned three hundred bucks on the jewelry last month. I know it's not super-much, but it's growing." Ethan bit his lip.

Robert sighed and put down the muffin. "Look, I know you're passionate about this, but what will I do if it doesn't pay off? I can't take that risk," he said, looking into Ethan's eye in search of understanding. The atmosphere in the car suddenly became all too dense.

"So what? It's better to go into debt, so you can do a course at college that you don't even like that much?" Ethan pouted and pulled away.

Robert frowned, unsure what to make of it. "That's what I have been working for all this time."

Ethan slouched in his seat, silent for a while too long. Rob knew well what that meant. Ethan was trying not to say something offensive.

At least he *was* trying. "But you're so good at the food stuff. Why wouldn't you try? It makes you happy."

Robert bit his lip. He couldn't deny any of that, and he was torn between Ethan's logic and his. "How many food bloggers are out there? It's not only about being good at it. You need to be lucky as well, and I'm not sure if it's a good idea to build a future on that alone. I can do this on the side in college and see how it goes."

Ethan turned the tablet to Rob. "Isn't this a good sign? You won't... *We* won't be able to do it on the same scale in college."

Robert pulled the tablet to his chest and sighed, the steady pulsing in his head starting to become unbearable. "But I don't want to push you into doing it my way. You know yourself that you are the star here. I just... make food. You can't even taste it on the photo," he muttered, slightly deflated as soon as those words left his mouth. It was all true.

"But you make it look so good, and you take the photos. It's most of the effect in that. I can't take photos for shit. Rob... where do you even want to go to college?" Ethan took a deep breath and turned his head away, as if suddenly finding the dashboard fascinating.

Rob let out a sharp breath, looking at the panda mascot painted on the entrance to Choco Panda. It didn't cheer him up for once. "I was thinking to go to the closest one so that I can save money on accommodation and all that..."

"But basically, we won't be able to do projects together? You won't have time for it..." It sounded like 'you won't have time for me' in Rob's mind, and he leaned closer to pull Ethan against his chest for a hug.

"Come on, I'll always have time for you. You know that, right?" He pressed a kiss to the side of Ethan's head. Disappointing Ethan gave him cramps, but he couldn't just go with a crazy plan. It was about his future.

"No, I don't." It felt like getting stabbed. "You're gonna spend your time at college, I'm not gonna be a part of that, and how often will we see each other? Twice a month?"

Robert pulled away, staring at him without words to say. "You're really moving all the way to Seattle? In a month?" he uttered, hardly hearing his own words as his whole body went into a cacophony of nerves.

Ethan clenched his hands on the cap with panda ears. "Yes. I can't just stay here. I've told you. Did you just think it was a fantasy?"

Robert drew in a sharp breath. It was as if there suddenly grew a wall between him and Ethan, and he had no clue how to penetrate it. Would Ethan really move out so soon, just leave him here? "I thought... it was just vague plans..."

"No, I've been saving up for this like crazy. I need you to be in this with me."

Rob wasn't even sure if Ethan's tone was more pleading or demanding.

"Whoa, hold on. You can't say things like that..." Robert swallowed the bile rising in his throat. "I let you live with me, I helped you... but you can't just assume I'll jump headfirst into this kind of idea."

Ethan took off his glasses and rubbed his eye. "I know, I know, but how do you see this thing working otherwise?"

Robert sighed and looked through the windshield. With his pulse drumming in his temples like it did, he doubted he could focus and come up with anything. "I... don't know. It's a bit sudden."

"It's not sudden. We talked about it when I was considering quitting high school. I just see this massive opportunity, an article about us on such a big website, and I wanna grab it, but you don't believe in yourself. I don't get it. Everyone thinks you're great. What's stopping you?"

"I'm just being practical, Ethan. There is no guarantee that it'll actually turn into a steady job. I've made a decision a few years ago, why are you questioning it?"

Ethan kicked the side of the door without much force. "Because I want to be with you."

Robert swallowed and leaned closer again. His hand found Ethan's, and he slowly moved his nose along Ethan's ear. How could he respond to that? Of course, he wanted that, too. Who wouldn't? He'd most likely never meet anyone quite like Ethan. There was no one else like him. "Me too…"

Ethan didn't respond to the touch, but didn't pull away either. "Let's just go home."

Robert stayed still for several moments, but when nothing happened, he straightened up in the seat and switched on the engine. He didn't know what to say so he chose to give Ethan time to think about all this in peace.

Ethan leaned his head against the window, and Rob was worried his head would bump on it if they took a sharp turn, so he drove with extra care.

Mom was working the night again, and with both Ethan and Robert not in the mood to talk, getting back home was like entering a tomb. Rob never stopped following Ethan with his gaze, and he leaned against the wall, with a dull pressure in his chest and throat. "You want to eat something?" he eventually asked.

Ethan took off the Choco Panda shirt as soon as they got in. "Nah, I had a muffin at work." He went to the kitchen and poured himself some juice.

Robert gravitated toward him but stopped at the threshold, unsure whether he should invade Ethan's personal space, which seemed to have grown to the size of a room.

Ethan leaned against the countertop in just his skinny jeans, making it impossible for Robert to focus properly without glancing at the pink nipples. "I'll do some more work later. Um... Maybe I'll sleep in the guest room to not wake you up," he said without looking up.

Robert stared at him, and cold phantom hands clenched around his neck. Since they'd moved in together, all nights had been spent in Robert's bed, and he was starting to take it for granted. Was Ethan really so upset with him?

Ethan put on a hoodie he'd left laying around in the kitchen and drank his juice. He finally looked up from above the glass, his single blue eye piercing right into Robert, and it was like standing in the polar wind with little shards of ice blowing his way.

Rob cleared his throat and pulled on his index finger. "Are you angry?"

"I don't know. I know I'm not happy, but I don't wanna force you into anything. I don't wanna lose you either, and at the moment, I'm not really sure where we're both heading." Ethan zipped up his hoodie and put away the empty glass.

Robert swallowed, and stepped into the kitchen. His feet felt as if he were wearing lead shoes, but he needed to be closer. "Even if we live in different cities, I could come over for the weekends," he uttered.

"We won't be able to do projects together anymore." Ethan took a few steps away with a miserable face.

Robert looked at his feet. He had no words to respond to that. He wanted to share his passions with Ethan, wake up next to him, make him dinner, and watch him succeed. But this whole thing was happening too quickly.

"Why don't you say anything?" Ethan groaned and took a deep breath. "Do you not care about this? Is a safety net all you want? Is that really what you're about?" Each question was louder, resonating within the walls of the empty house and threatening to hit Robert.

Rob opened his mouth, but with his lungs burning, it took him a while to be able to steady his voice enough to speak. "Of course I do. I love you."

"I don't know if I can just live away from you." Ethan frantically rubbed his eye. "You know me, I'm not good at socializing, I won't meet anyone else, but you'll be at college with tons of new people. You'll probably meet some hot footballer and soon enough you'll be visiting me once a month, and then even that will dry up." Ethan took deep breaths that couldn't hide his exasperation.

That stung. Robert inhaled sharply and looked away, fighting the prickling around his eyes. "Don't you trust me? Do you really think I would cheat on you?"

Ethan curled his hands into his sleeves. "I don't know! Look how much life has changed for us in just the last six months. How do I know what it's going to be like in a year's time?"

Robert pressed his lips together, and his jaw clenched so hard it hurt. Lightheaded, he'd love to just curl up in his lair and lick the wound.

"You don't want to even try and work with me?" Ethan groaned, a frown deepening on his face. "Couldn't you take the plunge just once? What's the worst that could happen? Jesus Christ!"

Robert folded his arms across his chest and swallowed, finding it hard to look up into the accusing eye. Ethan did not trust him. He believed Rob was a coward.

Ethan screamed in frustration and threw his hands in the air. "And you've got nothing to say!" He walked up to Rob and for a moment it seemed like he wanted to push him, but in the end just passed him in the door. "You're just as talkative as my rats!"

Robert looked over his arm, shocked by the comparison. He couldn't breathe. Was this Ethan leaving him? He had no idea, and he didn't know anyone he could ask.

He watched Ethan's tense silhouette disappear in the corridor, followed by muttering and a slamming door. The kitchen had never felt so empty and uninviting.

Robert slowly forced his muscles to move and walked up to the fridge. He got quicker by the second, and soon, his knife was dancing over the chopping board, leaving tiny particles of chocolate as the milk heated up in the pot. He didn't want to think about anything but this. He'd make delicious, smooth chocolate, thick enough to line his aching insides. Then, searing pain flashed through his hand, and he gasped, looking at the red pool, rapidly swallowing the chopped chocolate.

"Fuck," he uttered, moving toward the sink and leaving red droplets on the floor. He hissed when the cold water flooded the cut, and he turned his finger so that the stream wouldn't hit the inner side of the flap of skin on the tip of his index finger. Just like that, there were tears on his cheeks, and he couldn't hold back a sob as he watched the pinkish water going down the drain.

Chapter 20

ETHAN

ETHAN COULDN'T SLEEP IN the guest room. He tossed and turned all night, missing Robert's warm embrace, the strong arm around his waist, and the chats before falling asleep. The argument from a few hours before kept spinning in his head like that freaking spinning top from *Inception*. He wished he could have expressed himself differently, but it was too late now. Robert probably didn't want to see his face. It was the silence from Rob that brought out the monster in Ethan. They couldn't even have a proper conversation because Robert would just bottle it all up and stand there without a word.

Ethan couldn't get over the fact that their art projects received such recognition, with the comments and e-mails swelling overnight, yet Robert would still not want to give it a shot. Ethan knew Rob was happiest when he could work on his food stuff. Sure, Rob was also ridiculously pragmatic and cared too much about safety, but at the end of the day, his foodie blog was his passion, and it made Ethan physically ache when he thought Rob would give it up to study something he wasn't all that interested in and spend time playing a sport he wasn't that keen on either.

At one point in the night, Ethan noticed he was getting so worked up he clenched his fingers into fists so hard he scratched himself. He couldn't believe they would have such a horrible fight just before graduation, just when Ethan had finished a present he had made for Robert. Something that was to cement them as a couple. He felt like the biggest idiot. On the other hand, if Rob was so obsessed with a safety net that he was willing to give up his passion for some time and still make plans to visit Ethan as often as he could, then maybe Ethan was selfish to try and push him in another direction.

Since he couldn't sleep anyway, Ethan got the laptop into bed and started absentmindedly checking the e-mails received overnight. There were requests for features, some praise, a crazy vegan telling him his artwork was a disgrace to humanity, quite a few sales on his online store, and one e-mail that got him to sit up and blink.

An art gallery in Seattle wanted to buy *Of Mice and Elk*. His heart started pounding like mad. The price for it was ten thousand dollars. When he set it, he didn't really think he'd sell it quickly, or at all for that matter. It had to be the popularity of the magazine feature that made him look more legit, not like a teenager working out of his boyfriend's basement. The money made from a sale like that would help him rent a place in Seattle and work on other projects without struggling with money for a few months.

He answered the e-mail in the most professional manner he could muster, but what popped up in his mind in an instant was just how much he wanted to share the news with Robert. There was no one in his life who would appreciate it more. Sure, he would tell his parents later, but Rob was a priority. And he wouldn't do it by text just because he was embarrassed by the earlier outburst. He had to face the music and apologize. Only now it hit him that it wasn't fair for him to push Robert so hard. Rob was the one person to believe in him, support his decisions, even if they were risky, and love him despite his missing eye and other health problems. Ethan wished he could be more like Rob. His first step would be to accept Robert's decision about college, even if he didn't like it.

He couldn't cook for shit so breakfast in bed was out of the question, but he could think of something else to make amends for his nastiness.

He took a shower and washed his hair to look presentable. Just in case he would meet Rob's mom in the corridor, he put on a pair of jeans as he walked down to the basement. The present for Rob was something he had been working on for a while. It was a black weasel, to match the white one in a letter jacket. This one had an eye patch, tiny black-rimmed glasses Ethan had scavenged off a doll he bought at a garage sale, and Ethan had even made a bone necklace for it. It sat in a wooden chair and slouched over its paws, and he knew exactly what he intended to put into those tiny fingers.

With his nerves twisting and turning, he took his project over to Rob's room, nervous that all he might get could be an order to leave. He was about to prove that he really was a bit insane. He stood in front of the door, and the tension in his body was already making him sweat. He squeezed his fingers on the little chair he was holding and imagined Robert on the bed, curled into a ball on his right side, like he liked to sleep. On nights when Ethan worked downstairs till late, he would slip under the comforter and hug Rob from behind. Sometimes, Rob would even wake up, and they'd kiss or have sex, and fall asleep covered in sweat and come.

Ethan gently pressed on the door handle and peeked inside, cringing at the sight in front of him. The bed was at the center of the room, and in the moonlight streaming through the window, Robert seemed so small and lonely curled up beneath the comforter. He'd pulled the cover around him like a tight cocoon and lay on his left side for once. Ethan choked up when he realized Rob was facing the weasel figure on the nightstand, and lay on the furry bedspread they always had sex on.

He slipped inside and quietly walked over there. Both weasels wouldn't fit on top of the nightstand, so he kneeled and put the black one on the floor before reaching out to get the white one down as well.

"What are you doing?" Robert's voice was raspy and flat.

Ethan froze, suddenly overtaken by panic. He wasn't ready yet! "Just this... thing."

"Are you moving out?" whispered Robert, but his body didn't move by an inch. Suddenly, even the cool night air was burning hot against Ethan's skin.

He got the white weasel to the floor and let out a long breath. "No." He plopped to his ass and ran his fingers through his hair. Why was it so hard to find the words now when they were needed?

Finally, the rustle of covers made him look up at Rob, who sat cross-legged on the mattress, his face so blank Ethan wanted to cry in shame for making him like this.

"I just... I wanted to apologize," Ethan whispered. "I wasn't fair. I guess we just both deal with things differently. I shouldn't have pushed you, you'll do what you think is right," he said even though Rob's decision made him want to scream and shout.

The sigh that left Rob's chest carried so much relief, it made Ethan even more ashamed of his earlier reaction. Rob was like him in many ways, but he was not *him*, and Ethan needed to respect that.

Robert shifted closer on the bed and spoke his name.

Ethan took a deep breath, afraid he was getting close to hyperventilating over what he was about to do. "So, even if we end up living in different places for some time, I want our relationship to work. I want to make a commitment." He paused, too nervous for words, and picked up the black weasel which held a simple dark signet in its tiny paws. "Will you marry me one day?" Ethan looked into Rob's gorgeous green eyes and knew he never wanted another man in his life. Nobody else would be so understanding and caring. It wasn't just about Robert being insanely hot. Ethan wanted all of him, and would love him even if something damaged his good looks.

Robert let out a choked sound, and his eyes narrowed, but before Ethan could look away, Rob stretched out his hand, brushing the backs of his fingers over Ethan's cheek. The touch was brief and gentle but made Ethan's blood flow quicker. There was a tornado in his chest, and the only thing that could stop it was acceptance.

"You're for real..." whispered Rob, almost noiselessly.

Ethan nodded. "Take it or I'm gonna cry," he tried to make it sound like a joke, but only managed a nervous chuckle.

Rob snorted, his eyes closing, but a hint of a smile was there, and it grew until it was so wide, Rob looked almost like Joker. In a good way. "I can't believe you," he said, pulling on Ethan's shoulder to bring him closer.

Ethan scrambled up to the bed with the weasel in his hands, his stomach in twisted knots about Rob not taking the ring. It wasn't like he wanted to get married tomorrow, he just wanted them to commit to it, for Robert to know how important this was to him.

Robert's smile softened when he looked at the taxidermy, and for a long moment, he didn't say anything. He slowly petted the top of the weasel's head with his finger and traced his hand lower, to the ring. Ethan followed the movement with his heartbeat all the way in his throat, but when Rob raised his hand, the simple band was already on his ring finger, close to a thick layer of bandage on the index finger. There was no mistaking the glow in his bright eyes though. "I love you."

Ethan exhaled in relief and carefully put the weasel on the floor before rushing to hug Robert. "I love you too. I'm so sorry about yesterday." He wrapped his arms around Rob's neck and kissed his lips as if it had been ages since he'd done it. Robert pulled him into a tight hug and groaned as Ethan deepened the kiss, stroking Rob's palate with the tip of his tongue. It was positively carnivorous.

Robert fell back on the mattress, taking Ethan with him into a tumble of sheets and limbs. Ethan had to be the happiest man alive. He slid his fingers under Rob's T-shirt and onto his firm muscles. "What happened to your finger?" he whispered between one kiss and another, his dick already reacting with the same enthusiasm his mind had.

Robert chuckled and pulled on Ethan's shirt, apparently intent on yanking it over his head. "Cooking accident."

"I'll kiss it all better." Ethan smiled at him and pulled Rob's hand closer to deliver on his promise. He might be smaller, but he still enjoyed lying on top of his lover.

Robert laughed and nuzzled the tip of Ethan's nose as soon as he got the shirt off him. Rob's skin was always so warm and naturally smooth. Aside from the head and pubic area, Rob only had a bit of fair hair dusted over his legs and forearms. "Such a sweet fiancé I have…"

"Except for when he's throwing a fit." Ethan laughed and gently kissed the bandage. He never stopped roaming his hands over Rob's skin, enjoying the goose bumps under his fingertips.

Robert pushed Ethan to the side so they faced each other on the bed, and hid his warm face in Ethan's neck, making him shudder with excitement.

"As long as you're mine," whispered Rob.

"I want to make *you* mine tonight," Ethan uttered breathlessly, hoping it wasn't a too vague way to say he wanted to top, to see how it would feel and give Rob an experience he himself loved.

Air brushed against his neck as Rob inhaled sharply before pulling away just enough to look at Ethan. The moonlight reflected in his eyes, softening the gaze. He slowly chewed on his bottom lip and stroked Ethan's shoulder. "But I want the plain lube."

Ethan chuckled, leaned closer, and kissed Rob's lips. He knew that at school everyone thought of him as Rob's 'girl', but tonight, with his ring on Rob's finger, he felt like a real man. "You sure you don't want a chili pepper lube?"

Robert snorted and leaned forward, pressing a kiss to Ethan's chin. He didn't seem intimidated or displeased by Ethan's idea at all. "If there's one place on the body where chili peppers don't belong, it's my ass."

Ethan deepened the kiss feeling like the happiest weasel on the planet. "I love you," he whispered into Rob's lips, slowly rocking his hips on top of Rob, his dick already attentive.

Robert looked at him with a small smile, and when he nuzzled Ethan's nose, his mouth stretched even farther. "Should I be scared now?" he chuckled, and Ethan shivered, feeling the familiar warmth of Robert's fingers on his stomach, just above his waistband.

"I hope not." Excitement spurred on by the touch went all the way to his balls. He was really gonna do it, and Rob seemed more than happy to be taken for the ride. This was stuff wet dreams were made of.

Rob leaned even closer, and soon they were chest to chest, forehead to forehead, their legs entwining. His warm breath tickled Ethan's lips, and when those big, warm hands slipped inside Ethan's pants, it was like being touched by the heavens. Robert pushed the jeans low on Ethan's hips and pulled out his rapidly hardening cock.

"I'll make it good for you," Ethan stroked Rob's back and let his hands slip lower, to Rob's gorgeous ass, always so firm to the touch. It was going to be just them forever, and Ethan knew he would be Rob's first and only guy. He would fight for it if need be.

"I know. It's always good," muttered Robert. He pushed his hips back against Ethan's hands but kept up the gentle tugging at his cock, slowly working Ethan to full hardness. They always focused more on Ethan's ass by default so it was a bit unnerving to start something new for once, but Ethan knew it would bring them even closer.

Ethan closed his eye and let their lips melt together as he kneaded Rob's buttocks, with his fingers slightly in between them. The hand on his dick was only helping him imagine how it would be to lie on top of Rob, slide inside of him, and watch that broad, muscular back tense up.

Robert pulled on Ethan's lips and rolled over to his back, which also meant he had to let go of Ethan's cock. "Pull them off," he rasped.

Ethan grinned like a maniac and got rid of his jeans and pants like he was the express train to nakedness. "What are you waiting for?" He laughed and pulled on the waistband of Rob's pants. Rob's cock never ceased to amaze him with its awesomeness.

"You," chuckled Rob, lying back and wiggling his eyebrows in challenge. There was a healthy blush on his cheeks, and he pulled Ethan on top of him with a silly grin.

"Oh yeah, don't start without me." Ethan snorted and left a kiss on Rob's jaw. At least when they lay down, the difference in height wasn't that prominent. Ethan had grown to deal with the fact that he would most probably be short all his life.

"It's not nearly as fun without you." Robert grinned at him and jerked up his hips, giving Ethan the hint to pull. As soon as the pajama bottoms passed Rob's crotch, his half-erect cock said 'hello' to Ethan, just as sweet and juicy as always.

"I'll just…" Ethan looked at the plump cockhead and then back at Rob's face. "I'll be back, I'll just… yeah." He gave Rob a quick kiss and scrambled lower, kneeling above his thighs. His mouth was all too ready to do some sucking on that hot flesh. Ethan bent down and gave the slit at the tip a lick as his palms explored the firm thighs.

Robert gasped and slid his hand to Ethan's head. "Oh, God… I thought it would be an 'I'll be right back' thing," he uttered, his muscles bulging as he gently pressed his hips up.

"I'll be back when I've had enough," murmured Ethan into the hot cock and began sucking on the head with a groan of satisfaction. He loved going down on Rob, and a big part of the fun was the musky smell of Rob's pubes. It was as if the pheromones around his groin called out to Ethan with a promise of pleasure. The head was so smooth to the touch he just wanted to lap on it and drink the bitter essence. Robert's fingers played over Ethan's scalp, gently tugging on the hair, and his gasps became sharper as Ethan sucked harder.

He'd learned quite a lot about pleasing Robert in the past months, and he was putting his knowledge to good use, suckling on the tip, bobbing his head over the shaft in rapid moves. The throbbing on his tongue was delicious, but Ethan finally backed off and kissed the tip.

"Maybe it would be better on your stomach? You wanna do condoms?" Ethan asked, already reaching under the bed for lube.

Robert looked up at him with a broad smile and shook his head with vigor, already rolling over. He pulled up the fur spread, gathering it underneath his arms and chest. Ethan was surprised by his enthusiasm but took it as a good sign.

"You wanna feel me inside like I do you?" Ethan took a deep breath and lay on top of Rob, enjoying the firmness of his muscles and already getting lube on his fingers. His cock couldn't be more ready. He could sense his lover's strength with each stir of the powerful muscles under him.

Robert hummed in agreement, folded some of the comforter underneath his hips, and looked back at Ethan. "I want no barriers with you."

Ethan left kisses along Rob's spine and let his slippery fingers slide between the best buttocks ever created. Rob's skin had that salty taste Ethan enjoyed so much. As he gently rubbed on the anus, he kissed Rob's shoulder blade, completely lost in the moment. The puckered flesh was so delicate he was afraid to push his fingers against the hole, but Rob's approving murmurs encouraged him to explore. With lube, it didn't take that long for the gentle massage to relax Rob's sphincter enough to let in the tip of Ethan's finger.

"I want everything from you," Ethan whispered and pushed in one finger with ease, his heart beating in an ecstatic pulse. "And I'll give you anything."

Robert stretched his back and slowly, very slowly rocked his hips back. Ethan's cheeks went up in flames when his finger was gradually swallowed by that incredibly smooth, scorching hot channel. He could barely breathe.

With all the slippery lube, he worked a second finger in and whimpered at Rob's moves. His cock couldn't get any harder, and if this became any more exciting, he was at risk of coming before he even got to fuck Rob. And that couldn't happen.

Robert gathered the fur into a ball and held it against his cheek, slowly rocking his hips back and forth. He didn't seem to feel any discomfort, and was even experimenting with the angle. The view on the muscles playing under Rob's skin was making all of Ethan's body throb. "That's... nice..."

"Yeah? Tell me if something doesn't feel right." Ethan kissed Rob's nape, smelling the soft hair, and experimentally shoved the fingers in harder, in short jabs. They reminded him of the moments in fucking just when Rob was coming and thrusting in with more strength and less control. Robert stirred and pushed his ass higher with a low grunt. His toes curled, and to Ethan's surprise, the muscle around his fingers relaxed further.

"So hot," muttered Rob, sliding his thighs farther apart.

Those words didn't even begin to describe how Ethan felt. He backed off slightly and kneeled on the balls of his feet, taking in the most arousing image he'd seen in his life. Not only because Robert was extremely handsome, with a fit quarterback body, but also because Rob was *his* fiancé, his man, opening up and giving himself to Ethan with no shyness. He leaned over to turn on the bedside table lamp, so he could feast his eyes on every ridge of Rob's muscles.

"Don't stop. I like it," grunted Robert and poked Ethan's knee with his toe, all stretched out and willing. Ethan was curious what was really going on in that brown head because *he* had been quite nervous when they first had full-on sex.

"I know something you'll like more." Or at least he hoped, but he tried to be confident. The way the muscles of Rob's ass clamped down on his fingers made Ethan all too eager to experience it on his dick.

Rob exhaled and looked back at him with one of his cheeks flattened against the throw. He winked at Ethan and lowered the front of his body even farther, leaving his ass on a silver platter for Ethan. In this moment, Ethan could propose to Rob again. He felt his own nostrils flutter with the deep breaths he was taking.

He quickly drizzled some lube over his cock and positioned it between those hot, tense buttocks, all slippery and ready. Ethan lay down on top of Robert and instead of pushing in, he gripped the base of his cock, trying to calm down so he wouldn't come the moment he was in. That would have been an utter failure.

Rob groaned and stroked the fur, ready, beautiful, waiting for Ethan to take him. Looking down at his own cock at the entrance to Robert's body, Ethan was breathless with excitement and anxiety. Would he be enough, would Rob actually like it? He did seem incredibly welcoming and enthusiastic, and Ethan couldn't let him down.

He didn't want to repeat himself about Rob telling him if anything hurt. They knew each other enough to communicate about stuff like that so Ethan took the plunge and pushed his cockhead through the relaxed sphincter into the hottest, tightest cavity he could dream of. A moan escaped his lips, and he grazed Rob's shoulder with his teeth, lying on top of him to experience everything his hot body had to offer.

Robert's back tensed, and he grunted, turning his head into the throw. His calves and heels pressed against Ethan, but it wasn't clear whether Rob did that to stop or encourage him. Just in case, Ethan stopped, and it was the most excruciating act of self-control in his life. All he wanted was to push in farther, finally fuck the man he loved.

"That feels... big," uttered Rob in the end, his hand tightening in the fur.

A stupid grin exploded on Ethan's face, and he leaned down to kiss Rob's back all over, focusing on the warm skin rather than the tight ring around his cock. "I think I now love you even more."

"Just don't move yet," muttered Robert, but he did accept the caresses, and after a moment, his body started to loosen up. Only now did Ethan feel how tense Rob's asshole had been when he'd first pushed in.

Even now, when it began to relax, it was snug and throbbing around Ethan's dick. He tried to keep still but it wasn't easy with arousal steaming out of his ears. He almost sang 'Hallelujah' when Rob pushed back and impaled his ass on Ethan's cock. The warm sleeve of his body was taking more and more of Ethan each time they moved.

Robert hummed his pleasure and braced himself against Ethan, who watched, speechless, as his cock sank in with ease. Robert was accepting him so completely.

"Oh, fuck," Ethan groaned at the sight, completely lost in his own pleasure. He moved his hands along the sides of Rob's hips and gripped the flesh. His cock was so happy in the slippery tightness he could come all too fast if he weren't careful.

"Yeah. Strange but good," agreed Rob, slowly moving his hand lower, to palm his cock as Ethan fucked him. He was gasping like an exhausted engine.

Ethan slowly rocked his hips, now regretting that he hadn't pulled his hair back into a ponytail, but dark strands all over his face were nothing in comparison to the opportunity of being inside of his beloved boyfriend. He felt so complete, just like when he bottomed, yet totally different.

"I want us to come together," he muttered and leaned over Rob's back to leave kisses on his spine. Rob had the tightest, most perfect body. He never wanted to leave.

Rob nodded and looked back at Ethan, his face flushed with arousal as he chewed his lip. His ass moved forward, gently sliding off Ethan's dick, only to push back. Trying to kiss Rob's lips was a miserable failure, Ethan could only reach his nape, so he pretended that was his plan in the first place and pressed his lips to Rob's skin.

The moment he heard the slapping sound of Rob masturbating, it was his cue. Ethan started rocking his hips faster, pushing his cock into that glorious ass and feeling like the conqueror of the universe. Here he was, the first and only guy to have sex with Robert, the most amazing guy on the planet. One day, they would get married and be together forever. Life wasn't long enough for the number of orgasms he wanted to have with Rob.

Robert's moan tore him out of his fantasy, and Ethan watched all the glorious muscle arch beneath skin. In the same moment, the vise of Rob's ass clenched around Ethan so tight he saw white. Trembling, Robert was coming hard, pushing Ethan harder against his ass with his heels and furiously working his cock.

"Oh fuck, oh fuck," Ethan whimpered, caught off guard by the way Rob's ass milked him and seconds later, he came. His knees felt as if they turned into marshmallows and he hugged Rob's waist, gluing himself to the sweaty body with moans as background music to the first time worthy of a Hollywood remake.

Robert sprawled on the bed beneath him, his body going completely limp. He was still shaking with little tremors, but within a moment, his heels were back against Ethan's ass, pushing him closer, as if Rob were afraid to lose the dick inside of him. He looked back again with glossy eyes and a lobster red skin.

"How do you feel?" Ethan whispered with a blissful smile, stroking Rob's sides and enjoying the heat of his lover's skin.

Robert grinned at him, getting even redder. "Your cock's so good. It's like it turned my insides into marshmallow."

"I love you." Ethan smiled back and slowly slid out his dick, so he could actually reach Rob's lips for a kiss. "You know what else is great?"

"Yeah?" whispered Rob, nuzzling Ethan with a wide smile. He pushed him to the bed and pulled him close with one leg, straight into the radiator-like arms. It was all Ethan needed to melt into the embrace.

"*Of Mice and Elk* got sold." He gave Rob's neck a lick, and his heart leaped when he saw Robert's eyes light up even more, the sleepiness gone from them in an instant.

"Oh, my God, Ethan! That's amazing. They really paid ten thousand?" He was smiling wide, completely absorbed by their happiness.

Ethan looked into Rob's eyes. He was afraid his bragging would spoil the mood, but fortunately that wasn't the case. Rob was happy for him, as always. "Yes. I mean, they haven't transferred the money yet, but they made an offer for the full amount."

"Who is it then?" Robert's legs curled around Ethan's, and small, gentle kisses sprinkled all over his face followed. Robert was so incredibly tender and compassionate. He'd never let Ethan down. He was an idiot to think that Rob would cheat on him in college. Rob would at least have the decency to break up with him first.

"It's a gallery in Seattle. And who knows, maybe they would buy more stuff in the future. The money will be a start for me. I'll be able to work on my art for a while without worrying about paying rent."

"I'm so happy for you. Told you you're gonna make it," cheered Rob, curling his big, muscled body around Ethan.

"And we're gonna make it, too. Right?" Ethan kissed Rob's chin.

Robert chuckled, and all of a sudden, there was something incredibly raw and vulnerable at the bottom of his eyes. "As long as you don't forget me in the big, wide world out there."

"Yeah, right. Like that's ever going to happen. You're the only gay weasel I know." Ethan stroked Rob's back, enjoying their intimacy.

Robert looked away, but smiled as if a big weight was lifted off his shoulders and leaned his head on Ethan's shoulder. "We're like the Chinese harmony sign. Black and white weaseled together."

Ethan's heart melted at the comparison and he entwined their fingers. "Yin and Yang."

Chapter 21

ETHAN

BRIGHT SUNLIGHT CARESSED ETHAN'S face as he left the car, soon followed by Rob's mom, who took a rare day off to be present at her son's graduation. Shining with pride, she adjusted her hair in the wing mirror and grinned at Ethan, pulling him along to Rob's side.

"You both look so handsome today."

Robert blinked as he locked the car, but his lips spread into a bright smile. With his eyes drifting to Ethan, there was no doubt about what he was thinking. Ethan felt a few inches taller and all mature now that he had a fiancé, an art career in the making, and a future in Seattle ahead of him. Graduating was just a cherry on top of that cake of success. And he wouldn't have it without his lover's help.

"Thank you," he grinned and wrapped his arm around Rob's waist. The bigger body next to his shifted closer, yielding to his needs. Since the night he proposed, it seemed he and Rob had become even closer. They were in a proper adult relationship now, no matter what anyone said.

Students and their families were already swarming in the parking lot, slowly making their way into the school like ants carrying food into their colony. Rob's mother had been hard at work with her camera since early in the morning. She even insisted on photographing them as they brushed their teeth in the morning, and Ethan believed there were dozens of photos picturing them don their robes. And of course, the hug was yet another opportunity for her to snap a picture.

"Mooom," moaned Rob, but his smile was still firmly in place.

Ethan just smiled and entwined his fingers with Robert's. "Has Robert told you that I sold my elk piece?" he asked, too excited to hold that information in, he wanted to tell the whole world about it.

Her eyes twinkled, and she stepped closer, hugging him tight. "Of course he did! But he made me promise that I let you tell me yourself before I congratulate you."

Robert sighed and ruffled her hair as if she were the kid of the family.

"Oh, God, Rob! I need to look good in the pictures!" she complained, fleeing the caress, but there was no real anger in her voice.

"Maybe I can take one of you with your mom, Rob?" Ethan slipped out of his fiancé's embrace and got the camera from Rob's mom. He couldn't wait to be free of school and do his own thing full-time. "You think they'll miss me at Choco Panda?" He laughed and waited for them to smile.

Robert put an arm around his mom and leaned down so that their faces would be closer in the picture. "Who wouldn't miss that pretty scowl?"

Rob's mom snorted, covering the lower part of her face.

"I wasn't grumpy all the time," Ethan muttered as he took the photo.

"No, no, only in the panda ears." Rob's mom laughed.

"He looks cute in the panda ears." Robert wiggled his eyebrows at Ethan but eventually stepped away and looked at the entrance. He remained silent for several moments as he watched the building and their classmates swarming in front of it.

"I'm never wearing them again unless they're made out of real panda," Ethan grumbled.

"Ethan! They're endangered!" Rob's mom's eyes went wider, making Ethan realize that, as usual, his humor wasn't going down that well.

"I'm just kidding."

"What if it were one that died of old age, or something?" teased Rob, winking at Ethan over his mom's shoulder. Her mouth dropped open.

"That's horrible! I can't believe you said that!"

Ethan forced back his smile and kept a serious face. "Robert has a point though."

"Ethan!" he heard his own mother's voice and turned around to see his parents rushing through the busy parking lot. He swallowed, unsure what to think. With the tense family situation, he never knew whether meeting them wouldn't evolve into an argument. The familiar warmth of Robert's fingers closed around Ethan's hand, and he was pulled forward. Did Rob know Ethan's parents would be there? He did not seem all that surprised.

"Mom, Dad..." He turned around and smiled. "I wasn't sure if you'd make it."

Mother bit her lip, her eyes became wider, and for a moment, Ethan wasn't sure whether she'd cry or scream at him. Dad pulled her close and gave Ethan a tight smile. "It's your graduation day. Of course we're here."

Robert squeezed his hand over Ethan's arm. "I hope you can join us for dinner afterward."

Ethan lit up at the prospect, even though it could mean some uncomfortable conversations. As stifling as his parents were at times, they were his, and he didn't want to lose touch with them. He was sure his relationship with them would improve once they started seeing him as an adult.

"Robert is cooking. I'm sure he's prepared something amazing. He wouldn't tell." Ethan stroked Rob's chest.

"Oh, come on. It's not about my cooking today, is it?" asked Rob, nuzzling Ethan's temple. It was odd to be touched by a guy in front of their parents, but it also gave Ethan a strange sense of freedom.

"We'd love to have you both," confirmed Rob's mom with a wide smile.

"It's about both of us today." Ethan smiled up at his fiancé. "We've decided to make a commitment to each other." He looked back at his parents, hoping they wouldn't spoil the moment by some nasty comment. Robert squeezed his hand hard, and his body stiffened next to his.

Mom and Dad stared at him blankly. It was Rob's mother who spoke first. She made a step forward to be able to see them both and frowned. "What do you mean?"

Ethan grinned like the Cheshire cat and pulled up Rob's hand with the signet. "I proposed and Robert accepted. It's not gonna happen anytime soon, but we're engaged. We promised each other we'll make it work when I move to Seattle."

Robert's mom looked at them, her bosom pushing up as she took a big gulp of air. "Oh, my God, Robbie! You didn't say a thing!"

Ethan's parents seemed more shocked than happy, but eventually, Dad cleared his throat and gave Ethan an awkward pat on the shoulder. "We're happy for you. As long as you wait till you're more financially stable."

"Yeah, absolutely. Aaaand..." Ethan's heart pounded like crazy. "A gallery in Seattle bought my elk project, so I'll have a good start. And when Robert finishes his studies, we can live together." He had it all planned out. It had to work.

While the engagement didn't excite his parents as much as he hoped it would, this piece of information had them smiling with wonder. "Really?" Mom pulled him into a tight hug and gave Ethan a loud kiss on the cheek. It was as if the sale dispersed all the fears that had paralyzed her earlier. "That's wonderful, honey!"

"It is." Dad smiled. "You should sit down with us. We could read the contract together to make sure it's advantageous to you."

"You would?" Ethan slipped out of Rob's embrace and made the step to hug his dad. His head was getting that tingle of pain like before he was about to cry. "That would be super-helpful, Dad."

Mom nodded. "We know you're talented, but you're not experienced in business. Let's do it one day soon," she proposed with a smile so bright as if she had just invited him for a day out at the mall.

"I'd love that. Robert?" Ethan came back to his fiancé and hugged him. "You all right?"

Rob smiled and nodded, but there was something strange and dark in his eyes.

"Oh... Did you want to wait till dinner with telling everyone about the engagement?" Ethan blinked, lost in what was appropriate and what wasn't.

"No, told you I'm all right," said Rob, though to Ethan it was obvious he wasn't. The strange moment was broken by Rob's mom, who demanded they go to the auditorium already.

Soon, they were joined by Chris, Kelly, and more of Rob's friends. There was something serious about Robert and Ethan couldn't pinpoint it, but he didn't want to ask in public. He would try to work it out later. For now, he decided to enjoy the graduation day and an end of high school that was just the beginning of his adult life.

After the ceremony, and a few drinks courtesy of Rob's mom, Ethan's parents relaxed considerably. They were even making jokes and seemed to get on well with their hosts. At least one of them because Rob excused himself and wouldn't stick his nose out of the kitchen. Ethan was getting anxious about leaving him alone for so long, even though Rob insisted he just needed to take care of the food. So when the opportunity arose to take away some plates, he went to the kitchen. He would finally have some privacy to talk to Rob.

The corridor smelled of fresh herbs and fine beef, but Ethan couldn't enjoy it while Robert was so obviously upset. Ethan watched him through the half-open door, and Rob was in fact preparing food instead of brooding like any other person would, but his shoulders were much tenser than usual, and he wouldn't even whistle while chopping.

Ethan approached him quietly and wrapped his arms around Rob's waist from behind. He couldn't help a smile at the fact that he could barely reach to properly kiss Rob between his shoulder blades. "Hey, what's up?"

Rob stiffened at first, only to relax into Ethan's arms with a low sigh. He dropped the knife onto the counter and stroked Ethan's forearms. His shirt smelled of the delicious foods, but beneath it was the musk of Rob's body, so familiar and calming. "I thought you're talking to your parents. How is it?"

"They even offered to pay for my apartment in the first six months so I can see how it goes. I wouldn't say they're crazy about me not going to college, but they do see there's money to be made from my art, and that they seem to understand. Philistines!" Ethan laughed and kissed Rob's back again.

Rob smiled and brushed his thumb over the side of Ethan's hand. "I'm glad you are getting along with them again. They're really trying hard to help you, you know."

"Now they are. But I had to put my foot down first. I would have never got to finish my elk if it wasn't for you." Ethan stood to the side so he could look up into Rob's face.

Robert beamed at him and slowly lowered himself to brush his cheek against Ethan's. "You know you'll always have my full support."

"I love you," Ethan whispered with a smile and wrapped his arms around Rob's neck. "I promise that even if I forget stuff, I'll never forget how much I love you."

A chuckle rumbled through Rob's chest, but when he hugged Ethan back, the embrace was so tight and stiff it almost hurt. "I'm gonna miss you," he said after a while.

"Is that why you're upset?" Ethan hugged him back, lost in the embrace of those strong arms. "You know we'll visit each other as often as possible."

Rob swallowed and nodded against Ethan's shoulder. "I'm n ot... angry or anything. Just been thinking about it a lot recently."

"Soon enough I'll be making millions in modern art and I'll be taking private jets to visit you." Ethan chuckled and inhaled Rob's fresh, masculine scent, but soon, Robert's warm hands tilted his face up for the sweetest kiss imaginable. It was long, chaste, and yet is still managed to soften Ethan's knees.

Chapter 22

ROB

It had been two days since Ethan had left, taken to Seattle by his parents. Even though they talked on Skype for hours each day, Robert couldn't find a place for himself at home. It felt so empty without Ethan around. No one to watch TV with, no one to cuddle with at night. And with Chris away on vacation, Rob had never felt lonelier. Being alone with his thoughts wasn't helping. He kept imagining scenarios in which Ethan had one of his lapses while he was cooking and burned himself or the whole apartment down. Or that he fell down the stairs and broke his leg, and no one would be there to help him. Or that he got one of those horrible headaches, forgot to buy pills and there would be no one to get them for him. But they had all agreed Rob would give Ethan time to settle in the new space first, so he was grounded where he was.

At least Rob's mom was coming home early from work tonight, so he hoped dinner together would help him clear his mind. He breathed a sigh of relief as soon as he heard the door shut.

"Hi, Mom!" he shouted in the general direction of the entrance. "I've made some sushi. Hope you're hungry." With a smile, he cut through the *nori*-wrapped roll and carefully placed the newly finished *maki* on the wooden serving board. He hadn't intended to go all out today, but the opportunity to dine with someone was too tempting to miss out on with some basic foods. He also made a bowl of chocolate *mochi* for dessert, other kinds of sushi, and some yakitori. Japanese foods were his mom's favorites, and every time he made them, it ensured him a whole evening's company. Ethan was busy that night, so they would only be able to catch up later. It made Rob feel empty and stranded in a house that now seemed far too big.

"Hey, sweetie. Can I smell something nice?" she chirped and came into the kitchen with a broad smile.

Robert nodded, uplifted by her presence. Before Ethan moved in, he'd never noticed just how much he needed someone around when his mother wasn't home. "Good to see you, Mom."

"Japanese! My favorite! I have the best son in the whole world." Mom gave him a wide smile. "You want me to help with anything?"

"No, I'm all done here. Just change and wait in the living room." He winked at her and lifted the two first boards before making his way to the coffee table by the sofa. He even had relevant music waiting in the CD player, and he switched it on before heading back to the kitchen. He mixed the pulverized seaweed with warm water and put the small plate on top of a teapot warmer. He liked to add additional aromas to his meals, so that they would be complete experiences.

Mom grabbed a few candles and put them on the table with glee. "A date with my Robbie. I have you all to myself again." She sat down on the sofa and pushed her shoes off.

Rob froze, staring at the shaky water on top of the teapot warmer. All of a sudden, the need for Ethan's hand around his wrist was almost unbearable, but he smiled at his mom and straightened, eager to have a moment for himself in the kitchen. "Green tea?"

"Yes, please! Do I get sake for dessert?" She laughed and lit the candles on the table.

Robert gave her a half smile and moved to the kitchen. "You know I'm not old enough to buy it." He paid no attention to her answer and picked up his pace, almost tempted to slam the door shut when he entered the safe haven of his kitchen. He pulled out his phone and looked at the screen. Did he miss a message from Ethan?

There was a short text. 'My neighbors are holding a private party at the local Starbucks. How hipster is that? ha ha :*'

Rob's heart almost jumped out of his chest and he quickly typed an answer before putting on the kettle. However he looked at it, Ethan was having way more fun than he. Going places, meeting new people, being recognized for his talent. Rob's fans didn't even know his face. He would be the *Secret Foodie* forever.

"Rob? You all right there?" Mom asked from the living room.

"Yeah, just make yourself comfortable. I'll be right back," he said right away. It was hard to focus when he thought of all the guys Ethan was meeting every single day. He trusted Ethan not to cheat on him, but he was there alone, and was likely to form a friendship that could later erase Rob off his radar. They would split up, and Rob would take it with a fake smile and good-bye wishes.

He grabbed the tea and made his way back to the living room.

"Did you take photos first?" Mom asked from the comfort of the sofa. "Should I put the light on after all?"

Robert blinked. No, he just wanted to sit down and eat. When Ethan was there, he'd go all out to show him what he could do, but today he just wanted to stuff his face full of something delicious. "It's fine, Mom. It's not my first or last sushi."

She was silent for a moment and the sound of breaking up new chopsticks was like breaking the ice. "You did anything interesting today?" she finally asked.

Rob cleared his throat. "Hung out with a few of the guys at the gym, then I went to the farmer's market, watched some TV. You?" He looked at her with interest. "Any new freaky accidents around town?"

"There was actually. This guy got brought in with a spitroast in his thigh, with meat and vegetables still on. He was insanely lucky, but his wife kept saying that he shouldn't take it out himself because it could have punctured an artery. It made me think of how you dealt with Ethan's injury. Better safe than sorry."

Robert stared at her, his mouth going dry, and all of a sudden there were tears prickling at the corners of Rob's eyes.

Mom frowned and leaned to him over the table. "Hey, Robbie, what is it?"

He took a deep breath, squeezing his hand over the fabric of his sweats as the sushi blurred in front of him like an abstract painting. "It was my fault. Ethan's accident," he muttered, fighting the cold and hot waves tumbling through his body.

"No, you've done everything you could, sweetie." Mom reached out to stroke his shoulder. "He's lucky to be alive."

"No, you don't understand." Robert blinked away the tears and dragged his hands down his face. "I shoved him. I did that."

Mom was silent for a while. "Oh, Rob... you never said. Why would you do that?" her voice was quiet, but still resonated in the room.

Robert hid his face in his hands, afraid to look up at her. When he opened his eyes, all he could see were his own feet on the rug. He needed to hug Ethan so bad. "It was an accident. I didn't think he'd fall down."

He felt his mom's fingers on his knee. "I'm not proud to hear you would do something like that, but things happen. What matters is that you helped him up."

Rob stared at her slim hand and bit his lip to keep a sob at bay. "But he's my boyfriend, and I scarred him for life. And now he's gone."

"He's not gone. Remember how happy he was to announce the two of you got engaged? Whatever you did to him, you seemed to have amended for it in his mind." Her voice was calm and soothing, and it did help to hear some reassurance. To confine his guilt in somebody.

Robert swallowed and touched the ring on his finger. He didn't even remember putting it on after he finished cooking. It hadn't been there for a long time, but already felt like an integral part of Rob's hand. "Yeah."

"And you'll go to visit him next weekend, right?"

Robert gave a shaky breath. "Yeah, but he's there all alone. What if something happens? What if he meets someone who does something interesting with their life?" He slowly raised his eyes at his mom. His appetite was completely gone by now.

She put a piece of sushi in her mouth but never stopped watching him. "You're interesting, honey. You make these delicious things, play football, and you'll be studying medicine. How is that not interesting?"

The lump in Rob's throat grew large enough to start choking him. "Mom, I won't have time for the blog if I become a doctor. I'll need to give it all up. I'll be out all the time, like you." He winced as soon as those words left his mouth, but it was the truth. He had been struggling with her absence for such a long time that he started considering it normal.

She frowned slightly and swallowed. "Yes, it is a choice I made, but it's extremely satisfying to know you help people. It's a calling. And I have to be honest with you. Yes, it would be hard for you to keep your blog going." That concerned look never left her face, as if she wanted to dissect Rob's thoughts.

Ron bit his lip and pulled on his index finger, even more lost. He didn't want to be tied down like that, to never be able to go anywhere with Ethan, to always be on call. "I know. Maybe I should do something else?" he uttered, looking straight at her.

Mom stared at him but looked more curious than displeased. "Oh. Okay. You never said that before. Maybe something in medical research, or pharmacy work..."

Robert swallowed hard, and pulled on his index finger, trying to calm down his erratic body. "I just... if I could, I would like to work around food. But I know it's not an easy business. I know." He slouched with a deep sigh. "My blog's doing good now, but I have no idea how it's gonna develop."

"You know I wouldn't push you into something you didn't want." She let out a long sigh and slouched. "I was just suggesting. You never said you wanted to do it professionally. So your blog. It's popular?"

Robert swallowed, surprised by how calm she was. When he'd expressed interest in anatomy a few years ago, she had been ecstatic but now she didn't seem disappointed at all. "Yeah. I got even more popular after I included some of Ethan's works into my photos. That's why we got those tiny porcelain plates and cups for dolls."

"But can you monetize that somehow? I know you pay for your own gas, and some little things, but could you actually reach a level that allows you to live off it?"

Rob shrugged. "I earn from adverts, and I have some savings from that, but there's no guarantee I will continue to grow." He sighed. "So many people don't make it."

"But is this what you would really want to do? Because I see you spend so much time on it. Maybe you should give it a shot. It's just so sudden. It's not *just* because you're missing Ethan, is it?"

Robert blinked, hung up on the first sentence as his heart leaped in his chest. "You're... okay with it?" he muttered.

Mom pouted. "As long as you realize you're taking responsibility for what you're doing. If it doesn't work out, you'll have to start from scratch, but come on, Robert, you're eighteen. Sure, live a little. Since you have savings, you can take a gap year and see what happens. After I graduated from college, I took a few months to travel around Europe, and nothing horrible happened. I got my first proper job after I came back. Sure, I also brought you back from that trip." She snorted, and her face got a bit of a red tint. "But I don't regret it."

Robert swallowed, a bit shocked. "You said you met him at college..."

She took a deep breath. "No, we met in Italy. Traveled together a bit and... he went on to India, and I went to Spain. He didn't even know I was pregnant when he left."

Robert looked to the barely-touched sushi and combed his hair with his fingers. That was a development he hadn't predicted. "Oh..." When he looked at his mom again, it was through different eyes. She wasn't the most organized or conscientious person on the planet, but he hadn't expected her early years to have been this wild. His grandparents had never said anything either. "So it wasn't... a friend from college?"

Her smile became soft and she shook her head. "No, it wasn't."

Robert sighed and slowly leaned in, resting his head on her shoulder. She smelled so nice and homely it made him instantly calm down. "Was he hot?"

Mom snorted and swatted his knee. "Robert! He was indeed very hot." She couldn't stop laughing.

Rob smiled, relieved. He always wondered why his dad never kept in touch, now he knew. "Tell me more?"

"He was Scottish, handsome, my age, we met in Venice." She sighed, but there was no sadness in her expression. "Resisting him wasn't an option."

"Was he a chef?" Robert chuckled and squeezed her hand, oddly at ease with the new information. He could definitely live with that.

It was as if Mom remembered the food again and leaned down for more sushi. "Silly. He worked at his family's farm back in Scotland. This was his last trip before settling down."

Robert cleared his throat and had some tea. "And you know his name? And where he was from?"

"No, sweetie, you're not going to go looking for him. It's not why I told you this." She raised her eyebrows and stuffed her mouth with more sushi.

Robert opened his mouth, startled, but said something he hadn't initially thought of. "Are you saying I should do something crazy and not regret it?"

Mom looked up at him with her eyes twinkling. "As your mom, I would *never* advise something like that. After all, what if you get hurt? What if it doesn't work out? What if you and Ethan break up? What if you don't try to find out?" Only the last question sounded serious.

Robert bit his lip and hugged her tight. He took several deep breaths before he could speak again. "You're the best, you know that?"

She hugged him back and kissed his temple. "I'm trying, sweetie."

Robert sighed and looked at the delicious meal that he would surely wolf down now that he knew he needed lots of energy. Before he could get to it though, his phone beeped, and he picked it up just because he hoped it was a message from Ethan. It wasn't a text but an e-mail, and Rob wanted to dismiss it at first in favor of dining. Everything changed when he noticed who the sender was. His life was about to do a one-eighty flip.

Chapter 23

ETHAN

ETHAN WAS ALMOST DONE setting up a display for the letter-jacket-wearing white weasel that represented Robert. When they parted, Rob decided he would keep the black one and Ethan could have the white one so that each could have at least that symbolic version of the other. It didn't make Ethan miss Rob any less, but at least it made him smile any time he looked at the Rob-weasel holding that tiny football. The apartment wasn't big, but thanks to his parents' help, still a bit bigger than what he would be able to afford on his own. With the taxidermy, he needed to have a workshop at home or he'd have to rent a studio space anyway, so it just seemed more logical to have a bigger place to stay. Especially because his line of work wasn't exactly decoupage or quilting. He could imagine a lot of people wouldn't want to share a studio space with him. Here, in the post-industrial building, no one cared as long as he kept everything clean, at least that was the suggestion the landlord gave him. The flat he was occupying didn't have any next-door neighbors so there wouldn't be any complaints about chemical smells and the like.

He'd managed to make the place look nice with a few second-hand items his parents helped him to move into the apartment from the flea market. He had a large bed, a rail for his clothes that still had an 'H&M' sticker on it, even the living room was quite well equipped, and he'd managed to quickly connect to the Internet. Things were looking up now that he had the money for *Of Mice and Elk* in his account, but even that would eventually run out, and he needed to keep on working and connecting to people.

That was why even with his lack of interest in socializing, he had forced himself to go to the neighbor's party a few days ago. You never knew whom you could meet. Strangely enough, it was actually fun. There were all sorts of artsy types living in his building, and holding a conversation didn't turn out to be that hard. People actually thought that what he did was cool and that his eye patch made him unique. His headaches weren't that frequent anymore so even he was trying to see the bright side of things. He hadn't had a memory lapse in a week, and even the one before that had been less than a minute.

What wasn't cool though was having to cook for himself. He spent the last few days with pizza and Chinese takeouts, but that couldn't last for an infinity or the next time Rob saw him he'd look more like a piglet than a weasel.

Ethan approached the kitchen counter with a pack of chicken breasts and a knife. He had salt and pepper. It couldn't be that hard. He'd tried to reach Rob earlier for advice, but he wasn't available.

He was washing his hands when the doorbell rang, making Ethan wonder. He didn't remember ordering anything. It had to be one of his new neighbors. Hopefully one who could cook. He'd draw him or her in under the pretense of a chat and coffee, and extract all cooking knowledge out of them.

"Coming!" Ethan smiled and walked to the door.

He looked into the mirror to put his hair in order and looked through the peephole. His heart froze when he faced a black weasel in thick-rimmed glasses.

He couldn't open the door fast enough. He was all fingers and thumbs, struggling to pull back the chain on the door, but he finally managed. He was sure he'd only see Rob in a weeks' time, but there he was, it had to be him.

"Hey!" Ethan opened the door wide and faced the broad chest of his boyfriend, who smiled at him so wide, his mouth seemed close to splitting.

"Baby, we've missed you," he said, wiggling the black weasel in the air.

"You came early!" Ethan squealed and glued himself to Rob's chest, laying his head on the lovely pillows of his pecs.

"That's what he said," a familiar voice said behind Rob with a snort. Chris.

"May we come in?" asked Rob, squeezing Ethan tight with his free arm. He lowered his face and pressed a soft kiss to Ethan's forehead.

Ethan nodded quickly and led them in. "Is Chris *joining* us? I don't know if I'm up for that just yet." He poked Chris's chest with a pout.

"Just for dinner." Chris grabbed Ethan and flung him over his shoulder, carrying him deeper into the apartment. Ethan was now almost facing Chris's ass so he looked up, just to see Rob's shocked expression.

"Watch out for his head."

Chris snorted. "Yeah, yeah, he's safe with me, Robbie."

"Hey! I—" Ethan didn't know what to say in the end, so he just dangled from Chris's arm with his hair almost sweeping the floor. "Caveman."

Chris eventually put him back on the floor and grinned. He was ridiculously tanned after his vacation in Florida.

"Nice place you got here. Not very Eddie-like."

Robert rolled his eyes and put the black weasel on the cupboard to stand next to its white counterpart. He even pushed them close, as if they were about to touch.

Ethan couldn't help but pet the fur on that black head. "Not *yet*. I've got all sorts of plans. I'll bring my bone chandelier from home, maybe put up some cool wallpaper..."

"Let's do it then," said Rob, stepping closer. His face was tense despite the smile.

"You wanna help me?" Ethan pushed some of his hair back and looked up at Robert, unable to stop the need to hug him again.

Rob's Adam's apple bobbed, and he bit his lip, slowly lifting Ethan by the ass. His kiss was sweet, gentle yet tentative, as if there was something Robert wasn't telling Ethan yet.

"Am I a football or something? You guys just keep picking me up." Ethan laughed and didn't mind one bit how Robert got him to sit on the kitchen countertop. He looked at the chicken breasts. "Oh, yes! Now I've got someone to help me cook this. I'll share."

"Yeah! I could get crumbs while you two lovebirds reconnect." Chris grinned and knocked on the tabletop.

Robert sighed, looking straight into Ethan's eye, as if hypnotized.

Ethan swallowed, starting to get uneasy with the strange tension. "Am I missing something?"

"Yeah, he wants to move in with you, Eddie. There, someone had to say it." Chris shrugged off the glare Robert sent him, completely unbothered.

Ethan's lips parted. "For real? For the whole summer?" His heart picked up pace at the thought of all the things they could do if Rob lived with him. They could actually get a few more projects done together.

Robert drew in a sharp breath and shook his head. His eyes were so large and dark Ethan had to let him speak. "No. For good. I wanna stay."

Ethan's chest fluttered with how fast his heart beat. He wrapped his legs around Rob's waist and pulled him closer. "You would? Oh, my God, Rob, that would be so amazing! What about college?"

Robert sighed and held him close, digging his chin into Ethan's shoulder. "Fuck it. I wanna live a little before I go into debt. And maybe I can actually do something else?"

Ethan kissed his temple and hugged him close. His chest was swelling with pride at the courage Rob had found in himself. The last thing he'd wanted was to try to force him into this decision, so seeing him make it on his own in the end was beyond words. It meant that at least a part of Rob truly believed they could make it. "We'll work super-hard, we'll make it happen Rob, I promise!"

The smile that spread on Rob's face reached his eyes and shone so bright Ethan half-expected for them to start burning. Robert fumbled with one of his pockets and slowly lowered himself to one knee, spreading out a piece of paper.

Chris laughed and put his hand over his face. "Oh no, here we go, I can't look at this."

But all of Ethan's attention was on Robert. "What is it?"

With a grin that threatened to break his face, Robert handed Ethan the piece of paper, which was a printed-out email. "Etha n... will you be in Vogue with me?" he whispered.

Ethan began to read the text and with each sentence his ego bloated closer to the size of the Titanic. It was an offer for them to do styling for a photoshoot for Vogue. It mentioned the website their photos were featured on and how impressed the Vogue editor was with the crazy concoction of food and taxidermy.

"Oh, my God! Robert! Yes, yes, yes! I can't believe it!" he squealed and slid off the countertop, trying to hug Rob so fast he fell into his boyfriend's embrace.

Rob tilted backward, and only Ethan pulling him up saved them both from a fall to the floor. Their kiss was rushed and messy, but oh-so-good. Ethan wished it would never end, but eventually, he slid to sit between Rob's knees, pressed against the sweet-smelling chest.

Robert gently brushed some hair off Ethan's forehead and rested his chin on top of his head.

"When are you moving in? We have to get to work straight away!" Ethan was frantic and he cupped Rob's face, trying to get a grip on the situation. "Is there any deadline?"

"Why do you think he brought me here?" Chris helped himself to some juice. "All his shit is in my truck."

Robert chuckled and moved the tip of his nose over Ethan's cheek. "An hour?"

Ethan wrapped his arms tightly around Rob's neck. A part of him was afraid this was just a dream, and he would wake up any time now. "I love you so much, Robert. We're gonna have the coolest home ever, and"—he lowered his voice to a whisper—"we're gonna fuck like monkeys every day."

"Wait till I'm gone with that last part, okay?" grumbled Chris. "No one cares about my straight innocence."

Robert grinned at Ethan and winked. "Eavesdropping, are we?"

Ethan laughed. He couldn't care less about what Chris had heard. It was his house after all. Happiness sparkled in him like bubbles in a freshly popped bottle of champagne. He was sure Rob and he would make it work, both in the relationship and in professional life. Rob was the one person that completely 'got' him. His head began to tingle with pain at the approaching tears.

"And weasels. Can we get weasels?" Ethan asked as he rubbed his eye.

"You mean ferrets?" Robert sighed and gently massaged Ethan's cheekbone with his thumb.

"Yes, ferrets. They're so cute, Rob, they'd keep us company!"

Chris snorted. "And you'd stuff them when they die?"

Ethan frowned and hugged Rob harder. "That's not the point!"

Robert's cheeks reddened, and he hid his face in Ethan's hair. "I researched them, actually. They're really cute."

Ethan stroked Rob's head with a blissful smile. He was sure it would be tough sometimes, and that they both had a lot to learn about living on their own as adults, but he was sure that figuring it out together would make the struggles worth it. "We're gonna be the best ferret daddies."

The end

Thank you for reading our book! If you enjoyed your time with our story, we would really appreciate it if you took a few minutes to leave a review on your favorite platform. It is especially important for us as

self-publishing authors, who don't have the backing of an established
press.
Not to mention we simply love hearing from readers! :)
How about a free story? You can find several here:
https://www.kamerikan.com/freebies
If you want to stay in touch with us, follow us on Amazon and join
our Facebook group, the Merikan Playroom.

TAKEN
BY THE LORD OF THE
NOCTURNE
COURT
K.A. MERIKAN

Taken by the Lord of the Nocturne Court

K.A. Merikan

"I am yours, and I can be your prince as well as your beast."

Luke

I'm your typical small-town loser stuck in a dead-end job. Single, because dating is for well-adjusted human beings, not traumatized gay boys with trust issues. All I want is to leave my past behind and finally start living.

My wish comes true in the most bizarre way imaginable. One evening, a beautiful man with pointy ears and flowing dark locks appears out of nowhere. He proclaims I am to be his 'Dark Companion' based on some stupid deal I made in a dream. Oh, and apparently he's an elven prince, the Lord of Shadows, Protector of the Nightmare Realm and Knight of Grief Ocean.

Which is a weird way to ask me out, but okay.

It's a hard no from me, but this absolute psycho abducts me to his palace in a moonlit realm populated by vicious beasts and backstabbing courtiers.

If I am to ever get back home, I need to adapt, because our full moon wedding is approaching fast. I can't allow myself to buy into his seductive kisses, poet shirts made of spider silk and bouquets of sapphire roses. They hide poison and deception. A gilded cage is still a prison.

But...

What if I just never realized that what I need is a man with a cruel smile and a sword dipped in midnight? A man with secrets, and scars, and smoky eyes, and a past filled with darkness, and... have I mentioned he has a big d—

"Taken by the Lord of the Nocturne Court" is a standalone, scorching hot, dark gothic M/M romantasy filled with snark and dark humor, but also violence, peril, jealousy, and angst.

The book is a darkly romantic escape into the shadows where love and destiny collide. Dive into the pages to discover if a gilded cage can become a home when shared with a seductive elven prince devoted to his Dark Companion's every wish.

NOT LIKE OTHER BOYS

Themes: abduction, enemies to lovers, size difference, fake relationship, dark humor, snark, jealousy, hurt/comfort, afraid to commit, obsessive hero, forced marriage, isekai, fantasy elven prince, gothic castle, childhood trauma, shadow magic, monsters and fantastical creatures, fish-out-of-water, secrets, portal fantasy

WARNING: This story contains scenes of violence, abduction, offensive language and morally gray characters unafraid to burn the world down for their beloved.

Available on Amazon

MANIC
PIXIE
DREAM
BOY
K.A. MERIKAN

Manic Pixie Dream Boy

K.A. Merikan

Can you find the love of your life on a tour bus?

Dusk. Leader of The Underdogs. Destined for greatness. Lives in the now.**Abe.** AKA Lolly. Iridescent. Unicorn.

All Dusk wants out of life is for his band to become world famous. He also wants to have a lot of fun along the way. And to get his rocks off. When he wants something, he goes for it, consequences be damned. So when he sees a gorgeous pink-haired guy who is the human equivalent of tattooed cotton candy, he can't help but have a taste.

But it's when Lolly ends up on their tour bus that Dusk knows their meeting was destiny. Abe is the kind of guy who goes with the flow. He was hitchhiking anyway, so why not spend the week with a hot piece of rocker beefcake, getting smothered by his sexy long hair? And why not play the part of the supportive cutie while he's at it? It's not like he'd be sticking around for long anyway.

All plans hit a wall when photos of Abe and Dusk emerge online, suddenly pushing the band into the spotlight. To take advantage of the sudden popularity, the band offers Abe money for staying. Which means money for being in a fake relationship with Dusk. Which isn't even fake. Or is it?

Themes: rock band, alternative lifestyles, tattoos, bisexuality, commitment, instalove, abandonment issues, fame, outing, coming out, life on tour

Genre: Contemporary M/M Rocker Romance Heat level: Scorching hot scenes

Length: ~52,000 words (Can be read as standalone, HEA)

Available on Amazon

About the author

K.A. Merikan is a duo of queer writers who don't believe in following the well-trodden path. In their books you can dip your toe into dangerous romance with mafiosi, outlaw bikers and bad boys, all from the safety of your sofa. They love the weird and wonderful, stepping out of the box, and bending stereotypes both in life and in fiction. Their stories don't shy away from exploring the darker side of M/M romance, and feature a variety of anti-heroes, rebels, misfits, and underdogs who go against the grain.

Be prepared for shocking twists, dark humor, raw emotions, and sizzling hot scenes.

e-mail: **kamerikan@gmail.com**
http://kamerikan.com

More information about works in progress and publishing at:

Facebook: https://www.facebook.com/groups/1817541075240882

Patreon: https://www.patreon.com/kamerikan